Flashback

Michael Palmer is the international bestselling author of nine previous novels, including, most recently, *The Patient*. His novels have been translated into twenty-six languages and have been adapted for film and television. He trained in international medicine at Boston City and Massachusetts General Hospitals, spent twenty years as a full-time practitioner of internal and emergency medicine, and is now involved in the treatment of alcoholism and chemical dependence. He lives in Massachusetts.

FLASHBACK

Michael Palmer

arrow books

Published by Arrow Books in 2001

3 5 7 9 10 8 6 4 2

Copyright © Michael Palmer, 1988

Michael Palmer has asserted his right under the Copyright, Designs
and Patents Act, 1988 to be identified as the author of this work

First published in the United Kingdom in 2000 by Century

Arrow Books
The Random House Group Limited
20 Vauxhall Bridge Road, London SW1V 2SA

Random House Australia (Pty) Limited
20 Alfred Street, Milsons Point, Sydney
New South Wales 2061, Australia

Random House New Zealand Limited
18 Poland Road, Glenfield
Auckland 10, New Zealand

Random House (Pty) Limited
Endulini, 5a Jubilee Road, Parktown 2193, South Africa

The Random House Group Limited Reg. No. 954009

www.randomhouse.co.uk

A CIP catalogue record for this book
is available from the British Library

Papers used by Random House are natural, recyclable
products made from wood grown in sustainable forests.
The manufacturing processes conform to the environmental
regulations of the country of origin

ISBN 0 09 941077 X

Printed and bound in Great Britain by
Cox & Wyman Ltd, Reading, Berkshire

To. N.M.S.

Over the three-year birthing of *Flashback* a number of people have given me encouragement, criticism, and support. My agent, Jane Rotrosen Berkey; my publisher, Linda Grey; my editor, Beverly Lewis; my family; and many friends of Bill W. share my deepest gratitude.

M.S.P.
Falmouth, Massachusetts
1988

If I fulfill this oath and do not violate it, may it be granted to me to enjoy life and art, being honored with fame among all men for all time to come; if I transgress and swear falsely, may the opposite of all this be my lot.

—Conclusion of The Oath of Hippocrates; 377? B.C.

Saint Peter don't you call me
    'cause I can't go.
I owe my soul to
    The Company Store.

—Merle Travis

Prologue

January 10th

   Two . . . three . . . four . . .

Toby Nelms lay on his back and counted the lights as they flashed past overhead. He was eight years old, but small even for that age, with thick red-brown hair, and freckles that ran across the tops of his cheeks and over the bridge of his nose. For a time after his father's job relocation from upstate New York to the T.J. Carter Paper Company of Sterling, New Hampshire, Toby's classmates in the Bouquette Elementary School had called him 'dot face,' and 'shrimp,' and had pushed him around in the school cafeteria. But things were better now, much better, since the day he had held his ground and absorbed a beating at the hands of Jimmy Barnes, the school bully.

   Five . . . six . . . seven . . .

Toby rubbed at the lump at the top of his leg, next to his peenie, where the pain had started and still persisted. The doctors had said that the shot would take the pain away, but it hadn't.

The music that the nurses had promised would relax him wasn't helping, either. The song was okay, but there weren't any words. His hand shaking, Toby reached up and pulled the padded earphones off his head.

   Eight . . . nine . . . The lights turned from white to

yellow to pink, and finally to red. *Ten . . . eleven . . .*

Following the fight with Jimmy, the kids had stopped pushing him and had begun asking him to walk home with them after school. They had even elected him to be the class representative to the student council. After months of inventing illnesses to stay home, it felt so good to want to go to school again every day. Now, because of the lump, he would miss a whole week. *It wasn't fair.*

Twelve . . . thirteen . . . The red lights passing overhead grew brighter, more intense. Toby squeezed his eyes as tightly as he could, but the red grew warmer and brighter still. He tried putting his arm across them, but the hot, blood light bore through and began to sting them. Softly, he began to cry.

'Now, now, Toby, there's no need to cry. Doctor's going to fix that little bump, and then you'll be all better. Are you sure you don't want to listen to the music? Most of our patients say they feel much better because of it.'

Toby shook his head and then slowly lowered his arm. The lights were gone from overhead. Instead, he saw the face of the nurse, smiling down at him. She was gray-haired and wrinkled and old – as old as Aunt Amelia. Her teeth were yellowed at the tops, and smears of bright red makeup glowed off her cheeks. As he watched, the skin on her face drew tighter, more sunken. Her wrinkles disappeared and the spaces below the red makeup, and above, where her eyes had been, became dark and hollow.

'Now, now, Toby . . . now, now . . . now, now . . .'

Once again, Toby threw his arm across his eyes, and once again, it did no good. The nurse's skin tightened still further, and then began to peel away, until the white of her bones shone through. The red dripped like blood over her skeleton face, and the holes where her eyes had been glowed.

'Now, now . . . now, now . . .'

'Let me up. Please let me up.'

Toby screamed the words, but heard only a low growl, like the sound from the stereo when he turned the record with his finger.

'Let me up. Please, let me up.'

The sheet was pulled from his body, and he shook from the chilly air.

'I'm cold,' he cried wordlessly. 'Please cover me. Please let me up. Mommy. I want my mommy.'

'Okay, big fella. Up you go.'

It was a man's voice, deep and slow. Toby felt hands around his ankles and beneath his arms, lifting him higher and higher off the bed with wheels, higher and higher and higher. That same music was in the room. Now, even without the earphones, he could hear it.

'Easy does it, big fella. Just relax.'

Toby opened his eyes. The face above his was blurred. He blinked, then blinked once more. The face, beneath a blue cap, remained blurred. In fact, it wasn't a face at all – just skin where the eyes and nose and mouth should have been.

Again, Toby screamed. Again, there was only silence. He was floating, helpless. *Mommy, please. I want Mommy.*

'Down you go, big fella,' the faceless man said.

Toby felt the cold slab beneath his back. He felt the wide strap pulled tightly across his chest. *Just the lump*, his mind whimpered. *Don't hurt my peenie. You promised. Please, don't hurt me.*

'Okay, Toby, you're going to go to sleep now.

Just relax, listen to the music, and count back from one hundred like this. One hundred . . . ninety-nine . . . ninety-eight . . .'

'One hundred . . . ninety-nine . . .' Toby heard his own voice saying the words, but he knew he wasn't speaking. 'Ninety-eight . . . ninety-seven . . .' He felt icy cold water being swabbed over the space between his belly and the top of his leg – first over the lump, and then over his peenie. 'Ninety-six . . . ninety-five.' *Please stop. You're hurting me. Please.*

'That's it, y'all, he's under. Ready, Jack? Team?' The voice, a man's, was one Toby had heard before. But where? Where? 'Okay, Marie, turn up the speakers just a hair. Good, good. Okay, then, let's have at it. Knife, please . . .'

The doctor's voice. Yes, Toby thought. That was who. The doctor who had come to see him in the emergency ward. The doctor with the kind eyes. The doctor who had promised he wouldn't . . .

A knife? What kind of knife? What for?

Then Toby saw it. Light sparked off the blade of a small silver knife as it floated downward, closer and closer to the lump above his leg. He tried to move, to push himself away, but the strap across his chest pinned his arms tightly against his sides.

For a moment, Toby's fear was replaced by confusion and a strange curiosity. He watched the thin blade glide down until it just touched the skin next to his peenie. Then pain, unlike any he had ever known, exploded through his body from the spot.

'I can feel that! I can feel that,' he screamed. 'Wait! Stop! I can feel that!'

The knife cut deeper, then began to move, over the top of the lump, then back toward the base of his peenie. Blood spurted out from around the blade as it slid through his skin.

Again and again, Toby screamed.

'That's it. Suction now, suction,' he heard the doctor say calmly.

'Please, please, you're hurting me. I can feel that,' Toby pleaded hysterically.

He kicked his feet and struggled against the wide strap with all his strength. 'Mommy, Daddy. Please help me.'

'Metzenbaums.'

The blade of the shiny knife, now covered with blood, slid free of the gash it had made. In its place, Toby saw the points of a scissors pushing into the cut, first opening, then closing, then opening again, moving closer and closer to the base of his peenie. Each movement brought a pain so intense, it was almost beyond feeling. Almost.

'Don't you understand?' Toby screamed, struggling to speak with the reasoning tone of a grown-up, 'I can feel that. It hurts. It hurts me.'

The scissors drove deeper, around the base of his peenie.

'No! Don't touch that! Don't touch that!'

'Sponge, I need a sponge right here. Good, that's better. That's better.'

The scissors moved further. Toby felt his peenie and his balls come free of his body.

Don't do that ... don't do that ... The words were in his mind, no longer in his voice.

Again, with all his strength, Toby tried to push up against the strap across his chest. Overhead, he saw the doctor – the man whose eyes had been so kind, the man who had promised not to hurt him. He was holding something in his hand – something bloody

– and he was showing it to others in the room. Toby struggled to understand what it was that he was showing, what it was that was so interesting. Then, suddenly, he knew. Terrified, he looked down at where the lump had been. It was gone, but so was his peenie . . . and his balls. In their place was nothing but a gaping, bloody hole.

In that instant, the strap across Toby's chest snapped in two. Flailing with his arms and legs, he threw himself off the table, kicking at the doctors, at the nurses, at anything he could. The bright overhead light shattered. Trays of sparkling steel instruments crashed to the floor.

'Get him, get him,' he heard the doctor yell.

Toby lashed out with his feet and his fists, knocking over a shelf of bottles. Blood from one of them splattered across his legs. He ran toward the door, away from the hard table . . . away from the strap.

'Stop him! . . . Stop him!'

Strong hands caught him by the arms, but he kicked out with his feet and broke free. Moments later, the hands had him again. Powerful arms squeezed across his chest and under his chin.

'Easy, Toby, easy,' the doctor said. 'You're all right. You're safe. It's me. It's Daddy.'

Toby twisted and squirmed with all his might.

'Toby, please. Stop. Listen to me. You're having a nightmare. It's just a dream. That's all. Just a bad dream.'

Toby let up a bit, but continued to struggle. The voice wasn't the doctor's anymore.

'Okay, son, that's it. That's it. Just relax. It's Daddy. No one's going to hurt you. You're safe. No one's going to hurt you.'

Toby stopped struggling. The arms across his chest and under his chin relaxed. Slowly, they turned him around. Slowly, Toby opened his eyes. His father's face, dark with concern, was inches from his.

'Toby, can you see me? It's Daddy. Do you know who I am?'

'Toby, it's Mommy. I'm here, too.'

Toby Nelms stared first at his father, then at the worried face of his mother. Then, with an empty horror swelling in his chest, he slid his hand across the front of his pajama bottoms. His peenie was there, right where it was supposed to be. His balls, too.

Was this the dream?

Too weak, too confused to cry, Toby sank to the floor. His room was in shambles. Toys and books were everywhere. His bookcase had been pulled over, and the top of his desk swept clean. His radio was smashed. The small bowl, home of Benny, his goldfish, lay shattered on the rug. Benny lay dead amidst the glass.

Bob Nelms reached out to his son, but the boy pulled away.

His eyes still fixed on his parents, Toby pushed himself backward, and then up and onto his bed. Again, he touched himself.

'Toby, are you all right?' his mother asked softly.

The boy did not answer. Instead, he pulled his knees to his chest, rolled over, and stared vacantly at the wall.

Chapter 1

The day, Sunday, June 30, was warm and torpid. On New Hampshire 16, the serpentine roadway from Portsmouth almost to the Canadian border, light traffic wound lazily through waves of heated air. Far to the west, a border of heavy, violet storm clouds rimmed the horizon.

The drive north, especially on afternoons like this, was one Zack Iverson had loved for as long as he could remember. He had made the trip perhaps a hundred times, but each pass through the pastureland to the south, the villages and rolling hills, and finally, the White Mountains themselves, brought new visions, new feelings.

His van, a battered orange VW camper, was packed solid with boxes, clothes, and odd pieces of furniture. Perched on the passenger seat, Cheapdog rested his muzzle on the windowsill, savoring the infrequent opportunity to view the world with his hair blown back from in front of his eyes.

Zack reached across as he drove and scratched the animal behind one ear. With Connie gone from his life, and most of his furniture sold, Cheapdog was a rock – an island in a sea of change and uncertainty.

Change and uncertainty. Zack smiled tensely. For so many years, June the thirtieth and July the first had been synonymous with those words. Summer jobs in high school; four separate years in college, and four more in medical school; internship; eight years of surgical, then neurosurgical, residency – so many changes, so many significant June-the-thirtieths. Now, this day would be the last in that string – a clear slash between the first and second halves of his life.

Next year, the date would, in all likelihood, slip past as just another day.

Highway 16 narrowed and began its roller-coaster passage into the mountains. Zack glanced at his watch. Two-thirty. Frank and the Judge were at their club, probably on the fourth or fifth hole by now. Dinner wasn't until six. There was no need to hurry. He pulled off into a rest area.

Cheapdog, sensing that this was to be a stop of substance, shifted anxiously in his seat.

'That's right, mop-face,' Zack said. 'You get to escape for a while. But first . . .'

He took a frayed paperback from between the seats and propped it up on the dash. Instantly, the dog's squirming stopped. His head tilted.

'You appreciate, I can see, the price that must be paid for the freedom you are about to enjoy. Yes, dogs and girls, it's time for' – he took the silver dollar from his shirt pocket and read from the page – 'a classic palm and transfer, Italian style.'

The book, Rufo's *Magic with Coins*, was a 1950s reprint Zack had stumbled upon in a Cambridge secondhand bookstore.

Amaze your friends . . . Amuse your family . . . Impress members of the opposite sex . . . Sharpen your manual dexterity.

The four claims, embossed in faded gold leaf on the cover, each held a certain allure for him. But it was the last one of the group that clinched the sale.

'Don't you see?' he had tried to explain to a neurosurgical colleague, as he was fumbling through the exercises in Chapter One. 'We're only in the O.R. – what? – a few hours a day at best. We need something like this to keep our hands agile between cases – to sharpen our manual dexterity. The way things are, we're like athletes who never practice between games, right?'

Unfortunately, although the principle behind that thought was noble enough, the implementation had given rise to a most disconcerting problem. For while Zack's hands were quite remarkable in the operating room, even for a neurosurgeon, he had as yet been unable to master even the most elementary of Rufo's tricks, and had been reduced to practicing before mirrors, animals, and those children who were unaware of his vocation.

'Okay, dog,' he said, 'get ready. I'm going to omit the patter that goes with this one because I can see you eyeing those birches out there. Now, I place the coin here ... and snap my wrist like this, and ... and *voila*! the coin it is gone. .... Thank you, thank you. Now, I simply pass my other hand over like this, and ...'

The silver dollar slipped from his palm, bounced off the emergency-brake lever, and clattered beneath the seat.

The dog's head tilted to the other side.

'Shit,' Zack muttered. 'It was the sun. The sun got in my hands. Well, sorry, dog, but one trick's all you get.'

He retrieved the coin and then reached across and opened the passenger door.

Cheapdog bounded out of the camper, and in less than a minute had relieved himself on half a dozen trees, shambled down a steep, grassy slope, and belly flopped into the middle of a mountain stream.

Zack followed at a distance. He was a tall man with fine green eyes and rugged looks that Connie had once described as 'pretty damn handsome . . . in a thuggy sort of way.'

He wandered along the edge of the slope, working the stiffness of the drive from his bad knee and watching as Cheapdog made a kamikaze lunge at a blue jay and missed.

Do you know, boy? he wondered. *Do you know that the rehearsal's over? That we're not going back to the city again?*

He squinted up at the mountains. The Rockies, the Tetons, the Smokies, the Sierras, the northern Appalachians – an avid rock climber since his teens, he had climbed at one time or another in all of them. There was something special, though, something intimate and personal that he felt in the White Mountains and nowhere else; they seemed to be giving him a message – that the world, his life, were right where they should be.

The demands of surgical training had exacted a toll on every aspect of his existence. But of all those compromises and sacrifices, the unavoidable cutback in his climbing was the one he had accepted the most reluctantly. Now, at almost thirty-six, he was anxious to make up for lost time.

Thin Air . . . Turnabout and Fair Play . . . The Widow-Maker . . . Carson's Cliff . . . Each climb would be like rediscovering a long-lost friend.

Zack closed his eyes and breathed in the mountain air. For months he had wrestled with the choice of a career in academic medicine or one in private, small-town practice. Of all the decisions he had ever made – choosing a college, medical school, a specialty, a training program – this was the one that had proved the most trying.

And even after he had made it – after he had weighed all the pros and cons, gotten Connie's agreement, and opted to return to Sterling – his tenuous decision was challenged. The ink was barely dry on his contract with Ultramed Hospitals Corporation when Connie announced that she had been having serious second thoughts about relocating from the Back Bay to northern New Hampshire, and in fact, that she was developing a similar case of cold feet over being engaged to the sort of man who would even consider such a move.

Not two weeks later, the ring had arrived at his apartment in its original box, strapped to a bottle of Cold Duck.

Zack sighed and combed his dark brown hair back with his fingers. They were striking, expressive fingers – sinewy, and so long, even for the hands of a six-footer, that he had taken to sending to a medical supply house in Milwaukee for specially made gloves. Early on, those fingers had set him apart in the operating room, and even before that, on the rock face.

He gazed to the northwest and swore he had caught a glimpse of Mirror, an almost sheer granite face so studded with mica that summer sun exploded off it like a star going nova.

Lion Head . . . Tuckerman Ravine . . . Wall of Tears . . .

There was so much magic in the mountains, so much to look forward to. True, life in Sterling might prove less stimulating than in the city. But there would be peace and, as long as he could climb, more than enough excitement as well.

And, of course, there would be the practice itself – the challenges of being the first neurosurgeon ever in the area.

In less than twenty-four hours, he would be in his own office in the ultramodern Ultramed Physicians and Surgeons clinic, adjacent to the rejuvenated Ultramed-Davis Regional Hospital.

After three decades of preparation and sacrifice, he was finally set to get on with the business of his life – to show his world, and himself, exactly what he could do. The prospect blew gently across what apprehensions he had, scattering them like dry leaves.

Connie or no Connie, everything was going to work out fine.

Homemade bread and vegetable soup; goose paté on tiny sesame wafers; Waterford crystal wine-glasses and goblets; rack of lamb with mint jelly; Royal Doulton china; sweet potatoes and rice pilaf; fresh green beans with shaved almonds; fine Irish linen.

The meal was vintage Cinnie Iverson. Zack was aware of a familiar mixture of awe and discomfort as he watched his mother, wearing an apron she had embroidered herself, flutter between kitchen and dining room, setting one course after another on the huge cherrywood table, clearing dishes away, pausing to slip in and out of conversations, even pouring water; and all the while, skillfully and steadfastly refusing offers of assistance from Lisette and himself.

The table was set for eight, although Cinnie was

seldom at her seat. The Judge held sway from his immutable place at the head. His heavy, high-backed chair was not at all unlike the one behind the bench in his county courtroom. Zack had been assigned the place of honor, at the far end of the table, facing his father. Between them sat his older brother, Frank; Frank's wife, Lisette; their four-year-old twins, Lucy and Marthe; and Annie Doucette, the Iversons' housekeeper, now a widow in her late seventies and part of the family since shortly after Frank was born.

In sharp contrast to Cinnie Iverson's bustlings, the atmosphere at the table was, as usual, restrained, with periods of silence punctuating measured exchanges. Zack smiled to himself, picturing the noisy, animated chaos in the Boston Municipal Hospital cafeteria where, for the past seven years, he had eaten most of his meals. He had been raised in this house, this town, and in that respect, he belonged; but in most others, after almost seventeen years, it was as if he had packed up his belongings in Boston and moved to another planet.

Of those at the table, Zack observed, Lisette had changed the most over the years. Once a vibrant, if flighty, beauty, she had cut her hair short, eschewed any but the lightest makeup, and appeared to have settled in quite comfortably as a mother and wife. She was still trim, and certainly attractive, but the spark of adventure in her eyes, once a focus of fantasy for him, was missing. She sat between the twins, across from Frank and Annie, and reserved most of her conversation for the girls, carefully managing their etiquette, and smiling approvingly when one or the other of them entered the conversation without interrupting.

14

Lisette was a year younger than Zack, and for nearly two years – from the middle of his junior year at Sterling High until her one trip to visit him at Yale – she had been his first true love. The pain and confusion of that homecoming weekend in New Haven, the realization of how far apart just six weeks had taken them, marked a turning point in both their lives.

For a while after Lisette's return to Sterling, there were scattered calls from one to the other, and even a few letters. Finally, though, there was nothing.

Eventually, she moved away to Montreal and made brief stabs first at college, then marriage – to a podiatrist or optometrist, Zack thought. Following the breakup of her marriage, she had returned to Sterling, and within a year was engaged to Frank. Zack had been best man at their wedding and was godfather to the twins.

Like Lisette, Annie kept pretty much to herself, picking at, more than eating, her food, and speaking up only to bemoan, from time to time, the arthritis, or dizzy spells, or swollen ankles which kept her from being more of a help to 'Madame Cinnie.' It was difficult, and somewhat painful, for Zack to remember the wise, stocky woman of his boyhood, hunkered over a football then hiking it between her legs to Frank as he practiced passing to his little brother in the field behind their house.

One of the curses of being a physician was to see people, all too often, as diagnoses, and each time Zack returned home and saw Annie Doucette, he subconsciously added one or two to her list. Today Annie looked more drawn and haggard than he had ever seen her.

Frank, of all those in the room, had changed the

least over the years. Now thirty-eight, he was in his fourth year as the administrator of Ultramed-Davis Hospital. He was also, if anything, slimmer, handsomer, and more confident than ever.

'What are the possibilities,' Zack had once asked a genetics professor, 'of two brothers sharing none of the same genes?'

The old man had smiled and patiently explained that with millions of maternal and paternal genes segregating randomly into egg and sperm, all siblings, brother or sister, were, in essence, fifty percent the same and fifty percent different.

'You should meet my brother sometime,' Zack had said.

'If that's the case,' the professor had countered with a wink, 'then perhaps I should meet the family milkman, instead.'

In the end, science had prevailed, although the notion that he and Frank were fifty percent alike was only slightly less difficult for Zack to accept than the possibility of his mother having had a child by any gene pool other than the Judge's.

It was nearly seven o'clock and the meal was winding down. The twins were getting restless, but were held in place by Lisette's glances and the prospect of Grandmama's apple pie. Although snatches of conversation had dealt with Zack's upcoming practice, most of it had centered around golf. The Judge, blind to anyone else's boredom with the subject, was on the sixteenth green of a hole-by-hole account of his match with Frank.

'Thirty feet,' he said, nudging his wineglass, which in seconds was refilled by his wife. 'Maybe forty. I swear, Zachary, I have never seen your brother putt like that – Marthe, a young lady does not play with her dress at the dinner table. He steps up to the ball, then looks over at me and, just as calmly as you please, says "double or nothing." It was – what, Frank, three dollars . . . ?'

'Five,' Frank said, making no attempt to mask his ennui.

'*Mon dieu*, five. Well, I tell you, he just knocked that ball over hill and dale, right into the center of the cup for a three. The nerve. Say, maybe next weekend we can make it a threesome.'

'Hey, Judge,' Frank said, 'leave the man alone. He's an Ultramed surgeon now. It's in his contract: no golfing for the first year.' He turned to his brother, his hands raised in mock defense. 'Just kidding, Zack-o, just kidding. You play any down in Boston?'

'Only the kind where you shoot it into the whale's mouth and out its tail,' Zack said.

Annie laughed out loud and choked briefly on a piece of celery.

'We played that, Uncle Zack,' Lucy said excitedly. 'Mama took us. Marthe hit herself in the head with her club. Will you take us again sometime?'

'Of course I will.'

'You're not going away like all the other times, are you?'

'No, Lucy. I'm staying here.'

'See, Marthe. I told you he wasn't going away this time. Will you take us to McDonald's, too? We never get to go except when you take us.'

Zack shrunk in his seat before Lisette's reproving glare. 'They get confused sometimes,' he said.

'I spoke to Jess Bishop,' the Judge went on. 'He's membership chairman at the club. You remember him, Zachary? Well, no matter. Jess says that being as your father and brother are members in good standing, you won't even have to go through the application process.'

'Thank goodness,' Zack said, hoping, even as he heard his own words, that the Judge would miss the facetiousness in his voice. 'So, who finally won today?'

'Won? Why, me, of course,' the Judge said, shifting his bulk in his chair. His Christian name was Clayton, but even his wife rarely called him anything but Judge. He was, like both his sons, over six feet, but his athlete's body had, years before, yielded to his sedentary job and rich tastes. A civic leader and chairman of the board of Davis Regional Hospital until its sale to Ultramed, the Judge had no less than six plaques tacked up in the den proclaiming him Sterling Man of the Year. He was also, though in his mid-sixties, a ten handicap. 'It was close, though, Frank,' he went on. 'I'll give you that.'

'Close,' Frank humphed. 'Judge, you're the one who pounded it into us that close only counts in hand grenades and horseshoes.'

Again, Annie Doucette laughed out loud, and again her laugh was terminated by a fit of coughing. This time, Zack noted, she was massaging her chest after she had regained control, and her color was marginally more pale than it had been.

'You okay, Annie?' he asked.

'Fine, I'm fine,' the woman said in the Maurice Chevalier accent she had never shown the least inclination to change. She lowered her hand slightly, but not completely. 'Now you just stop eyeing me like you want to take out my liver or something, and

18

go on about your talking. There'll be plenty of time for you to play doctor starting tomorrow. All my friends are busy thinking up brain problems just so they can come in and see you in your office.'

Before Zack could respond, Cinnie Iverson reappeared, a pie in each hand, and began her rounds of the table, insisting that everyone take a slice half again larger than he or she desired. Annie flashed him a look that warned, 'Now don't you dare say anything that will upset your mother.' Still, there was something about her color, about the cast of her face, that made him uneasy.

Dessert conversation was dominated by the twins, who competed with each other to give 'Uncle Jacques' the more complete account of what had been happening in their lives. Completely Yankee on one side of their family and completely French-Canadian on the other, the girls were interchangeably bilingual, and as they became more and more animated, increasingly difficult to understand. What fascinated – and disturbed – Zack was the lack of outward interaction between the twins and their father, or, for that matter, between Frank and Lisette.

Perhaps it was the seating arrangement, perhaps Frank's preoccupation with issues at the hospital, in particular the arrival of his younger brother as the new neurosurgeon on the block. Whatever the reason, Zack noted that Frank had spoken scarcely a word to the girls and none, that he could recall, to Lisette. In all other respects, Frank was Frank – full of plans for expanding the scope and services of Ultramed-Davis, and tuned into every potential new real estate development and industrial move in the area.

Watching the man, listening to him expound on the risks and benefits of entering the bond market at this time, or on the possibilities of developing the meadows north of town into a shopping mall, Zack could not help but be impressed. Frank had overcome one of the most difficult obstacles in life: early success. And, Zack knew, it hadn't been easy.

A legend in three sports at Sterling High, voted class president and most likely to succeed, he had gone to Notre Dame amidst a flurry of press clippings touting him as one of the great quarterback prospects in the country. His high school grades and board scores were only average, if that, and his study habits were poor, but the coaching staff and administration at the Indiana school had promised him whatever tutoring help he might need to keep him on the field. And help him they did – at least until his passes began to fall short.

Midway through Frank's sophomore year, the angry, defensive calls and letters home began. There were too many quarterbacks. The coaches weren't paying enough attention to him. Teachers were discriminating against him because he was an athlete. Next came a series of nagging injuries – back spasms, a torn muscle, a twisted ankle. Finally, there was a visit to Cinnie and the Judge from one of the assistant coaches. Although his parents had never made him privilege to that conversation, Zack was able to piece together that Frank had developed an 'attitude problem' and had become more adept at hoisting a tankard than at directing an offense.

By the middle of Frank's junior season, he was back in Sterling, working construction, complaining about his ill treatment at Notre Dame, interviewing with the coaches and administration at the

University of New Hampshire, and partying. A knee injury midway through his first season at the state school put an end to his athletic career.

And as if those failures weren't enough, Frank had to endure the rising star of his younger brother, whose participation in all sports except climbing had been curtailed by a vicious skiing injury. Following that accident, Zack had suffered through a brief period of depression and rebellion, and then had quietly but steadily built a grade-point average that enabled him to be accepted at Yale – the first Sterling graduate to be so honored.

There was every reason for Frank to fold, to become embittered and jealous, to drop out. But he didn't. It took an extra year, but he got his degree. Then, to the surprise of many, he stayed on in school and earned a masters in business administration.

The walls of expectation erected by the Judge were sheer glass, but bit by bit, in his own way, Frank had scaled them, and now he was a success once again, at least in terms of lifestyle, power, and accomplishments.

Cinnie Iverson had poured the final round of coffee, and the twins had at last been allowed to leave their seats, when Frank stood and raised his half-filled wineglass.

'A toast,' he announced. The others raised their glasses, and the twins insisted that theirs be refilled with milk so they could join in. 'To my little brother, Zachary, who proved that brains are always better than brawn when it comes to making it in this world. It's good to have you back in Sterling.'

'Amen,' said the Judge.

'Amen,' the twins echoed.

Zack stood and raised his glass toward Frank, wondering if anyone at the table besides himself thought the message in the toast a bit strange. For a moment, his eyes and his brother's met. Almost imperceptibly, Frank nodded. The toast was no accident. For all of his status and accomplishments, Frank still measured himself against the MD degree of his younger brother, and found himself wanting.

'To you all,' Zack said finally. 'And especially to my new partner in crime. Frank, I'm proud to be working with you.'

'Amen,' shouted the twins. 'Amen.'

Chapter 2

The three of them, father and sons, sat alone at the table. Outside, the storm clouds had arrived, bringing with them a premature dusk. The women were in the kitchen; Annie in the breakfast nook, Cinnie and Lisette by the sink, loading the dishwasher for the second time, chatting about the upcoming Women's Club bake sale, and keeping watch on the twins, who had taken Cheapdog out back to play in the meadow.

In a manner quite consistent with his belief that business matters and women should be separated whenever possible, the Judge had kept the conversation light until the last of them, Annie, had left the room. Then, after a few sips of coffee, he turned abruptly to Frank.

'Guy Beaulieu came to see me yesterday,' he said.

'So?'

'He says Ultramed and that new surgeon, Mainwaring, have just about put him out of business at the hospital.'

'Jason Mainwaring's not new, Judge,' Frank said patiently. 'He's been here almost two years. And no one – not him, not Ultramed, not me, not anyone – is trying to put Beaulieu out of business. Except maybe Beaulieu himself. If he'd be a little more cooperative and a little more civil to people around the hospital, none of this would be happening.'

'Guy's a crusty old devil,' the Judge said, 'I'll grant you that. But he's also been around this town nearly as long as I have, and he's helped a lot of folks.'

'What's all this about?' Zack asked. The Judge was hardly a spontaneous man, and Zack could not help but wonder if there was a reason he had postponed this conversation through four hours of golf to have it now.

Frank and the Judge measured one another, silently debating whose version of the story Zack was to hear first. The contest lasted only a few seconds.

'A short while back,' the Judge began, obviously unwilling openly to concede Frank's 'almost two years,' 'Ultramed-Davis brought a new surgeon into town: this Jason Mainwaring.'

'I met him, I think,' Zack said. He turned to Frank. 'The tall, blond guy with the southern drawl?' Frank nodded. Zack remembered the man as somewhat distant, but polished, intense, and, during their brief contact, quite knowledgeable – more the type he would have expected to see as a university medical-center professor than as a mountain community-hospital general surgeon.

'Well,' the Judge went on, 'apparently Guy was already beginning to have some trouble getting a lot of his patients admitted to the hospital.'

Frank sighed audibly and bit at his lower lip, making it clear that only courtesy kept him from interrupting to contest the statement.

'More and more, his patients – especially the poor French-Canadian ones – were being shipped to the county hospital in Clarion. Then rumors started floating around town about Guy's competence and all of a sudden, all the surgical cases who could pay – those with insurance, or on Medicaid – were going to this Mainwaring. I've heard some of the rumors myself and, let me tell you, they are vicious. Drinking, doing unnecessary internal exams on women, taking powerful drugs because of a small stroke . . .'

'Is there truth to any of them?' Zack asked.

During the summer between his sophomore and junior years at Yale Med, he had worked as an extern at the then Davis Regional Hospital, and Beaulieu had gone out of his way to bring him into the operating room and to nurture his growing interest in surgery. It was a concern he had never forgotten.

The Judge shook his head. 'According to Guy, there have been no specific complaints from anyone. Just rumors. He says that about eighty percent of his work now is charity stuff at Clarion County, and that he hasn't operated on a non-French-Canadian patient at Ultramed for almost a year. He says the whole thing is a conspiracy to get back at him because he was so opposed to the sale of the hospital to Ultramed in the first place.'

'That's ridiculous,' Frank said. 'Mainwaring's getting the cases because he's good and he works like hell. It's as simple as that. You know, Judge, I don't think it's fair for you to take Beaulieu's side in this thing.'

Clayton Iverson slammed his hand down on the table. 'Don't you ever dare tell me what's fair, young man!' he snapped. 'The provisional phase in our contract with Ultramed still has a month to run. I convinced the board of trustees to sell out to them in the first place, and by God, the three weeks until our meeting and vote is more than enough time for me to convince them to exercise our option and buy the damn place back.'

He breathed deeply and calmed himself.

Zack glanced over at Frank. Though he was staring at their father impassively, his hands were clenched and his knuckles were bone-white.

'And let me make this clear,' the Judge went on, 'I haven't taken anyone's side. As a matter of fact, Frank, I resented his implications that you were in any way involved with his problems, and I told him so. He apologized and backed off some, but he's hurt, and he's angry. I promised him I'd speak to you – both of you – about it . . . ask you to keep your eyes and ears open. I feel we owe it to him. You were too young to remember, Frank, but that man all but saved your life when your appendix burst.'

Frank's fists relaxed a bit, though Zack could tell that he was still smarting from the Judge's threat. Personality clashes, power plays, and political machinations were, he knew all too well, as omni-present and as integral a part of hospital life as IVs and bedpans. But he sensed something more to all of this – something virulent.

'Annie!'

Cinnie Iverson's cry was followed instantly by the crash of dishes. With reflexes born of years of crisis, Zack was on his feet and headed toward the kitchen as Frank and the Judge were just beginning to react.

Annie Doucette was on the floor. Her back and neck were arched, and her limbs were flailing uncontrollably in a grand mal seizure.

As Zack knelt beside the woman, he felt *the*

change sweep over him. Early on, he had heard about the phenomenon from other, older docs, but did not undergo it himself until midway through his second year of residency, when he witnessed the cardiac arrest of a patient. In that moment, his world suddenly began to move in slow motion. His voice lowered and his words became more measured; he sensed his pulse rate drop and all his senses heighten. It was unlike anything he had ever experienced in similar emergencies. Movements became automatic, observations and orders instinctive. Dozens of facts and variables were processed instantly and simultaneously.

Later, with the patient successfully resuscitated and stabilized, he would learn from the nurses that he had acted quickly, decisively, and calmly. It was only after hearing their account of his performance that he realized fully what he had done.

The change had been part of him ever since.

'Mom, call an ambulance, please,' he said as he rolled Annie to one side to prevent her from aspirating her own stomach contents, should she vomit. His fingertips were already at the side of her neck, feeling for a carotid pulse.

As *the change* intensified, all sense of the woman as a friend, a loved one, a patient, yielded to the objectivity of assessment. If it became necessary, in any way, to hurt in order to heal, then hurt he would.

'Frank, my medical bag is in a large carton at the back of the van. Could you get it, please?' *Please. Thank you.* The use of these words during a crisis kept everybody calmer, including, he suspected, himself. Stroke; heart attack with arrhythmia; epilepsy; sudden internal hemorrhage causing shock;

hypoglycemia; simple faint mimicking a grand mal seizure; the most likely diagnostic possibilities flowed through his mind, each accompanied by an algorithm of required observations and reactions.

Annie's color was beginning to mottle. Her back remained arched and her arms and legs continued to spasm. Her jaw was clenched far too tightly to slip any buffer between her teeth. Again and again, Zack's fingertips probed up and down along the side of her windpipe, searching for a pulse. She had had chest pain at the table. Zack felt certain of that now. Heart attack with an irregular, ineffective beat or complete cardiac standstill moved ahead of all other possibilities in his mind.

'Judge, are you okay to come down here and help? Good. I'm going to put her over on her back. If she starts to vomit, please flip her back on her side, regardless of what I'm doing. Lisette, check the time, please, and keep an eye on it.'

Zack eased the woman onto her back. Her seizure was continuing, though her movements were becoming less violent. Again he checked for pulses, first at her neck, then in each groin. There were none. He delivered a sharp, two-fisted blow to the center of her chest and began rhythmic cardiac compressions as Frank arrived with his medical bag.

'Judge, please fold something up and put it beneath her neck, then lay that chair over and put her feet up on it if you can. That's it. Frank, there are some syringes with needles already attached in the bottom of the bag. I need two. Also, there's a little leather pouch with vials of medicines in it. I'll need Valium and adrenaline. That one may say 'epinephrine' on it. Mom, did you get the ambulance? Good. How long?'

'Five minutes at the most.'

'Frank, can you do CPR?'

'I took the course twice.'

'Good. Take over here, please, while I get some medicine into her to stop her seizing. Don't bother trying mouth-to-mouth until she stops. Just pump. You're doing fine. Everyone's doing fine.' Zack placed his fingertips over the femoral artery. 'A little harder, Frank, please,' he said. 'Time, Lisette?'

'Just over a minute.'

Without bothering with a tourniquet, Zack injected Valium and adrenaline into a vein in the crook of Annie Doucette's arm. In seconds, her seizure stopped. Frank continued pumping as Zack hunched over the woman and administered half a dozen mouth-to-mouth breaths. Moments later, Annie took one on her own.

'Hold it, Frank, please,' Zack said as he searched, once again, for a carotid artery pulse. This time he felt one – slow and faint, but definite. He checked in her groin. Both femoral artery pulses were palpable. Again, the woman took a breath, then another. *Come on, Annie,* his mind urged. *Do it again. Just one more. Just one more.*

He slipped a blood pressure cuff around her arm and then worked his stethoscope into place with one hand while he returned his other to the side of the woman's neck.

'I hear a pressure,' he announced softly. 'It ain't much, but for right now, it's enough.'

Annie's breathing was still shallow, but much more regular. Softly, but steadily, she began to moan. Her lips were dusky, but the terrible mottling of her skin had lessened. At that moment, they heard the whoop of the ambulance, and

29

seconds later, strobelike golden lights appeared in the living room window.

Zack looked up at his older brother, who knelt across the woman from him. For an instant, he flashed on two young boys kneeling opposite one another in a dusty, vacant lot, shooting marbles.

For ten seconds, twenty, neither man moved or spoke. Then Frank reached over and took his hand.

'Welcome to Sterling,' he said.

Chapter 3

The ambulance was one of several well-equipped vans owned by Ultramed-Davis and operated by the Sterling Fire Department. Zack sat beside Annie in the back, watching the monitor screen as the vehicle jounced down the narrow mountainside road toward the hospital. A young but impressively efficient paramedic knelt next to him, calling out a blood pressure reading every fifteen or twenty seconds.

Sterling, New Hampshire, was small in many ways, but Zack could see Ultramed's influence in the emergency team's response. This was big city medicine in the finest sense of the term. Annie was still unconscious, although her breathing seemed less labored and her blood pressure was inching upward.

'Eighty over sixty,' the paramedic said. 'It's getting a little easier to hear.'

Zack nodded and adjusted the IV which the young man had inserted flawlessly, and even more rapidly than he himself could have done.

Frank had stayed behind to tend to the family and contact a cardiologist. They would meet later at the hospital.

Zachary felt tense, but he was also charged and exhilarated. When it all came together, when it all worked right, there was no comparable feeling.

Come, Watson, Come! The game is afoot. Zack loved the quote, and often wondered if Arthur Conan Doyle, a physician, had transferred the energy of his experience with medical emergencies to his detective hero.

After a brief stretch on the highway, the ambulance slowed and turned into the long, circular driveway leading uphill to the hospital. A large, spotlighted sign at the base of the drive announced: ULTRAMED-DAVIS REGIONAL HOSPITAL – COMMUNITY AND CORPORATE AMERICA WORKING TOGETHER FOR THE BETTERMENT OF ALL.

Zack smiled to himself and wondered if he was the only one amused by the hubris of the pronouncement.

The Betterment of All.

Ultramed Hospitals Corporation and Davis Regional Hospital could certainly never be accused of setting their sights too low. Still, although he had a few lingering concerns about working for a component of what some had labeled the medical-industrial complex, his conversations with Frank and the Judge, and his investigations of the hospital and its parent company, had provided no cause to doubt the proclamation, however audacious.

Ultramed-Davis, now a modern, two-hundred-bed facility, had a proud history dating back to the turn of the century, when the Quebec-based Sisters of Charity placed ten beds in a large donated house and named it, in French, Hôpital St. Georges. Over the decades that followed, brick wings were added, until, ultimately, the old house was completely replaced. The hospital's capacity grew to fifty patients, and eventually, to eighty. In 1927, the St. Georges School of Nursing was established, and before its closing in the early seventies, produced more than 350 nurses.

In mid-1971, the ownership and administrative control of St. Georges was transferred from the Sisters of Charity to a community-based, nonprofit corporation headed by Clayton Iverson, already a Clarion County circuit judge, and was renamed after Reverend Louis Davis, the pastor who had donated the initial structure to the town.

Over the years that followed, a succession of inadequate administrators, most of them using Davis Regional as a stepping-stone to bigger and better places, made a succession of unfortunate decisions, opting too often for projects and personnel additions that looked progressive but could not support themselves financially.

Gradually, but inexorably, community support for the facility dwindled, and benefactors became scarce. Older physicians began retiring earlier than they had planned, and a lack of financial inducements kept young recruits from taking their places. Bankruptcy and closure became more than theoretical possibilities.

It was then, with the wolves howling at the hospital door, that the Ultramed Corporation appeared on the scene. A subsidiary of widely diversified RIATA International, Ultramed assailed the hospital board with slide shows, brochures, stock reports, pasteboard graphs, and more financial information on the facility than even the most diligent trustee possessed.

Suspicious of outsiders and wary of losing control of an enterprise that had, for most of a century, been at the very heart of their community, a majority of the board opposed the sale, favoring instead another bond issue and one more stab at doing things right.

Clayton Iverson, citing what he called 'the bloodred writing on the wall,' knew the community had no sensible alternative but to sell. By his own spirited account, he worked his way through the trustees one by one, cajoling, arguing, calling in markers. In the end, Zack had been told proudly, the vote was unanimous. Unanimous, that was, save one. Only Guy Beaulieu remained opposed, though out of respect for the Judge he declined to vote at all.

Never one to relinquish power with a hook, the Judge extracted two concessions from the corporation in exchange for the sale of the hospital: a provisional four-year period after which the board of trustees could repurchase the facility, including all improvements, for the original six-million-dollar price; and the serious consideration of his son for the position of administrator.

As near as Zack could tell from his father's account, following an exhaustive series of interviews, Ultramed had selected Frank over dozens of applicants – most with extensive hospital experience.

That decision, for whatever reasons it was made, had proved brilliant.

Orchestrated by Frank, and aided by time-tested business practices and public relations techniques, the turnabout in the hospital was immediate and impressive. New equipment and new physicians underscored the corporate theme of 'A Change for the Better,' and the remaining opponents of the facility – mostly in the poor and uninsured sectors of the community – experienced increasing difficulty in finding a platform from which to voice their concerns.

In just a few years, Ultramed-Davis Regional Hospital had been transported from the backwater of health care to the vanguard.

'Hang on, Doc,' the ambulance driver called over his shoulder to Zack. 'We're here.'

Zack braced himself against Annie's stretcher as the man swung a sharp turn and backed into the brightly lit ambulance bay. Alerted by the ambulance radio, a team of three nurses dressed in blue scrubs and an orderly wearing whites was poised on the concrete platform.

Before Zack could even identify himself, two of the nurses, with tight-lipped efficiency, had pulled Annie's stretcher from the ambulance and sped past him into the emergency ward.

Zack followed the stretcher to a well-equipped room marked simply, TRAUMA, and watched from the door as the team transferred Annie to a hospital litter, switched her oxygen tubing and monitor cables to the hospital console, and began a rapid assessment of her vital signs. One nurse, apparently in charge, listened briefly to Annie's chest, then took up a position at the foot of the bed, supervising the evaluation.

'Excuse me,' Zack said to the woman, who wore a white lab coat over her scrubs. 'Could I speak to you for a moment?'

The woman turned, and Zack felt an immediate spark of interest. She was in her early thirties, he guessed, if that, with short beach-sand hair, fine, very feminine features, and vibrant, almost iridescent, blue-green eyes. Instinctively, and quite out of character for him given the situation, Zack glanced at her left hand. There was no ring.

'I . . . I'm Dr. Iverson, Zachary Iverson,' he said.

Had he actually stammered? 'I'm a neurosurgeon due to start on the staff here tomorrow. That woman we just brought in is ... I mean was ... sort of like my governess when I was young. Mine and my brother Frank's.'

'Now there's a name I recognize,' the woman said, cocking her head to one side as if appraising a painting in a museum.

'Yes,' Zack said. Several seconds passed before he realized that he had not yet finished explaining what he wanted. He cleared his throat. 'Well. Frank said he would arrange for a cardiologist – a Dr. Cole, I think he said his name was – to come in and take over Annie's care. Has he arrived yet?'

'No,' the woman said thoughtfully. 'No, he hasn't, Doctor.'

Her expression was at once coy and challenging, and Zack, often oblivious to women's attempts at nonverbal interplay, felt ill-equipped to respond with an expression of his own.

'I see,' he said finally, wondering if he was looking as flustered and restless as he was feeling. His ego was goading him to be assertive – to remind the woman that, while he might have momentarily been taken aback by her, he was, at least until the arrival of Dr. Cole, in charge. He cleared his throat again and, unconsciously, stood more erect. 'Well, then,' he went on, with a bit more officiousness than he had intended, 'would you please have someone call him again. I'll be in there with Mrs. Doucette. Just send him in as soon as he gets here. Also, could you order an EKG and a portable chest X ray.'

'Certainly, Doctor,' the woman said as he strode past her and into the room.

Bravo, his ego cheered. *Well handled.* He glanced

36

back over his shoulder. The woman had not yet moved. 'Could you call the lab, too, please,' he ordered, wishing her eyes would stop smiling at him that way. 'Routine bloods.'

'Certainly,' she said. 'Cardiac enzymes, too?'

Damn her cool, Zack thought. 'Yes, of course,' he responded. 'Have them draw extra tubes as well. Dr. Cole can order whatever else he wants when he gets here.'

He walked to the bedside without waiting for an acknowledgment of his request, and forced himself not to look back.

Annie's eyes, still closed, were beginning to flutter.

'I'm Dr. Iverson,' he said to the two nurses who were attending her. 'How's she doing?'

'Her pressure's up to a hundred over sixty,' one of them, a husky, matronly woman in her fifties, said. 'She's moved both arms and both legs, and it looks like she's about to wake up.'

'Good,' Zack said, aware that a portion of his thoughts, at least, were not focused on the matter at hand. He slipped his stethoscope into place and checked Annie's heart and lungs. 'Annie, it's Zack,' he said into her ear. 'Can you hear me?'

Annie Doucette moaned softly. Then, almost imperceptibly, she nodded.

'You passed out, Annie. You're at the hospital now and you're going to be all right. Do you understand that?' Again, a nod. 'Good. Just relax and rest. You're doing fine.' He turned to the nurse. 'Dr. Cole's due here any minute. Until he gets here, we'll just keep doing what we're doing.'

The nurse looked at him queerly, then glanced over at the door. Zack followed her line of sight and found himself, once again, confronting the enig-matic ocean-green eyes. This time, though, the disconcerting woman behind them stepped forward and extended her hand.

'Dr. Iverson, I'm Dr. Suzanne Cole,' she said simply.

Her expression was totally professional, but there was an unmistakable playfulness in her eyes.

Zack felt the flush in his cheeks as he reached out and shook her hand.

'I'm sorry,' he mumbled. 'It was sort of dumb for me to assume . . . what I mean is, you weren't exactly . . .'

'I know,' she said. Her tone suggested an apology for having allowed him to dig such a hole for himself. 'I'm sure it was this outfit that confused you' – she indicated the blue scrubsuit – 'but I just finished putting in a pacemaker.' She nodded toward Annie, who was now fully awake and beginning to look around. 'You seem to have done quite a job bringing this woman back, Dr. Iverson. Congratulations.'

It was nearing midnight. Zack Iverson sat alone in the staff lounge at the back of the emergency ward, sipping tepid coffee, sorting through what had been, perhaps, the most remarkable June the thirtieth of them all, and trying to slow down his runaway fantasies concerning Suzanne Cole.

It had taken several hours to ready a bed for Annie in the coronary care unit and to effect her transfer there. During that time, Zack had stayed in the background, watching Suzanne as she managed one dangerous cardiac arrhythmia after another in the woman, balancing complex treatments against their side effects, checking monitor readouts, reviewing lab results, then, suddenly, stopping to mop Annie's brow, or to smooth errant wisps of gray hair from her forehead or simply to bend down and whisper encouragement in her ear.

Unlike what Zack had imagined from her cool composure during their initial meeting, she was actually quite tense and frenetic during critical moments, moving from one side of the bed to the other then back, checking and rechecking to ensure that her orders were being carried out correctly. Still, while she seemed frequently on edge, she was never out of control and it was clear that the nurses were comfortable with her ways, and even more important, trusted in them.

Who are you? his mind asked over and over as he watched her work. *What are you doing up here in the boondocks?*

The Judge and Cinnie had checked in twice by phone, and around ten, Frank had stopped by. He seemed restless and irritable, and although he mentioned nothing of the episode, Zack sensed that he was still quite upset by the Judge's outburst and thinly veiled threat. Citing the need to be near the twins during the violent thunderstorm that had just erupted, he had left for home after only half an hour. But before he left, Zack had managed, in what he hoped was an offhanded way, to pump a bit of information from him regarding Suzanne Cole.

Dartmouth-trained and a member of the Ultramed-Davis staff for almost two years, she was thirty-three or thirty-four, divorced, and the mother of a six-year-old girl. In addition, she was co-owner, along with another divorcée in town, of a small art gallery and crafts shop.

Zack had tried, with little success, for a more

subjective assessment of the woman, but Frank, distracted and anxious to leave, had completely missed the point.

Now, as he sat alone, Zack wondered if it was worth waiting any longer for the woman to finish her work in the unit and, as she had promised, stop by for 'a hit of decaf.' The nurses had told him that it was not that uncommon for Suzanne, as they called her, to spend the night in the hospital if she had a particularly sick patient, and this night – with Annie and her pacemaker case – she had two.

Who are you? What are you doing up here?

The state of infatuation with a woman was not something with which Zack was all that familiar or comfortable. A bookworm throughout his college years, and a virgin until his junior year, he had had a reasonable number of dates, and a few short-lived romances after Lisette, but no prolonged relationships until Connie. He had once described his social life in college as a succession of calls to women the day after they had met someone special.

Connie was five years younger than he, but possessed a worldliness and sophistication that he felt were missing from his life. She had an MBA degree from Northwestern, a management-track position at one of the big downtown companies, a condo in the Back Bay, a silver BMW, friends in the symphony, and an interest in impressionist painters ('Pissarro has more depth, more energy in one brush stroke, than Renoir has in a dozen canvases, don't you think?') and foreign films ('Zachary, if you would stop insisting on plot all the time, and concentrate more on the universality of the characters and the technical brilliance of the director, this film would mean more to you').

Friends of his spoke to him from time to time of what they perceived might be a mismatch, but he countered by enumerating the new awareness Connie had brought into his life. Whether he truly loved the woman or not, he was never sure, but there was no questioning that he was, for most of their time together, absolutely infatuated with her beauty, her confidence, and her style.

Her decision to break off their engagement had hurt him, but not as deeply as he first thought. And over the months that followed, he had spent what free time he had flying the radio-controlled airplane he had built in high school, exercising himself back into rock-climbing shape, hiking with Cheapdog, and horseback riding with friends along the seashore at the Cape – but not one minute at a gallery or locked in combat with a foreign film.

'Hi.'

Startled, Zack knocked over his Styrofoam cup, spilling what remained of his coffee into a small pool on the veneer tabletop.

'Hi, yourself,' he said as Suzanne Cole plucked a pad of napkins from the nearby counter and dabbed up the spill. Was there to be no end to his ineptitude in front of this woman?

'It would seem you might have reached the limit of your caffeine quota for the day,' she said.

She had changed into street clothes – gray slacks and a bulky fisherman-knit sweater – and she looked as fresh as if she had just started the day.

'Actually,' he said, 'I use caffeine to override my own inherent hyperness. I think it actually slows me down.'

She smiled. 'I know the syndrome. I'm surprised

to find you still here, what with tomorrow being your first day in the office and all.'

'I wanted to be sure Annie was out of the woods. She's been pretty special to me and my family. Besides, I just finished my residency yesterday. It'll probably be months before my internal chemistry demands anything more than a fifteen-minute nap in an institutional, Naugahyde easy chair.'

'I remember those chairs well,' Suzanne said, leaning against the counter. 'There's an old, ratty, maroon one in the cardiac fellows' room at Hitchcock that I suspected would one day have a sign on it proclaiming: "Suzanne Cole slept here – and only here. . . ." So, it's a progress report you're after. Well, the news is good. At least for the moment. Your Annie's awake and stable, with no neurologic deficit that I can identify, although you might want to go over her in the morning. In fact, I think I'll make her your first consult, if that's okay. You did say you were going to do neurology as well as neurosurgery, yes?'

'Absolutely. I actually enjoy the puzzles nearly as much as I do the blood and guts.'

Her eyes narrowed.

'You sure don't talk like a surgeon,' she said. 'The ones I know have signs in their rooms like: "To cut is to cure," and "All the world is pre-op."'

'Oh, I have those, too. Believe me. Only as an enlightened, Renaissance surgeon, mine say: "*Almost all the world is pre-op.*"' He pushed a chair from the table with his foot. 'Here, have a seat.'

'Sorry, but I can't,' she said. 'I've got to go. Mrs. Doucette was my third critical admission this weekend, and I have a full day tomorrow. You ought to get some sleep, too, so you'll be sharp for my consult. Good night, now.' She slipped on her coat and headed for the door.

'Wait,' Zack said, realizing even as he heard his own voice that the order was coming from somewhere outside his rational self – somewhere within his swirling fantasies.

'Yes?'

She turned back to him. The darkness in her eyes and the set of her face were warning him not to push matters further. He picked up on the message too late.

'I . . . um . . . I was wondering if we might have dinner or something together sometime.'

Suzanne sagged visibly. 'I'm sorry,' she said wearily. 'Thank you, but no.'

Zack's fantasies stopped swirling and began floating to earth like feathers. 'Oh,' he said, feeling suddenly very self-conscious. 'I didn't mean to . . . what I mean is, it seemed like—'

'Zack, I'm sorry for being so abrupt. It's late, and I'm bushed. I appreciate your asking me, really I do. And I'm flattered. But I . . . I just don't go out with people I work with. Besides, I'm involved with someone.'

The last of the feathers touched down.

Zack shrugged. 'Well, then,' he said with forced cheer, 'I guess I should just hope that a lot of folks show up at this hospital with combined cardiac and neurosurgical disease, shouldn't I?'

Suzanne reached out and shook his hand. 'I'm looking forward to working with you,' she said. 'I know we'll be terrific.'

At that moment, from the far end of the emergency ward, a man began screaming, again and again, 'No! I won't go! I'm going to die. I'm going to die!'

The two of them raced toward the commotion, which centered about an old man – in his seventies, Zack guessed – whom the nurse, the emergency physician, and a uniformed security guard were trying to move from a litter to a wheelchair.

The man, with striking, long, silver hair and a gnarled full beard, was struggling to remain where he was. Zack's gaze took in his chino pants and flannel shirt, stained with grit, sweat, and grease, and a pair of tattered, oily work boots. The old man's left arm was bound tightly across his chest with a shoulder immobilizer; the tissues over his cheek and around his right eye were badly swollen by fresh bruises.

'No!' he bellowed again. 'Don't move me. I'm going to die if I go back there tonight. Please. Just one night.'

'What gives?' Zack asked.

The emergency physician, a rotund, former GP in town, named Wilton Marshfield, released his hold, and the old man sank back on the litter.

'Oh, hi, Iverson, Dr. Cole,' he said, nodding. 'I thought you two had gone home.'

'We were about to,' said Zack. 'Everything okay?'

He had known Marshfield, a marginally competent graduate of a now-nonexistent medical school, for years, and had been surprised to find him working in the emergency room. During a conversation earlier in the evening, the man had explained that Frank had talked him out of retirement until a personnel problem in the E.R. could be stabilized. 'Plucked me off the scrap heap of medicine and offered me a salary as good as my best year in the office,' was how he had put it.

'Sure, sure, everything's fine,' Marshfield said. 'It's just that ol' Chris Gow here doesn't understand that Ultramed-Davis is a hospital, not a bloody hotel.'

'What happened to him?' Suzanne asked.

'Nothing as serious as it looks,' Marshfield answered, with unconcealed disdain. 'He just had a little too much of the hooch he brews up in that shack of his, and fell down his front steps. Fractured his upper arm near the shoulder, but there's not a damn thing we can do for that except ice and immobilization. Films of his facial bones are all negative, and so's the rest of his exam. Now, we've got an ambulance all set to cart him home, but the old geezer won't let us take him off the litter without a fight. We'll take care of it, though. Don't worry.'

Suzanne hesitated for a moment, as if she wanted to comment on the situation, but then nodded and backed off a step.

Zack, however, brushed past the portly physician to the bedside.

'Mr. Gow, I'm Dr. Iverson,' he said. The old man looked up at him, but didn't speak. His face, beneath the beard and the filth, had an ageless, almost serene quality to it, but there was a sadness in his eyes that Zack had seen many times during his years of caring for the largely indigent Boston Muni patients – a sadness born of loneliness and hopelessness. There was also no small measure of fear. 'Are you in much pain?'

'Not according to him, I ain't,' the man answered, still breathing heavily from his struggles. 'I wonder when the last time was *he* fell down the stairs like I did and broke his arm.'

'Who do you live with?'

The old man laughed mirthlessly, wincing from the pain. Then he turned his head away.

Zack looked to Marshfield for the answer.

'He lives by himself in a shack at the end of the old logging road off 219.'

'Do you have a phone, Chris?'

Again, the man laughed.

'How did you get here?'

'How do you think?'

'A trucker found him sitting by the highway and brought him in,' Marshfield explained. 'Chris is no stranger here. He's a woodcutter. Periodically, he goes on a toot and cuts up himself instead of the wood.' He laughed at his own humor and seemed not to notice that no one else joined in. 'We sew him up and ship him back home until the next time.'

Zack looked down at the old man. Could there be any sadder state than being sick or badly hurt, and being alone – of hoping, against hope, for someone to come and help, but knowing that no one would?

'Why can't he just be admitted for a day or two?' he asked. 'Are there empty beds in the house?'

'Oh, we have beds,' Marshfield said, 'but ol' Chris here doesn't have any kind of insurance, and unless his problem is life-threatening, which it isn't, he either goes to Clarion County, if we want to ship him out there, or he goes home.'

'What if a staff doctor insists on admitting someone who can't pay?'

Marshfield shrugged. 'It doesn't happen. If it did, I guess the physician would have to answer to the administration. Look, Iverson, you weren't around when this hospital admitted every Tom, Dick, and Harry who came down the pike, regardless of whether they could pay or not, but I'm here to tell you, it was one helluva mess. There were some weeks when the goddamn place couldn't even meet its payroll, let alone buy any new equipment.'

'This man's staying,' Zack said.

The emergency physician reddened. 'I told you we had things under control,' he said.

Zachary glanced down at the old man. Sending him home to an isolated shack with no phone and, as likely as not, no food, went against his every instinct as a physician.

'Under control or not,' he said evenly, 'he's staying. Admit him to me as . . . malnutrition and syncope. I'll write orders.'

Marshfield's jowly cheeks were now crimson. 'It's your goddamn funeral,' he said. 'You're the one who's going to get called on the carpet by the administration.'

'I think Frank will understand,' Zack said.

This time, Marshfield laughed out loud. 'There are a few docs beating the bushes out there for a job because they thought the same thing, Iverson.'

'Like I said, he's being admitted.'

'And like I said, it's your funeral. It's okay, Tommy,' he said to the guard. 'You can go on about your rounds. Dr. Social Service, here, is hell-bent on learning things the hard way.'

He turned on his heels and stalked away.

'Chris, you're going to stay, at least for the night,' Zack said, taking the old man's good hand in his. 'I'll be back to check you over in a few minutes.'

The man, bewildered by the sudden change in his fortune, could only stare up at him and nod. But the corners of his eyes were glistening.

Zack turned to Suzanne. 'Come on,' he said, 'I'll

walk you outside. I can use the fresh air.'

They walked through the electronically opened doorway and out onto the ambulance platform. A steady, windblown rain swept across the coal-black pavement.

'I guess I have a few adjustments to make if I'm to survive here,' he said, shivering momentarily against the chill.

Suzanne flipped the hood of her trench coat over her head. 'Do us all a favor,' she said, 'and don't make any ones you don't absolutely have to. That was a very kind thing you did in there.'

'Insurance or not, that old guy's paid his dues.'

'Perhaps,' Suzanne said. 'Yes, perhaps he has. Well, I'll see you in the morning.'

'Yeah.'

She turned and took several steps, then turned back. 'Zack, about that dinner. How about Wednesday night? My place.'

Zack felt his pulse skip. 'I thought you didn't date men you worked with?'

'No policy should be without exceptions,' she said. 'You just made that point in there yourself, didn't you?'

'Yes. Yes, I suppose I did. But how about your . . . other involvement?'

She pushed her hood back from her forehead and smiled at him, first with her eyes, then with her lips.

'I lied,' she said.

Chapter 4

Lisette Iverson stood by the glass doors of her bedroom balcony, wincing as half a dozen spears of lightning crackled through the jet sky over the Androscoggin River Valley. Far below and to the south, Sterling incandesced eerily beneath the strobe. A cannonade of thunder rumbled, then exploded, shaking the tall, hillside A-frame like a toy.

She tightened her robe and then tiptoed down the hall to check on the girls. Mercifully, after two fitful hours battling the ghosts of the storm, both were asleep. Lisette had never done well with thunderstorms herself, and felt no small guilt at having passed those fears on to her children.

God, how she wished Frank would come to bed, or at least talk to her. It was nearly one in the morning, and he was still downstairs in 'his' den, staring, she knew, at the embers in 'his' fireplace, and listening over and over to the album of morose, progressive jazz he favored when he was angry at her.

And as usual, she also knew, he would take his own sweet time in telling her why.

It was the job, the hospital, that kept him so tense. Lisette felt certain of it. For a year – no, much longer than that now, two at least – he had been a bear to live with. And with each passing week, each passing month, there seemed to be less and less she could do to please him. Silently, she cursed the day he had closed his business in Concord and moved back to Sterling, even if the little electronics firm was on the ropes.

To be sure, his success with Ultramed had given them more than she could ever have imagined. But as she reflected on the dashing dreamer she had fallen in love with and married, Lisette told herself the price they were paying was far too high.

For a time, she debated simply going to bed. If she did, of course, Frank would never come up. He would spend the night on the sofa in his den and would be in his office at the hospital by the time she and the twins awoke. With a sigh of resignation, she stepped into her slippers and headed down the stairs. There was no way she could outlast him. She cared, and he, for the moment at least, did not.

The situation was as simple as that.

GARFIELD MOUNTAIN
JUNIOR OLYMPIC TIME TRIALS

Sparkling like neon against the sunlit snow, the crimson and white banner said it all.

From his spot at the base of the main slope, Frankie Iverson squinted up at the giant slalom course – a rugged series of two-dozen gates marked with red and blue flags. *One more run*, he told himself. Just one more run like the last, and he would be on his way to Colorado.

The trip, the trophy, everything. After years of practice, years of frustration, they were so close now he could taste them.

'Next year will be yours,' the Judge had told him

during the agony and tears that had followed last year's race. 'Next year Tyler will be too old to compete, and you'll be number one.'

Tyler. What a joke. Why couldn't his father understand that it was the shitty way the slope had been groomed – the goddamn ruts that had caught his skis – that had caused him to lose by half a second. Not Tyler.

One more run.

'Hey, Frankie, you sleeping or what?'

Startled, Frank whirled. His brother, Zack, wearing black boots and a black racing suit, ambled towards him over a small mound of packed snow.

'Just studying the course, Zack-o,' Frank said.

'As if you needed to. You could ski backward and there's still no one in this field who could catch you.'

Frank jabbed a thumb toward the huge board where the times for the first run were posted. 'You could.'

Zack laughed out loud. 'Make up three seconds on you when I've never once beaten you on a run? You've got to be kidding. Listen, all I want to do is stay on my feet and get that second place trophy. There'll be plenty of time for me next year when you're racing Seniors.'

'Sure, Zack-o, sure. Lay it on any thicker and I'll slip on it. Since when did you get off thinking you could psych me?'

And psyching he was, too, the little worm, Frank thought.

They were just about two years apart in age, but Zack had hit a growth spurt just after his thirteenth birthday, and suddenly, over the year that had followed, the competition between them had intensified in all sports – especially in skiing, where the gap separating them had been narrowing all winter.

Again, Frank glanced at the time board. There was a wide margin between Zack and the boy in third place. The final run was a two-man race, and his brother knew it as well as he did. He was being psyched, all right. Zack would be skiing second, right after him, and he was getting set to pull out all the stops.

'Listen, Frankie,' Zack said, with that note of sincerity that Frank knew was a crock of shit, 'I mean it. I'll try my best, sure. But I'll be pulling for you, too. Believe me I will.' He reached out his hand. 'Good luck.'

Frank looked at his brother's hand and then at his face. There was something in Zack's eyes that made him almost shudder – a confidence, a determination he had never seen in them before. It was a look, though, that he knew well – a look he had faced many times in the eyes of their father. Frank hesitated for a fraction of a second and then pulled off his glove and gripped Zack's hand tightly.

'Go for it,' he said.

'I will. See you up top.'

Zack smiled at him, nodded, and wandered off to join a group of racers waiting for word that the second run was to begin.

Frank glanced over at the crowd of parents preparing to make their way to vantage points along the course. At that instant, the Judge, who was chatting with several friends, looked over. Frank smiled thinly, and his father responded with a hearty thumbs-up sign.

One more run.

Restless to get it over with, Frank crossed to retrieve his skis from the rack where they and those of the other competitors were lined up on end like pickets in a fence. He knew he was shaken by the brief encounter with his younger brother and by the look in his eyes. And that knowledge upset him even more.

Three seconds was a lot, true, but the way Zack had been coming on over the past few weeks, anything was possible. For a moment, Frank even toyed with the notion of asking him to back off, to wait his turn.

It wasn't fair, he thought. First that goddamn rut, now this. It was *his* year. The Judge had said so himself. Nothing was going to keep him from that trophy, that trip – nothing and no one.

He pulled his skis from the rack and ran his hand along the bottom, testing the wax.

Relax, he pleaded with himself. *Relax, but keep that edge the Judge is always talking about. That winning edge.*

It was then that he noticed Zack's black Rossignols, resting in the slot next to where his own skis had been. Trancelike, he set his skis back in their place and then took a coin – a dime – from his pocket.

This would be his year. Next year would be Zack's. That was the way it was meant to be.

He glanced about. No one was watching. Using the coin, he loosened the toe-binding screws on one of Zack's skis two turns – not enough to really feel different, just enough to lessen control a bit, to widen each turn a few inches, to preserve his three-second edge.

It was his year. His last chance. In fact, he was doing Zack a favor, ensuring that should he fall, the ski would come free and help keep him from a serious ankle injury.

But there would be no fall. No injury. Just a few inches at each gate. Just a few fractions of a second. Just enough. Next year was time enough for Zack. Then the Judge would have two Junior Olympians to boast about. It was the best way for everyone. The way things were meant to be. It was his year ... his year. ...

'Frank?'

The colors and sensations of that day faded as Lisette's voice nudged its way into the scene.

Frank rubbed at his eyes and then pushed himself upright on the sofa. The fire he had built against the chill of the summer storm had dwindled to a few smoldering embers. His mouth tasted foul from the two scotches – or was it three? – he had buried, and his head was pounding at the temples.

'Honey, are you all right?'

'I'm fine,' he mumbled, pawing at his eyes. 'Just great.' It had been years since he had had that nightmare. Years.

'Frank, please, come to bed. It's after one-thirty.'

'I'm not tired.'

'You were sleeping.'

'I wasn't fucking sleeping. I was thinking.'

'Do you want anything? Some milk? A sandwich?'

'I told you, I'm fine. Just leave me alone.'

It was going to be bad, he thought. He had fought the whole thing from the very beginning, but he hadn't fought hard enough. The last thing he needed in life was his brother moving back to Sterling. And now, thanks to the Judge and goddamn Leigh Baron, here Zack was, and already playing hero. He should have fought harder. Baron ran Ultramed, but

Davis was still *his* goddamn hospital, and he should have fought harder.

'Frank, honey,' Lisette said, 'you say you're fine, but I know that's not true. You haven't said a decent word to me all night.'

She tried to sweep his hair from his forehead, but he brushed her hand aside. Then he crossed unsteadily to the hearth, threw a log on the embers, and jabbed at it with the poker.

'That was quite a little show you put on this evening, Lisette,' he said thickly. 'Quite a little show.'

'I don't know what you're talking about. Really I don't.'

'Oh, give me a break. I saw you standing back there mooning over my brother. And I'm sure I wasn't the only one, either.'

'Honey, that's crazy. I never . . .'

'Sure, like you never made love with him, either. Christ, it's a wonder you didn't rip your dress off right then and there in the kitchen.'

'Frank, please. You've been drinking. You only say things like that to me when you've been drinking. What you know about me and Zack is all there ever was. Nothing more. And certainly nothing that didn't burn out years ago. I was excited about what he did for Annie, but so was everyone. Besides that I didn't say three words to him all night. Now please, come to bed. Let me rub your back or something.'

'You go to bed. I'll be up when I'm ready.'

'Frank, you believe me, don't you? I love you.'

'There's only one reason, one explanation why he would have passed up all those big-time job opportunities to come back here,' he said, more to himself than to her. 'One reason. And that's to rub it in to me.'

He splashed more scotch into his glass and downed it immediately.

'Frank, please don't have any more to—'

'He's a vindictive son of a bitch, Lisette. Beneath that mellow, do-gooder image of his, he's as vindictive as they come. And whether he admits it or not, he's got a score to settle for all those years he had to watch from the stands while everyone was cheering for me. He's got points he wants to make with Mom, with the Judge, with everyone in this damn town – even you.'

'That's crazy.'

'Yeah? Well, we'll see what's crazy?' He stumbled against the side of the sofa and then dropped heavily onto it. 'He can have this place. The hospital, the Judge, Leigh Baron, all of it except you – but only when I say so. Only after I've done what I've set out to do. Only after I've . . .'

His eyes closed and his head slumped to one side. In seconds, he was snoring.

Lisette took a blanket and drew it over him. It was the liquor talking. Nothing more. By morning it would be a wonder if Frank remembered anything of what he had just said. He loved his brother. Just as he loved her and the twins.

He just wasn't very good at showing it, that was all.

There was something tearing at him – something that had nothing to do with Zack.

Only after I've done what I set out to do. What in God's name had he meant by that?

Silently vowing to do whatever she could to get her husband through whatever it was that had him so on edge, Lisette turned and headed back up the stairs.

Chapter 5

The Carter Conference Room of Ultramed-Davis, refurbished by Ultramed but originally donated to the hospital by the paper company, was a large, all-purpose space, with deep-pile carpeting, a speaker's table and podium at one end, and seating for close to one hundred. Metal-framed, full-color lithographs of significant moments in medical history lined the room on either side, and photographic portraits of past presidents of the medical staff filled the rear wall by the door. Beneath each portrait was a small gold plaque engraved with the officer's name, year of birth and year of death. Beneath those photographs of past presidents still living, the date of birth had already been engraved, followed by a hyphen and a ghoulishly expectant space.

It was seven-thirty in the morning of Wednesday, July 3. The medical staff usually met on the first Thursday of the month, but because of the holiday, the staff had voted to hold its July session on Wednesday instead. The heated debate on the subject, typical for any group of MDs, had taken up more than half of its June meeting.

Forty physicians, nearly the whole staff of Ultramed-Davis, milled about the room, some exchanging pleasantries or bawdy stories, others obtaining 'curbside consultations' from various specialists. A few merely stood by a window, staring wistfully at the brilliant summer day they would never have the opportunity to enjoy.

Zack Iverson sat alone toward the back of the room, mentally trying to match the faces and demeanors of various doctors with their medical specialties (gray crew cut, red bow tie . . . pediatrician; forty-four long sportcoat, thirty-four-inch waist, slightly crooked nose . . . orthopedist), and musing on his first two days in practice.

They had gone quite smoothly, with a number of consultations in the office and several in the hospital. He had even spent a brief stretch in the operating room, assisting one of the orthopedists in the removal of a large calcium deposit that had entrapped a young carpenter's right ulnar nerve at the elbow.

Several times each day, he had visited with Annie, who was progressing reasonably well in the coronary unit. He had also discharged old Chris Gow after a day and a half of good nursing care and after arranging for social services to help him get medicare coverage, physical therapy, and one meal a day at home. Contrary to Wilton Marshfield's dire prediction, there had been no repercussions from Frank or anyone else regarding the old man's hospitalization.

All in all, they had been two interesting and rewarding days – the sort that more than made up for medicine's liabilities as a career.

This day, however, was the one Zack had been awaiting. It would start with his first major case in the O.R. – the removal of a woman's ruptured cervical disc – and it would end with dinner at Suzanne's. He smiled to think of how misguided his apprehension about coming to Sterling had been.

'Okay, everyone, find a seat.'

The staff president, a pale, doughy internist named Donald Norman, called out the order as he hand-shook his way to the front of the room.

Norman had interviewed Zack twice on behalf of Ultramed, and it was actually *in spite* of the man and those two sessions that Zack had decided to come to Davis at all. A graduate of one of the medical schools in the Caribbean, Norman had been subsidized and trained at Ultramed hospitals and was a company man right down the line. His portion of the interviews had consisted of little more than a mirthless litany of Ultramed procedural and medical policies, each accompanied by a set of statistics justifying the 'guideline' as beneficial to the welfare of both patient and hospital.

While Norman hailed the streamlined corporate approach as 'revolutionary and unquestionably necessary,' Zack wondered if it amounted to a sort of gentrification of health care.

And he made no points whatever with the man by saying so.

To make matters worse between the two of them, Zack's spontaneity and relaxed, eclectic approach to medicine sat poorly with Norman, who, though no more than a year or two older than Zack, wore a three-piece suit, smoked a curved meerschaum, and generally conducted himself like some sort of aging medical padrone.

In the end, with Zack's decision still very much in the air, several of the other physicians on staff managed to convince him that Ultramed-Davis was far more flexible in its policies and philosophy than Donald Norman liked to believe.

Norman took his place at the front table and

gaveled the meeting to order with the underside of an ashtray.

During the secretary's, treasurer's, and committees' reports, several latecomers straggled in, including Suzanne, looking lithe and beguiling in sandals and a floral-print dress. She was accompanied by Jason Mainwaring, who, Zack noticed in spite of himself, wore no wedding ring, although he did sport a sizable diamond on one little finger. The two took seats on the opposite side of the room and continued a whispered conversation, during which the charismatic general surgeon touched her on the arm or hand at least half a dozen times.

Zack spent a minute or two trying, unsuccessfully, to catch her eye, and then gave up and turned his attention to the meeting.

'Any additions or corrections to the committee reports?' Norman was saying. 'If not, they stand accepted as read. Old business?'

One hand went up, accompanied by low groans from several parts of the room.

'Yes, Dr. Beaulieu,' Norman said, taking no pains to mask the annoyance in his voice.

From his seat, five or six rows in front of Zack, Guy Beaulieu stood, looked deliberately about the room, and finally marched up to the speaker's podium – a move that prompted several more groans.

Zack, who had not seen Beaulieu in three or four years, was struck by the physical change in the man. Once energetic and robust, he was now almost pathologically thin. His suit was ill-fitting and his gaunt face had a sallow, grayish cast. Still, he held himself rigidly erect, as had always been his manner, and even at a distance, Zack could see the defiant spark behind his gold-rimmed bifocals.

'Thank you, Mr. President,' Beaulieu began, with a formality that probably would have sounded unnatural and patronizing coming from most in the room, but coming from him, did not. His speech still bore an unmistakable French-Canadian flavor, especially his 'th' diphthongs, which sounded more like *d*'s. 'I know that many of you are becoming a bit weary with my monthly statements on behalf of those who are not being cared for by this institution, as well as against those of you who have slandered my name in this community. Well, I promise you that this will be the last in that series. So, if you will just bear with me . . .'

He removed a couple of sheets of yellow legal paper from his suit-coat pocket and spread them out on the podium. Once again, there were muted groans from several spots in the room.

Zack glanced over at Jason Mainwaring, who now sat motionless, staring impassively at the man. At that moment Suzanne turned and caught his eye. Zack waved a subtle greeting with three fingers, and she nodded in return. She seemed, even at a distance, to be preoccupied.

'I would like to inform the medical staff of Ultramed-Davis Hospital,' Beaulieu read, adjusting his bifocals, 'that I have retained the Concord firm of Nordstrom and Perry, and have filed a class-action suit against this hospital, its administration, its medical staff, and the Ultramed Hospitals Corporation on behalf of the poor and uninsured people in the Ultramed-Davis treatment area. I am being joined in this effort by a number of present and former patients who fall into that group, including Mr. Jean Lemoux, Mr. Ivan MacGregor, and the family of Mme. Yvette Coulombe.

'The charges, which include unlawful and callous discharge from the hospital, improper patient transfer, and refusal to treat, are currently under review by Legal Assistance of New Hampshire, who have promised a decision in the next two weeks as to whether or not they will join our effort. As I have said many times before, sound, compassionate medical care is a right of all people, not a privilege. The attitude of this facility has, over the past three years, become one of, "Why should you get health care just because you are sick?" We intend to fight that policy.'

Zack glanced around the room and catalogued myriad reactions among the physicians; few, if any, of them, seemed sympathetic, and none of them appeared very threatened or upset. Some were openly exchanging looks and gestures of disgust, and one was actually circling a finger about one ear.

There are a few docs out there beating the bushes for a job because they thought the same thing, Iverson. Wilton Marshfield's warning against bucking the Ultramed system echoed in Zack's thoughts as he studied the sea of blank and disapproving expressions. Suzanne's, he noted, fell vaguely in the second group.

Beaulieu, too, paused and looked about, but then he continued as if unperturbed.

'In addition to the charges outlined above, we shall document a progressive and unethical blurring of the distinction between medical suppliers and providers, to the point where the care of patients throughout and without this facility is being compromised. We have evidence to back up our position, and every day we acquire more. It is my hope that those on the medical staff who have information which will further substantiate our claims will come forward and present such information to me or to our attorney, Mr. Everett Perry. I assure you that all such disclosures will be kept in the strictest confidence.'

The man, for all of his 'crustiness,' as the Judge had put it, had guts, Zack acknowledged. Again he scanned the room; guts, yes, but not a speck of visible support.

'Finally,' Beaulieu read on, 'I would like to announce that I, personally, have initiated legal action against a member of this staff, as well as against the administration of this hospital, who are, I believe, responsible for the slanderous, inaccurate, and highly damaging rumors regarding my personal and professional conduct. I call upon any physician who has knowledge of this matter to come forward. Again, I promise strictest confidence. Remember, there but for the grace of almighty God go any one of you.

'I thank you for your patience, and would welcome your questions and comments.'

Not a hand was raised. Beaulieu nodded in a calm and dignified manner, and then returned to his seat, apparently unmindful of the many annoyed and angry expressions that were fixed on him.

The staff meeting proceeded uneventfully. At the end of 'new business,' Zack was formally introduced and welcomed with brief, measured applause. Sensing that some verbal acknowledgment of the greeting was called for, he stood up.

'Thank you all very much,' he began. 'It feels great to be home again, and to be on the medical staff of the hospital in which I was born. As Dr. Norman noted in introducing me, in addition to my neurosurgical practice, I shall try to function as a medical neurologist until we are large enough, and lucky enough, to get one of our own. It is my hope to care for all those who need help in my area of expertise' – he glanced over at Guy Beaulieu – 'regardless of their ability to pay.

'I would also like to thank our radiologists, Drs. Moore and Tucker, as well as my brother Frank, for their work in obtaining our CT scanner. It's a beautiful piece of equipment, and both radiologists have gone out of their way to become versed in its use. Sometime soon, the three of us plan to present some sort of workshop on the interpretation and limitations of the technique.

'Since my nearest backup is close to a hundred miles away, I'll be on twenty-four-hour call, except during my vacation, which is scheduled from August third through August fifth . . . three years from now. Thank you.'

There was laughter and applause from around the room.

'Oh, one more thing,' Zack added as the reaction died away. 'I expected there might be some unusual problems arising from my decision to return and set up shop in the town where I was born and raised. So I'd like to make it perfectly clear that there is absolutely no truth to the rumor – started, I believe, by Dr. Blunt over there, who delivered me and was my pediatrician – that I won't go into the operating room without the one-eyed teddy bear I insisted on clinging to during his examinations.'

Suzanne, with Jason Mainwaring in tow, caught up with Zack in the corridor.

'Zack, hi,' she said. 'Thanks for the laughs in

there. Have you met Jason?'

'I think briefly, a few months ago,' Zack said, shaking the surgeon's hand. 'Nice to see you again.'

'Same here,' Mainwaring said, in a pronounced drawl. 'That was a cute little speech, Iverson. I was especially partial to the line about the teddy bear.'

'Thanks,' Zack said, wondering if the man was being facetious.

'I even liked that other one. About your next vacation being so far away. You're a funny man.'

'Thanks again.'

'However,' the surgeon continued, 'I would caution you against makin' any more inflammatory statements about this Beaulieu business until you know all the facts. Y'see, Iverson, I'm the staff member Beaulieu alluded to in there – the one he's suin'. And noble as you tried to sound in your little pronouncement there, you and Beaulieu aren't the only ones who do charity work. I operate on plenty of folks who can't pay, too.'

Zack was startled by the man's rudeness.

'Well,' he said, 'I'm glad to hear that. I only hope they get their money's worth.'

'You know,' Mainwaring countered, 'I've always heard that only the most arrogant and sadistic surgeons elect to spend their professional lives suckin' on brain. . . .'

'Hey, guys, what is this?' Suzanne cut in. 'This sounds like the sort of exchange you both should have put behind you when you climbed down from your tree houses and started high school. Jason, what's with you? Were you attacked in your crib by a mad neurosurgeon or something?'

Mainwaring smiled stiffly. 'My apologies, Iverson,' he said.

65

He extended his hand, but shielded from Suzanne the hostility in his eyes was icy.

'Hey, no big deal, Jason. No big deal.'

'Good. Well then, we'll have to see what we can do about drummin' up a little neurosurgical business for y'all.'

'Thanks.'

'Meanwhile, you might try to steer clear of politics around this place – at least until you've been here long enough to learn everyone's name.' He checked his gold Rolex. 'Suzanne, dear, I b'lieve we still have time to complete our business. Nice to see you, Iverson. I'm sure you'll make the adjustment to this sleepy little place just fine.'

Without waiting for a response, he took Suzanne's arm and strode down the hallway.

Andy O'Meara, red-cheeked, beer-bellied, and beaming, strolled among the tables of Gillie's Mountainside Tavern, shaking hands and exchanging slaps on the back with the twenty or so men enjoying their midday break in the smoky warmth. Over nearly twenty years he had come to know each and every one of them well, and was proud to call them his friends.

'Andy O, you old fart. Welcome back!' ... 'Hey, it's Mighty Mick. Way to go, Andy. Way to go. We knew you'd beat it.'

First the cards and candy and flowers when he was in the hospital, and now this welcome back. They were a hell of a bunch. The very best. And at that moment, as far as Andy O'Meara was concerned, he was the luckiest man alive. Tomorrow would be Independence Day – the day for celebrating the birth of freedom. And this day was one for celebrating his own rebirth.

'Hey, Gillie,' he called out, the lilt of a childhood in Kilkenny still coloring his speech. 'Suds around, on me.'

After three months of pain and worry, after more than a dozen trips to Manchester for radiation therapy, after sitting time and again in the doctor's office, waiting for the other shoe to fall, waiting for the news that 'We can't get it all,' he was back on the road, cured. The bowel cancer that had threatened his very existence was in some jar in the pathology department at Ultramed-Davis Hospital, and whatever evil cells had remained in his body had been burnt to hell by the amazing X-ray machines. The backseat and trunk of his green Chevy were once again filled with the boxes of shoes and boots and sneakers that he loved to lay out for the merchants along route 16, and the rhythm of his life had at last been restored.

'To the luck of the Irish,' he proclaimed as he hoisted the frosted mug over his head.

'And to you, Andy O,' Gillie responded. 'We're glad to have you back among the living.'

Andy O'Meara exchanged handshakes and hugs with each man in the place, and then set his half-filled tankard on the bar. It was his first frosty in more than twelve weeks, and with a full afternoon of calls ahead of him, there was no sense in putting his tolerance for the stuff to the test.

He settled up with Gillie and stepped out of the dim, pine-paneled tavern, into the sparkling afternoon sunlight. He prided himself on never being late for a call, and Colson's Factory Outlet was nearly a thirty-minute drive through the mountains.

He switched on the radio. Kenny Rogers was

admonishing him to know when to hold and know when to fold. The country/western music, usually Andy's staple, seemed somehow out of keeping with the peace and serenity of this day. At the edge of the driveway he stopped and changed to a classical program on WEVO, the public station.

Better, he thought. *Much better.*

The tune was familiar. Almost instantly, it conjured up images in Andy's mind – softly falling snow . . . a stone hearth . . . a roaring fire . . . family. As he hummed along, Andy tried to remember where he had heard the haunting melody before.

'. . . What child is thi-is, who laid to re-est in Mary's la-ap, lay slee-eeping? . . .'

He surprised himself by knowing many of the words.

'This, thi-is is Christ the Ki-ing, whom shepherds gua-ard and angels sing. . . .'

It was the Christmas carol, he suddenly realized. That was it. As a child in Ireland it had been one of his favorites. How strange to hear it in the middle of summer.

He paused to let a semi roar past. The noise of the truck was muted – almost as if it made no sound at all. Andy shrugged. As wonderful as it felt to be back on the road again, it also felt a little odd.

'. . . Haste, ha-aste to bring him lau-au-aud, the Ba-abe, the so-on of Ma-ry. . . .'

He closed the windows, turned on the air conditioner, and swung out of the drive onto route 110. The green of the mountainside seemed uncomfortably bright. He squinted, then rubbed at his eyes and wondered if perhaps he should stop someplace to pick up a pair of sunglasses. No, he decided. No stops. At least not until after Colson's.

Settle down, old boy, he said to himself. *Just settle down*.

He adjusted the signal on the radio and settled back in his seat, humming once again.

Route 110 was two lanes wide, with a narrow breakdown space on either side. It twisted and turned, rose and dropped like an amusement-park ride, from Groveton on the Vermont border, along the ridge of the Ammonoosuc River Valley, to Sterling and Route 16. A scarred, low, white guard-rail paralleled the road to Andy's right, and beyond the rail was the gorge, at places seven hundred feet deep.

Andy's restless, ill-at-ease sensation was inten-sifying, and he knew he was having difficulty concentrating. He adjusted his seatback and checked his safety harness. The guardrail had become something of a blur, and the solid center line kept working its way beneath his left front tire. He tightened his grip on the wheel and checked the speedometer. Forty-five. *Why did it feel like he was speeding?*

Subtly, he noticed, the trees on the mountainside had begun to darken – to develop a reddish tone. He rubbed at his eyes and, once again, forced the sedan back to the right-hand lane. Twenty-five years on the road without an accident. He was damned if he was going to have one now.

Ahead of him, the scenery dimmed. A tractor trailer approached, sunlight sparking brilliantly off its windshield.

Suddenly, Andy was aware of a voice echoing in his mind – a deep, slow, resonant, reassuring voice, at first too soft to understand, then louder . . . and louder still. 'Okay, Andy,' it said, 'now all I want you to do is count back from one hundred . . . count back from one hundred . . . count back from one hundred . . .'

Out loud, Andy began to count. 'One hundred . . . ninety-nine . . . ninety-eight . . .'

A blue drape drifted above him, then floated down over his abdomen.

'Ninety-seven . . . ninety-six . . .'

Hands, covered by rubber gloves, appeared in the space where the drape had been.

'Ninety-five . . . ninety-four . . . Why aren't I asleep?' his mind asked. 'Ninety-three . . . ninety-two.'

'Bove electrode, please,' the low voice said. 'Set it for cut and cauterize.'

Another pair of gloved hands appeared, one of them holding a gauze sponge, and the other, a small rod with a metal tip. Slowly, they lowered the metal tip toward his belly.

'Ninety-one . . . ninety—'

Suddenly a loud humming filled his mind. The metal tip of the rod touched his skin just below his navel, sending a searing, electric pain through to his back and down his legs.

'Jesus Christ, stop!' Andy screamed. 'I'm not asleep! I'm not asleep!'

The wall of his lower abdomen parted beneath the electric blade, exposing a bright yellow layer of fat.

'Eighty-nine! . . . Eighty-eight! . . . For God's sake, stop! It's not working! I'm awake! I can feel that! I can feel everything!'

'Metzenbaums and pick-ups, please.'

'No! Please, no!'

The Metzenbaum scissors sheared across Andy's

peritoneum, parting the shiny membrane like tissue paper and exposing the glistening pink rolls of his bowel.

Again, he screamed. But this time, the sound came from his voice, as well as from within his mind.

His vision cleared at the moment the right head-light of his automobile made contact with the guardrail. The Chevy, now traveling at nearly ninety miles an hour, tore through the protective steel as if it were cardboard, crossed a narrow stretch of grass and gravel, and then hurtled over the edge of the gorge.

Strapped to his seat, Andy O'Meara watched the emerald trees flash past. In the fourth second of his fall, he realized what was happening. In the fifth, the Chevy shattered on the jagged rocks below and exploded.

Chapter 6

The cafeteria of Ultramed-Davis, like most of the facility, had been renovated in an airy and modern, though quite predictable, style. The interior featured a large, well-provisioned salad bar, and a wall of sliding glass doors opened onto a neat flagstone terrace with a half-dozen cement tables and benches.

Pleasantly exhausted from his three-hour cervical disc case, Zack sat at the only table partially shaded by an overhanging tree and watched as Guy Beaulieu maneuvered toward him through the lunchtime crowd.

During the summer Zack had spent as an extern at the then Davis Regional Hospital, Beaulieu had been extremely busy with his practice and with his duties as president of the medical staff. Still, the man always seemed to have enough time to stop and teach, or to reassure a frightened patient, or to console a bereaved family.

And from that summer on, the surgeon's blend of skill and compassion had remained something of a role model for Zack.

'So,' Beaulieu said as he set down his tray and slid onto the stone bench opposite Zack, 'thank you for agreeing to dine with me.'

'Nonsense,' Zack replied. 'I've been looking forward to seeing you ever since I got back to town.

72

How is your wife doing? And Marie?'

'Clothilde, bless her heart, is as good as can be expected, considering the filthy stories she has had to contend with these past two years. And as for Marie, as you may have heard, she grew weary waiting for you to propose and went ahead and married a writer – a poet of all things – from Quebec.'

Zack smiled. He and Marie Beaulieu had been friends from their earliest days in grammar school, but had never been sweethearts in any sense of the word. 'Knowing Marie, I'm sure he's very special,' he said.

'You are correct. If she could not have you, then this man, Luc, is one I would have chosen for her. In an age when most young people seem to care for nothing but themselves, he is quite unique – consumed by the need to make a difference. He works for a village newspaper and crusades against all manner of social injustice while he waits for the world to discover his poems.'

'Kids?'

'They have two children, and I don't know how on earth they manage to feed them. But manage they do.'

'And they're happy,' Zack said.

'Yes. Poor and crusading, but happy, and as in love – more so, perhaps – than on the day they were married.'

Zack held his hands apart. '*C'est tout ce que conte, n'est ce pas?*'

Beaulieu's smile was bittersweet.

'Yes,' he said. 'That *is* all that matters.' He paused a beat for transition. 'So, your old friend Guy Beaulieu is a little short of allies in this place.'

'So it sounds,' Zack said, picking absently at his salad.

Beaulieu leaned forward, his eyes and his voice conspiratorial. 'There is much going on here that is not right, Zachary,' he whispered. 'Some of what is happening is simply wrong. Some of it is evil.'

Zack glanced about at the newly constructed west wing, at the helipad, at the clusters of nurses and doctors enjoying their noontime breaks on the terrace and inside the cafeteria.

'You'll understand, I hope, if I say that I see little evidence of that around me. Could you be more specific?'

'Your father spoke to you, yes?'

'Briefly.'

'So you know about the lies.'

'I know something of the rumors, if that's what you mean.'

Beaulieu leaned even closer. 'Zachary, I beg your confidence in this matter.'

'That goes without asking,' Zack said. 'But I have to warn you of something. The Judge on Sunday, and you again this morning, suggested that at least some of your quarrel might be with Frank. You should know that I have absolutely no desire to take sides in that disagreement. Your friendship means a great deal to me. I don't know if I'd even be a surgeon today if it weren't for your influence. But Frank's my brother. I can't imagine lining up against him.'

'Even if he was in the wrong?'

'In my experience, Guy, right and wrong are far more often shades of gray than black and white. Besides, I tried my hand at crusading during my years at Boston Muni. All it got me was a tension

74

headache the size of Alaska. I should have bought stock in Tylenol before I took my first complaint to the Muni administration. I'll listen if you want to talk, but please don't expect anything.'

'Thank you for the warning,' Beaulieu said. 'Even though I have a great fondness and respect for you, and even though, as you no doubt gathered, I haven't much support around this place, I was reluctant to share with you what I know, largely because of Frank. But then, when you said what you did at the meeting this morning – I mean about treating anyone, regardless of their ability to pay – well, I sort of took that as an invitation to talk.'

Zack sighed.

'You thought correctly,' he said finally. 'I fight it tooth and nail, but when I'm not looking, the part of me that can't stand seeing people get screwed always seems to sneak to the surface.'

'Yes, I heard what you did for that old wood-cutter the other night.'

'You did?'

'Don't be so surprised. This hospital, this entire town, in fact, has a communication system that would make the Department of Defense green with envy. You had best accept that fact and adjust to it if you're going to survive here. Drop a pebble in the lake and everyone – but everyone – will feel the ripple. That's why stories, such as those that have been spread about me, are so damning. In no time at all, everyone has heard a version.'

'Like that old game – telephone.'

'Pardon?'

'It's a party game we used to play. Everyone sits in a circle, and the first person whispers a secret to the one next to him. Then the secret goes all around the circle, and by the time it gets back to the one who started it, it has totally changed. It bothers me terribly to think that anyone would deliberately be doing anything to hurt you, especially making the sort of accusations the Judge says have been flying around.'

'They are lies, you know, Zachary. Every last one of them.'

Zack studied the Frenchman's face – the set of his jaw, the dark sadness engulfing his eyes. 'I know, old friend,' he said at last. 'I know they are.'

'So . . .' Beaulieu tapped his fingertips together, deciding where to begin. 'What did you think of my little prepared statement this morning?' he asked finally.

'Well, the truth is, I thought you handled yourself, and expressed yourself, very well.'

Beaulieu smiled. 'Diplomatically put, my boy. But please, continue, and remember, my feelings are quite beyond being hurt.'

Zack shrugged. 'Okay, if you really want to know the truth, I kept thinking that all that was missing from the whole scenario was a horse, a lance, a shaving-bowl helmet, and Sancho Panza.'

This time, the older surgeon laughed out loud.

'So, you think I am tilting at a windmill, is that it? Well, my young friend, let me give you a closer look at that windmill. Richard Coulombe. Do you know him?'

'The pharmacist? Of course I know him. I called in a prescription to him just yesterday.'

'And did you know that he does not own his pharmacy anymore?'

'The sign says Coulombe Drug.'

'I know what the sign says. I also know that

Richard is now an employee, and not a proprietor. He sold his store nearly two years ago to a chain outfit named Eagle Pharmaceuticals and Surgical Supplies. I do not know how that particular deal, with that particular company, was brought about, but I can guess now that it was no accident. Richard did not want to sell, but he needed the money to pay an enormous debt – a hospital bill and a surgeon's bill, Zachary – run up by his wife, now his late wife, Yvette, during a series of cancer operations.'

Beaulieu chewed on a bite of sandwich as he gauged Zack's reaction.

'Did you perform the operations?' Zack asked.

The surgeon shook his head. 'The Coulombes had been my patients for many years, but shortly before Yvette began having symptoms, the rumors about me began circulating. Like most of the other people in town, they decided, or were told – I'm still not exactly certain which – to go and see Jason Mainwaring, instead. They were also told that their insurance coverage was quite limited, but that barring complications, most of Yvette's bills would be covered.'

'But complications there were.'

'Four separate operations, all of them indicated and due to unforeseeable circumstances, as far as I can tell; but four nonetheless. Then there was a protracted stay in the Sterling Nursing Home. In fact, Yvette never did return home before she died.'

'And, of course, there were more bills for that. I get the picture.'

'Actually,' Beaulieu said gravely, 'you haven't gotten the picture at all . . . yet. You see, Ultramed Corporation not only owns our hospital, it now owns both nursing homes in town as well. Did you know that?'

'No,' Zack said. 'No, I didn't.'

'The corporate name is the Leeward Company. They own nursing homes and rehabilitation centers all over the east and midwest, and about three years ago they purchased the two here in Sterling. But what not so many people know, including me until just a few months ago, is that Leeward is a division of Ultramed, bought out by them precisely four years ago. The bills for all three institutions – Ultramed-Davis and the two nursing homes – are actually spit out of the same computer. I'm not going to tell you who's in charge of that computer, but you can guess if you wish.'

'I don't have to,' Zack said, wondering why Frank had never mentioned the purchase of the nursing homes to him. 'Coulombe's story is a very sad one, especially with the unfortunate outcome for his wife. But I see nothing evil or even immoral in it.'

'That is because you are missing a piece of the puzzle,' Beaulieu said. 'A crucial piece. And remember,' he added, 'what I am about to reveal to you is just the tip of the iceberg.'

'Go on,' Zack said, wishing now that the man would not.

Beaulieu pulled a folded typed sheet from his jacket pocket, smoothed it out on the table, and slid it across to Zack. 'As I mentioned before,' he said, 'I do not have too many allies in my little crusade. But I do have some. One of them has spent nearly six months traveling from place to place, trying to gather information for me. Just last week he came up with this. It's a list of the boards of directors of two companies.'

Zack scanned the parallel lists of names, headed simply R and EPSS. Five of the ten names on each list were identical.

'What do these letters stand for?' he asked.

The fire in Guy Beaulieu's eyes intensified. 'The R stands for RIATA of Boston, the megaglomerate that owns Ultramed. In a sense, they are our bosses, Zachary. Yours, mine, and every other doctor's in town.'

'And the other?'

'The other, my friend, stands for Eagle Pharmaceuticals and Surgical Supplies – the corporation that bought out Richard Coulombe. Their boards of directors interlock.'

Beaulieu illustrated his point by sliding the fingers of one hand between the fingers of the other.

Before he could respond, Zack saw movement at the corner of his eye. He slid the paper onto his lap at the instant a shadow fell across the table. He and Beaulieu looked up.

Frank, smiling benignly, stood not five feet away from them, holding a tray of food.

'Are you gentlemen having a heart-to-heart?' he asked. 'Or do you have room at the table for one more?'

Carefully, Zack folded the sheet of paper and slid it into his pocket, although he sensed the move was a fruitless one. Frank had heard at least part of their conversation. Of that, he was almost certain.

A Bach fugue was playing on the small cassette deck by the sink. Barbara Nelms, staring glumly at the bathroom mirror, ran a finger over the furrows in her forehead and the crow's feet at the corners of her eyes. The creases had, it seemed, appeared overnight. Instinctively, she reached for her makeup kit. Then, just as quickly, she snapped off the tape, turned and walked from the bathroom. If she was bone-tired, if she was stressed close to the breaking point, if frustration and fear had aged her six years in six months, why in the hell should she try to hide it anymore?

The product of a perfectly uncomplicated upbringing in Dayton, Ohio, and four idyllic years as a business and marketing major at tiny St. Mary's College in Missouri, she had always prided herself on being a model parent, wife, citizen, and member of society. She was a registered Democrat, a voting Republican, an officer in the PTO three years running, a scout leader, a reader at church, a better than average pianist and tennis player, and, at least according to her husband, the best lover a man could ever want.

But now, after six months of haggard guidance counselors and harried school resource workers, of evasive, pompous behavioral psychologists and bewildered pediatricians, none of that mattered. She had dropped off all committees, hadn't picked up a tennis racket in weeks, and couldn't remember the last time she and Jim had had sex.

Something was wrong, terribly wrong, with her son. And not only could none of the so-called specialists they had seen diagnose the boy's problem, but each seemed bound and determined to convince her that it fell in someone else's bailiwick.

The violent episodes, occurring at first monthly, but now almost once a week, had enveloped Toby in a pall of melancholy and fear so dense that he no longer smiled or played or even spoke, except for occasional monosyllables in answer to direct questions – and then only at home.

Situational depression; delayed autism; childhood schizophrenia; developmental arrest with paranoid ideation; acting out for secondary gain; the labels and explanations for Toby's condition were as varied – and as unacceptable – as the educators and clinical specialists who had applied them.

The boy was sick, and he was getting sicker.

He had lost nearly ten pounds from a frame that had not an ounce of fat to begin with. He had stopped growing. He had failed to satisfy the requirements for promotion to the fourth grade. He avoided interacting with other children.

He had been given vitamins, antidepressants, Thorazine, Ritalin, special diets. She had taken him to Concord, and then to Boston, where he had been hospitalized for four days. Nothing. Not a single objective clue. If anything, he had returned from the medical mecca even more uncommunicative than before.

Now, as she prepared to drag her son to yet another specialist – this one a young psychiatrist, new in town, named Brookings – Barbara Nelms felt the icy, all-too-familiar fingers of hopelessness begin to take hold.

Toby's episodes at first seemed like horrible nightmares. Several times she had actually witnessed them happen – watched helplessly as her son's eyes widened and grew glassy, as he withdrew into a corner, drifting into a terrifying world he would share with no one. She had listened to his cries and had tried to hold him, to comfort him, only to be battered about the head and face by his fists.

In the end, there was nothing she could do but stay close, try her best to see that he didn't hurt himself, and wait. Sometimes the episodes would last only half an hour, sometimes much longer than that. Always they would end with her son mute, cowering, and totally drained.

Perhaps this will be the day, she said to herself. Perhaps this man, Brookings, the first full-time psychiatrist in the valley, would have the answer.

But even as she focused on this optimistic thought, even as she buttoned her blouse and smoothed the wrinkles she should have ironed from her skirt, even as she went to her son's room to fetch him for yet another evaluation at yet another specialist's office, Barbara Nelms knew that nothing would come of it. Nothing, perhaps, except another label.

And time, she also knew, was running out.

The drive from their house to the Ultramed-Davis Physicians and Surgeons Clinic took fifteen minutes. For most of the ride, Barbara Nelms kept up a determined conversation with her son – a conversation that was essentially a monologue.

'This doctor's name is Brookings, Toby. He's new in town, and he specializes in helping people with attacks like yours. . . . We're going to get to the bottom of this, honey. We're going to find out what's wrong, and we're going to fix it. Do you understand?'

Toby sat placidly, hands folded in his lap, and stared out the window.

'It would make it easier for Dr. Brookings to do his job if you would talk to him – tell him what it is you see and feel when you have the attacks. Do you think you can try and do that? . . . Toby, please, answer me. Will you try and talk to Dr. Brookings?'

Almost imperceptibly, the boy nodded.

'That's good, honey. That's wonderful. We all just want to help. No one's going to hurt you.'

Barbara Nelms thought she saw her son shudder at those words.

She swung her station wagon into one of the few spaces left in the crowded parking lot, locked her door, and then walked around the car to let Toby out. It was a promising sign that he had unbuckled his safety belt himself. Instantly, hope resurfaced.

Perhaps this would be the day.

The only other time she and Toby had been in the Ultramed-Davis Physicians and Surgeons Clinic was for a brief follow-up visit with Dr. Mainwaring. Toby's pediatrician worked out of an old Victorian house on the north side of Sterling. A directory, framed by two large ficus trees in the gleaming, tiled lobby, listed two dozen or so doctors, along with their specialties. Phillip R. Brookings, MD: Child and Adult Psychiatry was on the second of the three floors.

'Toby, do you want to take the stairs or the elevator? . . . Honey, I promise you, Dr. Brookings just wants to talk. Now, which will it be? . . . Okay, we'll take the stairs, then.'

Barbara took his hand and led him up the stairs, half-wishing he would react, make some attempt to pull away. He was plastic, emotionless. Still, she could tell he was completely aware of what they were doing.

A small plaque by the door to room 202 read P.R. BROOKINGS, MD: RING BELL ONCE AND ENTER.

The waiting room was small and windowless, with textured wallpaper, an array of black-and-white photographs of mountain scenes, and seating for only four. At one side was a small children's play area, consisting primarily of dog-eared *Highlights* magazines, multicolored building blocks, and puzzles, none of which, Barbara knew, Toby would be interested in. She ached at the image of her son before it all began, huddled on the floor with his father, pouring excitedly over his Erector Set.

No, Daddy, this way . . . turn it this way . . . See?

At precisely three o'clock, Phillip Brookings emerged from the inner office, introduced himself stiffly to her with a handshake and to Toby with a nod. He looked even younger than she had anticipated – no more than thirty-two or -three, she guessed, although his thick moustache made it hard to tell.

As so often had happened over the preceding months, Barbara found herself wondering if she had aged so much, or if doctors were actually getting younger.

'So,' he said, taking one of the two remaining empty chairs, 'welcome to my office. Toby, I appreciate your coming to see me, and I hope we can help you to feel better.'

He wore a button-down shirt and tie, but no jacket, and Barbara's initial impression, despite his youth, was positive. If nothing else, he had started off on the right foot by not talking down to the boy. She glanced over at Toby, who sat gazing impassively at the photos on the wall.

'Here's the medical history form you sent us, Dr. Brookings,' she said, passing the paper over. 'You have the other reports I sent you?'

Brookings nodded and briefly scanned the sheet.

'I think,' he said, 'that if it is all right with Toby, I would like to speak with him alone in my office.

What do you say, Toby? . . . We can keep the door open if you want, okay?'

He stood up and stepped back to the doorway of his inner office.

'Are you coming?'

'Go ahead, honey,' Barbara urged. 'I'll be right here. Remember what I said. There's nothing to be afraid of.'

Slowly, Toby rose from his chair.

'Wonderful,' Brookings said. 'Come in. Come in.'

Silently, but with every fiber, Barbara Nelms cheered her son on. He was being more cooperative, more open to this man than he had been to anyone she had taken him to in some time.

Perhaps, at last, he was ready. Perhaps . . .

She watched as Brookings disappeared into his office. From where she sat, directly opposite the doorway, she could see a roomy, comfortably furnished office with a large picture window, and plants arranged on the floor and hanging from the ceiling.

Go on, darling. Go ahead in. It's okay. It's okay.

After a brief hesitation, Toby followed Brookings in.

Then, after a single, tentative step inside the door, he stopped, his gaze riveted on the broad picture window across from him.

'Come in, Toby,' Barbara heard Brookings say. 'I'm not going to hurt you.'

Barbara could see Toby's body stiffen. His hands, which had been hanging lifeless at his side, began to twitch.

Dear God, she thought, *he's going to have an attack. Right here. Right now.*

'Toby, are you all right?' Brookings asked.

Toby took several backward steps into the waiting room, his face chalk white, his eyes still fixed on the window.

'Honey, what's wrong?' Barbara felt her muscles tense. No one but she and her husband had ever witnessed one of the attacks before. Frightened as she was, she sensed a part of her was actually grateful for what was about to happen. At least someone else would know what they had been going through all these months.

Instinctively, she glanced about for any objects on which Toby might hurt himself.

Then, suddenly, the boy turned, threw open the outer office door, and raced out into the hall.

'Toby!' Barbara and Brookings, who had come out of his office, called out in unison.

The psychiatrist was across the waiting room and out the door before she had left her seat. Barbara reached the corridor just as he disappeared through the stairway door. Her pumps were almost impossible to run in. At the head of the stairs she kicked them off and skidded down to the first floor, falling the last three steps and skinning her shin.

As she limped into the lobby, Barbara heard the horrible screech of an automobile's tires and froze, anticipating the sickening thump of the car hitting her son. There was none. Instead, through the glass doorway, she saw him weaving through the parking lot, running as she had not seen him do in many months. Phillip Brookings was a dozen yards behind and closing.

Barbara raced across the drive, narrowly avoiding being hit by a car herself.

'Toby, stop! Please stop!'

The boy had made it beyond the parking lot and was sprinting across a stretch of thirty-or-so yards of lawn, toward the dense woods beyond. Brookings was now no more than a few steps behind him. With only a yard or two to go before the forest, the psychiatrist launched himself in a flying tackle, catching Toby at the waist and hauling him down heavily.

'Thank God,' Barbara panted, hurrying across the parking lot. This was the first time, in all of his attacks, that Toby had done anything like this. Even at a distance she could tell that, although he was pinned beneath the physician, Toby was struggling. As she neared she could see his efforts lessen.

'Toby, stop that,' she heard Brookings saying firmly, but gently. 'Stop fighting me and I'll let go.'

Barbara approached cautiously, expecting to see the familiar lost, glassy terror in her son's eyes. What she saw, instead, was a fierce, hot mix of anger and fear. It was almost as if he were snarling at the man.

Carefully, Brookings pushed himself away, although he still maintained a grip on the boy's belt.

As Barbara knelt beside her son, she realized that this was not one of his attacks after all – at least not a typical one. He was awake and alert. Whatever had set him off was in this world, not in the world locked within his mind.

'Toby, are you all right?' she asked. 'What happened? What frightened you so?'

The boy did not answer.

'I'm going to let you go, Toby,' Brookings said. 'Promise me you won't run?'

Again, there was no response.

Slowly, Brookings released his grip on Toby's

belt. The boy, still breathing heavily, did not move.

'What was it?' Barbara asked.

'Pardon?' Brookings's shirt and the knees of his tan trousers were stained with grass, and he, too, had not yet caught his breath.

'Dr. Brookings, Toby saw something out your window – something that frightened him. This wasn't one of his attacks.' She turned to her son. 'It wasn't, was it, honey?'

Tears glistening in his eyes, Toby stared up at her. Then he shook his head.

'Can you tell us what it was?'

This time there was no answer.

Phillip Brookings rubbed at his chin. 'Mrs. Nelms, I don't know what to say. I saw Toby staring out my window, and I followed his line of sight. But there was no one there, nothing.'

'Nothing?'

Brookings shook his head. 'Just a big oak tree, a parking lot, and beyond it the emergency ward of the hospital. Nothing else. I'm sure of it.'

The emergency ward. Barbara Nelms saw her son stiffen at the words.

'Toby, was that it? Was it the emergency ward?'

The boy remained mute.

'Dr. Brookings, what would you suggest?' she asked. 'Can you help us?'

The psychiatrist looked down at Toby. 'Perhaps,' he said. 'Perhaps with time I can. But I would like to insist on something before I begin.'

'Anything.'

'I want Toby to have a CT scan and a clean bill of health from a neurologist. As near as I can tell from reviewing the material you sent me, he has had neither. Correct?'

'I . . . I guess so.'

'Well, if his attacks are some sort of seizure disorder, I think a neurologist should be involved, don't you?'

'Doctor, I told you when I first called, we're willing to do anything. Absolutely anything. Is there someone you can recommend?'

Brookings nodded. 'There's a new man in town. Yale Med. Trained at Harvard hospitals. He's a neurosurgeon, actually, but he's doing neurology as well. His name's Iverson. Zachary Iverson. I'll give him a call and then get back to you.'

Barbara stroked her son's forehead. There was nothing in his expression to suggest he had followed any of their conversation. For a moment, studying the sunken hollows around his eyes and the tense, waxy skin over his cheeks, she felt as if she were looking at a corpse.

'Please, Doctor,' she said, 'just one thing.'

'Yes?'

'Do it quickly.'

Brookings nodded, and then rose and returned to his office.

Barbara took her son by the hand and led him back to their car. Desperately, she searched her thoughts for any unpleasantness or difficulty he had encountered at Ultramed-Davis or in any other emergency ward. There was none. Nothing but a gashed chin when he was five and, of course, the incarcerated hernia operation last year.

But Barbara Nelms knew – as the surgeon, Dr. Mainwaring, had told her – that the whole hernia affair had been as routine as routine could be.

89

Chapter 7

Suzanne Cole and her six-year-old daughter, Jennifer, shared an isolated, narrow two-story north of town with a fat, yellow cat named Gulliver ('... because,' Jennifer explained, 'he likes to travel') and a black Labrador retriever who seemed oblivious to any name.

The rooms in the modest place were cluttered and warm. Snow shoes, ski poles, tennis rackets, and even a pair of old stethoscopes hung on the smoke-darkened pine walls, interspersed with prints and original oils representing all manner of styles. There was a Franklin stove in the living room and a loom in one of the back bedrooms, as well as a battered spinet ('Mommy used to play a lot, but now she can only play "Deep Purple"') and dozens upon dozens of books.

The spaghetti dinner, Zack had been proudly informed, was largely Jennifer's creation, and she served it with a charm and enthusiasm that made almost as deep an impression on him as did her mother. She was a tall girl for her age, with an elegant nose, straight auburn hair that hung midway down her back, and Suzanne's magical eyes and smile. She talked of school and animals and ballet, and seemed quite pleased to show off her collections of rocks and stuffed animals.

In return, Zack had promised to introduce her to

Cheapdog and to teach her to fly his radio-controlled plane. He even completed a relatively smooth, Italian-style thumb palm and transfer, although when he was finished, Jennifer had smiled earnestly and said, 'That one could use a little more practice, Zack. I could see the coin.'

By dessert – chocolate brownies with ice cream – what self-consciousness he had arrived with had long since vanished, and he found himself feeling more like a friend of the family than a guest.

If there was an uncomfortable edge to the evening at all, it was due to Suzanne, who seemed, at times, distant, distracted, and content to let Jennifer keep the conversation afloat.

But unwilling to find any fault with the woman, Zack read into her mood swings an introspection and vulnerability that only made her that much more interesting and attractive.

She was returning to the table with some coffee when Jennifer hopped up and announced that she was leaving to watch *M*A*S*H* and wash her hair.

'There's only one thing that troubles me,' the girl said as she shook Zack's hand.

'What's that?'

'Well, it's your dog. I've heard of sheep dogs, but never a name like Cheapdog.'

'Well,' Zack said, 'they're sort of the same thing.' From the corner of his eye, he saw Suzanne stop and lean against the wall, watching. 'You see, I was walking on the beach one morning in a place called San Diego. Do you know where that is?'

'In California?'

Zack nodded. 'They have a great zoo out there and a killer whale who does advanced calculus and prepares his own tax returns. Well, there was this man on the beach – he was Mexican, but he was sort of . . . sleazy. Do you know that word? Well, it means, like, sneaky. Not all Mexicans are that way, by any means, but this guy sure was.

'Anyhow, there he was, with this big cardboard box, and in the box were a bunch of puppies – scruffy little mongrel puppies. He reached in and pulled this little fur ball up by the back of the neck. Like this. And he held him up for me to see.

'"Señor," he said, "how would you like to buy this leetle fellow. I geeve you my word, señor, he is purebred, ol' Eengleesh cheapdog. His papers are een my safe at home. Buy him now, and I breeng them to you tomorrow. Si?"'

'That means yes,' Jennifer said.

'Si.'

'And you said? . . .'

'Si.' The three of them said the word together and laughed.

'And that's how Cheapdog got his name.'

'Isn't there any old English sheep dog in him at all?' Jennifer asked.

'There must be some,' Zack said, 'because every time Princess Di or Prince Charles comes on the television, he stands up.'

'That's silly.' She thought for a moment, and then added, 'I like that story.' Again, she formally shook Zack's hand. Then she turned and raced up the stairs.

'Thanks again for dinner,' he called out after her.

'I like that story, too,' Suzanne said after the footsteps overhead had died away. 'And I really liked the way you talked to Jen. Person-to-person, not grown-up to child. No condescension. And believe me, she appreciated it, too.'

92

'Thanks. That girl doesn't encourage anything approaching kid talk, believe me.'

Suzanne nodded somewhat sadly. 'She's had to do a lot of growing up in a fairly short time. My marriage and divorce were a bit – how should I say – turbulent.'

'Oh?'

For a moment, she looked as if she might want to expand on the remark, but then she shook her head. 'Fodder for another evening,' she said.

She chewed at her lower lip, rested her chin on one hand, and stared into her cup of coffee. There was a sadness in her eyes, but there was also, Zack observed, something else – a restlessness, perhaps; a tenseness in the set of the muscles in her face and neck.

'Is anything the matter?' he asked.

Suzanne hesitated, and then pushed away from the table and stood up. 'I think we'd better call it a night,' she said. 'I have a really busy day tomorrow, and I have a lot of things to sort through before I go to bed. You've been great company – for both of us – but I guess I just need some time alone.'

Nonplussed, Zack glanced at his watch. It was not yet quarter to eight.

'That's it?'

She shrugged and nodded. For a few seconds it seemed as if she were about to cry.

'I'm sorry, Zack,' she said finally, 'but I guess this just wasn't a good night for me to be charming and entertaining. God, it seems like all I ever do around you is apologize. Well, forgive me, anyhow. I'll make it up to you some other time. I promise.'

She waited until he had stood up, and then locked her arm in his and guided him across the screened-in porch and down the wooden front steps. The subtle scent of her and the touch of her breast against his sleeve made his sudden dismissal that much more confusing and painful.

He shuffled along beside her, wishing he were less inexperienced in understanding women, and feeling totally inadequate and foolish for not knowing what to say.

At the camper, she once again apologized for cutting their evening short and promised him a rain check good for one after-dinner conversation some-time very soon. He reached for the handle and then stopped and turned back to her.

'Yes?' she asked, eyeing him appraisingly, as she had that first night.

'Suzanne, I . . . I know that something's bothering you,' he heard himself say. 'I only wanted to say that whatever it is, I hope it comes out the way you want.'

He hesitated, expecting her to thank him politely for his concern and send him on his way.

She did neither.

'I'm afraid I've been guilty of not paying attention,' he went on. 'I guess I was just too busy indulging my own fantasies. Look, I just want you to know I'm glad we've met, and I'm grateful as hell we're becoming friends.' He opened the door to the van. 'If you ever do want to talk about whatever it is, I'm available . . . no strings attached. In fact, for a modest fee I'll even omit the coin tricks.'

He moved to kiss her on the cheek, but then thought better of it and climbed up behind the wheel of the camper.

'Zack, wait a minute,' she called as he began to back away. He stopped and leaned out the window.

'There's a spot halfway up the hill behind the house where you can see almost the whole valley. It's really peaceful on an evening like this to sit up there and watch the lights of town wink on. If you'll give me a minute to check on Jen and get a blanket and some wine, I'd like very much to go up there with you.'

'It's okay not to, you know.'

She smiled in a way she hadn't all evening.

'I know,' she said.

The soft evening air was filled with the hum of cicada wings and the chirping of peepers and crickets. For nearly an hour they lay side by side in the noisy silence, watching the mountain shadows stretch out across the valley. High overhead, a solitary hawk glided in effortless loops, its silhouette a dark crucifix against the perfect, blue-gray sky.

'The girls in the O.R. said you did a beautiful job on that woman's neck this morning,' Suzanne said at last, sipping at what little remained of a bottle of chardonnay.

'You checked up on me?'

'Of course I checked up on you. Do you think you have a corner on the attraction-to-someone-you-just-met market?'

'No,' he said, trying to ignore the sudden pounding that seemed to be lifting his chest off the blanket. 'I guess not.'

'Technique, high marks; speed, high marks; looks, high marks.'

He grinned. 'Well, I'm glad I made a decent first impression on the nurses. After nine years in various O.R.s, and all that time on rock faces, there's not too much that rattles me. This morning, though, I'll admit I was a little nervous.'

'I can understand that. Doctors are *always* under a big magnifying glass of scrutiny, but never the way we are during the first few months at a new hospital. For a time after I arrived on the scene, I felt sort of like a new haircut. Everyone had to express an opinion. . . . The case you did is doing okay?'

'Pain free for the first time in a year, and moving all the parts that are supposed to move.' Zack held up crossed fingers for her to see.

'That's super. You know, I'm curious. You seem like the type who would thrive on an inner-city madhouse like Boston Muni – all that action.'

'Actually, I loved that part of it. But not just that there were so many cases and so much trauma to work on. I loved the patients – talking with them; getting a sense of their lives; becoming important to them; even growing into friendships with some of them. But I never was comfortable with the pressure in big teaching hospitals to become the world's expert in some little corner of neurosurgery.'

Suzanne nodded. 'And if you don't play it that way,' she said, 'then you end up being the world's expert at being passed over for promotion.'

'Exactly. I also confess that I was getting a little tired of the political bullshit – the empire building and back stabbing; having to grovel before a department head or administrator just to get a lousy piece of equipment that the hospital would have been able to purchase out of petty cash if it weren't so damn inefficient.'

'So you thought corporate medicine would be more streamlined – more responsive to the needs of the hospital and the patients?'

'That's what I thought.'

'You say that as if your opinion's already changed.'

Zack propped his chin on his hands and stared out over the valley.

'I don't know,' he said. 'A few things have happened since I arrived here that . . .'

His voice trailed away. Throughout the day, he had more and more come to realize that there was no way he could discount Guy Beaulieu's claims. And if they were true – if Ultramed or Mainwaring or Frank had conspired, for whatever reason, to drive the old surgeon out of practice – then the situation in Sterling was more virulent, more frightening, more . . . unacceptable than anything he had ever encountered at Boston Muni.

He also knew that if his old mentor's concerns about the ethics and practices of Ultramed proved accurate, there would be no way he could walk away from the problem. He had returned to Sterling to practice the best possible neurosurgery in the best possible setting, and that was that.

'Hey, Doc,' Suzanne said, 'do you know that that last sentence of yours never quite made it out of the womb?'

He looked at her. 'Fodder for another evening,' he said. 'I believe that's the established way out?'

'That's it, Charlie. 'Nuff said, then.'

Suzanne rolled onto her side, resting her cheek on one hand. After a time, she reached over and ran her fingers lightly over his face.

'You really are quite handsome, you know,' she said.

'Thanks. I have trouble believing that, especially having spent my life in the shadow of a man with Frank's looks, but it's nice to hear.'

'It's nice to say.'

Zack cleared his throat, which seemed to be getting drier and grittier with every passing moment. He was, at once, reluctant to touch her and even more reluctant not to.

'So,' he managed, struggling to pull his thoughts from her perfect mouth, 'what tale of crisis and resolution brought you to this place?'

Again, she touched his face, this time allowing her fingertips to linger on his lips. 'I guess I didn't make the law of the mountain clear to you,' she said. 'As long as we're lying on *my* little overlook at the base of *my* mountain, I get to ask the questions. That's the law. Take it or leave it.'

'But what happens to those unfortunates, like me, who don't have a mountain?'

Her eyes, and the very corners of that exquisite mouth, formed the smile that was, perhaps, her most alluring.

'In that case,' she said, 'you must adopt one. I'll send you the paperwork in the morning and have our social worker come by for an interview as soon as possible. Meanwhile, we'll save all that stuff from between the lines of my curriculum vitae until you get approved, okay?'

Zack shrugged. 'It's your mountain.'

'Exactly. It's my mountain. Do you think I'm too forward, touching you like this?'

'No. Not forward. Maybe a little tough to read, though, considering that a couple of hours ago you were trying to rush me out of the house and down the hill.'

'Ah,' she said, 'but that was before you said the magic word.'

'Oh, of course. The magic word. How stupid of

me. Why, I've used that damned magic word approach so often, it's become automatic. . . . In fact, it was so automatic this time that that ol' magic word just slipped right past me.'

She took his face in her hands and drew him toward her. Again, as at the dinner table, he saw a strange sadness in her eyes.

'The magic word, Zachary, was "friend."'

Her kisses, first on his eyes, then around his mouth, and finally over his lips, were as sweet and warm as the mountain air. For one minute, two, she held him, her tongue exploring gently beneath his lips, and then along his teeth and around the inside of his cheeks.

Finally, she drew away.

'Was that okay?' she asked.

Zack swallowed hard. 'There are at least a hundred words I would pick before settling for "okay."'

'I'm glad. You look a little bewildered, though. I suppose I owe you some kind of apology – or at least an explanation – for being so inconsistent.'

Zack ran his hand through her hair, then down her back and over the seat of her jeans. Her body was fuller than Connie's but tighter, and far, far more exciting to touch.

'You don't owe me anything,' he said. 'Shaw wrote that there are two tragedies in life. One is not to get one's heart's desire, and the other is to get it. At the moment, I think he was wrong about number two.'

'Zack, out by the camper before you said, "No strings attached." Does that promise apply if we make love – right here, right now?'

'It applies.' He slid his hand beneath her blouse and over her breast. Her nipple hardened instantly to his touch. 'Whatever's going on, I just want to make it better.'

'You're making it better,' she said.

Again and again, they kissed. There was an urgency and hunger in her lips and her touch. Zack knew that it was the secret of her sadness that was driving her into his arms. He knew that, this night at least, she needed him rather than loved him.

But this night, at least, it was more than enough.

She helped him slip off his shirt and nestled her face against the hair on his chest.

'Slowly,' she pleaded. 'Just make it last. Please, just make it last.'

Zack undid the buttons of her blouse, pausing between each one to kiss her lips and her wonderful breasts, then eased off her jeans. He worked his moistened fingertips over her nipples, then down her belly, along the edge of her soft hair, and finally to the tense nubbin of her clitoris.

'Touch me here,' she murmured. 'Two fingers. That's it. Oh, God, Zachary, that's it.'

Moment by moment, what questions he had faded in the smoothness of her skin and in her craving for him. With every touch, every kiss, he felt himself drawn closer to her.

He brushed his lips over her ankles and along the softness of her inner thighs, and then he drew his tongue over her again and again.

She dug her nails into the skin of his back, pulling him even more tightly against her. 'Don't stop. Oh, don't stop yet.'

She was an angel – at once vulnerable and knowing, chaste and worldly wise. And making love with her was unlike anything Zachary had ever experienced in his life.

She drew his face to hers as she eased him onto his back, caressing him, then sucking on him until he begged her to let up.

'Now, Zachary,' she whispered, her lips brushing his ear. 'You're so wonderful. Please, do it now.'

They made love – slowly at first, and then more fervidly; each immersed in the other; each focused on pleasing, rather than being pleased.

Darkness settled in across the valley. Far below them, the lights of Sterling flickered like so many stars, mirroring the expanse overhead.

'Zachary, what time is it?'

'Midnight. A little after, actually.'

They were half dressed, bundled in the blanket against a slight, early morning chill. The connection between them had already transcended their lovemaking, and each minute, every second, it grew.

'Do you know,' she said, 'that in my entire life I have never come like that? What a wonderful rush.'

He kissed her on the neck, then on the lips. 'It must have been that chardonnay.'

'Yes, of course,' she said, buttoning her jeans. 'How foolish of me to overlook that. Next time we'll have to try it without the wine. A controlled experiment. Just to be sure.'

'My mountain?'

She laughed. 'Your mountain it will be. You know, I keep saying it, but you are really a very kind and very sweet man.' She kissed him lightly on the mouth. 'I only hope you'll still respect me in the morning. Believe it or not, making love like this *is* a bit beyond my usual first-date fare.'

'Not to worry,' he said. 'Doing what one wants in situations like this is a payback for all of the headaches and responsibilities of having to be a grown-up.'

Her expression darkened. 'Zachary, I'd like you to know what's going on – why I've been acting so weird all night. Well, almost all night.'

'Listen, it's perfectly all right if—'

'No. I want to. Besides, by tomorrow night you'll know anyhow.'

She rolled onto her back, took his hand, and guided it to her right breast. 'The upper, outer quadrant,' she said. 'Fairly deep.'

It took his fingers only a moment to find the lump – a disc-like mass, the diameter, perhaps, of a half dollar, and as hard as the sidewall of a tire; which was to say, too hard. His first impulse was to reassure her, to label the mass a cyst. But he knew better. There was, without a biopsy, absolutely no way to tell.

Suddenly the whole night – her distraction, her mood swings, their passion, everything – made sense.

'How long since you first felt this?' he asked.

He ached for what he now realized she was going through. If, at that moment, the lump were offered as an exam question with only one correct answer, he would have to call it trouble, all the way down the line.

And so, he knew, would she.

'A month. Six weeks now, I guess,' she said. 'There's been no change over that time. Mammograms were equivocal. A needle biopsy came back "normal breast tissue," and rather than go through that procedure a second time, I elected to go ahead with an excision, and, if necessary, a modified radical.'

'When?'

'I'm going in tomorrow evening. Surgery's scheduled for Friday morning. And in case you couldn't tell, I'm scared stiff.'

He held her tightly.

'I'm just grateful you didn't send me away tonight, that's all. You've made arrangements for Jennifer?'

'My partner in the gallery is going to take her. She has a son two years older than Jen.'

'Good. It's going to be okay, you know.'

Suzanne nodded grimly. 'Just keep reminding me. I tell you, being a physician, I just know too goddamn much. And I'll tell you something else: no matter how much you read, no matter how many Donahue shows you watch, the prospect of what might happen just doesn't compute.'

'It's going to be okay,' he said again, forcing conviction into his voice. 'You've got a friend who's going to be with you all night tomorrow. Will they be doing the excision under local?'

She shook her head.

'No,' she said. 'The anesthesiologist and surgeon both recommended general. And frankly, I was relieved.'

'Who's the anesthesiologist?'

'Pearl. Jack Pearl.'

'Good. He did my case this morning. He's a little on the weird side, I think; sort of like a character out of a Gothic horror novel. But he sure as hell knows what he's doing in the O.R. And the surgeon?'

Suzanne sighed.

'It's your friend from this morning,' she said. 'Jason Mainwaring. Whatever you might think of him, Zack, he's by far the best technician around.'

'So I've heard. Well, I only hope his skill in the O.R. is more highly advanced than his skills in interpersonal relations.'

'Oh, it is.'

'In that case,' Zack said, 'we've only got one thing to worry about, right?'

Chapter 8

Frank Iverson's office was a spacious two-room suite on the ground floor of the west wing – the newest addition to the hospital. From his spot in one of three leather easy chairs, Zachary watched his brother's two secretaries go about their business with prim efficiency. One of the women was dark, with an air of sophistication and polish. The other was blond and wholesome. Both were young, well built, and remarkably good-looking – far beyond the run-of-the-mill in any setting, but near goddesses by Sterling's standards.

Gorgeous secretaries, a plush office, big-money business deals, a Porsche 911, a spectacular hillside A-frame – the man certainly had style, Zack mused. And while that particular style was not one Zack had ever really wished for himself, Frank had clearly come a hell of a long way from fraternity beer blasts.

Fifty percent identical. With each passing year, it seemed, the two of them were becoming less and less a validation of that genetic truth.

Still, there was a time, Zack knew, when their drives and their goals were not nearly so divergent, a time when the two brothers careened through their world along virtually parallel tracks, guided only by the beacons of early success: trophies, ribbons, medallions, and adulation.

It had become something of a game for him – a

recurring daydream – to imagine his life had he *not* fallen that winter day, had the ligaments of his young knee *not* shredded.

Accidents. Illness. The violent, uncaring acts of others. The daydream, as always, led him to acknowledging how fragile life was – how totally beyond control. A patch of ice, the fraction of an inch, and suddenly, in one agonizing instant, the blinders were stripped away from his protected view of life; his unswerving track was transformed into a twisting, rutted path negotiable only one uncertain step at a time.

Zack's eyes closed as he drifted back to that day. He was in a perfect spot, racing after Frank. Three seconds was a lot, but nothing he couldn't have made up – especially with his brother being so uncharacteristically cautious on his second run.

And he wanted it. He wanted it more than he would ever admit to anyone – even, he reflected, to himself.

The colors, the packed snow, the sudden disappearance of the steady crosswind that had been blowing all day – it was a moment frozen forever in his memory. The conditions were perfect for an upset, for a demonstration to all that Zachary Iverson had suddenly come into his own. The Judge, their mother, and most of the town, it seemed, were gathered along the slope, anticipating his run.

Waiting beyond the red and blue pennants marking the slalom course was a wonderful trophy, a savings bond, a trip to the Junior Olympics, and a huge piece of the praise and newsprint that he had watched being heaped on his older brother over the years.

It was time. It was, at last, *his* moment, *his* run.

He checked the course below. No problems. A few final seconds to mentally chart his line, and he lowered his goggles and glided to the electronic starting gate.

Then, suddenly, he stopped.

Something was wrong. Something simply didn't feel right. His boot? The wax? No, he realized at the last possible second, it was his ski – his right ski. Somehow, the binding on it had come loose.

He backed away and made the necessary adjustment on the screw, cursing himself for not being more meticulous in his preparation in the first place. The oversight could have been ruinous.

But now there was nothing to stop him. It was his run, and there was nothing but two minutes of skiing between him and Colorado.

Nothing, that was, except a small patch of ice.

Zack shuddered and sensed his body recoil and stiffen as he relived some of the pain and helplessness of that fall, the bouncing and tumbling over and over again down the matted slope.

The loose binding, while never a factor, had certainly been an omen.

'Dr. Iverson, can I get you something? Some coffee?' It was one of Frank's bookend secretaries – the blonde, scrubbed and sensual. The prototypical farmer's daughter.

The impotence and anguish lingered for a moment, and then drifted away. Unconsciously, Zack rubbed at the still-hypersensitive scar that ran along his knee.

'No,' he said hoarsely. 'No, thanks.'

He checked the time. Just four o'clock. Three forty-five, Frank had said; he had been quite specific about the time.

Zack had a consultation waiting and a small stack of paperwork in his office. Suzanne was due to sign herself into the hospital in less than two hours. The last thing in the world he needed at that moment was a meeting with Frank. However, the invitation had been couched in words that made it difficult for him to beg off, even for a day.

The fifteen-minute wait, while very annoying, was hardly surprising. Frank had never been one to pay too much attention to the schedules of others.

'Excuse me,' Zack said to the secretary, 'do you have any idea how much longer he's going to be?'

The woman smiled blandly. 'No, Dr. Iverson, I'm sorry, I don't. But it shouldn't be too much longer. Mr. Iverson is on the line with the Ultramed mainframe computer in Boston. He talks to it every day.' She sounded very proud to be working for someone who regularly talked to a mainframe computer. 'Are you sure you wouldn't like a cup of coffee? Or a Coke?'

Zack shook his head. 'What I'd like,' he said, standing, 'is to reschedule this appointment for a time when he's able to keep it. Just tell my brother to have me paged when he's through, okay?'

'That won't be necessary, old shoe,' Frank's voice boomed from the intercom on the blonde's desk. 'I was just calling Annette to have her send you in. The door's open.'

No explanations, no apologies.

Zack wondered how long the intercom had been turned on. The notion of being eavesdropped on did not sit well with him at all.

'Sit down, sit down,' Frank sang as Zack closed the door behind him. 'Are you sure you don't want the girls to get you something? A drink? Something to eat?'

'No, thanks, but go ahead if you want to.'

The office was richly paneled. A floor-to-ceiling bookcase, complete with a built-in bar and sound system, covered one wall, and a huge aerial photo of Ultramed-Davis filled much of another. A computer keyboard and screen occupied only a portion of the massive mahogany desk that Frank had once proudly described to him as 'a one-of-a-kind honey.'

Frank himself, seated in a high-backed, brown leather chair, and dressed in a tan linen suit, silk tie, and custom-tailored shirt, looked as if he had just stepped off a page of *Gentleman's Quarterly*.

'So,' he said, sliding a box of slim cigars across the desk, 'how goes it?'

Zack slid the box back. 'It goes fine, Frank.'

'The office okay?'

'Perfect.'

Zack's office, supplied and paid for by Ultramed for one year ('With the strong possibility of a second year, if all goes well'), was a neat, three-room space on the top floor of the Ultramed-Davis Physicians and Surgeons Clinic.

'Word has it you've been doing a hell of a job in the operating room.'

'That's nice to hear.'

'Nice for both of us. It's not too many hospitals the size of this one that can claim a full-time, Harvard-trained neurosurgeon. And, of course, I come off looking like some sort of health-care Iacocca for recruiting you.'

'Frank, you didn't exactly beat down my door to get me to come.'

'Nonsense. I just had some . . . some early misgivings, that's all. But the Judge and the Ultramed people helped me see the light, and now I'm really happy with the way things are turning out. You've been a real shot in the arm for the morale in this place.'

'I haven't encountered any morale problems,' Zack said, sensing the word was something of an introduction to the real business at hand.

'Well, we do our best to see that there are none,' Frank replied. 'And as you say, we do pretty well at it. But every once in a while, something or someone pops up that threatens to polarize our Ultramed-Davis family – turn brother against brother, as it were. And you know what they say about a house divided, right?'

'Right, Frank.'

'So, Zack-o . . . Speaking of houses, how's your place?'

Oh, for crying out loud, Zack wanted to shout, *this isn't some sleazeball business adversary you have to play cat and mouse with. This is your brother. Just say what in the hell it is you want, and let's get it over with.* Instead, he folded his hands together, crossed his legs, and settled back in his chair. It was Frank's show.

'The house is beautiful, Frank,' he said mechanically. 'I don't know how you stumbled on to the place, but I'm certainly glad you did.'

He wondered where Suzanne was at that moment, what she was doing, how she was feeling.

'Great,' Frank said. 'Remember what I said about the basement full of extra furniture we have. Just come by and take what you want until you get your own stuff, okay?'

110

'Sure.'

Zack reminded himself that his brother, for all of his straight-up-the-middle-with-power athletic skill, had always been an expert at hidden agendas. It was an art he had studied at the feet of a master: their father. If Frank was operating true to form, this small talk was anything but casual.

'The rent's pretty decent for a place like that, yes?'

Zack laughed. Decent was far too tame a word. The rent for his tiny apartment in Boston had been three times what it was for the house, which had a huge, wooded lot, two fireplaces, and several times as much space as the apartment.

'Don't tell the realty company that owns it,' Zack said, 'but they're getting killed on this deal. I sleep with my lease under my pillow for fear someone will sneak in and take it away.'

'Oh, we won't,' Frank said calmly.

'We?'

Zack realized that the hidden agenda was about to surface.

'Ultramed-Davis, Zack. You see, Pine Bough Realty Trust is a sort of, well, convenient way for the hospital to administer some property it owns hereabouts. We're your landlord.'

Frank beamed, obviously delighted with the way he had delivered the news.

'You know,' Zack said, now consciously working to keep his cynicism in check, 'somehow that little piece of information doesn't altogether surprise me. Not that it would have made any difference, Frank, but you could have told me when I rented the place that in addition to my salary, my office, my equipment, and my insurance, Ultramed was providing the roof over my head.'

111

Frank shrugged. 'This seemed like a more appropriate time.'

'Tell me, is it customary for a hospital to have such a – how should I say – proprietary role in a community?'

'I would use the word *progressive*.' Frank smiled and winked. 'You see, Zack, the bottom line of this or any other business is money. *Dinero*. The big D.' As he became immersed in his rhetoric, he grew more excited and animated, his gestures more professional. 'That's what the administrators and boards of directors of hospitals all over the country are just beginning to realize. Fortunately, Ultramed recognized it years ago. Eliminate nonprofitable programs and deadwood; increase receivables and collections. Change the red ink to black, no matter how, and the rest takes care of itself. If it's real estate, then it's real estate. If it's other investments, then it's other investments. Colleges like Harvard and Dartmouth have some of the biggest stock portfolios and real estate holdings around. Why shouldn't hospitals follow their example?'

'I . . . I don't know why they shouldn't,' Zack said. *But give me time*, he was thinking, *and I'm sure I can come up with something*.

The wedding of business and medicine was one with which he was simply not comfortable – at least not yet. He reflected on the new CT scanner . . . the incredible opportunity he had been given by Ultramed to set up a private practice. The marriage, he acknowledged, deserved, if not his blessing, at least his open mind.

Perhaps that was what his brother needed to hear.

'You know, Frank,' he went on, 'if I seem

112

uncomfortable with some of this corporate-medicine stuff, you've got to remember that I've spent the last eight years in a hospital where everything was always in incredibly short supply. Everything, that is, except for the dedication of the nurses and the doctors, and the love – I guess there really isn't any better word for it – that they had for their patients.

'I'm grateful to be in a situation like this. Believe me, I am. But there are some parts of those years I spent at Muni that are hard to get out of my system. Frank, I tell you, there was something so pure about the kind of caring that went on in that grimy old place, something so . . . I don't know, holy, that many times patients seemed to get better when every medical fact – all the odds – said they shouldn't. Does that make any sense?'

Frank held up his hands. 'Hey, Zack-o,' he said, 'that makes all the sense in the world. That's what makes you such a valuable addition to the staff here. So, you just do the doctoring and let me worry about the politics and the CT scanners and such. That way everyone benefits, right?'

Dignity, Zack was thinking, still immersed in his years at Boston Muni. *That's what it all boiled down to. The dignity that came from being cared for with love and respect: from being treated as something more than a credit or debit on a balance sheet.*

He flashed on the tears glistening in the eyes of Chris Gow at the realization that someone cared enough to stand up for him, regardless of the cost.

'Right?' Frank asked again.

'Huh? Oh, yes, exactly.'

'Good,' Frank said. 'Then I can assume you'll leave this Beaulieu business to me?'

'What?' Again, Zack warned himself not to drop his guard too low. Frank was, and probably always would be, the fiercest of competitors.

'Beaulieu, sport. Hey, are we on the same wavelength or not?'

'Frank, you haven't said one word about—'

'Well, what in the hell else do you think we've been talking about? I've let that business with the old man and Wil Marshfield slide by because I knew that you hadn't had time to learn the system around here. But Beaulieu is another story. Zack, that man is on a vendetta because he thinks the hospital's to blame for his inability to maintain a surgical practice. Have you heard that kind of paranoid talk from anyone else around here?'

'No, but—'

'Every time someone new has come on the staff over the last few years, Beaulieu buttonholes him with wild claims and stories about how we're railroading him out of business and how we forced Richard Coulombe to sell his pharmacy in order to pay his hospital bills. Christ, I'm surprised he hasn't tried to tie us in with the fucking famine in Ethiopia. Let me tell you something, Zack. No one has to try and force Guy Beaulieu into retirement. He's doing a perfectly adequate job of that all by himself.'

'And as for that Coulombe crap of his, ours wasn't the only debt the man had, believe me. He was in it up to here with everyone in town. Check it out yourself. Coulombe either sold that store or he spent the rest of his days in a courtroom.'

'But—' Zack stopped himself at the last moment from breaking his promise to Beaulieu by bringing up the connection between Ultramed-Davis and Eagle Pharmaceuticals and Surgical Supply. He also

114

found himself wondering if the former owner of the house he was renting had ever been a patient at the hospital.

'But what?' Frank demanded. There was a sudden harshness in his eyes, an edge to his voice.

'Nothing,' Zack said. 'Forget it.'

With his thoughts focused on Suzanne and on problems at the office, he was willing to do almost anything to avoid a clash. 'Forget it.'

Frank shook his head. 'You're holding out on me, Zack-o. It's written all over your face. Now, what's going on?'

'I said, *nothing*.'

Zack felt the skin tighten across the back of his neck.

Some of what is happening is simply wrong. Some of it is evil. . . . Guy Beaulieu's words, his anger and his sadness, took hold. *Your old friend Beaulieu is a little short of allies in this place. . . .*

'All right, Frank,' Zack suddenly heard himself saying. 'You want to know what's wrong? I'll tell you what. I believe Guy, that's what. I listened to him, and I looked in his eyes, and I know he's telling the truth. That's what's wrong. I don't know if it's Ultramed, or that pompous ass Mainwaring, or what. And I sure as hell don't know why. But I think Beaulieu *is* being railroaded out of practice, just like he says. And if that's true, then it pisses me off. It pisses me off a lot, and it makes me want to do whatever I can to help the man out. There, is that what you wanted to hear?'

Frank laughed out loud. Then he lit up a cigar and sent a smoke ring swirling toward the ceiling.

'Let's just say it's what I *expected* to hear,' he said. 'You always were something of a bleeding heart, Zack – a sucker for anybody's cause. Vietnam, Timmy Goyette's supposedly-stolen Junior Olympics entry fee, women's rights, not enough mashed potatoes in the school lunches. Give the boy a sob story, and he'll give you his guts . . . and his allowance. Remember all that? I sure do. So why should Guy Beaulieu and his paranoid stories be any different, right?'

'Frank, you can really be a bastard, do you know that?'

'Careful, boy,' Frank said, launching another perfect ring. 'That's your mother you're talking about. Besides, this time you're wrong. Dead wrong.'

'What?'

'This is one cause you'd best steer clear of, brother. Beaulieu's on his way off the plank, and if you're hanging onto him when he goes, then you're going to get awfully wet. I promise you that.'

He opened his desk drawer, withdrew an envelope, and slid it across.

'I've been keeping this letter quiet because I still hoped Beaulieu would back off. Now, I'm afraid, I have no choice but to present it to the ethics committee. There are people on the staff who wanted to do something months ago to limit or cut off his privileges, but I kept putting them off. Like the Judge said, the old guy did save my life. Here, have a read.'

The letter was handwritten and carried no heading other than the date, June 17.

Dear Mr. Iverson:

I am writing to share with you some allegations against Dr. Guy Beaulieu by myself and several other nurses on the emergency ward. Over the past several months, he has become increasingly inconsistent and indecisive in his dealings with patients. He has been quite forgetful, at times issuing the same set of orders more than once, and at other times, neglecting to order certain studies which we would consider routine and basic.

In addition, on more than one occasion his speech has been slurred and his manner inconsistent enough to raise the question of drugs, alcohol, small strokes, or some combination of the three. Fortunately, his case load has been small enough so that no one has been harmed – at least no one that we know of. Still, we feel some sort of investigation and action is called for.

I would welcome the chance to meet with you and discuss this matter further. Meanwhile, I feel you should have a talk with Dr. Beaulieu.

Sincerely yours,
Maureen Banas, R.N.
Head Nurse

Zack read and reread the letter in stunned silence, trying to match the charges with the eloquent, dedicated man he had listened to at the staff meeting and, later, over lunch. There was nothing in Beaulieu's manner, speech, or the content of his words that bore out the nurse's claims. Still, there was no way such charges could be dismissed.

Across the desk from him, Frank sat in smug silence, obviously savoring the moment.

'This is terrible,' Zack murmured, trying, as he read the letter for a third time, to get a fix on the

nurse, Maureen Banas. . . . *colorless, but efficient . . .
distant . . . knowledgeable . . .* he simply hadn't spent
enough time around her yet to have any real handle.

'Terrible, but true,' Frank said. 'I had hoped to
spare the old duffer any more humiliation, but after
hearing his little speech the other morning, and
seeing the way he's gotten to you, well, it seems I
have no—'

'Frank, does anything about this letter strike you
as strange?'

Frank set his cigar aside and leaned forward.

'What are you talking about?'

Zack slid the letter back across the desk.

'Well, for one thing, this woman doesn't substantiate her charges with one specific example.'

'Well, there's no doubt she has them. Zack, don't
you think you're grasping at straws?'

'And for another, the whole damn thing is just
too . . . too sterile.'

'What?'

'Just look at it, Frank. Not one bit of sensitivity
or poignancy. Not one indication that she understands the charges she's making could quite possibly
send a man's life down the drain – a man who has
practiced surgery in this town for thirty years.
Christ, for all the awareness she's showing, she
might just as well be writing to complain that a
neighbor's poodle is shitting in her flower bed. The
more I think about it, the more this letter smells. I
think that woman should be spoken with, face to
face.'

'You don't think I've done that?'

'Well, then, *I* want to. It's the only way I'm going
to even begin to believe all this.'

'You go to her or anyone else about this

118

business,' Frank said, jabbing a finger at him, 'and you'll be out on your ass quicker than you can say "scalpel." This is my affair – mine and Ultramed's. You really have it in your mind to fuck things up for me around here, don't you?'

'Frank, that's nonsense.'

'Is it?'

For several frozen moments, Zack could only sit and stare at his brother. Despite his tan, Frank looked pallid, his expression a disconcerting amalgam of anger and – what? Fear? They had had their differences over the years, true, and from time to time, some magnificent arguments. But Zack sensed something far more powerful at work here.

'Frank, please,' he managed. 'Stop sounding like I'm your goddamn enemy. I'm not. I just care about Beaulieu and I want to see that he gets a fair shake, okay?'

A margin of color returned to Frank's cheeks.

'Okay?' Zack asked again.

Frank smiled.

'Sure, sport,' he said, far too amicably. 'I understand. I'll tell you what, why don't we just leave it that I'll keep you posted and you'll keep an eye on things . . . from a distance. That way I get to do what I'm paid to do, and you get to keep from taking a fall. I promise you, Beaulieu will get every break that's coming to him. Yes?'

Zack gauged the intensity in his brother's eyes, and then nodded. Their session had gone far enough.

'So, that's taken care of,' Frank said, tilting back in his chair and folding his hands in his lap. His tone and expression gave no hint of their disagreement. 'Listen, how about we have dinner sometime this weekend? I'll have Lisette give you a call.'

'Sure, Frank. That'd be fine.'

'Excellent. Oh, and by the way,' he added, getting up from his chair as Zack stood to go, 'tell that new squeeze of yours that we're all praying everything goes well for her tomorrow.'

Now Zack felt the color drain from *his* face. 'How did you—'

His brother patted him on the shoulder.

'Sport, if someone who works for me so much as farts anywhere in this hospital, sooner or later I get a whiff. That's worth remembering. Trust me on that one and you'll be doing both of us a favor. She's a terrific lady. I'm glad she's finally coming out of her shell. I hope things work out between you.'

With that, he shook Zack's hand and ushered him out the door.

Chapter 9

Disturbed by a cart clattering past the door of her hospital room, Suzanne Cole rolled onto her back, floating in the twilight world between sleep and wakefulness.

For a time, she struggled to complete a dream she had been having – a romantic, storybook dream, in which Jason Mainwaring, dressed head to foot in ebony armor, sitting astride a coal-black stallion, was jousting with a knight clad equally spectacularly in gold. Again and again, the men sped past one another, their lances exploding off their opponent's shield. With each encounter, one or the other came close to falling from his mount, but each time, the stricken knight recovered and swung about for another pass.

Suzanne herself was seated in the grandstand, wearing a flowing gown of pink silk and clutching a single white rose.

Who are you? she called again and again to the gold knight. *Who are you? What do you want from me?*

As the dream faded, the knight turned toward her and lifted the visor of his golden helmet. Like flashing neon, the face of the man kept changing. One moment it was Zachary Iverson, and the next, Paul Cole – the pathologically self-possessed physiology professor who had picked her out of a

121

crowded lecture hall during her second year in medical school and had swept her up in a whirlwind of flowers and parties and romantic weekends in the country.

Less than a year later they were married. If there were signs of the man's sickness during those months, she had missed them completely. Later, when the recreational drugs, and the erratic behavior, and the lies – 'misunderstandings,' Paul had called them – began to surface, she had chosen to ignore them, to rationalize them away.

By the time she knew that her efforts to hold their marriage together had been a mistake, there was Jennifer. The years she spent trying to accommodate Paul for her daughter's sake had nearly cost Suzanne her career, and perhaps even more than that.

Why? she pleaded again. *What do you want from me?*

'Dr. Cole, it's morning.'

Why? . . .

'Dr. Cole?'

The nurse's gentle voice, and the touch of her hand, began to dispel what remained of the dream. The colors began fading into a sea of white.

How long had it been since Paul had last forced his way into one of her dreams? The arguments, the guilt trips, the hang-ups when *she* answered the phone, the missing prescription pads, the visits from the glib, condescending drug enforcement agents . . . *Why had she given the man so goddamn many benefits of the doubt?*

'Dr. Cole . . .'

Suzanne opened her eyes a slit.

'Hi,' she murmured. Instinctively, she reached up

and touched her breast, dreading the thick bandages she expected to find there.

'It's seven-fifteen,' the nurse said. 'Time for your pre-op meds.'

Pre-op. Damn, she thought. It was not over at all. It was just starting. Why was this happening? Life in Sterling had been everything she had hoped it would be – so peaceful, so uncomplicated, so good for Jen. Now, suddenly, everything seemed to be unraveling at once. Why?

She opened her eyes fully.

'Seven-fifteen?'

'Uh-huh. You're on call for twenty minutes from now. This is some atropine and Demerol.'

Atropine . . . Demerol. One to dry up secretions, and the other to help one not give a damn about the prospect of being disfigured, or worse. *What wonderful potions we doctors have at our fingertips,* she thought acidly. What wonderful potions, indeed. She turned onto her side and winced as the needle pierced her buttock. Then she rolled onto her back and smiled up weakly at the nurse.

'Nicely done,' she murmured.

The nurse, a kind, elderly woman named Carrie Adams, patted her hand. 'You're going to do fine,' she said. 'I've had a couple of cysts removed, and so has my daughter. The hardest part is the waiting to get it over with.'

'I'll try to remember that.'

Once again, this time in spite of herself, Suzanne reached up and touched her breast. It was all so crazy. This sort of thing happened to other people – to patients. She was trained to help them through their medical crises, not to go through one herself. She had bounced back so far, put so many pieces of her shattered world back together. Now this.

Helplessness ... panic ... rage ... her emotions, held in check over the weeks since that terrifying moment of discovery, swirled about like wind-blown snow.

Where in the hell was the acceptance that the textbooks all wrote about?

'That Demerol should start to work in just a few minutes,' the woman said, as if reading her thoughts.

'Good.'

'And here are your earphones.'

'Oh, yes,' Suzanne said, taking the set and placing it on the bed beside her. 'What's on today?'

'I don't know,' the woman replied, 'but Dr. Mainwaring's on channel ...' She took a three-by-five card from her uniform pocket. '... three.'

The system – tapes picked by the surgeons to be played in the operating rooms and broadcast to earphone receivers – was designed to reduce patient anxiety levels. Over the few years it had been in place, the innovation had received high marks from surgeons and patients alike. Suzanne flipped the dial on the phones to 3, and held one up against her ear.

'"Greensleeves,"' she said.

'Pardon?'

'"Greensleeves." That's the music. A really beautiful version of it. Here, listen.'

She passed the earphones up. The nurse politely listened for a few seconds, and then returned them.

'Very pretty,' she said. 'Well, I'll be back in a little while. Meanwhile, you just relax. Oh, by the way, there's an envelope for you on the bedside table. Perhaps you'd better read whatever's inside it before that medicine I gave you takes effect.'

Suzanne thanked the woman, and then waited until she had left the room.

The envelope, with the Ultramed-Davis heading and logo, read, *Dr. Suzanne Cole*. She peeled it open, knowing it was from Zack. Throughout much of the evening, he had sat there with her, reading out loud from magazines and newspapers, laughing, sharing stories of his life, and, when there was nothing to say, just holding her hand. He had been as open, as tender, and as understanding as any man she had ever met.

She wondered if he realized the resentment she was feeling at his intrusion into her life. Silently, she cursed herself for using him the way she had. She had no intention of allowing a man close enough to ruin her life again – not now, at least. Possibly not ever. Zack had said they could make love with no strings attached, but she knew damn well that there were always strings. When the operation was over, regardless of the outcome, she would do what she must to put distance between them.

For a moment, the fear of what might be growing within her breast seemed pale next to the fear that she might never again be able to trust.

Dear Doc—

It's now 2 a.m. The sleeper they gave you seems to have worked, because you've been out fairly solidly for about an hour. I'm going to leave now, and hope that you don't wake up until a minute or two before they bring you down to the O.R. I just wanted to thank you for Wednesday night, and even more, for letting me share this evening here with you. I don't know if my being here helped you, but it has surely helped me. It's not much of a secret that I think you're pretty special.

I know how frustrating and frightening this is for you – partly because it's frustrating and frightening for me, too. Just know that whatever happens, I'll be with you as much and as closely as you want me to be.

If there's a good, working definition of 'friend,' maybe it's someone who helps us find the tools to get through this kind of shit when we can't seem to find them for ourselves. Regardless of what happens, you've got one in me.

It's going to be benign. That's all I can say. It's going to be benign, and everything's going to be okay.

Be strong. You have an appointment on my mountain as soon as this is over.

Zack

'I'm sorry, Zack,' Suzanne whispered as she slipped the note back into its envelope, tucking it between the pages of the novel she had been reading for the past two weeks. 'I'm sorry I wasn't stronger. . . .'

She settled back onto her pillow and slipped on the earphones. Her mouth had become uncomfortably dry from the atropine, but the Demerol, too, was having its effect, so she did not really care.

Carrie Adams and an orderly wheeled a stretcher into the room and helped her slide onto it.

Please, God, Suzanne whispered to herself as the fluorescent lights flashed overhead, *let it be nothing. Let it be benign.*

Jason Mainwaring met her in the operating room,

his blue-gray eyes intent from between his aqua mask and hair cover. Suzanne pulled off her earphones. The same lovely piece she had been listening to filled the operating room.

'Welcome to my world, Suzanne,' he said.

Suzanne smiled weakly.

'I wish I could say I was pleased to be here.'

'I understand.' He patted her arm reassuringly. 'We'll take good care of you. Don't you worry.'

'Thanks.'

'How do y'all like my music?'

'It . . . it's beautiful.'

'The most beautiful music ever written, I think. It's called *Fantasia on Greensleeves*, an' it's by an English composer named Ralph Vaughan Williams. I begin every single case with it, an' then go on to some other pieces of his. If you want, I'll make a tape of it for you.'

'That would be very nice,' she managed.

Jack Pearl, the anesthesiologist, appeared at Mainwaring's side. Together with a nurse, they helped her from the litter onto the chilly operating table. Then, in a maneuver so quick and painless she barely realized it was happening, Pearl slipped an intravenous line into a vein at her left wrist.

Next, a broad strap was pulled across her abdomen and tightened.

A final pleasantry or two from Mainwaring, and they were ready to begin.

Jack Pearl came into Suzanne's field of vision, held up the rubber stopper of her intravenous line, and slipped in a needle attached to a syringe full of anesthetic.

Please, God, she prayed once again, *let Zack be right. Let it be okay.*

'All right, Suzanne,' Jack Pearl said. 'This is just some Pentothal.' He depressed the plunger, emptying the contents of the syringe into her intravenous line. 'All you have to do now is count back from one hundred.'

From the speakers overhead, Ralph Vaughan Williams's flowing fantasy filled the room.

'One hundred,' she said thickly. '. . . ninety-nine . . . ninety-eight . . .'

Above her, the huge, saucerlike operating light flashed on.

'Ready,' she heard someone say.

Takashi Yoshimura was one of seven Orientals living in Sterling, New Hampshire. The other six were his wife and five children. Though Japanese by birth, and, in fact, by birthplace, he had been raised and educated in lower Manhattan, and spoke both English and Japanese with a pronounced New York accent.

Like a number of the new Ultramed physicians Zack had met since his return to Sterling, Yoshimura, a pathologist who insisted on being called Kash, was young, well trained, and exceedingly capable.

It was just after eight in the morning. Yoshimura, diminutive, with close-cropped hair and Ben Franklin glasses, sat at his desk, with Zack peering over his shoulder. Before them, in a stainless-steel pan, was the fleshy, silver-dollar-sized mass that had just been removed from Suzanne Cole's right breast.

Zack watched in tense silence as the man maneuvered the tissue about beneath a bright light and magnifying glass. A floor above them lay Suzanne, adrift in the dreamless netherworld of general anesthesia. In minutes, the unimposing little pathologist would send word to the O.R. of his interpretation of the cells in the frozen sections of the specimen, and Suzanne would either have her incision sewn up, or a large portion of her breast and the surrounding lymph nodes removed.

If Kash Yoshimura was the least bit nervous about the awesome implications of this facet of his work, it certainly did not show in his face. He hummed a soft, almost tuneless melody as he scanned the surface of the mass, searching for any telltale dimpling or discoloration. Then, with a final, satisfied arpeggio, he used a scalpel to produce a thin slice from the core, and handed the pan with the exposed specimen to the histologist.

'Okay, George,' he said to the tissue technician, 'do your thing.'

'Well?' Zack asked, after the technician had left.

'What do I think?'

'Uh-huh.'

'You are, perhaps, familiar with the immutable medical law of eighty-five/fifteen?'

Zack shook his head.

'I'm surprised,' Yoshimura said, 'your being Harvard-trained and all. Well, simply put, the law states that every probability in medicine is either eighty-five percent likely or fifteen percent likely. Proper application of the law means one can never be wrong, as long as one knows whether the event in question seems remotely likely or not so remote.'

Zack smiled. 'I take it you scored well on your boards.'

Kash Yoshimura nodded. 'I did okay,' he said.

'And the biopsy is eighty-five percent likely to be . . .'

'Benign. An adenoma, I would guess.'

'Wonderful.' Zack pumped his fist.

'At this point, you may be eighty-five percent enthusiastic,' the pathologist cautioned. 'No more.'

'I understand.'

Yoshimura reached across and patted Zack understandingly on the shoulder. 'We'll have the answer in just a few minutes,' he said. 'Meanwhile, all I can tell you is that our mutual friend is in remarkably capable hands.'

'Mainwaring?' Zack flashed on his initial, unpleasant encounter with the man.

Kash nodded. 'I watched him work a number of times when I was a student and resident. He is a superb technician.'

'So I've heard. He's a little short on tact, though. In the first five minutes after we met, he managed to say something snide about virtually every aspect of my life.'

'Perhaps he finds a new neurosurgeon in town threatening to his ego.'

'Perhaps. Where was it you trained?'

'Hopkins.'

'Mainwaring was at Hopkins?'

'He was. No small fry, either. A full professor, if I'm not mistaken.'

Zack was surprised. 'I wonder what on earth he's doing up here in the boondocks,' he said. 'Especially the northern New England boondocks. That accent of his puts him well below the Mason-Dixon line.'

The pathologist shrugged. 'Beats me. Apparently, he doesn't deem pathologists threatening enough to insult. Aside from my reporting biopsies to him, we haven't had more than a one- or two-word 'conversation since he arrived a year or so ago.'

'Actually,' Zack said, suddenly anxious to learn more about the man Guy Beaulieu claimed was helping to drive him out of practice, 'it was closer to two years. Did you ever tell him you watched him operate at Hopkins?'

'As a matter of fact, I did. Once, shortly after he got here.'

'And what did he say?'

'Nothing, really. He glared at me for a moment with that steely look that I think surgeons practice in front of a mirror to use on nurses and anesthesiologists and the like.' He grimaced. 'I mean *some* surgeons,' he qualified. 'Then he just said, "That's nice," – something like that – and walked away.'

'And no mention of that since?'

Yoshimura shook his head.

'How weird. Mainwaring seems very much the old-boy type. I'd expect him to go out of his way for someone from *his* college or *his* hospital – especially a prestigious place like Hopkins.'

'Believe it or not,' Yoshimura said without rancor, 'there are still those about, even in our lofty profession, who are ... uncomfortable with certain aspects of certain anatomies.' He gestured toward his eyes. 'Whatever the reason, the social circle Jason Mainwaring runs in certainly does not include the Yoshimuras.'

'Well, I'd enjoy it very much if mine did,' Zack said.

Kash Yoshimura eyed him for a second, and then he smiled. 'I think we would like that, too,' he said.

The histology technician announced his return with a soft knock on the doorjamb.

'Ah,' Kash said. 'This is the moment we turn our eighty-five/fifteen into something quite a bit more certain. Good sections?'

The technician nodded proudly, and set down a cardboard holder containing a dozen or so glass slides.

Zack was struck by the remoteness of the unfolding scenario from the woman whose quality of life, and even, perhaps, whose very existence, was at the center of the drama – a marked contrast to the immediacy and intimacy of surgical medicine.

Still, he knew, in the moments to follow, Kash Yoshimura would hold as much power, as much responsibility, as if he were the man in the operating room with the scalpel.

The pathologist slid the first of the sections onto the stage of the dual-view teaching microscope, and motioned Zack to the second pair of oculars.

Silently, Zack watched, barely breathing as the multicolored cells slid through the brightly lit field.

One by one, Yoshimura worked his way through the slides. With the fifth or sixth one, he had resumed his humming. Finally, he stopped, and looked over at Zack.

'You have an opinion?' he asked.

Zack nodded. 'Uniform cell type, uniform pattern, no obvious foci of necrosis,' he said. 'I can't put a name on it, but I can say that it sure as hell looks benign.'

Yoshimura nodded. 'Should you ever tire of neurosurgery, Dr. Iverson, I would say you have quite a future as a pathologist.'

He picked up the phone and dialed the operating room. 'This is Dr. Yoshimura calling from pathology,' he said. 'You may inform Dr. Mainwaring that he has excised a totally benign, fibrous adenoma. Thank you.'

Zack pumped the man's hand as if he had been the cause of the tumor being noncancerous, rather than merely its interpreter.

Before it had really even begun, Suzanne's nightmare was over. Anxious to be at the bedside when she awoke, Zack hurried to the recovery room.

One story above, in operating room 3, Jason Mainwaring received the news of the biopsy impassively, and then looked over at his anesthesiologist.

'So, Jack,' he said, 'if it's all right with you, we are ready to close.'

Jack Pearl, a ferret-like man in his mid-forties, smiled at the surgeon from beneath his mask. Then he glanced down at the serene face of their patient.

'Everything is better than all right, Dr. Mainwaring,' he said. 'In fact, it's perfect. As always. Absolutely perfect.'

Subtly, unnoticed by anyone else in the room, Jason Mainwaring returned the smile and nodded his approval.

At that moment, both men were focused on precisely the same thought: *Four hundred ninety-one down. Only nine to go.*

Chapter 10

Over the more than thirteen years that Zack had spent as a medical student and surgeon, Suzanne represented, without doubt, the most striking recovery from general anesthesia he had ever encountered.

He was already in the recovery room, waiting by the nurse's station, when she was wheeled in from the surgical suite. She was awake, smiling, and totally alert. Her jubilant thumbs-up sign to him made clear that she was also well aware of the results of her operation.

'That is the most amazing wake-up I've ever seen,' Zack commented to one of the recovery room nurses as Suzanne, with very little help, transferred herself from the litter to her hospital bed. 'It's hard to believe she was ever really asleep.'

The nurse, an animated young redhead whom Zack knew only as Kara, beamed with pride.

'Oh, she was out, all right,' she said. 'Isn't it wonderful? Almost all of Dr. Pearl's cases come out of the operating room looking like that.'

'Mine didn't,' Zack said, recalling the prolonged, but quite typical recovery of his cervical disc case.

'Pardon?'

'Nothing. I'm just really impressed, that's all.'

'Everyone around here is,' the woman said. 'Part of it may be Dr. Mainwaring, too. He demands that his patients be anesthetized just so, and Dr. Pearl is the only one he'll allow to work with him. I used to scrub before I got the job in here, and I tell you, they are quite a pair. Things have really taken a turn for the better at this place since they teamed up.'

Across the recovery room, Zack saw Jack Pearl peering through an ophthalmoscope, examining the nerves and vessels on Suzanne's retinae while one of the nurses checked her vital signs. He was a slight, sallow man with a pencil-thin moustache and a broad, high forehead that dominated his nondescript eyes.

'What do you mean, "a turn for the better"?' Zack asked, knowing he was fishing for some opinion on Guy Beaulieu. 'I grew up in Sterling and then did an externship here. I always thought we were pretty fortunate with the surgeons we had.'

The nurse eyed him warily, suddenly uncertain as to whether she might have said too much to a virtual stranger. Zack tried his best to appear only marginally interested in her response.

After a beat or two, she shrugged and brushed a wisp of hair from her brow.

'Ormesby's okay,' she said, 'at least for routine things. But I think it might be time for Dr. Beaulieu to retire, especially with all the trouble he's been having, and with someone as good as Dr. Mainwaring around.'

'Is that the general feeling of the nurses?' Zack ventured.

Again, she appraised him.

'Dunno,' she said finally, although her eyes told him otherwise. 'But they like you. I can tell you that much. And we all like having a neurosurgeon on the staff. It makes Ultramed-Davis seem more – I don't know – special.'

'Thanks, Kara. Thanks for telling me that.'

The young nurse blushed.

'Well, I've got to get back to work,' she said. 'See you.'

'See you.'

Zack watched as the woman returned to her patient. Her opinion of Guy Beaulieu was, he suspected, typical of what he would encounter from most of the other nurses on the staff. Whether justifiably or not, the man's reputation at Ultramed-Davis was shot. And Zack knew that given the nature of medicine, gossip, and the intense microcosm of hospitals, there was probably nothing on God's earth that Beaulieu could do to reverse the situation.

Still, despite all the rumors and innuendoes, despite Frank's vehemence and the damning letter from Maureen Banas, Zack could not shake the belief that Guy was the victim of some sort of calculated effort to drive him from practice. The thought was so sad, so pathetic, that it almost defied comprehension. On some level, Zack realized, he was half hoping the charges against Beaulieu would prove true. At least then he could make some sense of it all.

Jack Pearl had finished his evaluation of Suzanne and was headed back toward the operating room when he noticed Zack.

'Morning, Iverson,' he said.

'Jack.' Zack nodded. 'How goes it?'

'Did you have a case this morning?'

'No. I just stopped by to see how Suzanne was making out. She looks great.'

Pearl glanced back at her. 'Pretty routine business,' he said.

'What did you use?'

For the fraction of a second, the anesthesiologist's expression seemed to tighten. Then, just as quickly, it relaxed.

'The usual,' he said. 'A little Pentothal, a little gas. Mainwaring likes his patients really light.'

'I guess. She doesn't look as if she's even been asleep.'

Again, tension flickered across Pearl's face.

'Well, she was,' he said simply. He glanced at the clock over the nurse's station. 'Got to go, Inverson. You have a good day, now.'

'Yeah, Jack. You, too.'

As the taciturn little man shuffled away, Zack realized that during this and all their previous encounters, Pearl had not once made direct eye contact with him. The trait was not that surprising, he acknowledged, given the nature of the breed. Although the exceptions were far too numerous for any generalization, many of the anesthesiologists he had known were introspective loners, skilled more in biochemistry and physiology than in the more subjective arts of clinical medicine, and committed to one of the specialties where conversation and interaction with patients – awake patients, at least – was at a minimum.

Still, there was something unusual about Jack Pearl, something furtive and arcane, that Zack found both curious and disconcerting. He wondered if perhaps the man had a past – trouble somewhere along the line – and he made a mental note to ask Frank about him sometime. Then he turned and headed to Suzanne's bedside.

Though a bit pale, she was still smiling, radiant and wide awake.

'Hi, lady,' he said. 'What's new?'

'Oh, nothing.' She feigned a yawn. 'A little this, a little that. You know. Just another routine, humdrum day.'

'Yeah, my day, too.'

'That's quite obvious from those dark circles around your eyes,' she said. 'Hey, before I forget to mention it, thanks for your note. It meant a lot.'

'You look fine. Are you in any pain?'

'Not really. At least not compared to what I would have been in if that biopsy had been positive.'

'It *does* seem a bit easier to deal with this way,' Zack said. 'I thought I'd have the chance to break the good news to you, or at least to remind you of it, but you came out of the O.R. as if you'd never been asleep. It's absolutely incredible how light you are so soon after general anesthesia.'

'I know. Jason said I would be. It's wonderful. I had my appendix out when I was seventeen, and I remember being totally out of it for a day. Jack Pearl said that if it was okay with Jason, I could go home this afternoon.'

'That's great.'

'Zack, God bless every woman who has to go through this madness. I know we're supposed to believe that there's some sort of grand, cosmic scheme operating in life, but cancer – especially breast cancer – just doesn't lend itself very easily to any philosophizing. I tell you, I'm so relieved, all I want to do is cry.'

'Well, go ahead and do it. In fact, I'm pretty relieved myself, so if you're free tomorrow night, I could come over with a bottle of wine and a box of Kleenex.'

Her eyes darkened.

'Zack, I . . .'

'Go ahead,' he said.

'I really owe you for staying with me the way you did last night. . . .'

'There's a "but" coming. I can feel it.'

'Zack, Wednesday night was wonderful,' she whispered. 'I really mean that. But it's just not like me to start things in the middle that way. Do you understand?'

'I guess so.'

'For weeks I've been so consumed with my damn lump, then suddenly you show up in my life and . . . Zack, I just need some time and a little space to sort some things out. You said the other night that you had no expectations. I hope you meant it.'

Zack swallowed hard. 'I hope so, too,' he said.

She smiled thinly and squeezed his hand.

'Thanks at least for trying. Listen, I have the next week off. I owe Jen some quality time with her mother and my partner a few days of help in the gallery. I'll call you toward the middle of the week, okay?'

'Middle meaning like Tuesday?'

'Zack, please.'

'Okay, sorry, sorry. Middle of the week is fine. Can I at least drive you home later?'

'I'll be fine. Besides, I don't even know if I'll be going home later. Zack, there'll be time. If it's supposed to be, there'll be plenty of time.'

There was a sadness in her eyes that helped keep him from pushing matters any further.

'Sure thing,' he said. 'Hey, for what it's worth, I just ran into your replacement in Annie's room.'

Suzanne smiled broadly, obviously relieved at the change in subject.

'Don Norman? Is he overwhelmed yet?'

'Hardly. Norman doesn't seem like the type to be overwhelmed very easily – at least not as long as there are guidelines and policies for him to follow. And Ultramed seems to have provided all the guidelines and policies he could ever want, so not to worry.'

'I won't,' she said. 'And I agree totally. The man is conscientious as hell, but he *is* a little medical robot. Julia Childs with a stethoscope – strictly cookbook. Annie okay?'

Zack nodded. 'When I stopped by, she was fighting with Norman about her sodium restriction, so I guess that's about as good a sign as any. Oh, get this: right in the middle of their little altercation he puffs himself up like he loves to do – you know, like this – and he says, "Mrs. Doucette, pull-eese. Whether you know it or not, I am the Chief of Staff at this hospital. I certainly know what is best for my patients.'

'Good imitation. Excellent. And what did Annie say?'

'Nothing too inflammatory. She just eyed him with this great Annie look, called him "Tubby," and suggested that he should lose weight so that he would be a better example for his patients.'

'Oh, no.'

'It was great. Norman turned ten shades of red, and looked for a moment as if he might haul off and pop her in the nose. Having been brought up by the woman, I can say that it's lucky for him he didn't. Even after cardiac arrest, my money would have been on Annie. Well, listen, I've got to go play doctor. If you change your mind about that ride home, give me a page.'

'Sure.'

'You know, I still can't get over it.'

'What?' she asked.

'How light you are. The nurse I was talking to said all of Mainwaring's patients come out of the O.R. like that. I've got to ask him his secret.'

'No secret, Doctor. Just good technique.'

Jason Mainwaring, sans mask and haircover, appraised them from the foot of the bed.

'Well,' Zack said casually, trying not to appear as startled by the intrusion as he was, 'whatever it is, it's impressive. I'd like to scrub with you sometime to learn firsthand how it's done.'

'My goodness,' Mainwaring mused, 'a neurosurgeon who doesn't know everything. What will the gods send us next?'

'Now just a minute,' Zack countered, again feeling his hackles stiffen at the man's superciliousness. 'I don't know if you're like this with everyone, or just with me, but I—'

'Hey, fellas,' Suzanne cut in, 'remember me? The patient?'

Mainwaring smiled down at her as if Zack were no longer there.

'Is everything still all right, my friend?' he asked.

'Perfect, Jason. I can't tell you how pleased I am.'

'That's fine. Just fine,' he drawled.

Zack, arms folded tightly, stood back from the bed a step, wondering if he should say good-bye or simply leave. It was obvious that Jason Mainwaring, for all of his glistening reputation and surgical skills, was too threatened by him to let up even for a moment.

Unless he could find some way of reassuring the man that they were playing for the same team – and his experience with similar egos told him that possibility was highly unlikely – the two of them seemed destined to be enemies.

Well, so be it, Zack thought. It would only make things that much easier if, in fact, Mainwaring did prove in any way responsible for Guy's difficulties.

'Can I go home this afternoon?' Suzanne asked.

Mainwaring smiled, walked to the bedside opposite Zack and took her hand.

'If there's no major bleeding from that incision,' he said, 'and you still feel the way you do right now, I don't see why not. Listen, I've got an emergency exploratory in just a few minutes, and a gall bladder at two. Why don't I stop by after that – say, four-thirty? Then, I'll not only discharge you, but I'll even drive you home. Your place isn't very far out of my way.'

Suzanne's eyes flicked toward Zack.

'Oh, Jason, I wouldn't think of—'

'No, no. It's settled.'

Don't you think driving your post-op patients home is carrying bedside manner a bit too far, Doctor?

Zack barely kept the snide rebuke in check. He was already irritated with the man and his ways, and now he realized he was jealous of him as well.

Suzanne had made no secret that she and her surgeon had a friendship that, at times, went beyond the hospital. But she had also been careful to add that Mainwaring had a wife and children living somewhere in the South, who were, for whatever reason, as yet unable to follow him to New England.

There was, Zack reminded himself angrily, never a valid excuse for jealousy. Nevertheless, jealous he

142

was. His reaction also reminded him that it was far more pleasant being threatening than feeling threatened.

'Well,' he said, clearing his throat, but still unable to fully expunge the hurt from his voice, 'you two seem to have everything pretty much under control, so I'll just get along. See you later, Suze. Nice job, Mainwaring.'

Before either of them could respond, a nurse whom Zack recognized as one of the emergency crew rushed across the recovery room to Mainwaring.

'Doctor,' she said breathlessly, 'there's some trouble in the emergency ward. It's Dr. Beaulieu. He's—' She glanced at Zack and Suzanne, and stopped in mid-sentence, obviously unsure of how much more to say. '. . . um . . . Mr. Iverson would like you to come down right away if you can.'

'Of course, Sandy,' Mainwaring responded with urbane calm. 'Tell Mr. Iverson I'll be right along.'

'Thank you, Doctor. Hi, Dr. Iverson. Hi, Suzanne. Are you okay?'

'I'm fine, Sandy, thanks,' Suzanne said. 'Everything's all right.'

'That's wonderful. I'll tell everyone downstairs the good news.'

She hurried off.

'So,' said Mainwaring, 'I'll see y'all at four-thirty, yes?'

He gave Suzanne's hand a final squeeze and then strode out of the recovery room.

'Are you going down there?' she asked Zack.

'Uh-huh.'

'Let me know what's going on, okay?'

'Sure.'

He made no move to touch her.

'Zack?' she said softly.

'What?'

'I'm sorry I didn't handle that situation better. Jason comes on a little strong sometimes. He caught me off balance. He's really a decent guy. Just don't let him get to you, okay?'

'Sure.'

'Talk to you later in the week?'

'Right.'

He turned to go.

'I hope the trouble with Guy is nothing big,' she called.

'You and me, both,' he muttered.

But as he headed for the emergency ward, feeling not a little deflated, Zack could not shake an ugly sense of foreboding.

Nothing that Zack had imagined about what was transpiring in the emergency ward prepared him for the reality.

There was commotion bordering on chaos. The hospital's three-man security force was there, as were the director of nursing, Mainwaring, Chief of Staff Donald Norman, and half a dozen embarrassed patients and their families. The epicenter of the turmoil was behind the closed door of the family quiet room, where brief periods of strained silence separated angry, easily audible outbursts in English and in French from Guy Beaulieu.

'Damn you, Frank, get out of my way before I strike you,' were the first words Zack heard. 'That woman is my patient, and I have every right to care for her. Now, out of my way!'

'Guy, sit down and quiet down, or I swear I'll

144

have the guards come in here and tie you down. I will not have you making a scene like this in my hospital.'

'Your hospital! If it's your hospital, Mr. High and Mighty, then why don't you see that this is all a plot to take my practice away? You're in on it, aren't you? That's why. You're one of them!'

'Dammit, Guy, shut up. There are patients out there.'

'I know there are. *My* patients! Now let me pass!'

Zack crossed to where Jason Mainwaring stood, leaning against a wall near the quiet room.

'What gives?' he asked.

Mainwaring glanced over at him and then looked back toward the source of the commotion.

'The old quack has gone berserk, that's what,' he said coolly. 'He's been unbalanced for some time, but at least he's had the presence and intelligence to limit his outbursts and paranoia to the staff meetings. This is disgraceful.'

'Do you know what happened?'

Mainwaring's response was preempted by yet another outburst from Beaulieu, followed by still another, though more constrained, response from Frank.

Moments later, the door to the quiet room opened and Frank slipped out. He appeared a bit more ruffled than usual, but was still impeccably dressed, with not one hair out of place.

'Stay with him, Henry,' he said to one of the security guards – a broad, neckless man with bad skin and close-cut hair, who looked to Zack like a mammoth fireplug. 'If he starts yelling again, cuff him to the chair and shove a rag in his mouth.'

'Mr. Iverson, I don't hurt people unless they hurt

145

me. I told them that when I started working here.'

'Look, Henry, if you want to keep on working here, you'll do as I say and keep that nutcase quiet until Chief Clifford and his men get here. Now get in there and do your job.'

Shaking his massive head, the guard entered the quiet room and closed the door behind them. There were no shouts of protest from Beaulieu.

Frank scanned the cubicles filled with patients. 'Christ,' he muttered. Spotting Zack and Mainwaring, he approached them, shaking his head.

'This is fucking insane,' he said, keeping his voice low. 'And you know what? It's my fault. I should have done something about him way back when his craziness started. Well, Zack-o, if there's one good thing to come out of all this, it's that at least you get to see him in action firsthand.'

'Exactly what's going on?' Zack asked. 'What tipped him over?'

Frank laughed sardonically. 'I keep telling you, brother, Guy Beaulieu tipped over a long time ago. This is just an example of how far. See that woman over there in bed five? Well, she's got some sort of bowel problem.'

'Probably a ruptured diverticulum,' Mainwaring interjected.

'Well,' Frank went on, 'Beaulieu's done some surgery on her in the past. On her husband, too, I think. This time, though, the woman and her internist apparently talked things over and decided that she might be better off with Jason, here, doing the surgery.'

'I evaluated her right before I did Suzanne,' Mainwaring explained, 'and had her scheduled to follow in the O.R.'

'Meanwhile, Beaulieu, the lunatic, comes strolling through the emergency ward, spots the woman, and without a word to anyone, begins examining her and issuing orders to the nurses. Needless to say, the poor lady, who's not too swift to begin with, was totally confused and absolutely terrified.' Frank looked impatiently toward the ambulance bay. 'Where in the hell are the goddamn cops? When you don't want them they're all over the place.'

'Frank, you don't need the police,' Zack said. 'Let me talk to him. Can't you see where this might be upsetting and humiliating for him? I'll just get him out of the hospital and he'll calm down.'

'He's out of the hospital anyway,' Frank said acidly. 'For good.'

'What?'

'This was the last fucking straw. I told him about the latest series of complaints, and about that letter from Maureen Banas. And I suspended his privileges.'

Zack's heart sank.

'Frank, is that when he went nuts?'

'What difference does it make?' Frank said. 'Nuts is nuts. Just listen to him.'

From within the quiet room, Beaulieu had again begun to shout.

'You ape, let go of me! Take your hands off me, goddamn it! Take your hands—' Suddenly, the surgeon's words were cut short.

Without waiting for Frank's permission, Zack bounded across to the quiet room and threw open the door. The guard, Henry, had balled a red bandanna in his fist, preparing to use it as a gag. Beaulieu was sitting, handcuffed to the arm of his chair. He was staring in wide-eyed terror, not at his tormentor, but at a vacant spot on one wall.

The right side of his face was starting to droop.

'Oh, Jesus,' Zack said as he knelt by the man. 'Guy, can you talk?'

Beaulieu turned to him slowly. His eyes were glassy and filled with tears.

'Head . . . hurts,' he moaned.

His speech was thick and slurred. His tongue seemed bunched at the corner of his mouth.

'Did you hit him?' Zack demanded of the guard.

'Not even a tap. I swear I didn't.'

'Undo these,' Zack snapped, jiggling the hand-cuffs. The man hesitated. 'Dammit, do as I say!'

'Do it, Henry,' Frank said from the doorway. 'What's happening, Zack?'

Zack turned slowly and looked up at his brother.

'He's having a stroke, Frank,' he said hoarsely. 'That's what. A cerebral hemorrhage, I would guess. I need a litter, a nurse, and an IV setup. And I want the CT scanner warmed up.' He turned to the guard. 'Tell me again, did you touch this man's head?' His voice was ice, his eyes fire.

'I didn't touch nothin' except his wrists,' the man said defensively. 'I swear, I don't hurt people unless they hurt me.'

'Undo these. Quickly now!'

The guard did as he was told, and instantly, as if made of rags, Guy Beaulieu's right arm flopped off the chair and dangled down. Zack lowered him to the floor and cradled his head in his lap.

'I need that litter, please,' he said, barely able to contain his anguish. He bent close to Beaulieu. 'Easy does it, old friend,' he whispered. 'Easy does it.'

Beaulieu's eyes opened, and Zack noted with horror and despair that the pupil of the right one

148

had already begun to dilate.

'Okay, Guy,' he whispered, stroking the older man's forehead and cheek, 'the litter will be here in a second. Just hang on. You're going to be okay.'

Suddenly, for a few frozen seconds, Beaulieu's eyes stopped their random drifting and focused on Zack's face.

'No . . . I'm . . . not,' he said, forming each word with the most excruciating effort. 'God . . . help . . . me . . . I'm . . . not.'

Slowly, his eyes closed.

'Damn you,' Zack hissed, looking first at the guard and then at Frank, Mainwaring, and Don Norman, who were clustered in the doorway. 'God damn you all.'

Chapter 11

Over the months since her son's attacks had first begun, Barbara Nelms's approach to housework had changed radically. Where once she had been meticulous almost to the point of obsession, now she cut corners wherever possible. She was never comfortable remaining out of range of the boy for more than five or ten minutes at a time.

With sitters unwilling to stay alone with Toby, and her husband drifting further and further into his work, the television set had become her closest ally. Only when Toby was engrossed in Saturday cartoons, or some of the programs on the children's cable network, did she dare spend any prolonged time doing laundry or preparing meals.

It was late afternoon, and Barbara had not even begun to think about dinner. All day Toby had been even more restless and remote than usual. She had read to him for a time and taken him to the store with her. She had pulled him around the block in his wagon and pushed him on the tire swing in the backyard.

Now, as she stared at the unwashed dishes in the sink and thought about the pile of ironing she had been avoiding, it was all she could do to keep from breaking down. Through the door to the living room she could see her son, lying on his back on the carpet, staring at the ceiling.

'Toby,' she called out, 'five more minutes and Robin's on. We missed him this morning while we were at the park. Why don't you go and get your bear, and I'll turn him on.'

That the boy did not react was upsetting. When Toby was at his worst, his most distant, the prospect of watching *Robin the Good* usually brought a response of some sort. The actor who played Robin was overweight for the role and as patronizing to the children, as inane and vapid, as anyone she had ever seen, but his half-hour show, aired three times a day, was bright and quick.

'Okay, honey,' she said, 'you just stay put, then. I'm going to do some dishes, and then I'll turn on Robin.'

Glancing almost continuously over her shoulder, she thrust her hand into the sink and snapped a nail off so low that it drew blood.

'Dammit,' she said, sucking at the wound. 'Dammit, dammit, dammit.'

She ran cold water over her finger. Then, as much from frustration as from pain, she began to cry.

She snatched up the phone, dialed the mill, and had her husband called out of a meeting.

'Bob, hi, it's me,' she said.

'I know. Has he done it again?'

'No. No, he's okay just now. But he's not acting right.'

'He never acts right. Honey, I'm sorry I can't talk now, but I'm in the middle of an important meeting. Was there something special?'

Barbara blotted her bleeding finger on a towel.

'I . . . I was hoping you might be able to come home early. I'd like to put a nice dinner together, but I'm worried about Toby.'

'Impossible,' Bob Nelms said too quickly. 'Honey, you just said he was okay. The people from Chicago are here. I've got a ton of stuff to go over with them. In fact, I was going to have Sharon call and tell you I'd be late.'

'Couldn't you postpone them for a day? Just this once?'

'Sweetie, you know I'd come if I could. But they're only going to be here for a day.'

'Please?' she whispered, fumbling through a cabinet for a Band-Aid.

'What?'

'Nothing. Nothing. When should I expect you?'

'Probably pretty late. How about you take Toby out for some pizza. I'll eat here.'

'Bob, isn't there any way you could—'

'Barbie, please. Don't make things any more difficult for me than they are. I'll be home as soon as I can, okay? . . . Okay? . . . Doggone it, Barb, don't do this . . .'

Slowly, Barbara Nelms replaced the receiver. Then she waited for her husband's return call. A minute passed, then another. Finally, she wrapped a Band-Aid around her finger and shuffled to the living room.

'Come on, my merry man,' she said hoarsely, 'it's time for Robin.'

Toby Nelms let his mother lead him into the den and then sank down on the floor by the couch. He wanted her to get his bear for him, but the words to ask wouldn't come.

'Okay, Tobe,' she said, switching on the television, 'I'll just be in the kitchen. Call if you need me.'

Stay, he thought. *Please stay with me.*

The cartoon that introduced Robin the Good's show appeared on the screen, along with a now-familiar voice that announced, 'Hey, merry men and merry maids, get out your longbows and your stout staffs. It's time to travel once again to those days long, long ago – to Sherwood Forest and that friend of the poor, Robin the Good.'

Toby watched quietly as his mother adjusted the color and then left the room. Moments later, she returned and set his tattered bear beside him.

'Enjoy the show,' she said, patting him on the head. 'I'll be in the kitchen.'

'Thank you,' Toby whispered. But she was already gone.

He stared toward the kitchen for a time, and then stuffed his bear between his legs and turned his attention to the television. Robin the Good, wearing a green suit and a hat with a feather, was dancing about and singing, while Alan-a-Dale played his guitar.

'. . . We welcome all you boys and girls. But don't bring any diamonds or pearls. 'Cause I take from the rich and give to the poor. Then I go right out and get some more. . . . What ho, merry men and maids. Welcome to Sherwood, where learning is always fun, fun, fun. Today we're going to do some drawing with Little John and take a ride on a camel with Maid Marian. But first, here's Friar Tuck. Tell us, pray thee, good friar, what letter we are going to learn about today.'

A fat man with a brown robe and a bald place on the top of his head hopped onto the screen.

'Hello, boys and girls,' he said. 'What ho, there, Robin. Today, we're going to learn about one of my favorite letters. It's the letter that starts off a lot of our favorite words like *candy* and *cartoon*. It's the third letter in the alphabet, and it's called C. So here're Robin and Alan to tell you about it.'

Robin the Good swung across the screen on a rope with leaves growing off it. Then he dropped to the ground as Alan-a-Dale began to play.

'Alas, my love, you do me wrong,' Robin sang, 'to cast me out so discourteously. Because today I sing this song about our friend the letter C. . . .'

Toby Nelms rubbed at his eyes as the color of the television set began growing brighter and brighter.

'. . . C, C, is all our joy. C's for carrot and car and cat. C, C starts club and cloud. Now what do you think of that? . . .'

Robin the Good danced around a tree.

Seated on the floor in his den, Toby Nelms's body grew rigid. His shoulders began to shake. The sound of Robin's voice grew softer as the music grew louder. Overhead, lights began to flash past. A face floated into view.

'. . . There's C for comet and C for crab; and C in front of the coat we wear. . . .'

'. . . Now, Toby,' the face said, 'there's nothing to worry about. You're going to go to sleep. Just relax. Relax and count back from one hundred. . . .'

Robin the Good was singing and prancing across the television screen as Toby Nelms began, in a soft, tremulous voice, to count.

He was on one knee, crooning the final lines of his ballad, as the boy began to scream.

Chapter 12

It was, all would later agree, a magnificent funeral. Standing room only. The crowd, sweltering in the brutally humid summer afternoon, filled the pews of St. Anne's Church and spilled out into the vestibule. The priests conducting the mass were not only from the predominantly French-Canadian St. Anne's, but from the crosstown parish, St. Sebastian's, as well.

'. . . Guy Beaulieu was not a *son* of Sterling,' Monsignor Tresche was declaring in his eulogy. 'He was one of its fathers – a gentle man, whose skill and caring hands have, through the years, touched each and every one of us. . . .'

Over the three days following Beaulieu's death, Zack had visited his widow, Clothilde, and daughter, Marie Fontaine, several times. Even so, he was surprised when Marie asked him to serve as a pall bearer. Although he would have preferred to remain less intimately involved with Guy's funeral than he had been with his death, accepting their request was the least he could do.

It had been at his desperate urging that Marie and her mother had put aside their biases against such things and had agreed to an autopsy.

'. . . a man of vision and conviction. A humble man, who faced mounting personal difficulties with courage and dignity. . . .'

The priest droned on, but Zack, seated in the first

row with the seven other pall bearers, heard only snatches. His thoughts kept drifting, as they had much of the time, to the agonizing scene with Guy in the emergency room, and to the equally unpleasant experience of viewing his post mortem examination.

As Zack had suspected, the man had died of a massive cerebral hemorrhage. There was, however, a major surprise. The arteries in Beaulieu's brain, and, in fact, in his whole body, were those of a man decades younger. The lethal stroke had resulted not from any crack in a hardened vessel but from the rupture of a small aneurysm – a pea-sized defect in one artery which, almost certainly, had been present without producing symptoms for many years.

The cause of that fatal tear, Zack knew, could only have been a sudden, drastic rise in blood pressure. That thought sent an angry jet of bile rasping in his throat, as it had over and over again since the autopsy. Guy Beaulieu's two years of difficulties at Ultramed-Davis, whether real or contrived, had loaded the weapon of his destruction.

The humiliating conflict in the emergency ward with Mainwaring, Frank, and the security guard had, in essence, pulled the trigger.

Frank, of course, saw things differently.

He had issued statements of shock and bereavement from the hospital, and from Ultramed, and had sent a basket of fruit to Guy's widow. But in the few minutes he and Zack had spent alone, he had made it clear that he considered Beaulieu's death nothing short of an act of Providence.

Unobtrusively, Zack glanced about the chapel. Suzanne, though dressed in sedate blue and wearing no makeup, sparkled in the midst of two rows of Ultramed-Davis physicians which did not include

156

Donald Norman, Jack Pearl, or Jason Mainwaring. Several pews behind her, between the Judge and Cinnie, sat Frank, resplendent in a beige summer suit and appearing, as usual, composed and in control. The mayor was there, along with several other area notables, including the region's congressman.

Guy Beaulieu had once described himself to Zack as 'just a plain, old, small-town Canuck, lucky enough to be born to parents who wouldn't let him quit school to work in the mills.'

It was good, at least, to see that so many people knew better.

Later, as Zack and the other pall bearers shuffled up the aisle with Guy's casket, his eyes and Frank's met briefly. He felt so distant from the man – so totally detached.

Had they really grown up in the same home, played in the same yard year after year? Had they really worn the same clothes, shared so many childhood dreams? Had they really once been fast friends?

The hope of reestablishing a friendship with his brother suddenly seemed naive. They would make do, perhaps, tolerate one another, even work together. They would spend sterile time together at family functions. But they would never be close.

The open hearse was festooned with flowers. Zack, feeling overwhelmed by the sadness and futility of it all, helped slide the heavy casket into place among them.

'Excuse me, Doctor,' a voice behind him said as he stepped back from the casket. 'Kin I talk to you?'

Zack turned and was surprised to find himself confronting the huge security guard, Henry Flowers, who seemed ill at ease in a dark suit and solid black tie. Looking on, several respectful steps behind him, was a petite, plain young woman in a white lace dress – almost certainly the man's wife.

'Yes?' Zack asked.

The guard shifted uncomfortably.

'I . . . uh . . . I wanted you to know that I'm real sorry for what happened to Dr. Beaulieu,' he said. 'He took care of my wife's mother once, real good care, and he's never done nothin' bad to me. . . . Dr. Iverson, I never laid a hand on him except to grab his wrist. I swear it. I . . .'

His voice drifted away. It took several moments before Zack realized that the man did not know the results of the autopsy, and if he did, he did not understand them.

Zack reached out and put a hand on the guard's shoulder.

'You didn't do anything that caused Dr. Beaulieu's death, Henry,' he said, loudly enough for the man's wife to hear. 'He had an aneurysm – a time bomb – in his head, and it just happened to go off while you were there.'

Relief flooded the guard's pocked face.

'Thanks, Doc,' he said, pumping Zack's hand as if it were the handle on a tractor-trailer jack. 'Oh, God, thanks a lot. If there's ever anything I can do for you, just ask. Anything.'

He backed away, and then grabbed his tiny wife by the arm and hurried off.

Zack watched until the incongruous couple had disappeared around the corner. Then he turned and headed to his camper, feeling marginally less morose. At least one other who had shared those awful moments in the quiet room had been affected by them.

*

The procession to All Saints Cemetery was, according to the Judge, as long as any Sterling had ever seen.

Following the service, Zack accompanied Frank and their parents to the shaded spot where Marie Fontaine and her mother were receiving final condolences.

Marie, who seemed to have aged a year in just the three days since her return home, accepted an embrace from Cinnie and a kiss on the cheek from the Judge. However, she barely touched Frank's outstretched hand before pulling away.

'It was good of you to come,' she said coolly.

'Your father meant a great deal to all of us,' Frank replied blandly.

She eyed him for a moment, and then said simply, 'That's nice to know.'

Zack glanced over at his parents, but saw nothing to suggest that they appreciated the tension in the brief exchange. Marie then turned to him, took both his hands in hers, and kissed him by the ear.

'Please stop by our limousine,' she whispered.

Imperceptible to the others, Zack nodded.

Half an hour later, Zack sat across from Marie Fontaine and Clothilde Beaulieu in the back of the mortuary's black stretch Cadillac. The smoked-glass windows, including the partition separating them from the driver, were closed, but the limo's air-conditioning system kept the steamy afternoon at bay.

Marie's husband, a gaunt, bearded man whose quiet dignity reminded Zack a little of her father, stood outside.

'We wanted you to know how grateful we are for all you've done,' Marie began.

'Your father was always very good to me.'

'He was very good to everyone,' she said. 'That's why it's so hard to understand why nobody stood up for him while he was being murdered.'

Zack's impulse was to correct her, but the intensity of her eyes told him not to bother.

'It upsets me a great deal to think that anyone might have deliberately set about to ruin him,' he said.

'Not anyone, Zack. Ultramed.'

'What?'

'Zack, we know Father confided in you. We know that even though your brother runs the hospital, he thought you would give him the benefit of an open mind. Was he right?'

'I told him I would listen and that I would respect his confidence, if that's what you mean.'

Marie glanced over at her mother, who nodded her approval of Zack's response.

'That's exactly what we mean,' she went on. 'Several years ago, Father opposed the sale of the hospital to Ultramed. He just didn't believe an outside corporation should be given such a vital foothold in this community – at least, not with so little community involvement or control. If it weren't for *your* father's influence, we think he would have succeeded in blocking it. But that is neither here nor there, now. Did you know that shortly after they took over at the hospital, Ultramed took legal action to fire him?'

'No,' Zack said. 'No, I didn't.'

'He was preparing to countersue them when they backed off. According to Father, they became frightened by a court decision in Florida that ended up costing one of the other corporations millions for trying to do the same thing to a pathologist who was working in a hospital they had acquired.

'Zack, Ultramed wants blind loyalty from everyone working for them – total acceptance of their policies. Father fought them at every turn. Less than a year after they dropped the suit against him, the rumors started. And within just a few months of that, a showy new surgeon was on the scene, snapping up chunks of Father's practice.'

'That would be Jason Mainwaring,' Zack said.

'Exactly.'

'Have you any proof that Ultramed engineered all of this?' he asked.

'Only this.' She reached beneath her seat, drew out a thick manila envelope and passed it across to him. 'Mother and I talked it over last night. Father liked you and trusted you. And frankly, we have nowhere else to turn. This is all the information he had been able to gather in his battle against Ultramed. It doesn't prove they were behind his murder, but it does show something of how they operate – some of the things they're capable of doing to turn a profit.'

'What am I to do with this?'

For the first time, Beaulieu's widow spoke.

'Dr. Iverson,' she said, in a soft accent virtually identical to Guy's, 'it was my husband's hope that the information contained in that envelope would convince the board of trustees, including your father, to exercise their option and order the repurchase of the hospital from Ultramed.'

Zack stared at her in disbelief.

'Mrs. Beaulieu, are you forgetting that I *work* for Ultramed? They pay my salary, my office expenses, insurance, everything. To say nothing of the administrator at the hospital being my brother.

What you are asking me to do isn't really fair.'

My husband is dead. Is that fair?

Zack saw the response flash in the woman's eyes and then vanish.

'We are asking you,' Clothilde Beaulieu said patiently, 'to do nothing more than study the contents of that envelope and use it – or not – as you see fit. I assure you there will be no hard feelings if you return the material to us after you have looked it over . . . or even right now.'

'We mean that, Zachary,' Marie said. 'We really do.'

For a time, there was only silence. Zack looked first at one woman and then the other, and finally at the envelope in his lap.

A sucker for anybody's cause.

Had Frank's terse assessment of him been so irritating because it was so close to the mark? Suzanne . . . the mountains . . . the Judge . . . his career. Any clash with Ultramed and Frank was almost certainly destined to be a losing proposition for him. And there was much, so very much, at stake.

The envelope was a Pandora's box. A bomb that might be nothing more than a dud, or nothing less than a lethal explosion.

A sucker for anybody's cause.

Slowly, deliberately, Zack slid the dead surgeon's legacy under his arm. Then he reached across and shook hands with both women.

'I'll be in touch,' he said.

Frank, Frank, he's our man. If he can't do it, no one can. . . .

Over the two decades since his graduation from Sterling High, not a day had passed that Frank

Iverson did not hear the chant echoing in his mind. Cheerleaders dancing on the sidelines, each one hoping Frank would at least spend a few minutes with her at the victory celebration after the game. Grandstands jammed with parents, teachers, students, and reporters, all screaming *his* name, all begging him for one more pass, one more score. The Judge and his mother, proudly accepting congratulations from those seated around them.

Driving through the streets of Sterling toward his hospital, Frank heard the cheering as clearly as if he were standing on the field, staring across the line of scrimmage at the opposition, knowing that, in just a few seconds, his play would swell those cheers to a deafening roar.

Frank, Frank, he's our man. . . .

They had been days of glory for him; days of strength and independence. It felt so good to realize that after all the difficult, humiliating years that had followed, after all the lousy breaks and the goddamn patronizing, demeaning lectures from his father, a return to the stature and influence of those times was so close at hand. Two weeks, that was all. Three at the most.

He had done his part, and done it well. Now, all he needed was patience – patience and constant vigilance. Three years before, he had made the mistake of complacency, of trusting, and it had cost him dearly. There would be no repeat of that fiasco this time. Nothing would be taken for granted. Nothing. Besides, he affirmed as he swung up the drive to Ultramed-Davis, there were reasons aplenty for keeping his eyes open and his guard up. A million reasons, to be exact.

. . . If he can't do it, no one can.

Chapter 13

'Helene, I don't know how to tell you this, but I think it's time we moved Mr. Gerard Morris's fabulous woodland scene out of the window and more toward the back – like in the storeroom.'

Suzanne propped Morris's huge oil against a display case and stepped back several paces, hoping that the change in lighting and perspective might thaw some of the feelings she had for the man and his work.

'The man's a legend,' Helene Meyer called out from the back.

'In his own mind, he is.'

'Suzanne, when are you going to come to grips with the reality that tourists don't come up to northern New Hampshire to buy abstract art? They want mallards.'

'Paint by numbers,' Suzanne muttered, remembering a tongue lashing she had received from the pompous artist for reducing the price of one of his 'masterpieces' by fifty dollars.

'What?'

'Nothing. Nothing.'

It was nearing three in the afternoon. Suzanne and her partner had been doing inventory nonstop since her return from Guy's funeral. Outside, muted midday sunshine filtered through a row of expansive, century-old sugar maples, turning Main

Street into a gentle work of art that far surpassed anything Gerard Morris had produced.

Immersing herself in the inventory and spending time with Helene had helped lift some of the melancholy Suzanne was feeling, but memories of Guy Beaulieu kept her mood somber. Although she had not known the man outside the hospital, she had shared several patients with him before his practice dwindled, and more than respected him as a person and a physician.

Nevertheless, the stories that had been circulating about him of late were disconcerting, and Suzanne had gradually come to agree with those who believed that it would be in everyone's best interest for Guy to retire. Now, reflecting on Zack's opinion that the aging surgeon seemed quite capable and mentally intact, and with the realization that the man had died defending himself, she was having second thoughts.

First Guy Beaulieu, and then the old woodsman Chris Gow – in both cases she had backed off, siding with Ultramed through her silence. True, the corporation had plucked her from a situation that had seemed totally hopeless and had given her a chance. For that alone she owed Ultramed her loyalty. But still, there had been a time, she knew, when she considered herself a liberal, a champion of the underdog. There had been a time when she would have gone to the mat for either man, just as Zack had done. It was hard to believe she had changed so much over just a few short years.

As she hefted Morris's painting off the floor and replaced it in the window, Suzanne silently cursed Paul Cole for the chaos he had brought to her life.

'So?'

Helene Meyer, dressed in jeans and a blue-print smock, emerged from the storeroom with a pair of ceramic vases that they had taken on consignment from a MicMac Indian potter. She was a short, dark, energetic woman with close-cut hair and just enough excess pounds to puff her cheeks and arms.

'So what?' Suzanne asked.

'So where are Morris's ducks?'

Suzanne nodded toward the window.

'Good, good. You're learning, child. You're learning.'

The White Mountain Olde Curiosity Shop and Gallery occupied the ground floor of a half-century-old, red-brick structure two blocks from the center of town. Three years before, when she received word that an uncle had died and left the place to her, Helene was working in a dead-end advertising job in Manhattan and competing with what seemed like several million other forty-year-old divorced women for any one of a minuscule pool of available men.

She took her inheritance as an omen for change.

Despite having 'taken her act on the road,' along with her two children, Helene had never given up on the notion that Mr. Perfect was, at any given moment, just one man away. Perhaps, Suzanne reflected, that was why the woman always had a smile and an encouraging word for even the bleakest situation.

'You okay?' Helene asked, setting the vases on a pair of lucite pedestals, and then reversing them.

'Huh? Oh, sure, I'm fine.'

'You look tired.'

'I always look tired.'

'You always look beautiful,' Helene corrected.

'Today you look beautiful and tired.'

'I'm fine. I'm just not sleeping too well.'

The explanation was an understatement. Since her discharge from the hospital, she had been almost continuously restless and ill at ease, sleeping no more than an hour or two at a time and often awakening with an intense, free-floating anxiety. It was hardly the mood she would have expected, given the outcome of her surgery.

'You need some sex,' Helene said.

'I don't need any sex. That's your cure for everything.'

'Well, have I had a sick day since you've known me? As long as there are ski lodges and contra dances and Thursday night single-mingles at the Holiday Inn, I intend to stay healthy as a horse. Don't you think it's time you—'

'No. No, I don't. Now let's change the subject. Besides—'

She caught herself after that one word, but it was too late. Helene leapt at the opening.

'Besides, what?'

'Nothing.'

'Oh, yes.' She squinted across at Suzanne. 'You did it, didn't you? The other night with that new doctor. What's his name?'

'Zachary. But—'

'Well, I'll be damned. No wonder you're so tired.'

'I thought that was supposed to perk me up.'

'Not when it's the first time in several years, it's not,' Helene said. 'You need to keep in shape for that sort of thing. Glory be. He must be something else, that's all I can say. Tell me about him.'

'There's nothing to tell. He's a nice guy. I was

frightened about my surgery and he was under-standing, and things . . . things just . . . got out of hand. It was a mistake – just one of those things. We're not even going to see one another again outside the hospital.'

'Glory be,' Helene said again.

'You stop that.'

Helene took Suzanne by the shoulders.

'No, you stop that,' she said. 'Suze, you're like my sister. Bringing you in as a partner in this place is the best thing I've ever done – except maybe for that furrier from White Plains. . . .'

She sighed wistfully, and Suzanne laughed.

'If I keep putting my two cents into your life,' she went on, 'it's because I love you. I know you had it rough with that jerk you were married to and all, but that's water under the bridge. He's gone. You can't keep letting him rule your life.'

'I don't let him rule my life. I'm doing just fine, thank you.'

'And you've got a great job and a great kid and a lot of interests and you don't need anyone messing things up for you again. I know. I know. You've said all that before.'

'So . . .'

'So there's more. It's out there waiting if you'd just stop running scared and give it a chance.'

'Helene, I'm perfectly happy, and my life is perfectly under control.'

'Okay, okay. But if you ask me, you could do with a little less control and a little more—'

'Meyer, enough.'

Helene held up her hands defensively.

'Just trying to help,' she said.

'I know.'

168

'So, this Zachary that you're not going to see again outside the hospital, tell me about him.'

'Helene, I thought we—'

'Tall? Kind of a Clint Eastwood face? Great eyes? Dark brown hair?'

'How did you—'

At that instant, the door behind Suzanne opened. She whirled, and tensed visibly.

'Hi,' Zack said.

'I thought so,' Helene muttered. 'Glory be . . .'

'I'm sorry to have popped in on you like this,' Zack said, sipping the cappuccino Suzanne had made him. 'I know you said Wednesday.'

'That's okay. I needed a break.'

They were perched on cherrywood stools on either side of a glass case that doubled as a sales counter and jewelry display. Following introductions, small talk, and a nudge that Suzanne had tried unsuccessfully to find annoying, Helene had gone off on 'errands.' Across the gallery, a dowager tourist and her diminutive husband were eyeing a Gerard Morris, entitled typically: *The Forest Is a Symphony. Life in Itself*.

'How's the incision?' Zack asked.

'No problem . . .'

The atmosphere between them was subdued, but not strained. And despite her efforts to pull away, Suzanne sensed that her connection to him, forged on the hillside behind her house and later in her hospital room, had not softened. Silently, she cautioned herself against giving off any encouraging signals. Helene meant well, but she simply didn't understand.

'I'm sorry about Guy,' she said. 'He was a nice man.'

169

'Yeah.'

Zack debated telling her about the envelope, but decided against it – especially since it still lay unopened on the seat of the camper.

'Are you off for the afternoon?' she asked.

'Nope. I'm due at the office in a couple of minutes. I . . . um . . . actually, I came by for a consultation.'

She eyed him suspiciously.

'Seriously,' he said.

She started to protest, but held back. Helene was right. He did have great eyes. *Damn you, Paul*, she thought.

'Annie?' she asked.

'No, thank goodness. Norman seems to be hanging in there all right with her. She doesn't care much for him, though. She says she doesn't trust him. No, I don't need advice from Suzanne Cole, cardiologist. I need it from Suzanne Cole, mother.'

'Interesting,' she said. 'In that case, let me just change my expression from knowledgeable and unflappable to disheveled, bewildered, and exhausted. Okay, you may proceed.'

Across the gallery, the dowager and her husband had shifted their attention to Morris's *Three Deer, a Stream, and the Cosmos*, a garish rendering with luminescent stars and tiny sparkles in the water.

'It's a consult I've got to do for Phil Brookings,' Zack said. 'An eight-year-old boy.'

'Name?'

Reflexively, Suzanne picked up a pen and doodled *8 years* on the corner of a pad.

'Nelms. Toby Nelms. The kid hasn't spoken more than a word or two to anyone in five months. Brookings is ready to enter therapy with him, but he wanted me to evaluate him first. I think he's terrified at the prospect of spending hour after hour locked in his office with a kid who won't talk.'

'That does sound awful – especially for a shrink. But the child doesn't exactly sound neurosurgical.'

'Probably not, but he might be neurological. Apparently he's been having some sort of psychomotor seizures.'

'Psychomotor?'

'Sort of a grab-bag diagnosis, meaning, I don't have a handle on what's going on. Some variant of temporal-lobe epilepsy is as close as I can come, based on what Brookings told me. During the first seizure, just before he stopped speaking, he destroyed his room. There have been a number of others since then.'

'So why isn't it temporal-lobe epilepsy?'

'Well, for one thing, although there is this rage component like we see in temporal-lobe patients, there's also an enormous fear component. The kid acts as if he's absolutely terrified of something. And for another – and this is what's really disturbing – the recovery time is getting longer and longer with each episode. It sounds as if these seizures, or whatever they are, are associated with some actual increased pressure in the boy's brain.'

'Cerebral edema?'

'Quite possibly.'

'That's frightening.'

'Until now, the swelling's been reversible, but as you know, at some point a vicious cycle sets in: edema causing high fever, causing more edema, and so on.'

'Are there any triggers?'

'Triggers?'

'You know, something that sets off an attack.'

'Oh, no. Not that anyone has picked up on. Brookings wants to put him on Dilantin or one of the temporal-lobe epilepsy drugs, but he wanted me to check the boy out first. I thought maybe you could give me some hints about dealing with kids around his age.'

'Has he had an EEG?'

'I want to get both that and a CT scan, but according to Brookings, the little guy gets so agitated when he gets anywhere near the hospital that it's been next to impossible to get any kind of technically satisfactory study.'

'The hospital?'

'Brookings swears that the kid looked through his office window at the hospital and bolted. He had to chase him across the parking lot and actually tackle him.'

Absently, Suzanne had scribbled the words *Nelms, psychomotor*, and *hospital* on her pad.

'I assume Brookings has looked for the obvious – a bad experience in the hospital, something like that?' she asked.

'Uh-huh. Repair of an incarcerated hernia a year or so ago is all. Your pal Mainwaring did the work. I reviewed the record. The boy was in overnight, but there were absolutely no problems.'

Suzanne added *hernia* and *no problems* to her list.

'Was it done under local?'

'Something like Pentothal and gas, I think it was. Why?'

'No reason. Just throwing out thoughts. I had the same anesthesia, and I'm still talking up a storm, so I don't think that's it.'

Across the room, the tourists were embroiled in a

heated debate, the dowager gesturing toward *Cosmos*, and her husband toward *Symphony*.

'Any suggestions?' Zack asked.

Suzanne scratched lines under several of the words on her pad.

'Just one off the top,' she said. 'Don't see him in your office.'

'What?'

'And do your best not to look like a doctor, either, or to call yourself "doctor." He'll probably know you are one, but there's no sense in making a big deal of it. Unlike most grown-ups, kids don't get impressed with our title. They just get scared.'

'You mean, see him at my place?'

'Or even his place. Or better still, somewhere neutral. What about that plane you were telling Jen about? She's very excited about that. Is there any way you could put on a show for this child?'

'Excellent idea,' Zack said. 'Of course I could. That's perfect. I have just the place. The Meadows up at the top of Gaston Street. You know where that is?'

'Uh-huh. We've been there. That sounds just right. When are you seeing him?'

'Wednesday. Wednesday at one-thirty. Say, listen, that being Wednesday and all, why don't we meet up there at, say, eleven-thirty. We can have some lunch – a picnic. You can bring Jen and—'

'I can't,' she said too quickly. 'What I mean is, we already have plans.'

'Oh.'

'Zack, I'm sorry.' *Why was she lying?* 'Another time.'

He smiled tightly.

'Yeah, sure. Another time ... Well, thanks for the

coffee.' He cleared his throat and pushed off the stool. 'I . . . um . . . I guess I'd better get back to the hospital.'

'Zack . . .' she said as he headed off.

He turned back.

'Zack, I . . . I really am sorry about Guy.'

'Yeah,' he said, the hurt in his eyes unmistakable. 'Me, too.'

He turned again and was gone.

Stonily, Suzanne tore the sheet from her pad and balled it in her fist. Perhaps it was time she herself made an appointment with Phil Brookings. Sterling had been every bit the refuge she had hoped it would be. Peace and beauty, a good job, and time to spend with Jen. That was all she had wanted, and all she needed. *Why was this happening now?*

'Excuse me, Miss?'

The dowager, her husband hovering behind, stood by the stool Zack had just vacated.

'Huh? Oh, sorry,' Suzanne said. 'I see you're interested in Gerard Morris's work?'

'Yes. Is he local?'

'One town over. He's growing more popular every year.'

Why had she lied to him about Wednesday? Jen *did* have plans with friends, but she was free. *Why had she lied?*

'Well,' the woman said, 'my husband and I are most interested in the work on the left. The one with those lovely deer. Could you tell me its price?'

'It's eighteen hundred.'

'Oh,' the woman said. 'I see.' She scanned Morris's mimeoed resumé. 'Has he had any gallery shows outside of this area? Boston? New York?'

'No,' Suzanne said, realizing that, despite her

174

taste in art, the woman was no novice at buying it. 'I don't believe he has.'

Maybe Helene was right. Maybe it was time to stop running scared.

'Well,' the woman said, 'that being the case, don't you think the asking price for his work is a bit high?'

Suzanne eyed her for a moment, and then flipped the crumpled list into the wastepaper basket.

'As a matter of fact,' she said, 'I do.'

For years people had called her the Witch of West Eighty-seventh Street. But Hattie Day had known better. They called her Batty Hattie and filed petitions claiming her cluttered apartment was a health menace and her family of cats against the law. But Hattie hadn't cared. On her infrequent trips to the store, children taunted her and even sometimes threw things at her. But Hattie had understood, and still loved them as much as she loved her cats.

For years, people had said that she was crazy. But because she had known better, Hattie had just smiled at them.

But now, since the terrifying events that had followed her trip to Quebec, Hattie smiled at no one. Because now Hattie knew they were right.

It was nearly two in the morning. Exhausted, but reluctant to sleep, Hattie hobbled to her stove, lit a cigarette from the burner, and then put on a pot of tea. She was only sixty-two, but with her pallor, her long, unkempt hair, and her cadaverous thinness, she looked eighty.

She sank into a tattered easy chair and studied her hands. There was nothing about the bony, nicotine-stained fingers and the long, curving nails to suggest the wonderful music they had once made. The death of her parents in an accident had, in effect, ripped the violin from her hands – pulled her out of Juilliard and into a succession of mental hospitals. But over the years, she had made do. She had her apartment, and her cats, and her battered stereo, and more than enough records to fill each day with music.

But that was before Quebec.

Shakily, Hattie stubbed out her cigarette, hesitated a moment, and then limped to the stove to light another. The water had not yet boiled.

If only she had refused the invitation to Martin's wedding, she thought; if only she had stayed home where she belonged, none of this would have happened. But Martin, her cousin's son, was really the only family she had. And when *he* was at Juilliard he had stopped by often, bringing food and usually a record or two, and staying long enough to tell her about his studies. Once he had even brought his guitar and played for her – Bach, and several wonderful Villa-Lobos pieces.

Hattie smiled grimly at the memory.

The bus ride up to Canada had been easy enough, and the wedding had been beautiful – especially the chamber groups made up of Martin's friends. It was during the ride home that the dreadful ache in her leg had begun. The bus driver had turned her over to the ambulance people in Sterling, New Hampshire, and within an hour she was in the operating room having a cloth artery put in to bypass the clot in her groin.

They had called her recovery a miracle. After just a week in the hospital and two weeks in a nursing home, she had gone home. Martin had driven her back to Manhattan and had even gotten one of her cats back for her from the animal protection people. A miracle.

It was just a day after Martin had dropped her off that the frightening episodes had begun. Without warning, her mind would go limp. For an hour or more at a time she would sit, staring at nothing, unable to move or to focus her thoughts, knowing what was happening but powerless to control it. The colors in the room would become uncomfortably bright, all sounds unnaturally muted. Sometimes she could force herself out of her chair. Other times, she could only sit and wait for the terribly unpleasant episodes to pass. Twice she had wet herself.

She knew she was becoming insane.

Then, as if verifying her fears, some of the bizarre episodes had begun exploding into horrible, vivid, distorted reenactments of her surgery.

The teapot began whistling. Hattie pushed herself upright, put a tea bag into a chipped stoneware mug, and poured in the boiling water. On the way back to her easy chair, she stopped and put on one of the albums Martin had left with her – Elizabethan music and English folk pieces, with Martin featured on his guitar.

Perhaps, she thought, it was worth calling Martin and telling him she was going mad. She looked about for Orange, the cat he had retrieved for her. During the last of her nightmares, she had hurt it somehow – knocked out a tooth and cut its lip. Since then, the animal had spent most of its time under the bed or behind the bookshelf.

Hattie sank heavily into her chair. For a brief time, Martin's playing brought her some serenity and even some sweet glimpses into her dim past. There was a set of dances that she felt sure she had once played at a recital, and a lovely rendition of a song by Thomas Stewart. Next came her favorite, a gentle and haunting flute and guitar duet of 'Greensleeves.'

Bit by bit, her fears began to loosen their grip. Then, as they had twice before that day, the colors in the room began to intensify.

No! Hattie's mind screamed. *Please, God, not again.*

The music grew faint, and gradually faded into the hum of traffic passing on nearby Columbus Avenue.

No . . .

Hattie felt the unpleasant inertia begin to settle in. The glow from the lamp across the room hurt her eyes.

Please, God . . .

Desperately, and with all her strength, she forced herself to her feet, and grabbed her cigarettes, and stumbled toward the stove.

'Not this time,' she said out loud. 'Goddamn it, not this time.'

She thrust a cigarette between her lips and shakily turned the burner knob. The gas flame flashed on.

'Hattie . . . Hattie, just relax.'

The voice, deep and soothing, seemed to be coming from everywhere at once. Then, from above her, Hattie saw the blue-gray eyes smiling at her over the mask.

'Just relax now. There's nothing to worry about. Nothing at all. I want you to begin counting back from one hundred.'

'Please . . .'

'Hattie, count!'

'One hundred . . . ninety-nine . . .'

'Good, Hattie. Keep counting. Keep counting.'

'Ninety-eight . . .'

'She's under.'

'Ninety-seven . . .'

'Ready, everyone. Okay.'

'Ninety-six . . . No, wait, please. You're wrong. I'm not asleep. I'm not asleep yet.'

'Suction up.'

'Wait!'

'Knife, please.'

'No! Not yet! Not yet!'

Hattie Day screamed as the scalpel cut into the wall of her lower abdomen. Her screams intensified as flame leapt from the stove and ignited first her hair and then her robe.

'Snap, please. Now another . . .'

Hattie reeled across her apartment, knocking away pieces of fiery cloth. The rug began to smolder. She fell to the floor as the scalpel cut down her abdomen and over her groin. Flames seared her face and scalp. She retched from the smoke and the acrid smell of her own burning flesh.

'Retractors ready, please . . .'

The voice bored through the pain. The knife cut deeper.

'Sponge. No, over here. Right here!'

Her clothes now a mass of flame, Hattie Day lurched to her feet and plunged toward the window.

'Okay. Now, retract here.'

Shrieking, and now engulfed in flame, the woman they all called the Witch of West Eighty-seventh Street hurled herself through the glass and out into the summer night, ten stories above the street.

Chapter 14

Tuesday morning descended on Zack in the guise of one of his sneakers, set neatly and carefully on the side of his face by Cheapdog.

'Self-centered brute,' he mumbled, working his eyes open one at a time. 'The world has to turn upside down just because you have to take a pee.'

Cheapdog responded to the rebuke by licking him on the mouth.

'Okay, okay, mop-face. You made your point.' Zack scratched the animal behind one ear and made yet another in a long series of promises to get him a haircut. 'I'm afraid I haven't been paying much attention to you lately, old boy. Thanks for being so understanding.'

Feeling sluggish, and less enthused about a day at work than he had in some time, he pulled on a pair of surgical scrub pants emblazoned PROPERTY OF MUNICIPAL HOSPITAL OF BOSTON – NOT TO BE REMOVED FOR ANY REASON, let Cheapdog out into the backyard, did fifteen minutes of lackluster calisthenics, and finally started water for coffee.

Suzanne's striking change of attitude toward him was, he knew, one reason for his unpleasant humor. And as wonderful as making love with her had been, he wished now that they had played things differently.

But weighing perhaps even more heavily at that moment was Guy Beaulieu's legacy.

For most of the prior evening, Guy's envelope had remained unopened in the camper. In fact, at various times throughout the day Zack had actually considered returning it in that state. In the end, though, he realized that his decision to do what he could for the man had been made well before meeting with his widow and daughter, and in fact, even before the terrible events in the quiet room.

As he dripped hot water through his Chemex filter and scrambled two eggs with some chopped peppers, onions, and bits of leftover bacon, Zack mulled over his initial impressions of the surgeon's strange and bitter legacy.

It was after midnight when he had finally returned home from a long walk with Cheapdog and brought in the envelope. Too tired to read with much comprehension, he had spent two hours sifting through the material and sorting it into piles on the dining room table. From what he could tell, the Ultramed Hospitals Corporation, whether responsible for Guy's difficulties or not, had had a tiger by the tail.

There were dozens of newspaper clippings and official documents, plus computer printouts, a number of typed and amended lists of corporate officers and boards of directors, and several smaller envelopes filled with hastily scrawled, handwritten notes.

Beaulieu and his researchers had been thoroughly preparing themselves for battle. Still, despite their diligence, it looked to Zack as if the evidence they had accumulated of Ultramed's avaricious business practices was circumstantial and vague.

Zack felt certain that although the assorted documents might raise some eyebrows among the hospital trustees, they were lacking the one, essential ingredient that might turn that concern into votes: a flesh-and-blood example – even one – of the dangers of such practices – what Rock Hudson had been to AIDS, or the Challenger explosion to the dangers of space exploration.

Without such a rallying point, such an emotional linchpin, Zack knew that Beaulieu's efforts were ultimately as doomed as the man himself.

In addition to the evidence against Ultramed, the envelope contained a diary.

During the early morning hours, Zack had done no more than scan the small, spiral-bound note-book. Now, after clearing a space on the table for his breakfast, he opened it randomly. Not surprisingly, the writing, almost all of it in fountain pen, was meticulous and precise.

December 11th: Several patients cancelled today, including Clarisse LaFrenniere. Spoke on phone to her. She was reluctant to say anything. Had to beg her. Finally admitted that her son Ricky had heard at school that I had seen one of the girls in his class for a lump on her neck, and had undressed her and made her lie on my examining table, and then that I had walked around and around the table, touching her. No such patient exists in my records or memory. Made several calls to parents of any young girls I had treated. They admitted to having heard rumors, but denied any of them dealt with their daughters. They were all quite distant and embarrassed. I feel I may have done myself more harm than good by contacting them. Called Ricky and

182

begged him to give me the girl's name. He could or would not. Finally, Clarisse took the phone from him, told me not to call again, and hung up. I will not stop trying.

Zack glanced at several other pages, some of which outlined more of Guy's efforts to dive beneath the murky sea of rumors. Others described clashes with members of the medical staff, the local newspaper, and even certain patients.

Taken as a whole, it was a chronicle of the agonizing disintegration of a man's life.

Allegations of malpractice, none of them substantiated or backed up with a suit . . . letters of complaint to the newspapers and the hospital, most of them anonymous . . . rumors of sexual misconduct . . . rumors of inappropriate behavior . . . patient defections . . .

Blow after blow, humiliation after humiliation, yet Guy Beaulieu had refused to knuckle under. On one page he seemed heroic, on the next, pathologically obstinate. As Zack scanned the notes, the fine line separating the two conditions grew even less distinct.

The chances that a man is in the right increase geometrically by the vigor with which others are trying to prove him wrong.

The maxim was one of Zack's favorites, and he had cited it any number of times over the years. But never had he felt it in his gut the way he did at this moment.

Still, there was more than gut instinct to consider. There was the incriminating letter from Maureen Banas, along with other damning evidence Frank claimed to have. There was also Guy's explosive and

183

irrational behavior in the emergency ward on the morning of his death. And finally, there was the lack of any really good explanation as to why the man might have been singled out for destruction in the first place.

Certainly, his widow's belief that Ultramed was trying to rid itself of a potential troublemaker was possible, but the response seemed absurdly out of proportion to the threat Guy posed – like shooting a fly with an elephant gun.

Zack retrieved Cheapdog from where he was lurking beneath the window of a neighbor's unspayed collie, and chained him on a long run in the yard. Then he showered, dressed, and headed for the hospital, wondering what he would do if he had to confront Marie Fontaine and her mother with hard evidence that Guy had been, in fact, irrational, unstable, and paranoid. Even with a negative autopsy, the man could have been in the early stages of Alzheimer's or struggling with nonanatomical mental illness.

As he was pulling into the small Doctors Only lot at the hospital, Zack flashed on another saying – this one from a poster he had tacked to the wall of his med school apartment.

Just because you're paranoid, doesn't mean they're not out to get you.

The emergency ward was in a louder-than-usual morning hum, with several private physicians doing minor procedures, and the E.R. physician of the day, Wilton Marshfield, huffing from one of four 'active' rooms to the next, clearly upset that things were not proceeding at a more gentle pace.

Zack stopped by the lounge for one final cup of

184

coffee, and was in the process of failing to confound two candy stripers with a thumb palm, when he was paged for an outside call.

'Zack, it's Brookings here, Phil Brookings.'

'Oh, yes, Phil. If you're calling about that youngster, Nelms, I had to postpone his appointment because of Guy Beaulieu's funeral. I'll be seeing him tomorrow afternoon.'

Zack glanced over at the candy stripers, one of whom was completing the more-than-passable thumb palm of a penny on her first try.

'I know,' the psychiatrist said. 'The boy's mother called me. She was, how can I say, a little concerned that you told her to meet you on the side of some mountain. I promised her I would check with you to see if . . . ah . . . if there was anything further I could do.'

'Actually,' Zack said, smiling at Brookings's discomfiture, 'it's near the base of the mountain. Not on the side.'

'Oh . . . I see. . . . Well, I'll just give Mrs. Nelms a call and reassure her that you're not the, how should I say, the eccentric she thinks you might be.'

This time, Zack laughed out loud.

'Phil, forgive me for being glib. The truth is, I probably *am* the eccentric she thinks I might be. But this time, at least, I'm just doing what I can to avoid the difficulty *you* had. It's a little tricky doing a detailed neurological exam on a moving target.'

'I understand,' Brookings said, although his tone suggested some lingering doubts. 'I'll speak with the boy's mother and make sure they show up. And just in case, perhaps you should wear your sneakers. The kid is fast.'

'Thanks, Phil. I'll be in touch.'

185

Zack hung up as the candy stripers, still practicing, were preparing to leave the lounge.

'Here you go, ladies,' he said. 'One more. This one's called a finger roll. In it, this perfectly normal American quarter will be magically transported across the tops of my fingers and back without the aid of a crane, bulldozer, or my other hand.'

Between the second and the third roll, the quarter slipped between his fingers and plunked into his coffee.

'Now, I suggest that you two stay away from this trick until you're old enough to work with hot coffee,' he warned.

He stood proudly by the cup and waited to retrieve his coin until the bewildered pair had left the room.

'Me, eccentric,' he muttered as he headed through the emergency ward. 'That's ridiculous. Absolutely ridiculous.'

A set of X rays, five views of a teenager's cervical spine, were wedged up on a four-paneled viewbox in the corridor. Hours later, when the tension and excitement had died down and there was time to reflect, Zack would be unable to explain what it was about those films that had caught his eye.

But in that one microsecond as he passed by, something did.

It might have been the widening of a shadow, or perhaps the slightly unusual curve in the lateral view. Or it might have been nothing more or less than the instinctive processing of the films against thirteen years of study and God only knew how many other C-spines in how many other settings.

Whatever it was, something made him stop, turn, and study the X rays in more detail.

186

The fractures of vertebrae C-1 and C-2 were far from the most obvious he had ever seen, but they were certainly present – and unquestionably unstable. If the spinal cord had not already been damaged, a sudden twist, or turn, or bump could be disastrous.

Either way, he certainly should have been called in on the case.

He checked the name and birthdate: *Stacy Mills, age 14.*

Next, he cut through the nurses' station, looking for Wilton Marshfield. The portly physician was hunched over a counter, hurriedly writing a set of discharge instructions. Next to the instruction sheet was a soft cervical collar.

'Hi,' Zack said, moving close enough to verify that the instructions were, in fact, for Stacy Mills.

He looked past the man to bed 3, where a dark, pretty girl in riding jodhpurs and a lavender T-shirt was waiting with her parents. She was sitting on the edge of the litter with her feet dangling down, and she was rubbing gently at the base of her skull.

'Oh, hi, Iverson,' Marshfield said. He glanced up only long enough to nod, and then returned to his writing. 'This is one bitch of a morning, I'll tell you. . . . Saw you at Beaulieu's funeral yesterday. . . . Terrible business. Terrible.'

'Wilton, could I talk to you for a moment?' Zack asked softly.

Marshfield shook his head.

'Can't stop right now,' he said, pulling a prescription pad from his clinic coat. 'I've got to get rid of this kid, and then I still have two more patients to see. I'm getting too old for this pace, Iverson. Too damn old. Tell your brother he'd better hurry up and get this place straightened out so I can get back to my trout stream and my grandchildren.'

'It's about that girl you're getting ready to send home,' Zack said. 'Stacy Mills.'

Marshfield squinted over at the girl, and then picked up the cervical collar and the instruction sheet, and began writing a prescription for a muscle relaxant.

'Fell off her horse and strained her neck muscles,' he said as he wrote. 'Look, Iverson,' he added curtly, 'I'm sorry I snapped at you the other night. But please, just don't make any trouble for me today. I'm too far behind to—'

'Listen, Marshfield,' Zack whispered. 'I just looked at her films over there. She has a fracture. Two of them, I think. C-one and C-two.'

The older man froze. In slow motion, his pen wobbled in his fingertips and then fell, clattering onto the counter.

'Are you sure?' he rasped.

Zack nodded.

'Jesus . . .'

'Come, let me show you.'

Moments later, Zack led a mute, badly shaken Wilton Marshfield across to Stacy Mills and her parents.

'Hello, Stacy, Mr. and Mrs. Mills,' he said. 'My name is Iverson. Zachary Iverson. I'm a neuro-surgeon.'

He glanced back at Marshfield, who looked as if he were listening blindfolded to the final counts from a firing squad.

Inwardly, Zack smiled. If the man was waiting for gunfire, he was in for a pleasant surprise.

Hey, Wilton, relax, he was thinking. *As far as I'm*

188

concerned, this business of ours has never been a contest or a game. It's life. It's the real banana. And it's hard enough to do right even without the bullshit and the oneupmanship. You did the best you could, and that's all we got – any of us. There's no way I would hang you out to dry.

'Dr. Marshfield, here, has just made an excellent pickup on Stacy's X rays,' he said. 'He spotted a shadow he didn't like, and wanted me to check it before he would consider sending her home. I'm afraid his suspicions were correct. Stacy, there is a small fracture – a broken bone right up here.'

'I knew it,' Stacy said. 'See Mother, I told you it was killing me.'

'Is it dangerous?' the girl's mother asked.

'It would have been,' Zack said, slipping the soft collar into place, 'if it had gone undetected. It could have been a blooming disaster. But everything is under control now. You're going to be just fine.'

Mrs. Mills reached over and squeezed a stunned Wilton Marshfield's hand. Her husband patted him on the shoulder.

'Now, Stacy,' Zack went on, 'first of all, I don't want you moving your head around, okay?'

'Okay.'

'Good. Then there are some things I must explain to you and to your parents about what we do for cervical fractures.'

'Dr. Iverson, please,' the girl's mother said. 'Before you start, I'd like to get Stacy's aunt – my sister – over here. Would that be okay?'

'Certainly, but I don't see—'

'She helps me understand medical things. I'm sure you know her. She's the head nurse here. Maureen. Maureen Banas.'

Chapter 15

Although operating room 2 at Ultramed-Davis was newer than some of the dozens Zack had worked in, the ambience was no different. The sounds, the lighting, the tile, the filtered air – tinged with the unique mix of antiseptic and talc and freshly laundered gowns – provided sensations as familiar to him, as reassuring, as the mountains.

The stabilization of Stacy Mills's neck was proceeding flawlessly. Standing by the head of the table, Zack paused, savoring the sensations – the wonder of what he was able to do, and the bond he was feeling with the rest of the O.R. team. The sound system – Frank's brainchild, now installed in nearly all Ultramed's hospitals – was playing George Winston's magical treatment of 'The Holly and the Ivy.'

'All set?' he asked the scrub nurse.

The woman nodded.

'All right, then,' he said evenly. 'Stacy, this is the part I told you about. We're going to twist those four screws into place on your head. I've put lots of novocaine in each spot, so they won't hurt, but it will feel funny, and you might hear the grinding noise. Everything is going just fine. I know it's scary for you, but there's really nothing to be frightened about.'

'I'm not frightened,' the girl said. 'At least, not too much.'

'Good. And you remember what you have to do?'

'Don't move,' she answered.

'Exactly . . .'

Zack checked the position of the cervical halo one last time, and worked the four screws farther into place through the small incisions he had made in the girl's scalp.

'Unless I tell you to, don't move.'

From a spot several feet behind the O.R. team, Wilton Marshfield watched, his every breath a sigh of relief. Even though Zack Iverson had publicly gone out of his way to share credit for the pickup with him and had privately assured him that this sort of cervical fracture was the toughest of all to diagnose, he sensed that he would never be truly comfortable in the emergency ward again.

He had come out of retirement and into the E.R. as a favor to Frank Iverson, and because he was bored. Now, he knew, it was time to stop. And thanks to Iverson's brother, after forty years of busting his hump, of doing his best to survive first the knowledge explosion, then medicare and the paperwork crunch, then the malpractice crisis, and now the goddamn corporate-policy crap, he could at least go out as something of a winner.

'God love ya, kid,' he said softly, as Zack tightened the apparatus in place. 'God love ya.'

'Okay, Stacy,' Zack was saying, 'that's one. Now, wiggle your toes the way I showed you. Good. Now your fingers. Good, good. We're almost there.'

He stepped back for a moment and shifted his focus from the metal frame to the fine features and peaceful face of the girl/woman. Biology; organic chemistry; anatomy and physiology; boards and more boards; endless nights and weekends on duty or on call; countless meals of cafeteria food or nondescript leftovers in cardboard containers; countless hours in the O.R. and on the wards; scattered days, and weeks, and even months of consuming self-doubt – at moments like this one, the choices he had made in his life and the price he had paid made so much sense.

And when it was over, when the girl who loved to ride horses walked away from the hospital and from the split second that could have paralyzed her forever, he would take that moment and bankroll it in his mind as vindication for all the years and all the anguish, and as a hedge against those outcomes yet-to-be which would not bring smiles and handshakes and pats on the back – outcomes that, as long as they were unavoidable, were no less a part of medicine than this one.

'That's it, Stacy,' he cooed as he tightened down the last of the screws. 'That's it. You're doing perfect. We're all doing perfect.'

With the elective surgery schedule now an hour behind, O.R. 2 was emptied out as soon as the last screw was in place and the proper position of the halo was verified. Zack accompanied Stacy Mills to the east-wing room where, for a few days, she would be observed for signs of spinal cord swelling or compression.

'Well, you just take it easy, Stacy,' he said. 'I'm going to go talk to your folks, and then I'll send them up. I'll be back to see you at the end of the day. Wearing this device won't be the most fun you've ever had, but like I said, it won't be forever.'

'Dr. Zack,' the girl called out as he was leaving, 'in the operating room I said that I wasn't scared. Well, now that it's all over, I can tell you that I really was. I just didn't want to sound like a baby.'

Zack returned to the bedside and smiled down at her.

'In that case,' he said, 'I've got something to tell *you* – something I've never told any patient before.' He bent over her bed and whispered, 'I'm always a little frightened and a little nervous when I operate.'

'You are? Really?'

'The truth. I think it helps my concentration never to forget that it's always possible that something could go wrong. There, I said it, and . . . hey, Dr. Mills, I feel better already!'

'You're very silly, do you know that?'

'I hope so,' he said.

As he was leaving the girl's room, Zack spotted Maureen Banas approaching down the corridor. She was in her late forties or early fifties, he guessed, with short, graying hair that looked as if it had been cut by an amateur. Although she carried herself with authority, the tension etched into her face and the lack of attention to ten or fifteen excess pounds hinted at a life that had, perhaps, not been an easy one.

'Congratulations, Dr. Iverson, and thanks,' she said with an almost clinical lack of emotion. 'Stacy is a very special child to a lot of people. We all owe you a great deal for what you did.'

In that case, he wanted to say, *tell me about the nail you helped hammer into Guy Beaulieu's coffin.*

'Listen,' he replied instead, 'just seeing her moving those arms and legs and piggies of hers is enough to get me through six months of the usual

193

neurosurgical nightmares. Besides, it's Wilton Marshfield you should be thanking. I was just the technician.'

'Nonsense. I know he missed those fractures. Sticking up for him was a very kind thing for you to do, especially with the altercation you two had last week. Wilton's really a sweet old guy most of the time. But he misses too much.'

He misses too much. The opening, however slight, was there.

Zack glanced past the nurse. The corridor was quiet. There might have been a more appropriate time and place, but one day after Guy's funeral, and only hours after reading his diary, thoughts of the man were too close to the surface for Zack to walk away from this opportunity.

'Sort of like Guy Beaulieu in that respect,' he said. 'Yes?'

Maureen Banas looked at him queerly. 'I beg your pardon?'

'I was asking about your impressions of Guy Beaulieu. I was with him when he died, you know.'

'Of course I know.' Her strange expression had not faded. 'I thought a lot of Dr. Beaulieu. To die the way he did was . . . was very tragic.' She averted her gaze and peered around the corner into Stacy's room. 'Well,' she said, 'I guess I'd better check on my niece and get back to the emergency ward. Thank you again, Doctor.'

'Mrs. Banas, wait, please,' Zack said.

The woman stopped, her back still to him, her posture rigid.

'Please?' he said again.

Slowly, she turned to face him. Her arms were folded grimly across her chest.

'Yes?'

'Mrs. Banas, I . . . I read the letter you wrote about Guy.'

What little color there was drained from the nurse's face.

'Your brother had no right to go passing that around,' she said.

'Why?'

The woman looked about restlessly.

'Dr. Iverson, I think I'd better go.'

'Mrs. Banas, just a minute ago you said that you owed me a great deal for what I did for Stacy. Well, I don't usually call in markers like this, but I need to know about Guy – what he's been like these past two years; what he did that prompted you to write those charges. Please. It's terribly important to me . . . and to his family.'

Maureen Banas's reaction was far from the anger or defensiveness Zack would have anticipated. She began to tremble, and quickly grew close to tears.

'I . . . please, I don't want to talk about it. Your brother said he would speak with me before showing that note to anyone. He had no right to give it to you.'

'Look,' Zack said. 'I didn't mean to upset you. I'm just trying to get to the bottom of things – to the truth.'

It took several breaths before the nurse began to regain her composure.

'Dr. Iverson, I've got three children, one of them retarded, and an ex-husband who hasn't sent a dime of support in ten years. I'm sorry I wrote that letter, but . . . but I had to. I had to. Now, you've got to leave it alone. For my sake. For my family. Leave it alone. I beg you.'

'I can't, Mrs. Banas . . . Maureen, I don't want to cause trouble for you or for anyone, but I've got to know if that letter contained the truth about Guy. . . . Please.'

The woman said nothing.

'What is it?' he asked. 'Did someone pressure you to write it? Threaten to take your job away?'

The nurse bit on her lower lip. Her eyes had filled with tears. She glanced nervously about. Two nurses were approaching down the hall.

'Come with me,' she said softly.

There was a small sitting area at the end of the corridor – a colonial-style maple settee and two matching chairs arranged beneath a huge picture window that faced southwest, toward the mountains. Maureen Banas took one of the chairs and motioned Zack to the edge of the settee closest to her.

'Dr. Iverson, I meant what I said about my family,' she began in a hoarse whisper. 'If you speak of this conversation to anyone and I lose my job, you will have hurt a number of people who do not deserve to be hurt.'

'You have my word.'

'I . . . I'm terrified about doing this.'

'Please . . .'

'At the beginning of the summer, I quarreled with Dr. Beaulieu in the E.R. We never got along all that well to begin with, but I think we more or less respected one another. It doesn't make any difference what we fought about. The whole incident was actually pretty mild. But there were a number of witnesses.

'A week or so later, there was an envelope stuck under my door at home. In it were ten one-hundred-dollar bills, a copy of the note you saw, and instructions that when I copied the note over in my own hand and sent it to Mr. Iverson, I would receive a second, equal payment.'

'No hint of who the note was from?'

Once again, the nurse seemed close to breaking down.

'None.'

'Well, did the note say what would happen if you refused?'

'It said that trouble would start happening in my life, and that I could count on being fired. Dr. Iverson, I know what I did was awful, but . . . but I had been doing so poorly with the kids, and the damn bills just keep coming in, and—'

'Please, Maureen. You don't have to explain,' Zack said. 'I understand that you did what you had to do. Do you still have the note?'

The nurse shook her head.

'I . . . I was afraid to keep it.'

'Any sense at all as to who sent it? Do you think it was my brother?' Zack felt sick at the thought.

'I . . . I don't believe so,' she said.

'Why do you say that?'

'Well, whoever wrote me added at the end that if Frank Iverson learned my note wasn't really my idea, he would be fired just as quickly as I would be. . . .'

She began to cry.

'You see why you can't say anything to anyone about this?'

'Yes, Maureen. I see. Telling me what you did was a very brave thing to do. I promise you that I'll honor your confidence.'

'Th-Thank you.'

She dabbed at her eyes with her uniform sleeve and then hurried back down the corridor.

Feeling more sadness toward the woman than anger, Zack propped his foot on one of the chairs and gazed across at the Presidential Range.

Hiking . . . climbing . . . camping . . . unique challenges in the office and in the O.R. . . . The projected life that had drawn him back to Sterling suddenly seemed so remote, so naive.

Guy, it appeared, had been right all along. Someone at Ultramed was committed to driving him from practice – and in the ugliest of ways. Zack was grateful that that someone did not appear to be Frank. But in the end, would it really matter? In Sterling, at least, Frank *was* Ultramed. And when push came to shove, it was hard to imagine him lining up against the company.

The situation was so crazy, so far removed from a patient needing help and a physician trained and ready to render it.

But for better or worse, Zack acknowledged, he was in it to stay. He had chosen this town and this hospital. And now, if he had to do battle with Ultramed to justify that decision, then battle there would be.

All he needed to complete the circle, to place himself once and for all squarely where Guy Beaulieu had stood, was proof – if not proof from Maureen Banas, then perhaps from the Ultramed system itself.

If Guy was right, if the policies and the climate created by the corporation were so ruthless and self-serving, if compromises were being made and corners cut in the name of profit, then somewhere there was the medical tragedy such a philosophy must inevitably bring. Somewhere, there was that emotional focal point that would translate possibilities and abstract concerns into flesh and blood.

And if such a tragedy existed, Zack vowed, sooner or later he would find it.

From his position at the nurses' station on West 2, Donald Norman, MD, propped Annie Doucette's chart on his ample lap and peered over the top of it at a Rubenesque young nurse named Doreen Lavalley. She was standing on tiptoes atop a small stool, stretching over her head for a bag of IV solution. The skirt of her uniform was at her mid-thigh and rising.

Doreen was the sexiest, most desirable woman in the hospital, at least to the Ultramed-Davis Chief of Staff. For months he had been cultivating her with small talk, friendly pats on the shoulder, an arm about the waist, and impromptu teaching sessions.

Since his arrival at the hospital four years before, Norman had gone out of his way to keep his reputation spotless and to portray the perfect, responsible family man and community servant. The powers at Ultramed rewarded such behavior just as vigorously as they punished actions that brought negative publicity down upon their house.

But after four consecutive yearly merit awards, he believed that the company would tolerate a few slips. And with his wife gaining weight and growing more involved with her school committees and steadily less involved with their physical relationship, Doreen Lavalley had become worth the risk.

Besides, Norman reasoned, Frank Iverson was rumored to have made it with half the decent-looking women in the hospital, and he had been made a member of the Golden Circle and had twice won the highest administrator's award that Ultramed offered.

Just as her skirt was about to reach the base of her panties, Doreen located the right IV solution and hopped down from the stool.

Donald Norman cursed under his breath.

'Morning, Doreen,' he said, tugging at the small bulge that had materialized behind Annie Doucette's chart. 'How goes it?'

'Oh, Dr. Norman, hi.'

'Hey, I told you,' he whispered, with a conspiratorial wink, 'when no one's around you can call me Don. Listen, I'd like you to make rounds with me, if that's okay. Mr. Rolfe has some interesting findings in his chest, and that . . . that harpy, Mrs. Doucette, should still have her murmur.'

The nurse glanced about.

'Well, I'm a little behind in my work, and—'

'Oh, come on,' he urged. 'I just have those two on this floor. It shouldn't take long.'

'I . . . well, okay. As long as it's just two. And Dr. Norman, Annie's a nice lady. Really she is. Just give her a chance.'

'It's Don, remember?' Norman said. 'And as far as Annie Doucette goes, she may be a sweet old lady to you, but she's been a harpy to me.' He checked the three by five file card he carried on her. 'Besides,' he added, 'it's all academic to all intents and purposes, she's out of here.'

'You're sending her home?' Doreen asked with disbelief.

Norman shook his head.

'Not home,' he said. 'To the Sterling Nursing Home, provided they can clear out a bed.

Remember, under the Diagnostically Related Group system – you know, the DRGs – medicare pays by the diagnosis, not the length of the hospital stay. Our job is to get patients out as quickly as possible.'

What Norman did not mention, although they were certainly on his mind at that moment, were the Ultramed incentive points awarded for discharging patients before the end of their DRG period, and the even greater number offered for a transfer to a Leeward-owned nursing facility.

'I don't think Annie's going to like that idea,' the nurse said. 'She's very independent.'

'Well, then,' Norman said, tucking her chart under his arm and adjusting his tie, 'we'll just have to reason with her, won't we? Bring your order book along just in case. By the way,' he added as they started off, 'I'm giving an in-service on hepatitis next Thursday evening. I hope you'll be there.'

Well, actually, I—'

'I think Flo Bergman, the Ultramed nursing director, will be up from Boston. I'd like her to meet you. With the Ultramed director of nursing and the Davis chief of staff on your side, there's no telling what opportunities might open up for you. . . .'

Annie Doucette flipped off the quiz show she had been trying to watch, settled back on her pillow and stared up at the ceiling.

The pains in her chest, little more than twinges throughout the previous day, had begun to intensify, and for the first time since the horrible night of her admission, she was frightened. There were gaping holes in her recollection of that night, but not gaping enough to erase the agony and the humiliation she felt, to say nothing of the disruption she had caused Cinnie Iverson, the Judge, and their family.

She should never have accepted their invitation to dinner, she told herself. Never. After twenty-odd years of doing her work proudly and well, of being the glue that held the Iverson household together, she had become nothing but a burden – an imposition and source of worry for everyone.

If only she could have just gone as her husband had, quickly and painlessly in his sleep.

She chewed two Rolaids from the pack her son had bought for her and tried to focus her thoughts on the sweaters for her grandchildren and the afghan for the church bazaar – unfinished projects waiting for her at home in her flat.

All she needed was a few more days – a week, maybe – in the hospital, and everything would be okay. She had not given in to the aches and pains and the passing years yet, and she would not this time. The rumblings in her chest were probably nothing more than indigestion, anyhow.

Annie closed her eyes as bit by bit the discomfort yielded to a gentle sleep. . . . *A week . . . That was all she needed. . . . A week to get her strength back. . . . Then everything would be okay . . . everything would be back to normal again. . . . If felt so good to nap. . . . So good to drift off . . . so good . . .*

'So, Mrs. Doucette, how are we doing this morning?' Donald Norman boomed.

Startled, Annie felt another, slightly more urgent twinge in her chest.

'*We* have felt better, Dr. Norman,' Annie said, opening her eyes only after the last vapor of sleep had drifted away. 'Oh, hello, Doreen, dear.'

'Hi, Annie.'

'And what seems to be the trouble?' Norman asked.

Annie debated whether or not to repeat what she had already told the nurses about the pains. Donald Norman had never paid much attention to her complaints, anyway.

'I'm getting some pains,' she said finally.

Norman thumbed through her chart.

'Doreen, look. Here's the description I wrote of that murmur. Right here. A grade-two systolic. Let's listen and see if it's changed.'

He slipped his stethoscope down Annie's night-gown, listened for a few moments, and then guided the nurse to the bedside with his arm around her waist and gave her a turn.

'Here it?'

The young woman looked at Annie uncomfortably and nodded.

'Dr. Norman,' she said, 'Annie's been having chest pain on and off since yesterday morning.'

'Of course she has,' Norman said, as if he and the nurse were the only two in the room. 'I would bet dollars to doughnuts that they started right after I mentioned her discharge from the hospital. It happens all the time. People get anxious. Did you order an EKG?'

'It's right there in the front of her chart.'

'Good,' he said. 'Good work.' He scanned the tracing. 'Well, it shows nothing to be alarmed at. Just the same T-wave changes in the anterior leads. Here. See? Right here. I'll explain how they're different from other T-wave changes after we finish seeing these two patients.' He turned back to Annie. 'So, if everything else is okay, I think we should begin to plan for your discharge.'

'I'm not feeling well enough to leave yet, Dr. Norman.'

'I know, dear. I know.' Norman took her hand to pat it, but Annie pulled away. 'You're bound to be nervous at the prospect. That's why I've arranged for you to—'

'I wish to stay in the hospital for another week or so,' she said. 'Then I should be ready to go home.'

'Mrs. Doucette, you didn't let me finish. I was saying that I'm in the process of arranging a bed for you at the Sterling Nur – uh, a convalescent facility. A couple of weeks there, and you should be ready to go home.'

'I won't go,' Annie said flatly, sitting up in bed to confront the man. 'You are not going to stick me in any nursing home. I shall stay here for one more week, and then I shall go to my own home.'

'I'm afraid that's not possible, Mrs. Doucette.'

'Well,' she said, 'I'll just speak with Mr. Frank Iverson, and we'll see what is possible and what is not.'

'Feel free to do that if you wish, Mrs. Doucette. But Frank Iverson is not taking care of you. I am. And I am telling you that your hospitalization is about to run out and you will not be able to remain here for another week. That is the rule. In fact, it is one of the rules Frank Iverson is paid to uphold. Now, please calm down and try to realize that what I'm doing is in your best interests.'

Before she could respond, Annie felt another stab beneath her breastbone. Under the sheet, her fists clenched.

'You're not a very good doctor, you know,' she managed finally. 'You not only don't take very good care of yourself, you don't take very good care of your patients, either.'

Donald Norman glanced back at Doreen Lavalley, his face flushed with anger and embarrassment. The old woman *was* a goddamn harpy, there were no two ways about it. Not only was she jeopardizing a hefty set of bonus points for him, but she was making him look like a goddamn asshole in front of Doreen, as well.

'Mrs. Doucette,' he said sternly, 'we'll discuss this later. Meanwhile, lie back and get some rest. Doreen, come with me, please.'

He turned on his heel and stalked from the room. The nurse looked down at Annie and shrugged helplessly.

'I'll be back a little later,' she said.

'I want her to get some Valium,' Norman ordered when they were out of earshot. 'No, no, on second thought, make it Haldol, one point five by mouth every eight hours. Give her the first dose now.'

Doreen Lavalley hesitated.

Norman smiled at her and patted her shoulder.

'Hey, Doreen, don't worry,' he said. 'This is absolutely routine stuff. Nobody *wants* to go to a nursing home, but some people have to. And listen, I didn't get to be chief of staff in this system by not caring about my patients. If anything, I care *too* much.

'Believe me, it's all for the best. The Haldol will calm her down, and by this evening she'll be a thousand times easier to reason with. You just watch. Okay? . . . Now, about my in-service talk next Thursday. What do you say we. . . .'

Chapter 16

The 1938 Fleet monoplane cut through the warm midday air like an arrow, soared over the dense forest panoply and then across the broad, grassy field. It dipped and looped like a yo-yo, barrel rolling again and again, sunlight exploding off the hand-polished, crimson butyrate paint of its wings. At the far edge of the meadow it nosed upward, streaking toward a solitary puff of cloud in an otherwise flawless sky.

From his spot on a large boulder, Zachary watched intently as his fingers, through minute movements of the stick atop his radio control, choreographed the flight.

A stall, a spin, a roll out, a second pass over the field; Zack had built the Fleet as a high schooler, and although he had sometimes gone a year or more without the opportunity to fly her, he had kept the engine and the finish in perfect condition.

With a final, wide bank, he eased the model upwind and set her down sweetly in the grass. The plane was, as always, fascinating to watch, and this day, with any luck, she would be more than just a hobby. This day, she would be a tool to help him unlock the tortured silence of a young boy.

'Hey, Ace, that was a nifty piece of flying.'

Suzanne, dressed in snug white shorts and a Dartmouth T-shirt, stood on a small rise, looking as if she might have just drifted down from the sun. She had a plaid blanket draped over one arm and a wicker picnic basket hanging from the other.

'You know,' he said, squinting up at her, 'about twenty minutes ago I started getting this funny feeling you might show up.'

'Do we have time for lunch?' she asked, making her way down the slope.

Zack glanced at his watch.

'About forty-five minutes. I'm glad you're here.'

Suzanne stretched on her tiptoes and kissed him lightly on the mouth.

'Me, too,' she said. 'Can I set this food out, or is Cheapdog lurking somewhere?'

'No, no. Mop-face and the Fleet out there are avowed enemies. Sort of like sibling rivalry. He's home digging up the yard.'

She spread the blanket and set out dishes of fried chicken, smoked fish, and salad. Then she extracted a small portable radio, set it on the grass, and fiddled with the dial until she found WEVO. The announcer was thanking his guests for participating in *Midday Roundtable* and inviting listeners to stay tuned for a special edition of *Music of the Masters*.

'You must think I'm a little crazy for the way I've been acting around you,' she said as she poured lemonade. 'I wanted to apologize.'

Zack shrugged.

'No need,' he said. 'You've had a few more important things to deal with than me.'

'Perhaps. Just the same, I've been acting like a jerk, and I'm sorry.'

He reached over and brushed her cheek with the back of his hand.

207

'Fair enough,' he said. 'If that's what you need, then apology accepted. There, do you feel better?'

'Zack, I . . . I want to explain.'

'Hey, I don't require any—'

'No, I want to.' She studied her hands. 'At least I think I do.'

For much of the night she had sat with Helene, struggling to come to grips with the past.

'Nothing matters except the truth,' her friend had said. 'Nothing matters except how you really, truly feel. Right here, in your gut. I go out the way I do, see men the way I do, because I honestly know, in my heart, that I hate being alone. Otherwise I'd stay at home or join the Ammonoosuc Valley Quilters. Believe me I would. You don't have to do it my way, or anyone else's way for that matter, but your own, Suze. But – and it's a big but – you can't keep fighting your feelings. You can't fight who you are. If you think you care about the man, tell him who you are, where you've been. If he can deal with it, fine. If he can't, that's his problem.'

It all had made so much sense while they were talking. Now, Suzanne was not so sure. There was more than a little to be said for living the safe life.

The meadow, abutting the low hills southwest of town, glowed verdant and golden in the dry afternoon sun. For a time they ate in silence, save for the deep, cultured voice of the WEVO announcer, who was extolling the virtues of an English composer whose name Zack missed.

'Zachary,' Suzanne said suddenly, 'the other night was the first time I've made love in more than three years.'

'Well, you certainly haven't gotten rusty,' he replied. 'I would also guess that whatever the reason for those three years of celibacy, it wasn't a lack of offers.'

She smiled at him wistfully.

'You're sweet. Actually, there haven't been that many. I haven't been able to trust any man enough even to be encouraging.'

'If you're trying to make me feel special, you're doing a great job.'

'You *are* special. . . . Zack, my husband – my ex-husband – did an incredible hatchet job on my life, and then left me for dead. The scars that formed just don't seem to want to heal. I don't put all the blame on him for what happened. I could have put my foot down when I figured out what was going on. I could have gotten out. But I stayed. I always told myself it was for Jen, but looking back, I realize that I simply couldn't admit to myself how blind I had been – how badly I had misjudged the man I had married. And I couldn't accept that he didn't care enough about me to change.'

'You were young.'

'Twenty-three, if you call that young. And not a very worldly twenty-three at that. Paul was a Ph.D. Brilliant, handsome, charming as hell. Already an associate professor at thirty-five. Every woman in school had a crush on him. Unfortunately, what they didn't know – what *I* didn't know – was how sick he was inside. He was a sociopath, Zachary. A womanizer, a drug addict, and a glib, an unbelievably glib liar. He used me. In every way imaginable, he used me.'

She searched Zack's eyes for any signs of judgment or revulsion, but saw only sadness.

'You don't have to share any more of this if you don't want to,' he said, taking her hand.

'No, I'm okay. Much better than I thought I'd be. You're really very easy to talk to.

'For several years,' she went on, 'Paul stole prescriptions from the hospital, made them out to his women or his cronies or to people who didn't even exist, and signed my name. He had my signature down even better than I did. He hit up a dozen or more wholesale houses and worked his way through just about every pharmacy in the state.'

'Jesus . . .'

Suzanne gazed off toward the mountains to the south and began rubbing at her eyes.

'Are you okay?' Zack asked.

'Huh? . . . Oh, sure. I'm fine. Fine.'

She fished through her purse and put on her sunglasses.

'Where was I?'

'You were telling me about the prescriptions. Listen, if you want to change the subject, it's perfectly—'

'No, no. It feels good to be able to talk about it.' She reached beneath her sunglasses and again rubbed her eyes. 'Besides, there's not that much more to tell. Somehow Paul must have found out that the DEA people were on to me, because a week before they showed up at our door, he emptied out our bank account, sold everything we had of value, and took off. No note, no call, nothing. Jen was only two at the time. A year or so later, I heard that he was teaching at a medical school in Mexico. Somebody else said they saw him at an international conference in Milan. But by that time all I wanted was never to hear his name again.'

'What happened to you?'

'Pardon?'

'I asked what happened to you. Suze, are you sure you're all right?'

'Is the glare bothering you?'

'No. Why?'

'Nothing . . . nothing. What did you ask?'

'Suzanne, let's just leave it for another time—'

'No! Now, wh-what was it?'

She continued to stare off at the mountains. The muscles in her face had grown lax and expressionless. Her hands had begun to tremble.

Zack studied her uncomfortably. He glanced at his watch. Barbara Nelms and her son were due in ten minutes.

'Suzanne?'

She did not respond.

'Listen,' he said, shutting off the radio and putting it back into the wicker basket, 'I think maybe you've shared enough for one day.' He began repacking the leftovers. 'I'm just happy you felt able to talk about it with—'

'You know, ridiculous as it may sound,' Suzanne went on fluidly, 'I'm not sure I know exactly what happened next. . . .'

Zack looked at her queerly. The lifelessness was gone from her face and her voice, and she was as animated as ever. He battled back the urge to again ask her if she was okay.

'. . . One minute, I was suspended from the hospital, sitting in lawyers' offices, fighting with the child welfare people and trying to fend off the DEA animals, and the next I was here in Sterling, putting in pacemakers.'

Zack studied her for any lingering sign of distraction, but saw none. It was as if a cloud had passed briefly across the sun and then had suddenly released it. He forced concern from his mind. She seemed, as she had claimed, to be absolutely fine.

'Did Frank have a hand in that?' he managed.

'I guess. One day he called, the next day he came down and interviewed me, and the next day, it seemed, the pressure that had been on me from all those sides began to disappear.'

'Well, good for Frank.' Zack felt his tension recede. 'We haven't been getting along too well lately. I think I'll have to try a little harder.'

'I'm not really sure if it was him or Ultramed,' she said, 'but someone got the wolves off my back.'

'That's a horrible story.'

'Except for the ending, it is.'

'Call that part of it the beginning,' Zack said.

'I hope telling you all of that helps you see why I've had a little problem with letting a man back into my life. And also why I feel obligated to support Ultramed wherever I can. Thanks to Paul, loyalty has moved ahead of just about everything else on my list of qualities that matter in a person.'

'I understand.'

She kissed him – once, and then again. The last drop of his worry vanished.

'So,' she said, still cradling his face in her hands, 'just be patient with me, okay?'

'Just once in more than three years, huh?'

'Yup.'

He repacked the last of their lunch and pulled her down to him.

'As soon as we have a little time, I'd like to help you improve on that average.'

She brushed her lips across his neck.

'In that case, just don't stop trying. My

horoscope told me to be on the lookout for a tall, dark stranger who did coin tricks.'

He ran his fingers slowly down the back of her thigh and over her calf.

'Thanks for the picnic,' he said.

'Thanks for dessert. And listen, good luck with the Nelms boy. I hope this works out. If you get anywhere today, I think we should consider writing up our technique for some journal. We can title the article "Pediatric Neurology Alfresco."'

She pushed herself to her feet.

Zack walked her to her car and watched until she had disappeared down the hill. Then he returned to the field, absently humming a passage from *Fantasia on Greensleeves* by Ralph Vaughan Williams.

Toby Nelms looked chronically ill. His skin was midwinter pale, with several small patches of impetigo alongside his nose and at the corner of his lips. He was thin as a war orphan and carried himself with a dispirited posture, his gaze nearly fixed on the ground. But it was the listless, dull gray of his eyes that worried Zack the most. They were the eyes of utter defeat which he had encountered so many times in terminally ill patients – the eyes of death.

At Zack's request, Barbara Nelms hugged her son, promised to return for him as soon as she had finished shopping, and drove back down the hill to town. If Toby was frightened at her departure, his dispassionate expression hid the fact well. He had spotted the Fleet almost immediately, and had glanced over at it twice before she had even started to drive off.

Zack reflected on Brookings's account of the child's terrified dash across the clinic parking lot,

213

and knew that, for the moment at least, he was making progress.

A tumor, a seizure disorder, a congenital, slowly developing vascular abnormality, a toxic reaction to something the boy was consuming without anyone's knowledge – Zack had balanced the possibilities against the psychiatric diagnoses and found all of them wanting. He had even made a brief drive around the boy's neighborhood, searching for a landfill or other dumping site where Toby might be sustaining a chemical exposure. Nothing.

'Hi, kiddo,' Zack said, kneeling on the grass, two yards away from the boy. 'My name is Zack.' There was curiosity in the boy's eyes, but no other reaction. 'I'm a doctor, but I'm not going to examine you, or do any tests, or even touch you. Please believe that. I would like you to learn to trust that I would never lie to you, and that I mean exactly what I say, okay? I'll say it once more. I will *never, ever* lie to you. I asked your mom to bring you here because I thought it might be easier for us to get to know one another outside the hospital.'

At the mention of the word hospital, a shadow of fear darkened the boy's expression.

'Your mom will be back as soon as she finishes her shopping,' Zack added quickly. 'Meanwhile, we can lie around, or explore, or even climb up to that little cliff over there. This place is called the Meadows. I used to play here when I was a boy.' He flashed momentarily on Suzanne. 'I still do, in fact,' he added.

Toby's eyes darted again toward the Fleet.

'I built that plane over there a long time ago,' Zack explained. 'It flies by remote control.' He held up the control box for the boy to see. 'She loops, and rolls over, and zooms up to the clouds. Go ahead. Take a look at her.'

Toby Nelms remained where he was, but there could be no mistaking his interest.

'Go on. It's okay. I'm going back to the car for a second to get some fuel for her.'

Only when he had reached the van did Zack turn back. The boy was kneeling by the Fleet, and was, ever so gently, running his fingers over the shiny, lacquered finish of her wings.

Too anxious to stay away for the last fifteen minutes of the agreed-upon hour, Barbara Nelms rolled to stop some distance downhill from the meadow and made her way quietly toward Zack's van, half expecting to find her son waiting there, in near hysterics, for her return. What she found, instead, was a note, taped to the rear window.

Mrs. Nelms—
   Take a peek if you want, but please, try not to be seen. No words from Toby yet, but we're getting there. I need another hour. Please call my office and ask my receptionist to do the best she can with my schedule. See you later.
                                        Z. Iverson

From just beyond a small rise, she could hear the high-pitched whine of the model-airplane engine. Crouching low, she worked her way up. Near the crest of the hillock, she flattened herself in the tall grass and then peered over. Zachary Iverson sat alone, his back toward her. Her son was nowhere in sight.

Suddenly terrified at what she might have done

by trusting a man who was little more than a voice on the phone, she began to scramble to her feet.

Then, just as quickly, she dropped back down.

The boy was there, nestled between the physician's legs, sharing the stick of the radio-control device.

'That's it, fella,' she heard Zack cry over the noise. 'A little more, a little more, and . . . now!'

The plane, which had begun a slow roll across the grass, shot forward and then up, climbing at a steep angle toward the treetops at the far end of the meadow.

'That's it. You've got it. Now ease off. Ease off. Terrific! Hold her right there.'

Now well above the trees, the model banked smoothly to the south and began a lazy circle of the field.

'I did it! I did it!'

It took several seconds for Barbara Nelms to realize that the excited voice she had just heard was her son's. With a joyful fullness in her throat and tears in her eyes, she slipped back out of sight and hurried down the hill.

Zack and Toby Nelms lay opposite one another on the warm grass, a few yards from the Fleet, chewing on stalks of wild barley and watching a red-tailed hawk glide in effortless loops atop high, midday thermals.

'Now, just who do you suppose is working the radio-control box for *that* model?' Zack asked. 'Whoever it is has sure built one quiet engine.'

'That's goofy,' Toby Nelms said.

'Of course it is. Anyone with half a brain could tell that's just a kite. Now, if only I could see the string . . .'

Once the logjam of silence – of fear and mistrust – had been broken, the boy's words had come with surprising ease, and even occasional spontaneity. Zack had been reluctant to test the progress they had made with any pointed questions, but now, with just a few minutes left in their two hours together, he felt comfortable enough to try.

'You know, kiddo,' he began, 'a lot of people have been very worried about you these past few months.'

'I know.'

'But you still won't talk to anyone?'

Toby shook his head.

'Not even your parents?'

The boy stared vacantly at the crucifix soaring overhead.

'They never help me,' he said suddenly. 'I scream for them, and beg them to stop the . . . the man from hurting me. But they never come until it's too late. They never stop him.'

'What man?' Zack asked, at once repulsed and fearful at the thought of the boy being molested. 'Who's been hurting you?'

Toby turned away.

'Hey, kiddo, I'm sorry. I didn't mean to say anything to upset you or frighten you.'

For a few, anxious seconds, Zack feared he had pushed too hard and slammed the door he had, so gingerly, just opened.

'The man with the mask,' Toby said without turning back.

'Mask?'

The boy shifted restlessly, and then drew his knees and elbows in tightly to his body.

Zack decided he had gone far enough for one day.

217

He reached in his pocket for a coin. One good thumb palm and they would call it quits.

'He . . . he cuts it off,' Toby said, in almost a whimper. 'And . . . and then it grows back . . . and then he cuts it off again.'

'Cuts what off, Toby? . . . Look, I know it's hard for you to talk about, but you've got to try.'

He moved to put his hand on the boy's shoulder, but then thought better of it. He felt his heart pounding. *Don't stop now, kiddo. Don't give up on me now.*

'My . . . my peenie. And my balls, too.'

'Do you mean he touches you?'

'No, he cuts it off. He promises he won't hurt me. He promises he'll fix my lump, and then he cuts it off. And it hurts. It hurts and I scream at him, and he won't stop. And I scream for my mommy and daddy, and they never come.'

The boy began to cry, his shoulders jerking spasmodically with each heavy sob.

Again, Zack moved to touch him, but before he could, the child spun and flung his arms around him.

'Please, Zack,' he cried softly. 'Please don't let him do it anymore.'

He promises he'll fix my lump. . . . Suddenly, the child's words registered.

'Toby,' Zack whispered, still holding the boy tightly, 'the lump you're talking about, is it your hernia? That place here you had fixed?'

The boy nodded, his mind still racked with sobs.

'And the man with the mask . . . Is that the doctor?'

Again, a nod.

Zack eased him away, but continued to hold him by the shoulders.

'Toby, look at me. I think you've just been having nightmares. Bad, horrible dreams, but dreams that often go away as soon as you see them for what they are. The operation was perfect. All that's left is a little scar. The lump is gone for good.'

'No,' the boy said angrily. 'It isn't. It grows back. So does my peenie, and my balls. But then he cuts them off again, and it hurts – worse each time.'

Inwardly, Zack sighed relief. The boy's profound disturbance was rooted in a nightmare – the expression of pent-up fears surrounding a procedure now nearly a year in the past. Fascinating, but certainly neither difficult to understand nor as bad a situation as he had feared. At least Brookings would have something to work with.

'You don't believe me, do you?' Toby said. 'It's not a dream. He cuts them off, and they grow back, and then he takes those Metzenbaums and cuts them off again.'

Zack felt a sudden, vicious chill.

'He takes what?' There was no hiding the incredulity in his voice.

'The Metzenbaums. He asks for them from the nurse, and then he sticks them into me right here, and it kills me. Then he just cuts and cuts.'

'Toby, think,' Zack said urgently. 'Have you ever heard anyone else say that word?'

'What word?'

'Metzenbaums, Toby. Have you ever heard anyone except the doctor in your nightmare say that word?'

Toby Nelms shook his head.

Zack released the boy and sank back on his hands. Something was wrong. Something was terribly wrong. Metzenbaum scissors were commonly used in surgery, but rarely, if ever, until after the initial skin incision had been made. Toby Nelms would have been asleep at the time they were called for. Anesthetized. There was no way he could have heard that term, let alone so accurately understood what it meant. No way.

But somehow, he had.

Chapter 17

By the time Zack had finished rounds and headed from the hospital to his office, evening had settled in over the valley. To the southwest, the silhouetted mountains were ebony cutouts against the deepening indigo sky. It was a quiet, awesome evening, perfect for a run by Schroon Lake or for a horseback ride into the foothills to watch the moonrise. It was an evening to celebrate the joy of living.

But for Zack, the magic of the evening was lost in reflection on the agonized struggles of an old surgeon and the desperate plea of the nurse who had condemned him; and in concern as to how much to tell the waiting parents of a child who was sinking deeper and deeper into a hell of dreams that were not dreams – dreams that cut and hurt and maimed.

As he crossed the parking lot, Zack noticed Frank's Porsche, tucked in its reserved slot. Early mornings, late evenings, weekends – for whatever his shortcomings and the failings of his past, the man had become a demon of a worker.

Soon, Zack knew, the two of them would have to talk.

There were things Frank needed to learn of and to understand about Ultramed, about Guy Beaulieu . . . and now, especially, about Toby Nelms.

The boy's condition was clearly on a downward spiral, and each passing day was a lost ally in the struggle to uncover the truth. With Frank's help, the odds of finding answers in time to make a difference would be considerably shorter.

But would he listen?

Over the years, the two of them had drifted far apart in many ways. The disagreement over Guy Beaulieu had only underscored their differences. Still, Zack reasoned, they *were* brothers, and they each had a significant stake in Ultramed-Davis and in Sterling.

He glanced back at the Porsche. At seven that morning, when he had arrived for work, it was already there. Now, after more than thirteen hours, Frank was still at it. What more testimony did he need? The man had hitched his wagon to the Ultramed-Davis star. If there was a threat to the integrity of the hospital, he would listen.

Zack felt sure, at least, of that much. But he also knew that all he had were theories – gut sensations plus a few million questions. His brother was a company man. If there were trouble in his paradise, it would take more than suspicions to enlist his help – much more.

Barbara Nelms and her husband were waiting on one of the stone benches that flanked the entrance to the Physicians and Surgeons Clinic. Bob Nelms, clean-cut, fit, and hardy, had clearly borne less of the day-to-day strain of Toby's illness than had his wife. He greeted Zack with a firm hand.

'Pleasure to meet you,' he said. 'Barbara tells me you made some real progress with our boy. That's excellent. Excellent. Using that plane of yours was just a super idea.'

'Thank you, but—'

'You know, I'm no professional, but I've been

trying to tell Barbara all along that this was all just a nasty phase, and that when that kid of ours was doggone good and ready he would get through it. It sounds like you two made quite a large step in that direction today.'

'Call it a baby step,' Zack said.

Despite the machismo in Bob Nelms's words and manner, one look in his eyes and Zack knew the man was whistling in the dark. As a supervisor at the mill, he was used to accepting the burden of difficult problems and solving them. His thin-shelled denial would require delicate handling and constant awareness that Toby's condition was no less baffling and frightening to Bob Nelms than his impotence in the face of it.

As Zack followed the couple into the elevator, he wondered once again how much to share with them. It had never been his way to withhold information from his patients or, when the patient was comatose or a juvenile, from their families. But this was not information. It was the purest conjecture.

And even when he tested the explanation on himself, it sounded nothing short of phantasmagoric.

Mr. and Mrs. Nelms, I don't know how to tell you this, but I believe that your son was not asleep during his hernia operation last year. He appeared to his surgeon and anesthesiologist to be fully anesthetized. But somehow, at some level, he not only 'saw' his operation from within his body, but, it would seem, he fully experienced the pain of it as well.

Now, in some perverted, distorted way, he is reliving that surgery in terrifying flashbacks, much like those described in LSD users. . . . No. I don't have any idea how that could happen. . . . No, to the best of

223

my knowledge, such a phenomenon has never been reported with the anesthetics he received. . . . No, I don't have any hard evidence to back up what I say. . . . No, I don't know what could possibly be triggering the attacks. . . . No, I don't have any idea. . . . I don't know . . . I don't know . . . I don't know. . . .

His suspicions were vague, fantastic, and virtually without proof. Disclosure of them to the boy's parents would almost certainly precipitate premature action by them against Ultramed, the hospital, and the physicians involved in Toby's surgery – action Zack was in no position yet to support, and which could well lead to a coverup of the truth . . . whatever that was.

'Mr. and Mrs. Nelms,' he began once the couple was settled in across the desk from him, 'I'm afraid I don't have very much to tell you at this point. Toby did not share a great deal with me. However, he did say enough for me to suspect that he is having very severe fright reactions, and that while these reactions are occurring he is completely unable to distinguish them from reality. In other words, in just a few seconds, apparently with very little warning, he is transported from wherever he happens to be into another reality – a very distorted, very terrifying reality.'

'Are you saying he becomes insane?' Barbara Nelms asked.

'You've observed him,' Zack responded, still feeling his way along. 'What do you think?'

'But . . . but insanity is a condition, isn't it? A state of being. How can it possibly flick on and off like a light?'

'And what has the hospital got to do with it?' Bob Nelms added.

'I don't know,' Zack said, wondering how many more times he would hear himself repeat that phrase.

'Well, what do you think?'

Zack tapped his fingers together, stalling for a few more seconds to sort his thoughts. As much as he hated deception, this simply was not the time to air his theory.

'I assume you are both somewhat familiar with epilepsy?' he began. 'Well, most people think of epilepsy as an electrical disorder of the brain which causes periodic fits. The seizures we are most familiar with are motor seizures – that is, they involve the muscles and the extremities. But supposing the electrical explosion occurs in one or more of the cognitive areas of the brain – the thinking areas. What would result would still be a seizure, but it would be a sensory seizure rather than a motor one.'

'Are you trying to tell us that Toby has petit mal or temporal-lobe epilepsy?' Barbara asked. 'I've read everything I could get my hands on about both conditions, and quite frankly, Dr. Iverson, I don't think Toby's condition fits either one. He is aggressive like temporal-lobe epileptics, but only because he is absolutely terrified. And very little of his behavior resembles the detached, fugue reactions that I've read about in petit mal. And although the resting electroencephalogram is not that accurate in making either diagnosis, Toby's was normal the one time he had it done.'

Zack felt his cheeks flush and cautioned himself against any elaborate untruths. Barbara Nelms was too desperate and too bright. She was tired of getting the runaround from medical and mental health professionals, and she had done her homework well.

'I don't know what to say, Mrs. Nelms,' he countered, 'except to point out that if Toby's case were straightforward and typical, someone would have diagnosed it before now.'

'What about the hospital?' Bob Nelms asked again. 'Didn't the boy say anything to you to explain why he seems so frightened?'

'Nothing specific,' Zack lied. 'But since that's the main clue we have, I do feel that's the direction our investigation should go.'

Barbara Nelms slumped visibly.

'Dr. Iverson, investigations are fine, but you saw Toby. He's like a stick. His skin is getting infected. He gets bruises from almost nothing. He gets fevers with no evidence of infections. He's dying, Dr. Iverson. I swear, time is running out. Our son is dying.'

'Barbara, don't say that!' Bob Nelms blurted.

His outburst hit a raw nerve.

'Don't tell me what to say and what not to say,' she snapped back. 'You're in that damn mill until seven every night. You don't see him.'

'Doggone it, Barbara, I'm doing everything I can. You're the one who hasn't paid a bit of attention to anything but Toby these past—'

'Please,' Zack said. 'Please. I know this is hard on you both. But sniping at each other isn't helping anyone – least of all Toby.'

The couple stopped abruptly and exchanged sheepish looks.

'We're sorry,' Barbara said. She reached over and squeezed her husband's hand. 'We never used to fight, even at home alone. But this has just got us all . . .' She looked away.

'I understand, Mrs. Nelms. All I can ask is that

you both just do your best to keep it together, and give me a little time to do some reading and talk to some people. I'll work as rapidly as I can. I promise you that. And I'll plan on seeing Toby again next week. Same time. Same field.'

'Meanwhile?'

Zack shrugged.

'Meanwhile, I don't think any specific treatment is indicated. Especially since I don't really know yet what's going on. I will tell you that I don't take my responsibility for my patients lightly, and I'm fully aware that we don't have all the time in the world. I'll do my very best to get to the bottom of things quickly.'

He stood, hoping to bring the exchange to a merciful end before Barbara Nelms could hone in on the inadequacies in his explanation.

'Thank you,' Bob said, standing as Zack did and shaking his hand.

Zack walked them to the outer door of his office and again promised to work as quickly as possible.

'Dr. Iverson, could you just tell me one thing?' Barbara Nelms asked.

'Of course.'

'Are you holding anything at all back from us?'

Zack had to force himself to maintain contact with the woman's eyes. It was a technique at which, unlike Frank, he had never excelled.

'No, Mrs. Nelms,' he said flatly. 'No, I'm not.'

The woman hesitated, and for a moment seemed poised to challenge the denial. Then she reached out and shook his hand.

'That being the case, then, thank you, Doctor. You will keep us posted, yes?'

She took her husband's arm and walked away with him, down the darkened corridor.

Zack watched until the elevator doors had closed behind them. He ached from his lies and from the graphic reminder of the power of illness over the lives of whole families. He also knew, from her parting look, that Barbara Nelms would never again allow him to hide behind evasions and half-truths.

He would review Toby Nelms's record again, and then contact the National Institutes of Health library in Bethesda for a complete search of the reported adverse reactions to the anesthetics he had received. Finally, he would meet with Jack Pearl and Jason Mainwaring.

Beyond those steps, there was nowhere to go – nowhere except another session with Toby himself and then the sharing of his suspicions with Frank. Something had happened to the boy during his hospitalization at Ultramed-Davis – something devastating. If nothing else panned out, Frank would have to realize that it was in everyone's best interests that he pursue the matter. He would cooperate, or face Barbara Nelms and her attorney.

'Frank, don't move, honey, please. You feel so good. I want to do a little while you're still inside me. Just a line. Okay?'

Frank's secretary, the blond one, was named Annette Dolan. She had moved with her child to live with her mother in Sterling, and had been working as a hostess in the Mountain Laurel Restaurant when Frank first spotted her and offered her a job. Her qualification for the position was, quite plainly, that she looked better in a sweater than any woman he had ever seen.

She was a mediocre receptionist, and a far-worse-than-that secretary, but she was sweet and polite to everyone, and had proved a wonderful, undemanding diversion, especially on those occasions when he was able to indulge her passion for cocaine.

'Go ahead, baby,' he said, running his thumbs over her nipples. 'But hustle. I don't have much time left.'

For more than an hour, first on the oriental rug in his office, and then on the couch, Annette had screwed him as only she could – purely and passionately, without any of the head games he tolerated but hated in brighter women.

He cradled her breasts in his hands as she slipped one end of a straw into her nose and lowered the other onto the mirror that she had rested on his chest.

'That's it,' he whispered as she inhaled the dust. 'Get it all, baby. Get it all.'

He glanced across at the Lucite clock on his bookshelf. Twenty after eight. Less than an hour until Mainwaring was due. Less than an hour until the beginning of the end. Annette had been the perfect appetizer for that session. Now, however, it was time to pack her up and ship her home.

Frank waited until she had wiped the last grains of powder off the mirror and onto her gums. Then he skimmed the mirror across the room and pulled her magnificent, glistening body close to his. Slowly, he toppled off the couch and on top of her on the rug.

She was beautiful to the eye and to the touch, but after an hour and a hundred dollars worth of cocaine, she held little excitement for him. All that remained was the mechanical need to climax. He grabbed her corn-silk hair tightly in his fists, buried his chest against her breasts, and rammed himself into her again and again until, in less than a minute, it was over.

If only Lisette knew how much he needed this sort of uncomplicated, unquestioning sex, everything would be much better for them, he thought. Much better.

He took a minute to stroke the woman's clit, her tight, flat stomach, and finally her perfect ass. Then he moved to the chair behind his desk and watched as she dressed. Once every week or two was perfect – just enough to keep the adventure fresh and the woman from becoming tiresome.

Absently, he thumbed through the papers on his desk – papers that included the application of the surgeon who would be Mainwaring's replacement. The whole business had gone down like clockwork, Frank mused, just as he had promised it would. He and Mainwaring had estimated two years, and precisely two years it had been.

Now, there was less than an hour until the final phase of their project would start. Less than an hour until the beginning of the end, until the beginning of everything good for him.

Frank wrapped up what was left of the cocaine and flipped the plastic bag across to the woman.

'Here you go, baby,' he said. 'Enjoy.'

'You promised you would try some with me sometime, Frank. Remember?'

'Sometime, maybe. For now, you just get on home and enjoy it,' he answered. 'I don't have much use for that shit. There are enough other things I get off on. Like you.'

And, he was thinking, *like a million dollars.*

*

Frank showered in the bathroom off his office, dressed, and cleaned up the last vestiges of his session with Annette Dolan. Then he settled in before the computer terminal on his desk. There were still twenty minutes before Mainwaring was due – just enough time to check in with Mother.

And, Frank noted, it was especially fitting that he should.

For at a time when his back was to the wall, when the absence of $250,000 he had borrowed from the hospital accounts and then lost in that foolish land deal stared at him every day like a gaping, black hole of doom, Mother had provided him with the answer.

Mother was UltraMA, the Ultramed mainframe computer housed in the home offices in Boston. She was the fiber that held the expanding Ultramed empire together, providing it with consistency, rapid exchange of information, and a seemingly endless pool of physicians.

And in Frank's darkest, most desperate hour, Mother had served up both Jack Pearl and Jason Mainwaring.

Frank activated the terminal, dialed the network number, and flipped the toggle switch on his phone. In seconds,

Good evening, welcome to UltraMA—
Please enter access code

appeared on the screen.

Frank typed in the code and then, when requested, his own password. In a week or so his regional director would receive a printout of UltraMA users and would note on the appropriate evaluation form

231

that at nine o'clock in the evening of that day, Frank had been hard at work in his office.

Good evening, Mr. Iverson. We trust all is well in Sterling, New Hampshire. Do you wish to see your menu?

Frank typed *Y*.

Immediately, ADMINISTRATOR'S MENU flashed on, followed by a list:

1. Changes in procedures and policies manual.
2. Ultramed current staff physicians and salaries (your hospital only)
3. Ultramed current staff physicians and salaries (your region only)
4. Available physicians (by specialty)
5. Promotions, reassignments, terminations (past 30 days)
6. National health news of note.
7. Regional health news of note.
8. Preferred suppliers and services (your region only)
9. Performance ratings (region)
10. Performance ratings (nation)
11. Golden Circle Administrators

As he invariably did when communicating with Mother, Frank began by affirming his membership in the Golden Circle and his position as the leading administrator in the northeast region.

Leading administrator. Golden Circle. It was laughable now to think of how close he had come to not even applying for the Ultramed-Davis job. But with his electronics firm going down the tubes, the

Judge refusing to help him out, and Leigh Baron insisting that he would get serious consideration in the search process despite his lack of hospital experience, he really had nothing to lose.

It had been a mild shock when he was finally offered the position. And although there could be no arguing his remarkable success with the corporation, it remained something of a mystery to him why Leigh had picked him over many more experienced candidates.

Frank scanned the regional and national rankings and then returned to the Administrator's Menu and summoned up item four.

The physicians of possible interest to the Ultramed system were listed by specialty and sub-specialty, along with a detailed but straightforward summary of their education and work experience.

However, item four was hardly a typical employment bulletin board. Included with many of the names was a paragraph summarizing the professional and/or personal difficulties that had made the physician available.

Drugs, alcohol, sexual entanglements, financial improprieties, professional misconduct of one sort or another – compiling the roster was the full-time job of an obsessively diligent investigator in the home office. Primary among her responsibilities was the weeding out of those physicians for whom there was little or no hope of rehabilitation. Those remaining on the list, many of them excellent practitioners, were of particular interest to the corporation. More often than not, they proved to be devoted employees, grateful for a second chance, totally loyal to the company and its policies, and willing to work for any salary that was reasonable.

Steve Baumgarten in the emergency ward had been recruited through UltraMA's unique bulletin board. So had Suzanne Cole, a real prize, who almost from the start had generated an income many times greater than her salary.

But for Frank, it was the one-two parlay of Jack Pearl and Jason Mainwaring that had made Mother worth her megabytes in gold.

For at a time when Frank's back was to the wall, when he was becoming so desperate about the $250,000 that he was actually considering approaching the Judge for help, Jack Pearl's name appeared in item four.

The description of Pearl's problem, which Frank eventually had memorized, read:

Holds patent on what he has claimed is revolutionary new general anesthetic. Texas license suspended pending investigation of alleged illegal clinical testing of the substance and falsification of information on experimental drug application. Physician with same name registered 1984 from Wilkes Community Hospital, Akron, Ohio, because of alleged sexual involvement with a ten-year-old boy. Further information currently being sought.

Mildly intrigued, Frank had made a note to do some checking on the man, but had not put much energy into the project until, not a month later, UltraMA served up a brief item on a professor of surgery from Baltimore. Jason Mainwaring had been found to be an officer and partner in a Georgia pharmaceutical house, and subsequently had resigned his position due to charges of conflict of interest and illegal use of an unapproved drug.

It had taken trips to Maryland, Georgia, Texas, and Ohio; an additional twenty thousand dollars in Ultramed-Davis funds to gather information and secure the cooperation of a certain politician in Akron; and finally, a series of the most delicate negotiations with both physicians. But in the end, Frank had forged the key to his future. And now, within the next two weeks, the rest was about to become history.

For several minutes Frank scanned the electronic roster of physicians. He was amazed, as always, at how so many who held the ultimate ticket to success and prestige could have made such pathetic shambles of their lives.

A pediatrician from Hartford about to complete four months in an alcohol rehabilitation center; a gynecologist from D.C. who had resigned his hospital appointment amid a cloud of accusations that his examinations were too prolonged and included house calls; an oral surgeon facing revocation of his license for writing too many narcotic prescriptions for himself; Frank jotted down several names, along with a memo to himself to make some preliminary calls.

Ultramed and its parent corporation had the clout to make any physician's background difficulties disappear to all but the most intensive investigation. However, its administrators had been well warned against using that service indiscriminately.

Frank had just terminated with Mother when, with a discreet knock, Jason Mainwaring entered the office. He was dressed in a light cotton suit, monogrammed shirt, and white topsiders, and looked very much like the plantation owner he planned to become as soon as his pharmaceutical company had successfully produced and marketed Jack Pearl's Serenyl.

'Drink?' Mainwaring asked, setting his briefcase down and then striding directly to the small wet bar in Frank's bookcase.

'Sure,' Frank said, quietly resenting the way the man, as always, stepped into a room and took charge. 'Bourbon's fine.'

The surgeon gestured at the huge aerial photo of the Ultramed-Davis complex.

'Nice little operation y'all have here, Frank,' he said. 'I think I'm actually going to miss it some. But home is where the heart is, right?'

'Of course,' Frank countered. 'Although I knew you had been up here too long when I heard a little Yankee accent creep into that drawl of yours the other day.'

Mainwaring snorted a laugh as he scanned Frank's collection of cassettes.

'Mantovani, Mantovani, Mantovani,' he said disdainfully, tossing them aside one at a time. 'You know, the closest thing you have here to Beethoven is Mantovani.'

'I like Mantovani,' Frank said.

'I know.'

Mainwaring thought for a moment and then snapped open his briefcase, removed two cassettes, and flipped them onto Frank's desk.

'I know I'm prob'ly tossin' pearls to a razorback,' he said, 'but here are some examples of *real* music for you. It's what I listen to in the O.R. Call 'em a good-bye present. This one's Beethoven's Third. It's called the *Eroica*. And this one's by an English composer named Vaughan Williams. It's a fantasia on "Greensleeves." Listen to these two pieces, and I suspect even you will appreciate the difference between real music and the Burger King brand you've been listening to.'

'Sure thing, Jase,' Frank said, dropping the tapes into his desk drawer. 'I'll start my reeducation first thing in the morning.'

'I won't hold my breath.' Mainwaring settled in on the sofa Frank and Annette Dolan had so recently vacated, and motioned Frank to take the easy chair opposite him.

'I hate doin' business with anyone across a desk,' he explained.

Unless it's yours, right? Frank thought. He hesitated, and then did as the man asked. There was no sense in making an issue of it at this stage of the game.

'So, Jason,' he said. 'I assume you're still satisfied.'

Mainwaring took a file from his briefcase and opened it.

'With this kind of money involved,' he said, 'I won't be satisfied until our little anesthetic is in every operating room of every hospital in the world. But I am certainly pleased with the' – he consulted the file – 'four hundred ninety-six cases Jack and I have completed. I must say, Frank, you've done all right. You promised me five hundred cases in two years, and you delivered.'

'Like I told you when we first met, Jason, I know this town.'

The key to the whole project had been the rapid takeover by Mainwaring of Guy Beaulieu's practice. And only Frank, and to some extent, Mainwaring, knew how skillfully Frank had engineered that feat. Details: that's what it all came down to. Attention to

237

touches like the letter to Maureen Banas threatening his own position should she ever disclose to anyone, including him, what was being done to her. The sort of details he had neglected to attend to three years before.

'Pity about ol' Beaulieu,' Mainwaring said blandly.

Frank could not tell if the man was being facetious or not. Again, he opted to avoid an altercation. In the morning, Mainwaring would be gone. And in a week or so he would be back to officially tender his resignation and to offer proof of a million dollars in Frank's Cayman Islands account and half a million in Pearl's, in exchange for the patent Frank now shared with Pearl and all future rights to Serenyl.

And that, Frank knew, was what it was all about.

He would, at last, have squared away the $250,000 shortfall in the Ultramed-Davis books, and there would be a nifty little bundle left over to build on.

'Well,' he said dispassionately, 'at least the old guy didn't suffer. When my number comes up, I want to go the same way. . . . So, I assume you have everything you need to conclude this business with your company in Atlanta?'

Mainwaring skimmed through his notes.

'It would appear so, Frank. Here's that, ah, little agreement you insisted upon.'

He passed the document over.

Frank scanned the page to be certain it included Mainwaring's admission to having illegally used Serenyl on five hundred patients. It was Frank's insurance policy against any kind of deal being made behind his back. In the morning, the two of them would jointly place the confession, along with similar ones from Frank and Jack Pearl, in a safe deposit box at the Sterling National Bank, and upon Mainwaring's return to town, the three of them would retrieve and destroy the documents together.

'Remember, Frank,' Mainwaring warned, 'I don't have the final say in all this. My partners are still calculatin' what it's gonna cost us to go backward and do all the animal and clinical trials the FDA insists on, and—'

Frank laughed out loud.

'Jason, please,' he said. 'It costs tens of millions to develop and test new drugs that you don't even know are going to work, let alone work safely. You've got a gold mine here, and you know it, and I know it, and your partners know it, and even our little fairy friend Pearl knows it.

'After five hundred perfect cases without so much as one problem, the only money you're going to spend is whatever it costs to grease a palm or two at the FDA and to put together a few folders of bogus animal and clinical trials. So don't try to shit me, okay? It's unbecoming for a man of your class.'

Mainwaring shook his head ruefully.

'There are a number of things I'm going to miss around here, Frank,' he said, perhaps purposely intensifying his drawl, 'but I confess you won't be among them. Be sure Jack has all the paperwork and formulas ready for me in the morning, y'hear? Assumin' my partners and our chemists give their okay, I'll be back in eight or ten days. Meanwhile, I shall assume that you or Jack'll let me know if any problems crop up.'

'Of course, Jason, old shoe,' Frank said. 'But after two years and five hundred cases, I don't think you have to camp by the phone waiting to hear from us. Next to birth, death, and taxes, Serenyl is as close as life gets to a sure thing. . . . And you know that, don't you.'

Mainwaring's eyes narrowed.

'What I know,' he said evenly, 'is that this little tête-à-tête has gone on long enough.'

Without offering his hand, the surgeon snapped up his briefcase and left.

Not until the office door clicked shut did Frank's smile become more natural. In the interests of their deal, he had allowed the pompous ass to walk over him any number of times during the past two years. The son of a bitch even tried to tell him what music to listen to. Now, with the work completed and so successful, there was no longer any reason to defer to him, and Frank felt exhilarated that he hadn't.

After years of operating in the shadows of men like Mainwaring and the Judge, it was time to start casting some shadows of his own. His life had finally turned the corner. He was a rising star in a powerful corporation, and soon he would have the independence and prestige that only money could bring.

'God bless you, Serenyl,' he murmured.

Softly at first, then louder and louder, the familiar chant worked its way into his thoughts.

Frank, Frank, he's our man. If he can't do it, no one can. . . .

Four miles to the north, Suzanne Cole screamed and leapt up from the couch where she had been dozing. A vicious, searing pain had exploded through her chest from beside her right breast. Bathed in a chilly sweat, she tore open her blouse and ripped apart the clasps on her bra.

The scar from her surgery was red, but not disturbingly so, and the tissue beneath it was not the least bit tender.

Still, the pain had been like nothing she had ever experienced before.

Desperately, she searched her cloudy thoughts for some logical medical explanation. Perhaps a neuritis, she reasoned – the single, violent electrical discharge from a regenerating nerve.

Yes, of course, a neuritis. That had to be it. No other diagnosis made sense.

Shaken, but relieved, she sank back onto the pillow. Then she checked her watch. Forty-five minutes. That was all she had napped. She needed more than that – much more – if she was going to catch up with the sleep she kept losing every night. It was lucky she had taken time off after her surgery. The strain of the whole affair seemed to have taken more of a toll on her than she had anticipated.

Slowly, her eyes closed.

Perhaps she should get up and take something before she slipped off again. An aspirin or even some codeine. At least then, if the irritated nerve fired off again, the pain would be blunted.

No, she decided. As long as she knew what it was, there was nothing to be frightened about. It had only lasted ten or twelve seconds, anyhow. If it happened again, she could handle it. For that short a time, she could handle almost anything. What she needed most was sleep.

Relax . . . Breathe deeply . . . Breathe deeply . . . Good . . . That's it . . . That's it . . .

Now, she thought, as she drifted off, just what was it she had been dreaming about . . . ?

Chapter 18

The White Pines Golf Club course, designed by
Robert Trent Jones, was the pride, joy, and status
symbol of its select shareholders. Sculpted along a
narrow valley between two massive granite escarp-
ments, the layout was short but exceedingly tight,
and members still delighted in recalling the day in
'sixty-two when Sam Snead, playing an exhibition
round from the championship tees, shot an eighty-
six and lost two balls.

It was early Saturday afternoon, and for the first
time in years, Zack was preparing to play a round of
golf – his opponent: Judge Clayton Iverson.

Zack had originally planned to spend the
morning meeting with Jason Mainwaring and Jack
Pearl, and then the rest of the day not *between* the
granite cliffs, but *on* them, climbing with a small
group from the local mountaineering club. However, Mainwaring had signed out for a week to Greg
Ormesby, the only general surgeon remaining in
Sterling, and Pearl, too, was away until Monday
morning.

And in truth, as much as Zack had been looking
forward to making a climb, he was pleased with the
chance to spend a few hours alone with his father for
the first time since his return to Sterling.

Typically, the Judge's invitation to play had been
couched in words that made refusal difficult. He

had also intimated that there might be more on his mind than just golf. There would be, he had made it quite clear, just the two of them, although whether Frank was unable to come or had not been invited, he did not say.

Earlier in the day, after making rounds, thumbing once again through Toby Nelms's chart, and trying to locate Mainwaring and Pearl, Zack had spent an hour on the practice range. It had been a pleasant surprise to find that some vestige of his swing, developed over dozens of childhood lessons, remained.

Like most sports that involve doing something with a ball, golf had never held any great fascination for him. But the rolling fairways, perfectly manicured greens, and even the sprawling Tudor clubhouse with its shaded veranda and oriental rugs, had always brought him a certain serenity, especially on warm, cloudless, summer afternoons.

'So, Zachary,' Clayton Iverson said as they approached the first tee, 'just how interesting should we make it?'

He was dressed in white slacks, a gold LaCoste shirt, and his trademark – brown and white saddle golf shoes. Although he could hardly be said to be in shape, he carried his husky bulk with the easy grace of a natural athlete. Set off by a gnarled thicket of pure silver hair, his tanned, weathered face exuded confidence and authority.

'That depends on how badly you need money, Judge,' Zack said, knowing that it was both fruitless and in bad form to argue with his father against a wager of some sort.

'Well, then, suppose we make it, say, a dollar a hole with carryovers? I'll give you a stroke on the par fives and the two long par fours.'

'Let's see . . .' Zack made the pretext of counting on his fingers. 'Eighteen dollars. I guess I can handle that. Okay, sir, a dollar a hole it is. I assume you'll take it easy on me, as always.'

The Judge set his ball on the tee and looked up at his son with a predatory smile.

'Of course,' he said. 'Just like always.'

It was the most basic truth of the man's relationship with his sons, and almost a standing joke among them over the years, that he had never given them even the slightest quarter in anything competitive, whether gin rummy, at which he was a vicious profiteer, golf, or even business. Victories were to be earned, or not to be had; loans of even the smallest amounts of money were invariably accompanied by IOUs and were to be paid back in full, and always with some interest.

Zack knew that on this day, as always, not one punch would be pulled, not one edge given away.

The Judge's drive, to the genteel applause of a dozen or so onlookers, split the fairway and rolled to a stop well past the discreet two-hundred-yard marker.

Aware that he often felt less tension operating on a brain tumor than he did at that moment, Zack shanked his drive into the goldfish pond.

'I hope you don't have any pressing engagements, Judge,' he said, teeing up another ball. 'We could be here for a while.'

'Slow your backswing and drop your left shoulder a bit,' his father said.

Zack did as was suggested and hit a bullet that bounced almost on top of the Judge's ball and then rolled several yards beyond.

'Thanks for the help,' he whispered, tipping an

imaginary cap in response to the applause from the small gallery.

'Enjoy it,' the Judge said as they walked off the tee. 'At a buck a hole, that's all you get.'

By the end of the front nine, Zachary was seven dollars behind and was getting blisters on the sides of both heels from his decade-old golf shoes. Still, the afternoon was warm and relaxing, and he was enjoying a seldom-experienced sense of connection to his father, born largely, it seemed, of casual snippets of conversation and brief flashes to afternoons, long past, like this one.

Clayton Iverson had asked about his new practice and shared a few anecdotes from the courtroom, but otherwise had given no real indication that there were any items on the afternoon's agenda other than golf.

Following a brief stop in the clubhouse for a beer, the Judge dropped off the motorized cart he had used on the front nine and arrived at the tenth tee pulling his clubs on a two-wheeled aluminum caddy.

'I need the exercise,' he explained. 'And besides, with me riding and you walking and chasing those shots of yours all over hell and gone, it didn't seem like we had much chance to talk out there.'

'Very witty, Judge,' Zachary said. 'Well, just watch thee out. To quote the words of General Custer at the Little Big Horn, "We have not yet begun to fight."'

He led off the tenth hole with a decent drive, but his father's shot, sliced badly, flew far to the right and disappeared into a bank of tall rough. While they were scuffing through the heavy grass looking for the ball, the Judge waved the foursome behind them to play through.

'If we don't find it by the time those four have putted out, I'll drop one.'

'Fair enough.'

Zack wondered briefly about the amicable concession, which was out of character for the man.

'Zachary, tell me something,' the Judge went on, still searching through the rough. 'Have you encountered any problems with Ultramed since you started working at the hospital?'

'Problems?'

'Hey, you know what I'll bet? I'll bet my shot went a little farther right than we thought. Let's try looking over that way.'

'Judge?'

'Yes?'

'What sort of problems are you talking about?'

Clayton Iverson hesitated for a time, apparently uncertain whether or not to continue the conversation.

'Guy Beaulieu came to see me a few days before he died,' he said finally.

'Oh?'

'It was the second time he had been by in just two or three weeks.'

'He was very angry and upset.'

'He certainly was,' the Judge said, now leaning on his club and making no attempt to look for his ball. 'He was also quite determined to prove that Ultramed and Frank had railroaded him out of practice as a means of setting up their own man, this Mainwaring, in his place. He claimed to have evidence that such underhanded dealings are typical of the company.'

'I know what he claimed. What I don't know is why on earth he kept coming to you when you made it clear to him how strongly you supported Frank and the excellent job he's done at the hospital.'

They watched in silence as each of the passing foursome hit his approach shot. Three of the balls landed neatly on the green, and the fourth, hit by a grizzled old man whom Zack placed somewhere in his mid-eighties, landed in a sand trap. As he invariably did when around very old people, Zack found himself praying that the man's coronary and cerebral circulations were, at least at that moment, functioning as nature intended.

'The answer to your question, Zachary,' the Judge said after the old man had hit, 'is that Guy was convinced that Frank or no Frank, I would not want to see him go under for acts he never committed. Remember, he and I went back a hell of a long way. I can't count the number of committees and projects we worked on together over the past thirty years, struggling to pull Sterling up from the dying little mill town it once was. As often as not we were on opposite sides of the fence on an issue, but that never mattered. We both fought like hell, but we fought within the rules.'

'I understand.'

'So, I guess he believed that based on the way we handled our differences, and on my record as a judge, I would champion any cause I felt was just.'

'And was he right?'

The Judge took a new ball from his bag and dropped it backward, over his shoulder.

'Of course he was right,' he said. 'You should know that as well as anyone.'

'Sorry.'

'Beaulieu's dead, but the issues he was fighting against, if, in fact, they are issues at all, remain very much unresolved – at least until the deadline to repurchase the hospital passes. After that we are all, quite literally, at Ultramed's mercy.'

The buyback. Zack suddenly understood why Frank had been excluded from the afternoon. Silently, he cautioned himself against expressing any opinions until the Judge's position had become quite a bit clearer. Where Clayton Iverson and his scion were concerned, interactions and reactions had seldom, if ever, been simple and straightforward.

While Zack's schoolboy years, especially after his accident, had passed by quietly and, by comparison, virtually unnoticed, the relationship between the Judge and Frank had been a turbulent, volatile affair. The man had soaked in his older son's accomplishments like an insatuable sponge, and inevitably, when Frank's heroics were slow in coming, or worse, when he did anything outside of the persona the Judge had created for him, there was friction.

Thinking back, Zack wondered if either of the two ever truly appreciated the dynamics of those clashes.

If being Judge Clayton Iverson's second son had engendered certain problems for him, being his first had proven something of a curse for Frank.

He recalled the day when Frank, then a freshman or sophomore in high school, had received an A on a history paper. The teacher, in her comments, had noted that the writing style and content of the report were far beyond anything he had ever done before.

248

Suspicious of the sudden improvement, the Judge had confronted Frank in what he liked to call an eyeball-to-eyeball showdown. It was a technique that had seldom failed to uncover a lie from either of his sons, and on that occasion Frank was beaten decisively. After an hour of confrontation, he shuffled to his room and produced the senior's paper from which he had plagiarized.

The look in his eyes at that moment, a frightening olio of fear, hatred, humiliation, and anger, was one Zack would never forget.

The result of that showdown had been a zero on the report from the teacher and a four-game suspension from basketball by the Judge, although he subsequently rescinded his punishment after the coach pleaded that the team would suffer more from it than Frank.

That confrontation, and its aftermath, said much of both father and son. The Judge, feeling he had made his point regarding dishonesty in any form, never again brought up the incident.

For his part, Frank *was*, in fact, discouraged from further academic shortcuts, but only temporarily. Instead of responding to their father's leniency with change, he reacted with defiance. And one boastful day, not long after, he disclosed to his younger brother that he had dedicated himself to learning how to win in an eyeball-to-eyeball showdown. At first, he literally practiced before a mirror. Next came a series of what he called 'test fibs.' With time, even in the most critical situations he was able impassively to meet the man's piercing gaze and to hold it.

In the years that immediately followed, his conflicts with the Judge fell off markedly, due in part to Frank's mastery of his new craft, and in larger measure to his athletic accomplishments. Then, with Frank's repeated failures prior to Ultramed-Davis, their relationship again became strained.

Now, after four years of relative concord, a clash between the two men – possibly a monumental one – seemed to be in the making. And as always in the past, at the very heart of the matter were the Judge's expectations. Frank's performance had to be the very best, his conduct above reproach.

The foursome ahead of them finished putting and left the green. The Judge addressed his ball, but after several seconds he checked back down the fairway to ensure that no one was approaching, and stepped away.

'Zachary, you look troubled,' he said. 'What is it?'

'I'm not troubled. It's just that . . .'

'What?'

Zack shook his head.

'It's nothing, Judge. Go ahead and hit.'

'You're worried that I'm taking sides against Frank. Is that it?'

'He *is* your son.'

'And you think that because of that, I should turn my back on the possibility that he might be involved in something unethical, or even dishonest.'

'I didn't say that.'

'What, then?'

Zack stopped himself at the last moment from sharing details of Guy Beaulieu's legacy, of his encounter with Maureen Banas, and of his mounting distrust of Ultramed. There were still simply too many uncertainties to open those cans of worms before he had had the chance to discuss them with Frank.

'Judge,' he said, carefully choosing his words, 'Guy Beaulieu was trying his damnedest to bring down Ultramed. If Frank fell with it, that was no concern of his. I appreciate your commitment to doing what's right, but—'

'But what?'

Again, Zack hesitated. One slip, one misplaced thought, and the Judge would be off and running on another of his crusades.

In Frank's eyes, the two of them would be aligned against him and Ultramed, and any chance of enlisting his help, either in exposing the corporation or in solving the mystery of Toby Nelms, would likely be lost for good.

'Judge, Frank has his quirks and his faults,' he said finally, 'just like the rest of us. But considering the expectations and the pressures he's had to overcome since those days at Sterling High, I think he's done some things we should both be proud of. At the very least, we should be going out of our way to give him the benefit of the doubt in this business.'

'So you think I'm being disloyal by wanting to know whether my son and the corporation he works for are making a profit at the expense of my community?'

'I didn't say that.'

'And you think it's disloyalty to question whether Frank might have had a role in the destruction of a man's reputation?'

'Judge, please.'

'I'm sorry, Zachary, but I've spent more than thirty years as a lawyer, half of them as a judge. As far as I'm concerned, doing what is right is far more important than any of that kind of so-called loyalty.'

'I'm not arguing with that. It's just that from what I can see, this whole business isn't all that simple. Did you know that if it weren't for Frank's using his influence at the hospital, Beaulieu would have been suspended some time ago?'

The Judge looked shaken.

'No,' he said. 'I didn't.'

'Well, it's true.'

Of course, the story of Frank's intercession had come from Frank himself, but Zack saw no point in sharing that piece of information, or for that matter, his displeasure with Frank's behavior on the day of Beaulieu's death. He was enjoying the chance to play his brother's advocate. He also sensed that in arguing on Frank's behalf, he was, in some ways, making a case for their father's recognition of his own accomplishments in life.

The Judge seemed surprised and upset by his stand.

Again, he addressed his ball, although Zack could see from his stance and his bloodless knuckles that his concentration was broken. And suddenly Zack understood: his father had done something, or at least was contemplating doing something, that would not sit well with Frank, and now, all at once, he had doubts.

His swing was rushed and awkward. The ball, never really leaving the ground, skimmed across the fairway and slammed into the recently vacated sand trap. Clayton Iverson barely reacted to the horrible shot.

'You know,' he said as they trudged toward the bunker, 'from the day your mother and I first learned she was pregnant with Frank, we began to share visions of greatness for our children. I don't suppose that makes us unique, but I tell you, son, we spent many an hour by the fire that winter sharing our dreams. We even named Frank, and then you, after presidents – little-known presidents, but ones who did leave their marks on history.'

Inwardly, Zack sighed. This talk was one he had endured many times over the years. Franklin Pierce, the only president born in New Hampshire, and Zachary Taylor, the much-maligned warrior who, despite four historically undistinguished years in office, established the Department of the Interior, were special favorites of the Judge.

'Believe me, Judge,' Zack said, in what had become his standard response to the discussion, 'both Frank and I appreciate the values and the drive you instilled in us.'

He paused to chip his approach shot onto the edge of the green and then watched as his father, now totally off his game, took two shots to get out of the sand trap.

By the end of the hole, Zack had cut his deficit to six dollars, and following two tiers and a disastrous seven by the Judge on the thirteenth, he had pared it by three dollars more.

'Judge,' he said, motioning to the small refreshment kiosk by the fourteenth tee, 'let's take a break. Anything that could upset you enough to play like this ought to be talked out.'

'I'm not upset,' Clayton Iverson said.

'Okay, you're not upset. You only went from shooting four over par for the whole front nine, to shooting eight over for the first four holes since you brought up this business about the hospital. Why don't you have a seat at that little table over there and let me buy you a beer.'

The Judge started to protest, but then relented.

'Maybe I am a *little* upset,' he muttered.

Zack left him at the wrought-iron table and returned with two frosted mugs and two bottles of Lowenbrau.

'So, what's going on?' Zack asked as he sipped his beer.

'What do you mean?'

'I mean Frank, Judge. I know you helped him get considered for the job with Ultramed. Is that why you're being hard on him? Because you feel responsible?'

'Zachary, the mess your brother made of that damn electronics company of his wasn't his first fiasco. He just didn't have the patience for that kind of business. He was constantly trying to go directly from step one to step twenty. He was lucky the Ultramed opportunity came along when it did. I told him that when he—' Clayton Iverson stopped in mid-sentence.

'When he what, Judge?'

'Nothing. It doesn't matter.'

'He asked you for a loan, didn't he?' Zachary said.

Suddenly pieces of conversation he had had with his brother over the years began falling into place. Although Frank had never shared the details of his company's failure, he had made it clear that he felt their father was, at least in part, at fault.

'It was a foolish request. He was already in it up to here. It would have been throwing good money after bad.'

'Frank didn't see it that way, Judge.'

'Well, I did. I agreed to help him out of the hole he had gotten himself in, but only on condition that he get rid of that company. The hospital job gave him a chance to get out from underneath that nonsense and to show everyone in town just what he could do.'

To say nothing of bringing him back here, under your thumb, Zack thought angrily.

'So, he got the job, and he's done it well. What more could you want from him?'

'I could want him to bring the same values to his position that I bring to mine. That's what I could want. I could want him to stand up for what's right.'

Despite the warm afternoon, Zachary felt suddenly cold.

'What's right?' *I'm the one with Beaulieu's evidence*, he wanted to shout. *I'm the one who confronted Maureen Banas. How can you be so damned sure of what's right?* 'Dad,' he said, 'exactly what have you done?'

'You know, Zachary, I don't particularly like that tone of yours. You may be a big-shot surgeon, but you're still my son.'

Zack sensed himself backing away from his father's glare. He couldn't remember the last time he had pushed against the man this hard.

'Sorry,' he mumbled.

'Apology accepted. I think that thirty years on the bench more than qualifies me to tell when someone's handing me a line of bull. There was just too much smoke surrounding Beaulieu's complaints for there to be no fire. I . . . I didn't know until you told me that Frank had intervened on his behalf.'

He hesitated, and then reached into the pocket of

his golf bag, withdrew an envelope, and passed it over.

'Here,' he said, 'read this.'

Mrs. Leigh Baron
Director, Operations
Ultramed Hospitals Corporation
Boston Place
Boston, Massachusetts 02108

Dear Mrs. Baron:

The contract effecting the sale of Davis Regional Hospital to Ultramed Hospitals Corporation is now in its fourth and final year. As you are no doubt aware, the agreement contains provisions for the reacquisition of the facility by the community-based board, of which I am chairman, provided the board meets no less than five months prior to the termination date of the contract and agrees by a vote of no less than 51% of its members to return to Ultramed the original purchase price – a sum currently held in escrow in the Sterling National Bank – in exchange for resuming control of the hospital.

Until recently, I had no intention of convening the board to consider such a vote. However, a situation has developed that greatly concerns me – a conflict between Dr. Guy Beaulieu, one of the first physicians to settle in Sterling, and your corporation. It was the late Dr. Beaulieu's contention that the hospital administration, and ultimately, Ultramed Hospitals Corporation itself, was responsible for machinations calculated to drive him out of medical practice. He further claimed knowledge of actions by your corporation, through Ultramed-Davis, which have been contrary to the best interests of our community. I know that he had conveyed his feelings to you on several occasions, and that he had, in fact, instituted legal action against both the hospital and Ultramed Hospitals Corporation.

Dr. Beaulieu's widow has contacted me and has requested that the board seriously consider Dr. Beaulieu's allegations before the end of our provisional period at noon on July 19. I have asked Mrs. Beaulieu to make every effort, in advance of that date, to supply me with details of her husband's claims and the evidence behind them.

Meanwhile, please consider this letter notification that I intend to convene the board at 11 a.m. on Friday, July 19, for the purpose of discussing our options. Also, as provided in our contract, I have commissioned a full, independent audit of the hospital, which I expect to be initiated within the next few days. As you know, according to section 4B of the contract, 15 percent of the hospital's profits over the past four years should have been funneled back into the community through the treatment of indigent patients, and another 3 percent through support of various civic projects enumerated in section 4C. Violation of that section, even if uncovered after the July 19 deadline, will nullify our contract with you.

Meanwhile, if you have any information or thoughts on this matter, I would welcome hearing from you.

Hoping for an amicable resolution of this issue, I remain,

> Sincerely yours,
> Clayton C. Iverson

Zack was incredulous. Beaulieu's widow and daughter had given him no indication that they planned to contact the board directly.

'Judge, just when did Mrs. Beaulieu call you?' he asked.

'Well . . . actually, she didn't call me. . . . I called her.'

'And has she contacted other members of the board?'

'I, um, suggested she might want to do so.'

'Oh, Judge, why?'

'Because ol' Guy might have been right, that's why.'

'But Frank said he wasn't. Why couldn't you have just given him the benefit of the doubt?'

'I . . . I felt that if he hadn't done anything wrong, he didn't have anything to worry about.'

'Of course he does. He's got to worry about how to explain to the people at Ultramed why his own father would be trying to sabotage their hospital. You don't even know what kind of so-called evidence Guy had, do you? . . . Well, do you?'

Clayton Iverson shook his head.

'I didn't think so. Well, I do, Judge. I know exactly what he had. Clothilde Beaulieu gave it all to me at his funeral. And I tell you there isn't enough proof of wrongdoing even to dent Ultramed. Circumstantial stuff. That's all he had accumulated. Just a pile of inferential lists, anecdotes, and newspaper clippings.

'I'll admit that I have some strong reservations about that company, but up till now there's no hard evidence – not one person that I know of – who was directly hurt by the corporation's policies. Why couldn't you have just gone to Frank? Talked to him? That's what I had planned to do. Did he even see this letter before you sent it?'

The Judge took a long swallow of beer and wiped the foam from his lips with the back of his hand. Then he smiled.

'I haven't sent it,' he said simply.

'What?'

'The letter is being held by my lawyer in Boston until I decide what to do. I was thinking about having him send it over to Ultramed on Monday. I wanted to talk with you first. Now I'm glad I did.'

Zack felt drained and exhausted – a yo-yo on the string of a master.

'You could have just told me what you wanted in the first place,' he said. 'You can't play with people like that, Judge.'

'Nonsense. I haven't been playing with anyone. I needed your candid opinion, and I got it. I'm not committed to opposing turning the hospital over to Ultramed for good next week. I'm just reluctant to totally give up our leverage. You never know when you'll wish you had it. The truth is, it would take a hell of a lot more than anything I've learned so far to make me turn against Frank and send that letter. There, do you feel better?'

'What I feel,' Zack said, 'is wasted.'

'Good. In that case, suppose we play us some golf.'

The Judge set his beer down, took his driver from his bag, and wiped its head with a cloth.

259

'I'm pleased with the things you've told me about your brother, Zachary,' he said. 'I haven't made any secret of my disappointment with him over the years. But as long as he keeps acting for the benefit of our town, then he and Ultramed have nothing to worry about from me. However, if you learn of something, anything, that I should know, then dammit, you owe it to all of us to speak up. Clear?'

'Clear,' Zack said numbly.

'Including anything in that material of Guy's.'

'Right.'

The Judge set his ball on the tee. Once again in control, he looked relaxed and confident.

'Okay if I hit first?' he asked.

His swing was loose, compact, and smooth as velvet. The drive was arrow straight and by far the longest of the day.

An hour later, Zack stood on the eighteenth green and watched as his father rolled in a twelve-foot putt for a birdie.

'Five straight holes for me,' the Judge said. 'That's eight bucks. I just love this game, don't you?'

Chapter 19

Dose by dose, microgram by microgram, the Haldol level in Annie Doucette's blood had been rising. The input from her senses, barely adequate to keep her oriented *before* the tranquilizer was started, had become blunted and distorted. Her periods of lucidity, even in the bright, noisy daylight hours, had all but disappeared.

Now, as the muted stillness of late Sunday evening drifted over the hospital, what little hold she had been able to maintain on reality had begun to slip away.

One moment, she was home, in her own room, her own bed; in the next, she was someplace else, someplace at once foreign and familiar. It was evening, it was morning. Desperately, she struggled against the madness. Desperately, she tried to focus her thoughts. Still, nothing was certain – nothing except the realization that somehow, she had wet and soiled herself.

Call Zack . . . Call Suzanne, her mind urged. *Tell them to come and clean you up. Tell them to get you out of this place.*

She turned to search for a telephone, but a wave of dizziness and nausea forced her back onto the pillow.

Lifting the sheet, she stared down at her legs. Foul-smelling, loose excrement was smeared over the insides of her thighs. So disgusting. So humiliating.

Must get washed . . . Must get showered before someone comes.

Annie peered through a gray mist toward the door of her bathroom. *Shower . . . Clean up . . . Then call – who? What was his name?*

With all her strength she struggled onto her side. There were metal railings along both sides of her bed. Using one of them, and battling the constant spinning, she pulled herself up.

How disgusting . . . How humiliating . . .

There was no guard railing at the end of the bed. With agonizing slowness she worked her way over the feces-soaked sheet. Then she dropped one leg over the low footboard and onto the chilly linoleum floor. The dizziness was becoming unbearable.

Still, she knew she had to get clean.

An inch at a time, she slid her other leg onto the floor. With every ounce of her strength, she tried to stand. Momentarily, her leg held. But then suddenly, it gave way, and for the briefest time she was floating in air.

She landed heavily and gracelessly, air exploding from her lungs with a loud grunt. There was another sound as well – a sharp, snapping sound coming from somewhere within her body.

An instant later, unimaginable pain shot through her from her left hip.

Second by second, the pain intensified. Then, a heaviness settled onto her chest. Slowly, the dim light in the room faded, and Annie felt a merciful, peaceful darkness settle in.

*

The night was heavy – overcast and humid, with not quite enough breeze for comfort. It was nearing eleven when Zack eased the Judges' Chrysler into the largely empty parking lot outside the Ultramed-Davis emergency ward. The Judge, hands folded stoically in his lap, sat next to him. His mother, grim and silent, rod in the backseat, working over the handkerchief she had balled in her fists.

Annie Doucette was in trouble.

Zack would have much preferred to evaluate the woman's situation before involving his parents, but a well-meaning nurse, unable to reach Annie's son in Connecticut, had noted that they were listed in her record as "employer," and had called them.

A fractured hip and new coronary were the only snatches a shaken Cinnie Iverson could remember to repeat to Zack from that conversation.

'Zachary, dear,' she said now, as he helped her from the car, 'do you think they'll operate on her tonight?'

'I don't know, Mom. It's doubtful, though. Especially if the nurse I spoke to is right about her having had a new heart attack.'

'Her doctor – what is his name?'

'Norman, Mom. Don Norman.'

'Dr. Norman. Did you speak to him?'

'He was in working on Annie. I didn't see any sense in bothering him.'

'And did Frank say he'd be right in?'

'Yes, Mom. He's waiting for Lisette to get back from her sister's, and then he'll be in.'

Cinnie gave her handkerchief one last squeeze and then stuffed it in her purse.

'Well,' she said, 'I just hope Annie's okay.'

'Okay?' Clayton Iverson laughed disdainfully.

'Jesus, Cynthia, what world do you live in? The woman's almost eighty years old and she just fell out of bed, broke her hip, and had a heart attack. How in the hell could you possibly think she'd be okay?'

'Sorry,' Cinnie said. 'There's no need to cuss,' she added in a whisper directed more to herself than to her husband.

They entered the hospital through the emergency ward and took the elevator to the second floor. Annie had been moved back to the intensive care unit.

'Why don't you two wait in there,' Zack said, motioning them into the small waiting room just outside the unit. 'I'll be back as soon as I find out what's going on.'

Anger and tension had knotted the muscles at the base of his neck and were gnawing at the pit of his stomach. To be sure, over the years of his training he had had patients fall out of bed, even when strict precautions had been taken. The risk was always there, especially with so many hospitalized patients being old and infirm.

But this situation was different. Since he was a consultant on her case, Annie Doucette *was*, technically, his patient; but even more than that, she was his friend. In some ways she had been as much a parent to him as had Cinnie and the Judge. And even beyond that, he knew, was the special, proprietary feeling experienced by every physician toward a patient whose life he or she had saved.

He was on edge, his physician's detachment and objectivity hanging by the thinnest of threads.

From the moment Cinnie had called him with the news, he had been reminding himself that, while it was reasonable for him to be upset, there was

264

seldom, if ever, justification for a physician to lose objectivity – even when confronting oversight or negligence. In the microcosm of the hospital, explosions by physicians helped no one.

As he was heading into the unit, Sam Christian, one of three staff orthopedic surgeons, emerged. He was a tall, gaunt man, in his mid-fifties, who walked with a slight limp. Twenty-two years before, Zack and his mangled left knee had been one of his first cases.

'Evening Zack,' he said. He glanced into the small waiting room. 'Judge, Cinnie.'

'Hello, Sam.' The Judge came out to shake his hand. 'What's the story?'

Christian shrugged.

'She needs a new hip,' he said matter-of-factly. 'But until her cardiac situation gets straightened out, that's out of the question. Tomorrow, if she's still – I mean, if she's settled down, I'll put some pins across the joint to stabilize it until we can do something definitive.'

'Do you know what happened?' Zack asked. 'Were the side rails up on her bed?'

Christian's expression darkened.

'You'd best talk to Don Norman about all that. But yes, apparently the railings were up. She went off the end.'

'Oh, dear God,' Cinnie gasped.

'Thanks, Sam,' Zack said. He turned to his parents. 'I'll be out in a little bit.'

As he entered the unit he heard the Judge say, 'So, Sam, level with me, now. Who screwed up here?'

Zack had seen Annie briefly during morning rounds. At that time, she was awake and responsive,

265

but somewhat depressed and more lethargic than she had been. He suggested that she try spending more time out of bed, and had actually offered to walk down the hall with her. She refused, citing a headache and lack of sleep.

The change in her over just fourteen hours, even allowing for her accident, was terrifying. She was disoriented and combative; her speech was thick and slurred. Her gray hair was matted against her scalp with perspiration and bits of feces.

From the doorway, Zack watched as Don Norman struggled to examine Annie's chest. The portly internist had stripped off his suitcoat and rolled up his shirt-sleeves, but he was still wearing his tie, vest, and gold watch fob. Beads of sweat dotted his fleshy forehead and upper lip.

A young nurse stood off to one side, her face drawn and pale.

'Need an extra pair of hands?' Zack asked as Norman stepped back from the bed.

The man looked down at Annie and then shook his head.

'No, thank you, Doctor,' he said. 'I'm just about done.'

'She okay?'

'If you mean is she going to die, the answer is no . . . at least not tonight. Since we got a line in and gave her some fluid, her pressure has come up. But she's extended her old coronary. There's not much question about that. And I guess you know that she's fractured her hip.'

She's extended her coronary. *She*'s fractured her hip. Noman's emotionless statement – his tacit implication that Annie was responsible for her own misfortune – instantly rekindled the dislike Zack had developed toward the man during their interview many months before.

Still, there could be no arguing the truth in his grim assessment of her situation and prognosis. Pneumonia, stroke, embolism, heart failure; while orthopedists could work near-miracles with hips in the operating room, physicians and nurses knew all too well that immobilization of any sort was the deadliest enemy of advancing age.

Zack moved to within two feet of the bed.

'Is she making any sense?'

'Nope. Strictly word salad.'

'Stroke?'

'I don't think so.'

'Is there any evidence she hit her head?'

Norman shifted uncomfortably.

'I . . . I haven't really checked,' he said. 'As you can see, she's not the easiest thing in the world to examine right now.'

'Mind if I try?'

'Try anything you want,' Norman responded somewhat testily. Then he glanced over at the nurse.

Zack caught the look and warned himself against doing anything that would embarrass the man. He took Annie's hand. Instantly, she dug her nails into his palm.

'Hey, Annie D, *leggo*! It's me. It's Zack. I need that hand for my coin tricks.'

She looked up at him, blinking as if struggling to peer through a haze. Then, slowly, she loosened her grip.

'Do you recognize me?' Zack said, already speeding through a neurologic exam.

Annie did not respond.

'Well, you should.' He checked her scalp for any

telltale lumps, and her neck for any points of tenderness. 'You used to wipe my runny nose and drag me back to the bathroom to wash behind my ears. Remember that?'

Although it remained uncertain whether or not Annie recognized him, there could be no doubt that his words had calmed her down. She lay reasonably still as he checked her eardrums and retinae.

'Well?' Norman asked. His arms were folded tightly across his chest.

Zack smoothed Annie's matted hair off her forehead. 'There are no focal neurologic signs. Let's go out to the nurses' station and talk, okay?'

'Is it . . . all right if I listen in?' the nurse asked, pausing between words to clear a huskiness from her voice.

'Fine with me, if Dr. Norman doesn't mind.'

Norman hesitated and then shook his head.

'We haven't met,' Zack went on. 'My name's Iverson, Zack Iverson. I'm the new neurosurgeon on the block.'

'I'm Doreen Lavalley,' she said. 'Annie was my patient up on four. I feel sick about what happened. We had her tucked in with the side rails up. She soiled herself. I think she was trying to get to the bathroom when she fell. We were all in with a post-op patient who had started hemorrhaging, and our routine bed check was delayed almost an hour, and . . . and we're just . . .' She bit at her lower lip and looked away.

'Go on,' Zack said as they walked from the cubicle to the nurses' station.

For a moment, it seemed as if the young woman was going to cry. Then a flash of anger mixed with the anguish in her eyes.

'Dammit,' she said, 'I knew something like this was going to happen.'

'What do you mean?'

She glanced over at Donald Norman and then turned again to Zack.

'We're short,' she blurted. 'That's what I mean. We're short a nurse on every shift on every floor except the unit here. It's been that way for more than a year. First they got rid of the union with all those promises of increased pay and benefits and staffing. Then, just slowly enough so that none of us could organize to complain, they began to cut back on nursing. I knew something like this was going to happen. I just knew it . . .' Her firsts were clenched in frustration.

'Who's "they"?' Zack asked.

'The hospital, that's who . . . the administration . . . Mr. Iver—' She stopped in midword and looked sheepishly at Zack. 'Oh, great . . . Way to go, Doreen. . . . Brother?'

Zack nodded.

'Sorry,' she said.

'Don't be. Don, you're the chief of staff. Are the physicians aware that this has been going on?'

Norman's face was pinched and flushed. However, his indignation was directed not at the situation, but at the nurse.

'If Miss Lavalley has complaints about this hospital or the way it is run,' he said, his back almost turned to her, 'there are channels established for her to voice those concerns. She's worked here for enough years to know that – and also to know that airing her own distorted point of view in the middle of the intensive care unit is not one of those channels. Now, Doctor, if you'd care to share your thoughts on Mrs. Doucette with me, I can get on with the business of trying to save her life.'

The woman tensed at Norman's rebuke, but said nothing.

Zack wrestled against the urge to defend her, and won a narrow victory. The issue at hand was getting Annie Doucette diagnosed, treated, and stabilized. The nurse's charges, disturbing though they were, could wait.

He thought about calling Suzanne in, but quickly tabled the notion. Annie's monitor pattern was regular, at least for the moment, and Donald Norman, as thin-skinned as he was thick-waisted, seemed hardly the sort to welcome any encroachment on his authority.

'So?' Norman asked impatiently.

'Well, there's no evidence for a stroke or for head trauma,' Zack said, 'but she's clearly disoriented. I guess if I had to put a label on what's going on, I would say she's sundowning – especially if her blood chemistries all come back normal.'

Out the corner of his eye, Zack saw Doreen Lavalley nodding in vigorous agreement.

Sundowning was not a medical diagnosis in the pure sense. Nevertheless, to anyone dealing with elderly, hospitalized patients, the disorientation and psychotic behavior stemming from unfamiliar surroundings and the diminished sensory input of evening were as real and reproducible a phenomenon as a strep throat.

'Excellent,' Norman said, his expression and patronizing tone making it clear that Zack had added nothing to his assessment of the case. 'Good job. Listen, Doctor, why don't you dictate a note, and I'll put a formal request for a consultation in her chart.' He unrolled his sleeves and retrieved his suitcoat. 'If there's nothing else, I'm going to see another patient. I'll stop back on my way out.'

Zack, engrossed in Annie's chart, did not respond.

'What are you looking for?' Norman asked.

'An explanation.'

'For what?'

Zack glanced up.

'Don, this woman's been here almost two weeks, during which time she's been totally with it. Don't you think it's a little strange that she should have taken this long to sundown?'

'On second thought,' Norman said, 'why don't you just forget about the consult. We'll discuss this whole thing in the morning.'

'It's there, Dr. Iverson,' the nurse said.

Norman shot her a withering glare.

'What is?' Zack asked.

'The explanation. Look on the med sheet.'

'Give me that chart,' Norman snapped. 'Miss Lavalley, you don't know a good thing when you have it, do you? You just get the hell out of here. I'll deal with you tomorrow.'

'You can deal with me tonight, Dr. Norman, because I've had enough. I quit.'

'Haldol!' Zack exclaimed, slamming his fist on the page. 'What in the hell is she doing on Haldol?'

The nurse's fury was now uncontained.

'Dr. Norman – excuse me, *Don*—' she corrected herself sweetly, 'put her on it Tuesday when she complained about his plan to transfer her to a nursing home. He called her a harpy.'

'Damn you,' Norman hissed, his face now puffed and crimson.

271

'A nursing home? Norman, are you crazy?'

'Is *who* crazy?' Frank Iverson, hands on hips, stood just inside the unit door.

Zack rubbed at the grit of fatigue and tension that had begun to sting his eyes.

'This whole place, that's who,' he said to no one and to everyone. 'This whole place is crazy.'

'Easy, Zack-o,' Frank warned. 'Just stay cool. How's Annie?'

Zack lowered his hand and looked up at his brother.

'She's crazy. That's how she is. She's crazy because for the last five days she's been receiving a major tranquilizer. Her blood levels have been rising and she's been drifting further and further from reality until it's doubtful she even knew where she was when all this happened. She lost control of her bowels and was trying to crawl over the end of the bed to the bathroom when she fell. The nurse, here, tells me they didn't get in to check on her as soon as they should have because there's been such a staffing cutback that they're shorthanded. What kind of a goddamn place is this, Frank?'

'I . . . I think I'd better get back to my floor,' Doreen Lavalley said softly. 'Mr. Iverson, my resignation will be in the nursing office tomorrow morning.' Without waiting for a response, she whirled and hurried out.

'Don, what in the hell's going on here?' Frank asked.

'Your brother, that's what,' Norman answered. 'He barged in here, starts examining my patient without even being consulted, badgers the nurse into making some rash statements about the hospital, and then accuses me of causing the woman

272

to fall.' He turned to Zack. 'You've been trouble since the day you got here, and don't think we don't all know it. This hospital needs team players, Iverson. You're a grandstander. Ultramed-Davis ran perfectly smoothly before you showed up, and it will do just as well after you've gone.'

'I'm not going anywhere,' Zack said.

'Don't bank on it,' Norman shot back.

'Easy, both of you,' Frank said. 'First of all, just tell me, is that woman in there going to die tonight?'

'It was touch and go for a while,' Norman said. 'But I've gotten things under control. She's a bit disoriented, but she's not in any immediate danger. We'll wait a few days to let her cardiac situation calm down, and then Sam Christian'll fix her hip.'

'Zack?'

'What?'

'Do you think that's the way it is?'

'I think,' Zack said wearily, still resting his head on his hand, 'that Suzanne ought to be called in to take care of Annie. That's what I think.'

'Over my dead body, you arrogant son of a bitch,' Norman rasped.

'Careful, Don,' Zack said. 'That's Frank's mother you're talking about.'

'Will you two please stop it? There are nurses and patients all over this place. Now, Don, tell me, did you have Annie on a tranquilizer or not? And for God's sake, keep your voice down.'

Donald Norman was losing what little control he had left.

'First of all, Frank,' he said, 'I'll thank you not to tell me what to do with my voice. Second of all, I'll thank you and your brother, here, not to go questioning the therapy I choose for my patients.

You may be the administrator here, but I'm the chief of the medical staff.'

Frank stepped forward until his face was less than a foot from Norman's. His eyes were steely.

'Donald, one call from me, one' – he held up a finger for emphasis – 'and you'll be lucky to have a job scrubbing bedpans. You should know that. And if you don't think I have that kind of clout at Ultramed, just try me. Now take that chief of staff crap and stuff it. Then tell me what in the hell you were thinking when you put Annie Doucette on tranks.'

'Yeah, Don,' Zack urged acidly, 'tell him.'

'Zack, will you please shut the fuck up for a minute and let me get to the bottom of this?'

Norman was visibly cowed.

'Frank,' he pleaded, 'I was just trying to follow policy. The woman's DRG payments are about to run out. I have a bed lined up for her at the nursing home. That's just what I'm supposed to do. When I told her what was planned, she went berserk. She demanded more time in the hospital. That was out of the question. You know the rules as well as I do.'

'What rules?' Zack asked.

Frank ignored him.

'So you sedated her,' he said. 'Jesus, Don. She worked for my goddamn family. Couldn't you have just called me?'

'I . . . I didn't think to.'

'What rules?' Zack asked again.

'Yes, what rules?'

The three men spun toward the voice. Clayton Iverson was just a few feet away, calmly appraising them all. His expression was nonthreatening, but Zack could see anger smoldering in his eyes.

'Judge,' Frank said. 'You said you were going to wait out there with Mom.'

'I got impatient.'

'Well . . . well, good enough. I'm sure it's no great news to you that we can't always agree on everything in a hospital. Right?'

'Right.'

Frank smiled cheerily, but Zack knew he was shaken.

'Don, here, tells us Annie's still disoriented, but that her condition has stabilized. Isn't that so, Zack? Listen, Judge, why don't you get Mom and bring her in. It's getting late, and I'm sure you both want to get on home.'

The Judge confronted him in a brief eyeball-to-eyeball showdown, but Frank easily held his own.

'All right, Frank,' Clayton said evenly. 'As long as things are under control.'

'Don's an excellent internist, Judge, and Annie's getting his best shot. Right, Zack?'

'Right.' Zack nearly choked on the word.

'Don, come,' Frank said. 'Let's you and I go over some things before you call it a day.'

Without waiting for an answer, Frank took Norman by the arm and led him from the unit.

'How much of all that did you hear, Judge?' Zack whispered.

Clayton Iverson looked over at Annie, who was clumsily picking at the restraint that was holding her to the bed.

'Enough, Zachary,' he said. 'I heard quite enough. I'm going to have that letter in Leigh Baron's hands tomorrow. Are you going to try and talk me out of it?'

Once again, Zack rubbed at the burning in his

eyes. Even faced with this new reality, it was painful to accept that the promise of Ultramed-Davis – the sparkling physical plant and progressive approach to medicine – was no more than a veneer. Beneath the sheen, beneath the new equipment, the new specialists, and the intense public relations effort, the hospital had no soul.

'No, Judge,' he said finally. 'Tomorrow I'm going to give you a look at the material Guy had put together against Ultramed. You go ahead and do whatever you feel you have to do. I'm not going to try and talk you out of anything.'

Zack waited until the Judge had left, and then called Suzanne.

'Zachary, do you know what time it is?' she said blearily.

'Gee, no,' he said, 'but give me a minute, and I'll see if I can find someone who does.'

'That's not funny.'

'Sorry. You don't sound so hot.'

'I'm not. I have a splitting headache, and sixty milligrams of Dalmane had me barely asleep when you called.'

'Sorry again.'

'I've just got to get some rest. Was there anything special you wanted?'

'No,' he lied. 'Nothing special. I just wanted to see how you were.'

'Oh . . . well, can you call me in the morning?'

'Sure.'

'Thanks. I should go before this Dalmane wears off.'

'Good—'

The dial tone cut him off.

*

276

The atmosphere in the shingled ranch Zack had leased from Pine Bough Realty was kept musty and comfortable by the lingering aroma of decades of hardwood fires.

It was after one in the morning. Seated in a frayed easy chair by the dormant hearth, Zack sipped from the cup of Constant Comment tea, absently scratched Cheapdog in his favorite behind-the-ear spot, and waited.

Frank had asked him to stay up to talk, and had promised to be right over. But Zack knew that his brother had never marched to anything other than Frank Iverson's time.

In truth, it made little difference how late Frank would be. Zack was too keyed up by the events of the evening to sleep. His feelings – disappointment, anger, frustration – were strangely akin to those of the dreadful night when Connie had finally leveled with him about her decision to break off their engagement and not to accompany him to New Hampshire.

'It wasn't supposed to be like this, Cheap,' he said. 'It wasn't supposed to be like this at all.'

So much of him wanted to just pack up and run – load the camper and go back to Muni. For all of its underfinanced, stretched-to-the-limit turmoil, the place at least had heart. The bottom line there was never anything but sick or hurting patients and a crew of nurses, technicians, and docs determined to help them get well.

But even as he heard the crunch of his brother's Porsche on the gravel drive, Zack knew that he would stay. For Suzanne and the mountains; for Guy and Toby Nelms and all of the Stacy Millses yet to be in his life, he would see things through.

Frank's visit did not last long.

He was speaking even before the screen door had shut behind him.

'You really stuck it to me tonight, Zack-o,' he said breathlessly. 'You really stuck it to me.'

'Have a seat, Frank. You want something to drink? Some tea? A beer?'

At that moment, Zack caught the odor of whiskey and noted the fine, red flush at the corner of Frank's eyes.

'I don't want anything except a little goddamn loyalty and help from my brother,' Frank said, making no move to sit. 'A good nurse has quit; my father, who also happens to be the chairman of the hospital board, is furious; and my chief of staff wants to shoot me, to say nothing of what he wants to do to you. That's great, Zachary. That's a hell of a night's work.'

'Easy, Frank. Okay?'

'No, dammit! Not okay. Norman's right. From the minute you got back here there's been nothing but trouble. Playing Sir Lancelot all over the goddamn hospital, undermining my authority and Ultramed's policies, even flirting with my wife, for Chrissake.'

'That's ridiculous. Frank, you've been drinking. Why don't we both just sit on this and we'll talk in the morning.'

'I'll talk about it now,' Frank snapped.

Having, perhaps, seen and heard enough, Cheapdog growled a soft warning and from somewhere beneath the shag of his face, bared his teeth.

Zack glanced over at the animal, but made no attempt to quiet him down. With Frank less than totally rational already, Cheapdog was some insurance against a major blowup. That the dog was basically a coward would remain his secret.

'All right,' he said wearily, 'so talk.'

Frank was pacing, clenching and unclenching his fists and then rubbing his hands on the sides of his trousers.

'For years now, ever since you fell on that ski slope and I got to go to Colorado, you've been waiting for the chance to get back, to ruin me. Sitting in the stands all those years cheering and clapping with the others, and all the while hating my guts because you couldn't stay on your skis—'

'Frank, that's crazy.'

Revising upward his estimate of how much Frank had had to drink, Zack could only settle back in his chair and watch.

'I told them things were going just fine up here,' Frank ranted on. 'I told them we didn't need any goddamn neurosurgeon, least of all you. Well, let me tell you something, Zack-o. Tougher nuts than you have tried to fuck with me. Where are they now?'

He whirled and leveled a finger at Zack's face. From the corner of his eye, Zack saw Cheapdog again stiffen.

'Now just listen, and listen to me good,' Frank said. 'Things are going to change around here or you're out. I've worked too hard to get this place the way I want it to have anyone screw it all up – especially someone with a twenty-year-old chip on his shoulder. So just back off. Let up on the staff, on the Judge, and on Lisette, or I swear, Zack-o, I'll come down on you like a ton of bricks.'

Without waiting for a response, he spun on his heel and stormed from the house. Moments later, the Porsche screeched away.

Zack sat in numb disbelief. A twenty-year-past skiing accident; an innocent, unfulfilled high school romance. Was Frank merely drunk and tired, or was he truly crazy?

Let up on the staff. The warning would have gone unheeded under any circumstances. But now, there was not even room for dialogue or tact. An eight-year-old boy was drifting toward insanity and possibly death, and, consciously or not, someone at Ultramed-Davis knew why.

Zack glanced at his watch. It was after two. He picked up a book of crossword puzzles that were far enough beyond his ability to be soporific, and shuffled to the bedroom.

What he needed now, more than anything else, was some sleep; because warning or no warning, Frank or no Frank, he was going to get some answers – beginning in less than seven hours with Jack Pearl.

Chapter 20

The surgical residents at Boston Muni traditionally spoke of exhaustion in terms of the Wall – the moment when a physician ceased to function with any creative effectiveness. Throughout training, one was either approaching the Wall, up against it, or, when operating solely on the gritty-eyed fuel of caffeine and nervous energy, beyond it.

At 6:45, when his clock radio switched in on the final two verses of an a cappella version of 'Au Clair de la Fontaine,' Zack could distinctly remember seeing three, four, and five o'clock flash on its digital display. His bedside light was still on. The cross-word puzzle book with, perhaps, a dozen or so items out of one hundred thirty filled in, rested on his chest. The pencil was still wedged between his fingers.

Across the room, Cheapdog, quite ready to begin the day, was perched on his hind legs, his paws resting on the windowsill, the nub of his tail twitching at the prospect of joining some action in the backyard.

It wasn't supposed to be like this.

Zack's first thought of the morning was the same as the last he could remember from the night just past.

Boards of trustees . . . hospital buybacks . . . rules on length of stay . . . policies on who gets admitted and who doesn't . . . enemies . . . allies . . . realty trusts . . . Golden Circles . . . interlocking directorates . . . as if the stresses, pressures, and crises of day-to-day medicine weren't enough.

Perhaps, he mused, the real villain in the piece wasn't Frank, or the Judge, or Norman, or even Ultramed. Perhaps it was his own naiveté – his idealistic notions of illness and injury and the healing arts. Perhaps *that* was what needed overhauling.

Emotionally as well as physically drained, he shuffled to the bathroom to shave and shower, pausing to pull a quarter from behind Cheapdog's ear before letting him out.

The Wall, he knew, was just a few hours away.

Save for the lone librarian, the Ultramed-Davis record room was deserted. With thirty minutes remaining before his appointment with Jack Pearl, Zack had decided to give Toby Nelms's chart one last go-through.

Although he still felt numb and deflated from the madness of the previous night, the morning, at least, had gotten off to a decent start.

After getting Cheapdog settled on his run, he had chosen a route to the hospital that took him past a broad field of tiger lilies, lavender, and black-eyed Susans. For years Annie Doucette had allowed scarcely a day to pass without setting fresh flowers on the dining room table and mantel of the Iverson home. During her hospitalization, the family had done its best to repay her in kind.

Gathering up an armload bouquet, Zack had amused himself by composing cards he would have liked to have propped up by the vase in her ICU cubicle.

282

To Annie, with deepest apologies. Ultramed ... To Annie, my temporary patient: from Don, your temporary doctor. In repayment for your humiliation, heart attack, and broken hip.

In sharp contrast to the surreal chaos of the early morning hours, the unit had been bright and tranquil.

Annie, the Haldol largely out of her system, was fully oriented and even a bit feisty. Although she was sluggish from the analgesia she was receiving for her hip, she had talked in detail of her son and grandchildren, and of Zack's family. Of the thirty-six hours preceding her fall, she remembered nothing, except to reiterate her determination not to be sent to 'any death-trap nursing home.'

Donald Norman's cookbook cardiology had, for the moment at least, proven adequate, and while Annie's cardiac status remained shaky, it was not critical.

All in all, Zack had left the unit sensing that if anyone her age could make it through the ordeal she was facing, Annie Doucette could.

The record room librarian, an alert young brunette who was nearing the end of a pregnancy, seemed grateful to have company.

Zack signed for Toby's chart and brought it to one of several Formica-walled dictation carrels. The manila folder he set to one side contained the notes and the trickle of articles he had begun to amass on the more obscure complications of the two anesthetics the boy had received. None of those sources had offered so much as a clue to his bizarre condition.

Word by word, more meticulously even than on previous efforts, he picked through the chart.

283

Family history – unremarkable; past medical history – usual childhood immunizations and diseases, nothing else of consequence; physical exam – normal except for an incarcerated inguinal hernia; operative and anesthesia notes – routine. Nurses' notes: 'patient brought into recovery from O.R. awake, alert, and smiling; vital signs normal, no evidence for respiratory depression; pupils equal and reactive; lungs clear.'

Remarkable. Absolutely remarkable. Zack read the notes once, and then again. Toby's total stay in the recovery room was less than thirty minutes.

He asked for Suzanne's chart. Her anesthetics and doses, when adjusted for weight, were virtually identical to Toby's; so were her recovery room nurses' notes. Total time in the recovery room: forty-five minutes.

The germ of an idea began to take root. Zack checked the time. Thirteen minutes until he met with Pearl.

'Excuse me,' he called over to the librarian, 'are these records completely computerized?'

'For the last five years, yes,' she said, setting aside the romance saga she was reading. 'I think they're working on the five years before that.'

'Well, supposing I wanted to get, say, a list of all the gallbladder patients operated on in the last three years?'

'No problem. Cholecystectomy is one of our codes, 3982, I think.'

'How about just the ones where Dr. Pearl was the anesthesiologist?'

The woman checked her manual.

'Dr. Jack Pearl. Physician 914. I can get the printout for you in just a minute, but it will take a while if you want me to pull the charts.' She patted her belly. 'As you can see, I'm walking for two.'

'Your last month?'

'Last two weeks, I hope.'

'Well, if it's too much trouble—'

'No, no. We both need the exercise.'

'I hate to make it harder on you, but could I have the first few right away, and them come back in, say, an hour to check on the rest?'

'Sure. At this hour of the morning, this place isn't exactly humming.'

She was already typing commands into the computer.

By eight-thirty, Zack had scanned nine charts out of thirty-one. He slipped the notes he had taken into his folder and promised to return for the rest. Despite his lack of sleep, he felt energized – keyed up and very sharp.

His idea had provided no definite answers. But now, at last, he knew he had some damn good questions.

If Jack Pearl had made any attempt to straighten up his office before Jack's arrival, he had failed miserably. The small, windowless space between the O.R. suite and the recovery room was cluttered with journals and scraps of paper, and smelled heavily of coffee and stale cigarettes. Half-filled ashtrays, one with a butt still smoldering, graced two corners of the desk, and opened, cellophane-wrapped packets of Kleenex were everywhere.

Pearl himself, sporting a wrinkled green polo shirt, was nearly dwarfed behind the pile of reprints, texts, and notebooks on his desk. The hand he extended was cadaverous.

Regardless of how skillful an anesthesiologist Pearl was, it was difficult for Zack to imagine his fastidious brother hiring such a man.

'So,' Pearl said, his voice an annoying cross between Peter Lorre and, perhaps, Carol Channing, 'I see you are an early morning person, too.'

'Actually, I'm more a mid-afternoon person,' Zack replied. 'Thanks for making the time to see me.'

'No big deal. You want some coffee? There's a machine right down the hall.'

'No. Thanks, though.'

Zack noticed a stained Mr. Coffee crammed to the side of one bookshelf, but saw no evidence of filters or coffee.

'So, Iverson, what's on your mind?'

Pearl, sniffling every twenty or thirty seconds, stubbed out what was left of the smoldering cigarette as he was cuing up a fresh one. He was a man in constant motion, wiping his nose, smoking, or fiddling with the papers on his desk. He was also, Zack felt, somewhat effeminate.

Though they had done one case together, and had spoken briefly after Suzanne's surgery, this was their first contact of any substance.

The office, for all its disarray, was somehow barren and sterile. There were no diplomas or certificates on the wall, no photographs or mementos on the shelves. Zack felt an instant, immense curiosity about the little man, but he had already abandoned any notion of small talk – even nonthreatening questions about his background. Nothing in Pearl's manner encouraged such an approach.

'I need to discuss a case with you,' Zack began.

'Okay, shoot.'

'It's an eight-year-old boy named Toby Nelms. Jason Mainwaring repaired an incarcerated hernia in him almost a year ago. You did the anesthesia.'

'No bells,' Pearl said.

'Here's a Xerox of most of his chart.'

Zack passed the copy across and waited as Pearl flipped through it.

'Seems pretty cut and dried to me.' Pearl hesitated, and then looked up, his brow pinched in thought. 'Cut and dried. That was sort of a joke, wasn't it?' He thought some more. 'Pretty good joke, too, if I do say so myself. Pretty good.'

His laugh was a cackle. Zack smiled, but otherwise made no attempt to join in.

'Pentothal and isoflurane. Is that pretty routine for cases like Toby's?'

'Routine enough,' Pearl said. 'Why?'

'Well . . .' Zack rubbed at his chin and silently counted to five. 'I have reason to believe that the kid wasn't asleep during his surgery.'

Pearl's listless eyes flashed.

'That's ridiculous!' he snapped.

'Maybe, but I think it's true. He remembers details of the operation that there's no reason for him to know. And to make matters even more interesting, for the past six months he's been reliving the whole thing.'

Pearl was ashen.

'What?'

'He's having flashbacks in which he reexperiences his surgery, only in a terrifying, distorted way. It's as if his preoperative fears have become fused with the actual procedure. Instead of having his hernia fixed, he has his testicles and his penis cut off, again

287

and again. And each time, Jack, he feels the pain. Every bit of it.'

'That's . . . that's insane.'

'Is it?'

'Of course it is.' Pearl took a nervous drag from his cigarette and then blew his nose. 'He's lying, or . . . or he's been watching too much television.'

'I don't think so, Jack. And neither do the boy's parents. They're *this* close to instituting some sort of action against the hospital, and, I assume, against you and Mainwaring as well.'

'And you're encouraging them in this?'

'Hell, no. The opposite.'

'Well, thank God for that,' Pearl muttered.

'But I'm determined to get to the bottom of things. That's why I'm here. The kid's very sick from what he's going through. Very sick. In fact, he may be dying.'

Pearl whistled softly through his teeth.

'Well,' he said, 'I can't help you much except to tell you that whatever is going on has nothing to do with his anesthesia. I've done thousands of cases with exactly the same stuff this boy got, and . . . nothing like this has ever happened. Nothing.'

'As far as you know,' Zack corrected.

Pearl's expression was strange.

Zack tried to gauge the reaction against those he had anticipated. Anger? Arrogance? Confusion? Concern? Defensiveness? There was no real match. Something was going on, though. Of that he was almost certain.

The man was . . . was what?

'Look, Iverson . . .' Pearl ground out his cigarette and folded his hands on the desk. His fidgeting stopped. His gaze became more direct. '. . . I want to help you, I truly do. I want to help that kid. But there's really nothing I can say. He got routine anesthesia and had a routine operation. It's as simple as that. If you want to get to the bottom of whatever's going on, then you'll just have to head off in another direction, okay?'

In that moment, Zack understood.

His muscles tensed. The sensation was so familiar. It was being on the side of a steep drop, looking for the handholds and crevasses that would guide the traverse of a rock, and then suddenly seeing the perfect line across.

Jack Pearl's attempt at sounding concerned and accommodating had missed badly. He was frightened – absolutely white with fear.

The quieter and more composed he became, the more Zack knew he was squirming. Something *was* going on. His blade had hit a nerve. Now, it was time to give it a twist.

'Jack, I'm interested in something,' he said. 'Suzanne Cole was wide awake when she reached the recovery room. The nurse's notes in his chart say that Toby Nelms was, too. How do you do that?'

Pearl shrugged.

'I just pay attention, that's all. I monitor vital signs more frequently than most anesthesiologists, so I can keep the level of anesthesia right on the edge. A rise in pulse or blood pressure, and I just turn up the gas a bit. It's a matter of experience and technique.'

'But why is it that you only seem to use that technique and experience on Mainwaring's cases?'

The anesthesiologist's hand flickered toward the pack of cigarettes and then drew back. Where minutes before he had been in constant motion, now he was rigid.

'That's nonsense,' he said.

'The recovery room nurses don't think so. They tell me his cases always come out of the O.R. lighter than the rest of ours.'

'Iverson, just what is it you're driving at?'

Easy, now, Zack warned himself. *One step at a time. No slips.*

'Look, Jack,' he said. 'I don't want to make trouble for anyone. I just want to help this kid.'

'Well, throwing darts at me isn't helping anyone. You're . . . you're barking up the wrong tree. And frankly, your innuendoes are starting to annoy me.'

Zack sighed. 'Listen, just give me a couple more minutes and I'll be out of your hair. All I want you to do is look this over and tell me what you make of it.'

With what he hoped was just enough theatrical flair, Zack slid the notes he had just prepared from his folder and handed them across.

Pearl scanned the sheet for only a few seconds before he snatched up his cigarettes. His hands were shaking and his heavy breathing blew out the match before it could ignite his smoke.

'Just what in the hell is this supposed to be?' he asked.

'You know what it is, Jack. It's a summary of nine of the gallbladder cases you've done the past two years. I have another twenty or so charts being pulled right now, and I suspect they'll confirm what this list already suggests.'

Pearl looked ill. 'Which is?'

'Which is, Jack, that despite having the same procedure, and receiving, at least according to your notes, exactly the same anesthesia, Jason Mainwaring's cases came out of the O.R. looking as if they had never been asleep, whereas Greg Ormesby's were normal. Look at the recovery room times. Mainwaring's cases were transferred out anywhere from one to six hours faster than Ormesby's. . . . They didn't get the same anesthesia, Jack, did they.'

It was a statement, not a question.

'You're crazy,' Pearl said, thrusting the chart back at him. 'Those patients got exactly what I said they got. Now why don't you just take this . . . this garbage, and get out of here.'

'Okay, Jack. But you know I can't let this thing lie.'

Pearl's hands were again folded tightly on his desk.

'You do whatever you want, Iverson. I've got nothing to worry about because I haven't done anything.'

For the first time since their session began, Zack began to have some doubts. A boy was dying. He had laid that on the table. Yet Jack Pearl, if he knew anything, had refused to budge. Could he have been that far off base about the anesthetic? About the whole situation? Or was the pallid little anesthesiologist some sort of monster?

Only minutes before, answers had seemed so close. Now . . .

'Have it your way, Jack,' he said, rising. 'You know how to reach me if you think of anything.'

'I won't,' Pearl said. 'So just take your witch-hunt somewhere else.'

'He's eight, Jack. Eight years old.'

'Get out.'

Chapter 21

Frank Iverson loved his Porsche 911 with a passion and intensity beyond that which he felt for any human being, including his children. The connection, he believed, was a spiritual one – man at his finest and man's finest machine, linked in style, flexibility, and speed. There were times, in fact, like this clear, windless Monday afternoon, when he felt certain the machine was actually sensing his mood and responding to it.

With a four-hundred-dollar Minuet radar detector scanning the road, and a mental map of favorite State Police hiding spots, he swept down route 16 toward the Massachusetts state line and Leigh Baron, nudging the Porsche through eighty-mile-an-hour turns with his fingertips.

The Ultramed managing director's call to meet her at the Yankee Seaside Inn, just over the border, had come this morning, only minutes after Frank had learned from Mother of his two-place leap in the national standings. Almost certainly, a promotion of some sort – probably to regional director – was in the offing.

The place for their meeting, a good hour north of Boston, had been chosen to accommodate Leigh, who would be attending a management seminar there – or so she had said. There were, Frank acknowledged excitedly, other possibilities.

Time and again, over the years of their association, the spectacular redhead had hinted at an attraction for him. Perhaps now, with his stature rising in the company like a rocket, she was ready. And what an incredible prize she would be. Looks in a league with Annette Dolan's, money, power, and a brain to boot – the ultimate perk for the new Ultramed regional director.

Regional director. Frank beamed. The timing couldn't have been better. With Mainwaring's money as good as in the bank, and the nightmarish chore of juggling the hospital accounts to hide that quarter-million-dollar deficit nearly behind him, he would need the flexibility of offices in New Hampshire and Boston to set up some of the deals he had in mind.

Although the northeast region wasn't Ultramed's most lucrative, it was the fastest growing. He would be functioning in the center of the corporate spotlight. The company had set its sights on the prestige that involvement with established medical schools would bring, and there were ten of the world's most respected institutions in New England alone. In fact, only a year before, Ultramed had narrowly missed purchasing a major university psychiatric facility.

Success in getting the company's foot in *that* door, and he could pretty much write his own ticket.

And, Frank pledged, as he cruised around the Portsmouth rotary and south toward Newburyport, the first piece of business he would attend to with his newly acquired clout would be the removal from Ultramed of one Zachary Iverson. Since being taken to the cleaners in that disastrous land deal, he hadn't made too many mistakes in life. But allowing the Judge and Leigh Baron to pressure him into bringing Zack back to Sterling was easily the worst.

Frank screeched through a ninety-degree turn onto the ocean road. It might, he mused, even be worth making Zack's dismissal the condition of his accepting the new appointment. Leigh would agree or risk losing him. Making such a demand was certainly worth considering – if not now, then soon. In a matter of months, when his involvement with Ultramed amounted to little more than icing on his cake, he would have that kind of leverage anyhow.

And as the Judge loved to say, over and over again, leverage was the name of the game.

The Yankee Seaside, a two-story hotel laid out in a wide V above the rugged coast, was opulent but not garish. Frank stopped in the lobby men's room for a final check in the mirror – just in case – and then mounted the wide, circular staircase to the second floor.

The notion that Leigh Baron's call might have been social began to dissolve the moment she opened the door.

Suite 200 was a meeting room – richly appointed, with a fireplace and conversation area at one end, and an oval conference table with seating for ten nestled in the V. Huge plate-glass windows revealed a breathtaking vista of the North Atlantic.

Leigh herself was dressed for business in a lightweight burgundy suit and plain silk blouse. Her wonderful titian hair was pulled back in a tight bun, and she was wearing the tortoiseshell glasses that were sometimes replaced by contact lenses.

Still, there was no hairstyle nor manner of dress

that could obscure her spectacular good looks. And there was no way, Frank promised himself, that they would not become lovers. If not that day, then before too long.

'Frank, welcome,' she said, shaking his hand firmly, and warning him with her eyes against any other contact. 'I'm pleased you could make it down on such short notice.'

At, perhaps, five-foot-seven, she was shorter than he was by more than half a foot, but her bearing and manner neutralized that difference.

Frank felt off balance and edgy with the coolness of her greeting.

'You call, I come,' he said, taking a seat in the conversation area, across a low marble coffee table from her. He gestured to the room. 'Nice place.'

'Thanks. We own it.'

'Ultramed?'

'A subsidiary – Whiteside Travel Services.'

'Whiteside Travel? I didn't know that was Ultramed.'

'Not many people do.'

There was a door across from the one Frank had entered, and in spite of himself, his mind kept flicking to the possibility that it led to a bedroom. It would fit her style, he was thinking: a stiff, businesslike greeting, followed by mention of his recent rise in the Ultramed rankings, then word of his promotion. Suddenly, just as it seemed they were through for the day, she would reach up casually and shake free her hair.

'So, Frank,' she began, crossing her phenomenal legs and then consciously adjusting her skirt, 'you're looking well. How are things going?'

'I'm doing all right,' he answered cautiously. 'My

brother's been a bit of a pain, but it's nothing I can't handle as long as you and Ultramed back me up.'

'We always back up our administrators, especially those with the sort of track record you have. I assume you saw the new figures we just posted in Mother?'

Frank smiled. Step two of the scenario was unfolding.

'I told you I'd make it,' he said, feeling a surge of confidence.

'No, Frank,' she corrected. 'I told *you*. Remember? I want you to know how pleased we all are with the job you've done. Especially me, since I'm the one who first saw your potential and pushed for your appointment. Your success makes me look good.'

And my promotion will make you look even better, he thought.

The scent of her, even at a distance, had begun to fill his head, making it hard to concentrate. He would be the best – the very best she ever had.

'Now,' she said, 'what's this about your brother?'

'Oh, nothing.' He wished he had not brought up Zack until their business was concluded. 'He just doesn't have, I don't know, the team attitude, I guess, to make it with Ultramed. He's been nothing but a disruption since he arrived in Sterling.'

'What sort of disruption?'

Oh, Christ, never mind him. Just get on with it. A hundred miles from Sterling, and his brother was getting in the goddamn way.

'Hey, it's no big deal, Leigh. Like I said, I can handle it.'

'Tell me, please.'

Frank sighed.

'Okay,' he said. 'It's your dime. Zack's been constantly clashing with other doctors. He goes out of his way to undermine my authority, and he won't listen to anyone's reason. I tried to tell you he was going to be trouble.'

'Yes, I remember.'

'He always has been. I'll take care of it, though. Just as soon as we finish our business here, I'll take care of it.' He gestured about the room again. 'You know, this place sort of reminds me of a great little inn in Provincetown. I think you'd love it.'

Her eyes hardened.

'Frank,' she said, 'I want you to listen to me, and listen carefully. At this particular moment, as far as you're concerned, I'm Ultramed. You work for me. If you want to continue working for me, you'll stop mentally undressing me and pay attention to what this meeting's all about.'

'But—'

'It's not going to happen, Frank. Get that through your head. I have a husband I'm perfectly happy with. Understand?'

Numbly, Frank nodded.

'Good.' She reached across and squeezed his hand. 'Now just settle back and let's get down to business, because I'm afraid you have a problem to take care of.'

Her voice was grim.

Frank sensed a dreadful sinking in his gut.

'What sort of problem?' he asked.

'This letter arrived early this morning by messenger,' she said. 'I assume, since you haven't mentioned it yet, that it will come as a surprise.'

The moment Frank recognized the Judge's letterhead, an annoying whine began building in his head. By the time he had finished reading, the noise was a screech.

He scanned the document, and then read it again more slowly. It was, as Leigh had surmised, a total surprise.

An audit . . . When? . . . It was crazy.

Frank squeezed his temples, trying to quiet the noise as he struggled to concentrate, to understand what was happening, and why.

The whole thing was crazy . . . fucking crazy. . . .

The buyback threat he could deal with. The Judge was a bastard, but he was still only one vote. The board could be had. A member at a time, the board could be had. But until Mainwaring came through, an audit was out of the question. Absolutely out!

'Frank?'

. . . It was Zack again. It was that goddamn scene with Norman that had pushed the Judge over. . . .

Frank's teeth were clenched so tightly that his jaw ached.

. . . Who in the hell did they think they were dealing with?

'Frank, are you all right?'

'Huh? Oh, sure. I'm just furious, that's all.'

'I'm not too happy about it, either. Any idea why your father wouldn't have spoken to you about this?'

Frank snorted a laugh.

'Only dozens,' he said.

. . . Regional director . . . Leigh . . . the flexibility . . . the leverage . . . the power . . .

He had driven down with such high hopes. He would be driving back with nothing – nothing but headaches.

Fuck 'em, he thought viciously. The Judge *and* his brother. *Fuck 'em both.*

'Do you have anything to drink in this place?' he asked.

'Just coffee, Frank. You want that?'

'Yeah, okay. No, no, forget it.'

He stood and stalked to the window, his fists opening and closing at his sides.

'Frank,' Leigh said evenly, 'you have to calm down. We've got to know we can count on you to take care of this. Ultramed has too much at stake right now to take any backward steps. The competition is just waiting for a screw-up that they can use to turn prospective acquisitions against us. So just stay calm. This isn't such a big surprise, if you think about it. We expected when your father insisted on a buyback clause that he'd probably make some sort of move like this. He's a controller. That's his style.'

'Tell me about it,' Frank said bitterly, still staring out at the Atlantic.

'The question is whether he's just playing his game, or whether he really intends to fight. Any ideas about that?'

Frank turned back to her.

'It's a bluff,' he said.

'And that business about Beaulieu's widow?'

'Also a bluff. If Beaulieu had anything of substance, I would have heard about it long before this. It's the same sort of crap my father's been pulling since as far back as I can remember.'

'Can you handle him?'

'You're damn right I can. There isn't going to be any goddamn audit.'

'What?'

'I said I'll take care of it.'

He cursed his slip, and silently cautioned himself to be more alert.

'This is just another of his little tests,' he said. 'I've taken them before.'

They were underestimating him. Zack, the Judge, even Leigh. They were underestimating him badly, and they would see. They would all see. He was younger and stronger than his father, and he had learned the lessons of the man well.

'We're counting on you,' Leigh said. 'We want this whole business resolved before the board meets.'

'It will be.'

'Good. I'll be watching. It means a great deal to me to have you do this right. And it goes without saying that it means a great deal to you, too, yes?'

'When this is all over,' Frank said stonily, 'I want my goddamn brother out of Ultramed. I would fire him right now, but until this business with my father is resolved, I don't want to make any moves that might set off the Judge all over again.'

'I agree. Above all, you've got to keep things cool. . . .'

Her tone softened.

'. . . Listen, Frank, you deal with this smoothly, and you'll have our blessing to get rid of your brother if that's what you want. In fact, prove you can handle your father, and you can consider your potential with this company unlimited.' She smiled at him. 'Unlimited, Frank . . .'

'I understand.'

'Good.' She stood then. 'I want to be kept abreast of what's going on.' She nodded toward the Judge's letter. 'I don't like surprises.'

'I understand,' he said again. 'There won't be any.'

'In that case, Frank, you have a very bright future with our company.'

A minute passed after the door to suite 200 closed behind Frank. Leigh Baron poured a weak bourbon and water from the room's well-stocked credenza. Then she turned to the intercom, inconspicuously placed on an end table.

'It's okay, Ed,' she said. 'He's gone.'

Edison Blair, the CEO of RIATA International, entered the room from the inner office where he had been listening and crossed directly to the bar. He was nearing fifty but looked ten years younger, with close-cut, sandy hair, a lean, almost slight frame, and a deceptively boyish face.

His personal worth, estimated by various sources to be between twenty and thirty million, was actually closer to twice that, and was growing as rapidly as his young corporation.

'Unlimited potential. I like that little touch at the end,' he said. 'He thinks you were referring to yourself, you know.'

'Of course I know. I picked up all the tools I needed to deal with Frank Iverson in Men 101. Take away his vanity, and he's got nothing. With men like him, you've always got to leave the carrot.'

'I'll remember that. So,' he went on, 'what do you think?'

'Dunno. I have my doubts.'

'I've only met this Judge Iverson once, but from what I sensed of the man, my money's on him.'

Blair poured a shot of José Cuervo Gold Tequila, sniffed it once, and downed it in a single, quick gulp.

'I agree,' Leigh said, 'but I think it's worth waiting a bit before we play out our hand. Who knows? Maybe Frank'll pull it off. He's been a hell of a surprise so far – to everyone but me, that is.'

'It's lucky we don't have too many more surprises like him working for us, Leigh. It's not exactly optimal business practice to carry an administrator who embezzles a quarter of a million dollars from you.'

'Come on, Ed. He's made ten times that much for us already, and you know it. Our accountants haven't found so much as a missing penny since that one time. From the scrambling he's been doing, they think he's buying time to replace that money, and so do I. Either way, it's our ace in the hole.'

'So we wait?'

'We wait.'

'Leigh, I don't want us losing that hospital.'

'We're not going to lose anything. You can count on it.'

Edison Blair eyed her for a moment.

'I am,' he said.

Chapter 22

Disappointments and hard times had dogged Jack Pearl most of his life. From as far back as he could remember, he had been different – an outsider.

For one thing, he was an insomniac, a pathologic insomniac.

As a youth, his parents would scold him for being in the basement at four o'clock in the morning, fiddling with his chemistry set. Later that same day, he would be reprimanded and sent home for falling asleep in class. His condition had led to threats of expulsion on any number of occasions, and he well might have been expelled were he not, thanks to an IQ in the 160s, the best student in his school.

Making matters even more difficult for Pearl during those school years was the gradual emergence of his homosexuality. And even within that subset he was a fringe player, preferring much younger boys and their photographs to any more threatening entanglements.

In college, no roommate lasted more than a few weeks with his bizarre biologic rhythms and deepening melancholia. His dormitory room walls were decorated with posters and photos of his special heroes: Napoleon, Dickens, Edison, Churchill, Kafka, and Proust, none of whom, according to the first of his therapists, had ever enjoyed so much as one normal night's sleep.

That an insomniac should have chosen anesthesia as his life's work was one of the few pleasant ironies in Pearl's life; that one should have developed Serenyl, the quintessential sleep-inducing agent, was the ultimate irony of all.

The Serenyl odyssey had begun years before, in Iquitos, a jungle village by the headwaters of the Peruvian Amazon, where Pearl had accepted a six-month medical mission appointment as a means of escaping yet another disastrous situation in yet another hospital. Within a few weeks of his arrival, he had developed an intense fascination with the drugs used by medicine men, and in particular, with a plant alkaloid used by the most mystical 'doctors' in the region to induce a purgative state of deep hypnosis in their followers.

The moment Pearl first witnessed the incredible substance in action, the lack of direction and purpose in his life was at an end.

Two years of meticulously dissecting the active component in the alkaloid and modifying its composition led him to the synthesis of Serenyl – a structurally unique anesthetic, fully as remarkable as was its chemical forebear.

Now, for the first time since he conceived of its application, synthesized it, patented it, and adjusted its delivery and dosage in actual O.R. situations, Pearl's Serenyl was under attack.

It was five in the morning. An hour before, Pearl had given up trying to sleep and had brewed himself a pot of coffee. In the nearly twenty-four hours since his confrontation with Zack Iverson, he had slept, perhaps, two. Familiar feelings of loneliness and isolation – feelings he had been able to keep reasonably in check since moving to Sterling – had surfaced and were beginning to smother him.

The first glow of dawn was spilling over the valley as he wrapped himself in a blanket, padded across his dew-slicked yard, and settled onto a slat-backed chair. He wondered if a sleeping pill of some sort might be in order. With Mainwaring gone to Atlanta, the surgical load was light enough for his associate and their nurse anesthetist to handle.

He could call in sick and take a couple of hundred milligrams of Seconal. It had been years since he had taken a drug of any kind – he hated feeling the loss of control – but this might well be the time.

He had been thinking too hard, his mind poring over and over the evidence Frank's brother had thrown at him, frantically trying to assess the extent of the threat and to find fault in the man's logic.

Pinpointing even potential errors in Zack Iverson's reasoning had not been easy.

Pearl lit his fifth cigarette of the hour, searched about for a packet of Kleenex, and finally wiped his nose on the corner of the blanket. Why was it, he wondered, that every time life had started looking the least bit bright for him, every goddamn time, something or someone had come along to screw it up? *Why?*

Most aggravating of all to him was that this time, from the very beginning, he had seen the potential for trouble and had discussed his concerns with his partners.

He had warned them that Serenyl's marvelously diminished recovery time – the most distinctive of its many attributes – was also its Achilles' heel. The rest of the properties that set it apart from other anesthetics, injected or inhaled, were all unwanted side effects it did *not* have. He had even suggested using the anesthetic on other surgeon's patients, so that should questions arise, his technique, and not the drug, would be the focus of any suspicion.

But Frank and Mainwaring had been obstinate in their demand for absolute secrecy. In fact, both men had pooh-poohed his concerns and had laughed at the notion that anyone at Ultramed-Davis might be sharp enough, or interested enough, to put things together.

They hadn't counted on Zachary Iverson.

Pearl knew that he was drifting in over his head. Over a lifetime of turmoil he had developed something of a sixth sense about such things.

He should have been on the phone to Frank the moment Zack Iverson walked out of his office. But he had needed time to think – not so much about the gallbladder cases Iverson was reviewing, or even about the implications of the possible discovery of Serenyl, but about the chances that this child, this Toby Nelms was, in fact, suffering from a complication of his anesthesia.

Serenyl was the achievement of Pearl's lifetime – the validation of his entire chaotic and harried existence. It simply had to be flawless.

It was Mainwaring's promise, in writing, that Pearl would eventually receive credit for his work, that had brought him to Sterling. That Frank Iverson had arranged for him to be paid handsomely for his discovery when others had threatened to prosecute him for even working on it, was only icing on the cake.

Of course, Pearl acknowledged grudgingly, Frank Iverson had also smoothed over his past difficulties – most notably a dicey piece of business involving a politician's son in Akron. But without

Mainwaring's promise, even the lure of escaping *that* mess would not have been enough to make him move to a place like Sterling, much less to share the Serenyl patent.

But share that patent he had.

And now, like it or not, Pearl knew that he had to talk to Frank about his brother *and* Toby Nelms. They had looked at every possible immediate complication of Serenyl – renal effects, liver function, pulmonary function – and had found none. It had been sloppy not to have been conducting a long-range retrospective survey as well.

But dammit, Pearl rationalized, the drug had persistently functioned so perfectly....

Well, now he would simply have to make his partners understand that they had made a mistake; thank God it was not a fatal one. They merely had to go back and do the study they should have been doing from the beginning.

With just a little investigation, just a hundred or so calls to patients who had received the anesthetic, Pearl knew he could determine if Toby Nelms was a coincidence or a problem. Nobody would even have to know why he was conducting the survey.

And if there was a problem with Serenyl – if a second case like Toby Nelms was identified – almost certainly, he could fix it. He knew every molecule of the drug.

All he needed was the chance.

Pearl stood and paced nervously about the yard, mindless of the damp, which had already soaked through his cloth slippers.

He had a decent handle on Jason Mainwaring. In a sense, they were allies. The surgeon was a haughty, privileged bastard, but he was far more bark than bite. In fact, with his company's money on the line, he would probably demand that this loose end be tied up before consummating their deal.

Pearl stubbed his cigarette into the lawn and shakily lit another.

It was Frank Iverson he feared.

For as long as he could remember, wherever he had lived, whatever he had been doing, there had been Frank Iversons. They had pushed him in the schoolyard and called him names; they had sent flunkies to trip him and had stood laughing with their girlfriends as he clutched at the bloody scrapes on his knees and elbows; later in life they had loomed behind their desks, shaking their manicured fingers at him and telling him that there was no room in their institutions for 'his type.'

And however much *this* Frank Iverson's outward concern and intervention had helped him, Pearl knew better than to trust him. It was Serenyl, and Serenyl alone, that maintained the man's civility and support.

For nearly two years their work had gone on without a single hitch. It would take care and patience to convince Iverson of the need to hold off on the sale.

But what were a few weeks, Pearl reasoned desperately, or even a few months, compared with the importance of the anesthetic to medicine? In the end, even Frank would have to understand that.

Understand. Pearl shuddered at the notion. One of the more unpleasant constants in life had been that, where he and the things that were important to him were concerned, the Frank Iversons had never understood.

There were still several hours before Iverson

would even be at his office. Until then, there was nothing he could do.

He badly needed to relax.

Glancing at his watch, he crossed the yard and entered the cellar of his rented bungalow through the metal bulkhead. The basement, dusty and unfinished, was illuminated by a single, bare bulb, suspended from the ceiling.

Pearl took a screwdriver from his toolbox, knelt down behind the oil burner and pried out a loosened segment from the cinderblock wall. Creating the hiding place had been one of his first priorities after moving in.

He moved several dozen vials of Serenyl and the notebook outlining its synthesis off to one side of the space and withdrew one of two cigar boxes stuffed with photographs. Next, he carefully replaced the cinderblock and shuffled to his room.

Settling onto his bed, he undid his robe, and then, one at a time, drew certain photos from the box.

By the third one, Pearl's hand had slipped down the front of his pajama pants and begun gently to massage himself. Iverson had demanded, none too kindly, that he steer absolutely clear of any involvement with boys, or for that matter, with any men in the area. Without the photographs, he would have gone insane.

The ones he selected this morning were the very best in his collection – those he had taken himself.

In minutes, his growing arousal had begun to dispel some of the fears and loneliness. It would all work out, he told himself. Whatever words he had to find to convince Iverson, he would find.

He produced a five-by-seven in which three beautiful boys were frozen in a montage he had carefully designed. That afternoon in East St. Louis had been incredible – one of the very best.

Slowly, Pearl's eyes closed, his movements intensifying as his fantasies took flight.

Being different wasn't easy. It never had been. But as best he could, as he always had, he was making do.

And for once in his life, for once in his goddamned, troubled life, something was going to work out.

'Frank, come in, come in.'

Judge Clayton Iverson's chambers, a huge, high-ceilinged room with dark oak paneling and three walls of immaculately, aligned tomes, was as somber and intimidating as was the man himself. On the wall behind the desk, surrounding a portrait of the chief justice of the Supreme Court, were dozens of framed photographs of the Judge in variations of the same pose with three presidents, half a dozen governors, and virtually every New Hampshire politician of substance for the past half century.

There was also, near the center of the display, a colour photo of Frank, dressed in his purple and gold Sterling High School uniform, his left arm extended, his right cocked behind his ear, ready to throw.

The draperies were drawn against the midday sun.

Seated behind his massive oak desk, his thick, silver hair fairly glowing in the dim light, the Judge looked bigger than life.

Frank had feared it was an error not to have pushed for a meeting in some more neutral site. And now, as he sensed the awe that had always accompanied his visits to that room, he cursed himself for not having been more insistent.

Well, no matter, he decided. It was time for a new

Iverson to take charge. He had set passing records on the fields of a dozen different rivals; his play had quieted scores of enemy crowds. He would meet the man in his lair, or anywhere else for that matter, and he would prevail.

'So, Judge,' he began, matching, then just exceeding the firmness of the man's handshake. 'How goes it? Mom okay?'

'She's still upset about Annie, but otherwise, she's fine. In it up to here in that garden of hers.'

'She certainly does love that ol' garden. Lisette's been working on one, too, you know. You and Mom'll have to come see it. Speaking of Annie, have you by any chance seen her today?'

'Nope, tonight. I promised your mother I'd take her over.'

'Well, you're in for a pleasant surprise. She's doing great. Don Norman tells me they'll probably operate on her hip before the week's out. Now Suzanne Cole is back on the case, so Annie's got the benefit of both doctors.'

'That's good to hear, Frank. It's a shame, though, a crying shame that she had to fall like that.'

Frank tensed. As always, the man had gone right for the jugular. No bullshit, no finesse. The key to handling him would be to stay cool and not allow himself to get rattled.

'No one feels worse about what happened than I do, Judge,' he said. 'But what's done is done. Now, our job is to get her back on her feet, right? And thanks to Ultramed, we've got one of the best physical therapy departments in the state.'

'You didn't keep a tight enough rein on that doctor of yours, Frank. You're in charge. It's your hospital, just like this is my courtroom.'

311

Oh, give me a fucking break, Frank thought.

'You're right, Judge,' he said. 'Your point's well taken. I've spoken to Don, and he knows his behind is on the griddle from now on. Also, he's making arrangements to pay for any expenses Annie runs up in getting home care after her surgery.'

'Excellent, son. That's an excellent move.'

'Our hospital's come a long way since Ultramed took over, Judge. I'll do anything I have to to keep it on the right track.'

Clayton Iverson loosened his tie and ran his thumbs beneath the black suspenders that had always been part of his courtroom dress.

'I assume,' he said, 'that statement of purpose is your roundabout way of asking me to withdraw the notice I dispatched to your friend, Ms. Baron.'

Damn, but the man was tough.

'Well, as long as you brought it up . . .'

The Judge swiveled in his seat, lifted the picture of Frank from the wall, and appraised it thoughtfully.

'Remember when this was taken?' he asked. 'It was right before the state championship game against Bloomfield. The best game you ever played, I think. Six touchdown passes against the team people were calling the toughest ever in the state.'

'Five,' Frank corrected.

The Judge smiled.

'You're forgetting the thirty yarder in the third quarter that was called back for a holding penalty. On the very next play, you threw that forty-five-yard bomb to Brian Cullen. Three men hanging all over you, and you heaved that ball downfield like . . . like you were playing in the backyard.'

'That was a long time ago, Judge.' Frank was genuinely surprised and touched by the detail in the

312

man's recollection. 'You have quite a memory.'

'Son,' Clayton Iverson said, 'you'd be amazed at how much I remember from those days.' His tone was uncharacteristically wistful. 'There was a toughness to you then, Frank – a determination to be the best. You had the whole world right in the palm of your hand. Somewhere along the line, though, you started backing off, making bad choices. No, not bad,' he corrected, '*terrible*. Somewhere along the line, you lost that edge.'

'But—'

'I'm not through. The worst part of it all is that the more you struggled, the less willing you became to listen to advice. You ran up against problems, and instead of plowing through them like you used to, you tried to run around them.

'I want you to succeed here, Frank. I want that very much. But I'm not going to make it easy for you. I'm going through with that letter, and I'm going to try and find out just what went on with Guy.'

'I've told you before, Judge. Nothing went on with Guy.'

'I hope not, Frank. Don't you see? I want you to show up at that board meeting with a case for Ultramed that's so strong and so polished, no one on the board would even *think* about voting against you. This is one problem you're going to meet head on, son. And I pray to God you roll right over me.'

Frank held up his hands in frustration.

'Judge, you're just making a mess of everything. Checking up on me and the hospital, auditing our books. The people at Ultramed are watching. If they see that I can't even reason with my own father, everything I've gained these past four years will be headed down the drain. Just the fact that I was the last one to know about your letter has already made me look like an idiot.'

'Well, when Ms. Baron and her associates see the case you put together for their corporation, you will be a hero.'

'But—'

'That's the way it is, Frank.'

He swung back and replaced the photograph.

Frank felt an all-too-familiar anger and frustration begin to well up. He cautioned himself against any outburst, and reminded himself to meet strength with strength.

'Okay, Judge,' he said. 'You obviously have your mind set on this thing.'

'I do.'

'Well, then, I'd like you at least to compromise on one thing – the audit. We weren't scheduled for our general audit until next February. It will take me days to put everything together as it is, and it will throw my staff into chaos. Either cancel it or . . . or at least postpone it until next month.'

The Judge shook his head.

'Farley Berger says it's got to be done in the next day or two in order for his team to have all the figures checked over by the meeting on Friday.'

'But there's nothing in the contract that says the audit has to be done by the board meeting. Make it two weeks.'

Clayton Iverson thought for a minute.

'Okay, Frank,' he relented, 'you want two weeks, you've got two weeks.'

That's it, Judge, Frank thought exultantly. *That's it: that's all I need.*

'I'm going to beat you, you know,' he said.

'I hope so, son,' the Judge responded. 'I truly do.'

Chapter 23

For Zack, the day had resembled some of those during his residency. Two consults on the floors; assisting one of the orthopedists with a back case; admitting a three-year-old who had fallen off a swing, hit her head, and then had a seizure; and finally, seeing half a dozen patients in the office. It was the sort of pace on which, ordinarily, he thrived.

This day, it was all he could do to maintain his concentration.

Six days had passed since his initial contact with Toby Nelms, and he was still unable to put together the pieces of the child's diagnosis. For a time after his abortive interview with Jack Pearl, he had tried, as an exercise, to give the anesthesiologist the benefit of the doubt – to concoct another explanation that would jibe with the facts.

He had cancelled his schedule for the day and driven to Boston for consultations with several anesthesiologists at Muni. He had also spent four hours in the Countway Medical Library at Harvard, reviewing every article he could find on Penthothal, isoflurane, and their complications.

By the end of his search, he considered himself qualified as one of the experts in the field. Always, though, his efforts brought him back to his original hypothesis, and back to a single word: *Metzenbaums*.

Now, in a few days, he would meet again with the boy and his mother. This time, Zack knew, Barbara Nelms would not settle for evasions and half-truths. The woman was desperate. She had every right to be.

It was just after four in the afternoon. From the west, dusky mountain shadows inched up the valley toward Sterling. Zack had just finished a detailed discussion of Menière's disease with the last of his office patients.

'I know exactly what you have,' he had told the elderly man, who had come because of intermittent dizziness and a persistent, most unpleasant hum in his ears. 'Unfortunately, I also know there is very little we are going to be able to do beyond teaching you how to live with it.'

He had ordered some tests in hopes of coming upon one of the rare, treatable causes of the condition, had passed on the address of the national society dealing with Menière's, and had expressed his regret at not being able to do more. The man's disappointment was predictable and understandable, but it was nonetheless painful for Zack.

It's not going to get you, Toby, Zack vowed as he watched his crestfallen patient shuffle from the office. The practice of medicine provided more than enough of the frustration and heartache that came from having no answers. In Toby Nelms's case, the answers were there. And somehow, someone was going to supply them. *Just hang in there, kid. Whatever's going on, whatever they've done to you, it's not going to get you.*

Zack sent his office nurse home early, alerted the answering service that he would be on his beeper, and spread the boy's folder on his desk. Most of what he was rereading he knew by heart. After just a few minutes, he snatched up the phone and called Frank's office. There was no alternative but to share his suspicions with his brother and try to enlist his help in another confrontation with Pearl.

Frank was gone for the day, and his secretary had no idea where he was or when he would be back.

A call to Mainwaring's office gave him only the answering service, and the information he already had, that the surgeon was out of the state until the following Monday and was being covered by Greg Ormesby.

'Answers,' he canted, drumming a pen on the edge of his desk. 'There have got to be answers. . . . Where are you, Jason? . . . Who are you? . . . What do you know?'

On an impulse, he checked his hospital directory and dialed the pathology department. Takashi Yoshimura answered on the first ring.

'Kash,' he said, 'if you can do it, and if it wouldn't put you on the spot, I need a name. . . .'

Ten minutes later, Zack was on the line with a Dr. Darryl Tarberry at Johns Hopkins.

'Dr. Tarberry,' he said after explaining how he had come by the man's name, and after listening patiently to ebullient praise of Kash Yoshimura and his work, 'I *am* calling for a recommendation, but not for Dr. Yoshimura. Fortunately, we already have him on our staff. The man I'm interested in is Dr. Jason Mainwaring. Kash said you might have worked with him when he was at Hopkins.'

For a few seconds there was only silence.

'Who did you say you were?' Darryl Tarberry asked finally.

From his recollection of the man, Yoshimura had

guessed that Tarberry was in his mid-sixties by now. But from the harsh crackle in his voice, Zack wondered if he might be years older than that.

'My name's Iverson. Zachary Iverson,' he repeated. 'I'm a neurosurgeon, and I'm on the credentials committee here.'

Again there was a pause.

'Mainwaring's applying for surgical privileges at your place?'

'That's right.'

'Well, I'll be,' Tarberry said. 'Where did you say that hospital of yours was?'

'New Hampshire, sir. Listen, I don't want to put you on the spot, Dr. Tarberry, but we would certainly appreciate any information you can give us.'

'This call being recorded?'

Zack groaned.

'No, I promise you it isn't.'

'I'm not putting anything on paper, now.'

'That's fine.'

'Mainwaring and his lawyers had this place tied up in knots for I don't know how long. Damn lawyers. Ended up costing the hospital a small fortune to settle even though we were one hundred percent in the right as far as I'm concerned. One of my colleagues got ulcers from it. I swear he did. I don't want that happening to me. I'm too damn old for that kind of nonsense.'

'You have my word.'

'Your word . . . Iverson, huh. That Swedish?'

'English. It's English,' Zack said, staring upward for some sort of celestial help.

'Well, Iverson, I don't know all the details.'

'That's okay.'

'And as far as I'm concerned, we never had this conversation.'

'Promise.'

'Well,' the man said, drawing out every letter of the word, 'let me tell you first that Mainwaring may be the most ambitious sonofabitch God ever put in a mask and gown, but he is one fine surgeon. Maybe the best I've seen, and I've seen plenty.'

'Go on,' Zack said. . . .

After fifteen minutes of prodding and cajoling, Zack felt he had extracted as much from Darryl Tarberry as he was likely to – at least over the phone. There was more to the story, he knew. Probably much more. But even so, a huge piece had fallen into place in the puzzle of Toby Nelms.

Zack was just finishing writing a synopsis of the interrogation when the door to his waiting room opened and closed.

'I'm here,' he called out.

'What a coincidence. So am I.'

Suzanne appeared at his office door, wearing a lab coat over an ivory blouse and ankle-length, madras skirt.

'Got a minute?' she asked.

'For you? Years.' He set the Tarberry notes in Toby Nelms's folder and pushed it to one side of the desk. 'Trouble with Annie?'

'No, no. Nothing like that. She's doing amazingly well. I think Sam Christian's going to do her hip tomorrow.'

'Excellent. I'm so pissed off about what's happened to her. Everytime I think about what Don Norman did, I want to hunt him down and flatten that pudgy little nose of his.'

'Zack, I'm as upset as you are about Annie, but I

don't see how you can lay all the blame on Don. He didn't do anything with malicious intent.'

'That depends on your definition of malicious. He was sedating her so that she wouldn't object to being sent to a nursing home, so that Ultramed could continue to rake in profits from her care. If that's not malicious, I don't know what is.'

'Hey, easy does it, okay?'

'What do you mean?'

'That's your opinion. But it happens not to be everyone's. Couldn't you just let up on this place a bit?'

'Huh?'

'Zack, Frank just left my office.'

'So, that's where he's been. I've been trying to reach him.'

'He's really upset with you.'

'I know. Is that why he went to see you?'

'As a matter of fact, it is. He . . . he wanted me to talk to you – to ask you to let up on your criticism of this place.'

'He could have come and asked me himself.'

'He says he tried.'

'He was drunk. He threatened me. That's not what I would call the optimal approach. . . . So, now he's chosen to involve you. I can't believe this place.'

'Zachary, I didn't come up here to pick a fight. I just wanted to do what I could to smooth things over between you two. I owe Frank a lot. I thought you understood that from all I told you of what happened to me.'

'Sorry,' Zack mumbled. 'If I'm touchy, I guess it's that I just wish things were different between me and Frank.'

'Well?'

'Suzanne, I can't help it if Frank thinks it's my fault that the Judge is pushing the board of trustees to buy back the hospital from Ultramed.'

It was clearly the first she had heard of that development.

'My God, Zack, you can't let him do that.'

'First of all,' he said. 'I have no more control over that man than Frank or anybody else does. And second, why not?'

'Well . . . well because,' she stammered. 'If the board threw Ultramed out, Frank would be ruined.'

'Nonsense. He knows his job. He could do it just as well for a community corporation as he could for an operation like Ultramed. Better, probably. Suzanne, listen to me. Something's wrong around here. Something's terribly wrong.'

'Dammit, Zachary, what is the matter with you? Don't you have regard for anyone but yourself? I come here to ask you to let up on a man who is partly responsible for saving my career, to say nothing of his being your brother, and all you can do is . . . is tear down his hospital.'

'It's not *his* hospital. Look, I don't want to get into a fight. I have too much on my mind.'

'Like what?'

Every instinct was clamoring for him to change the subject, to keep his theories to himself – at least as long as they were no more than that. He stared down at his hands. Darryl Tarberry's revelations about Jason Mainwaring were too fresh in his mind.

'Suzanne,' he said slowly, 'I have reason – good reason – to believe that human experimentation is being conducted at this hospital.'

'Now that is the wildest—'

'And,' he cut in, 'I have just as much reason to believe that you might have been one of the subjects.'

Suzanne listened in wide-eyed disbelief as he recounted his experiences with Toby Nelms and Jack Pearl, his brief study of the gallbladder surgery performed by Mainwaring and Greg Ormesby, and finally, his conversation with Tarberry.

'Apparently, a woman died of an anaphylactic reaction to a local anesthetic she received in Mainwaring's office. Mainwaring claimed it was Xylocaine, but there was plenty of documentation that the woman had received that drug on numerous occasions with no problems. A nurse of his, who was very upset with what happened, charged that Mainwaring had been testing something out that wasn't Xylocaine. Although investigators could never prove that was true, they did apparently discover that our friend Jason was part owner of a pharmaceutical house somewhere in the South.'

'This is crazy!' Suzanne said. 'Did that man you talked to at Hopkins happen to know what company this might have been?'

'He couldn't remember.'

'He . . . couldn't . . . remember . . . Zack, this is exactly the sort of thing Frank was protesting. These are terrible, disruptive charges you're making on very little hard evidence.'

'I'm not making any charges,' he said, feeling his composure beginning to slip. 'I'm sharing a disturbing theory with a friend whose clinical judgment I value and trust. I would think you'd be frantic at the thought that someone might have been fooling around with your body while you were asleep.'

'Well, I'm not frantic, I'm worried – about you.

Zack, you've only been here a couple of weeks. In that time, you've clashed with Wil Marshfield, had words with Jason, fought with Don Norman, upset your brother, fostered a move to buy back the hospital, and now, on nothing more than the flimsiest circumstantial evidence, you're accusing the finest surgeon and anesthesiologist on the staff of a terrible crime.'

Zack pushed back his chair.

'Suzanne, listen to me—'

'No, you listen. How do you explain the fact that there hasn't been one other case like Toby Nelms's?'

'I . . . I don't know. Maybe it's a rare complication of whatever it is they're using. Maybe people have had episodes like this but they've happened in other places, or haven't been brought to a doctor's attention. Maybe there's some sort of sensory trigger involved that just doesn't happen to everyone. You told me yourself that you hadn't been feeling right since your operation.'

'I've been tired. That's a far cry from having a psychotic seizure.'

'What about that episode in the field?'

'What are you talking about?'

'You went blank.'

'I did nothing of the sort.'

'You did. It was as if someone threw a switch, and all of a sudden you weren't there.'

'Zack, this is crazy. You've got to back off. You've hit this place like an earthquake.'

'Suzanne, that child is dying.'

'Maybe so. But it's not from something Jason or Jack Pearl did to him. One other case, Zachary. Just find me one other case like Toby Nelms and I'll

323

listen. Even then I may not believe you, but I'll listen. In the meantime, I think you owe your brother, and all the rest of us for that matter, a little breathing room.' She stood up. 'Back off, Zack. Please. Do what you can to keep your father from destroying what your brother has worked so hard to build, and give us all a rest.'

She snatched up her handbag and, without waiting for a response, raced from the office.

For a time, Zack sat numbly, staring out the window at the waning afternoon. *A trigger, or a sequence of triggers.* Perhaps that was the key. Suzanne had no recollection of the episode at the Meadows during their picnic, but something weird had happened to her. A switch *had* been thrown. But what? A word? A sound? A smell?

Zach drummed his long fingers on the desk. He felt his thoughts darting out at the answer again and again, like the tongue of a snake. But each time not quite far enough . . . not quite far enough. . . .

Finally, he slid Toby Nelms's file back in front of him and opened it, once again, to the first page.

'They're not going to get you, kid,' he whispered. 'I swear, they're not going to get you.'

Even among the best of the old New England inns, the Granite House was special. The slanting, hard-wood floors, beamed ceilings, and oddly shaped rooms, each with a stone hearth, were rated by the guides as only slightly less wonderful than the cuisine and service.

Frank Iverson had chosen the spot carefully for his first encounter with the Davis Regional trustees; specifically, this night, a successful banker named Bill Crook, and Whitey Bourque, the rotund, often outspoken manger of the local A & P.

The evening had gone well – better than he had dared hope.

He had orchestrated the conversation beautifully, weaving accounts of Ultramed's successes and plans in with reminiscences of some golf games he had shared with Crook, and some interested queries about Bourque's daughter, Renée, one of the finest young horsewomen in the area.

Now, as they sat in the otherwise deserted Colonial Room, sipping cognac and smoking after-dinner cigars, he felt ready to nail the two men down.

There were twenty-one members of the board. Frank considered six of them to be all but in the bag – either because of their relationship with him or because of business they would lose if Ultramed was forced out of Sterling. Allowing for two no-shows at the meeting – and given the board's track record, that was a conservative estimate – he would need only three or four more votes to block the buyback regardless of the Judge's position.

And at least half of those votes were right there at the table, sitting, it seemed, in the palm of his hand. All he needed to do, ever so carefully, was close his fingers.

Unlimited potential . . .

Frank allowed himself the flicker of a smile.

Don't go too far away, Ms. Baron, he thought, eyeing the two men over his snifter. *I'm coming.*

'They sure know how to do it right here, don't they,' he began.

Bill Crook, logy from the meal and the drinks, mumbled agreement. He was a slap-on-the-back Ivy Leaguer with a reputation for enthusiastically supporting the ideas of others while never coming up with an original one of any substance.

Whitey Bourque belched and dabbed at his lips with the corner of his napkin. Frank noticed the tangles of fine veins reddening his cheeks.

'Good beef,' he humphed. 'Nothing we don't have at the store, but good.'

'Lisette always said yours is the only place in town to buy meat, Whitey,' Frank aid. 'As a matter of fact, I think I'll have her stop by tomorrow and stock up our freezer. . . . So, now, before we break up and head home to our families, I want to be sure I've answered all the questions either of you might have about just what Ultramed has on the drawing board for our hospital. Bill?'

The banker thought for a moment, and then shook his head.

'Sounds like a pretty ambitious and exciting set of objectives to me, Frank,' he said.

'And don't forget for a moment that Ultramed plans to finance every one of these projects with local money. Sterling National Bank money, if I have my way. Whitey?'

Bourque shook three sugars into a cup of coffee and drank it in one gulp.

'No questions,' he said.

'I'll have details of our proposal for competitive bidding on our dietary service in your hands by the end of the month.'

'That'll be fine, Frank. Fine.'

'Excellent.' Frank glanced at the check, and then handed it and his Gold Card to the waitress. 'Bring us a few more of those little mints, honey,' he said. He cleared his throat and turned back to the table. 'So, gentlemen, I've enjoyed sharing this meal with you both, and I presume Ultramed and I can count on your support at the board meeting Friday.'

The two men looked at one another, silently selecting a spokesman. Whitey Bourque was chosen.

'Well, Frank,' he said, 'all we can tell you at this time is: that depends.'

Frank felt suddenly cold. 'Depends on what?'

'On what your father comes up with these next couple of days. He called us yesterday, Frank, and asked us to keep our minds open on this business until he had checked up on a few things. I felt that considering how much help he was to me during last year's fund raiser for the new parish house, that was the least I could do.'

'And I owe him for the way he stepped in when my boy Ted experimented with that damn dago red wine and had that accident,' Crook chimed in. 'He saved the kid's buns for sure.'

'Gentlemen, please,' Frank said, struggling to keep any note of desperation from his voice. 'I'm not arguing against the good works the Judge does around this town. For goodness sakes, that's a given. And I'm proud to be his son. But it's apples and oranges. What we're talking about here is support for your hospital and the good works *we've* been doing. Renée's broken wrist, Whitey. Remember that? Or . . . or how about that coronary your mother had last year, Bill? People say that if it weren't for our new unit and our new cardiologist, she would have died.'

'I . . . I understand,' Crook said, staring down into his empty glass.

'Well?'

Whitey Bourque sighed.

'Frank, we're sorry,' he said. 'We'd like to help you out, but we gave the Judge our word we'd wait and follow his recommendation. He's the chairman of the board, and he's doin' all the legwork on this thing. All we want is what's best for Sterling. Since we're all too busy to do in-depth research of any kind, we're sort of counting on him to steer us in the right direction. I hope things work out. And whatever happens, I intend to help you and the hospital in any way I can.'

'Ditto for me, Frank,' Crook said.

'Well, then ... I guess there's nothing more I can say, is there.'

'You gave a good presentation, Frank,' Bourque said, standing. 'A damn good presentation. Your father'd be proud.'

'Hey, what the heck. We'll work it out, Whitey. I'm sure of it.'

Frank forced the words through a noose of anger and frustration tightening about his throat.

He walked the two men to the dirt parking lot, shook their hands amiably, and watched until their taillights had disappeared into the night. Then he turned and landed a vicious kick on the door of the Porsche, leaving a dent and a small scrape.

Heedless of the damage, he leapt behind the wheel and skidded from the lot, spraying a retired salesman and his wife with sand and stones.

From the moment she had heard the Porsche screech into the drive and the screen door slam, Lisette knew it was going to be another one of those nights.

With a mumbled greeting and not so much as a peck on the cheek, Frank stormed past her and into his den. She stood in the darkened hallway, waiting for the clink of ice in his glass. Frank did not disappoint her.

Now, as she brewed a pot of the herbal tea that Frank had once introduced to her as 'the only drink I ever touch after ten,' she battled the urge to bury herself in bed.

She set the pot, two cups, some sliced lemon, and some sugar wafers on a tray and carried them to the study. Frank was standing in one corner, his back to her, reading.

'Hi, what's the book?' she asked.

'Nothing.'

He shoved the volume back into the bookcase and turned to her, but she had caught enough of a glimpse to know. It was his high school yearbook.

'Frank, are you okay?'

'Yeah, sure, I'm great. Do me a favor and just leave me alone, will you?' His words were already beginning to slur.

'I brought you some tea.'

'I don't want any fucking tea.'

'Frank, please.'

'I said I don't want any goddamn tea!'

He swiped his arm across hers, sending the tray spinning across the room. Tea splattered on the wall. The fine china, a wedding gift from her mother, shattered.

Stunned, she stared at the mess.

'Frank, something's wrong with you,' she said as calmly as she could. 'You need help. Please, honey. I love you. The girls love you. For our sake, you've got to get some help.' She stepped toward him, her arms extended.

'I don't need any help!' he screamed. 'What I need is to be left alone!'

'Please.'

She took one more tentative step forward, and he hit her – a swift, backhand slap to the side of the face that sent her reeling against a chair.

'I don't need you. I don't need my fucking father. I don't need goddamn Ultramed. I don't need anyone! I'm going to make it, and nothing any of you can do is—'

He stopped in mid-sentence and looked down at her as if noticing her for the first time. Instantly, the fury in his face vanished.

'Baby. Oh, Jesus, are you all right?' he asked, moving toward her.

Lisette backed away, forcing herself not to touch the burning in her cheek.

Then she turned and bolted from the room.

Chapter 24

Leigh Baron stared thoughtfully at the receiver in her hand, and then set it gently in its cradle.

'Frank just lied to me, Ed,' she said. 'I don't like it. I don't like it at all.'

As she sipped her coffee, she gazed out of her thirtieth-story office window, across Boston harbor to the airport. It was just after eight in the morning, and traffic was, as usual, badly backed up coming into the Sumner Tunnel. She had spent the night in the city, working into the early morning on several impending Ultramed acquisitions and then catching a few hours of sleep on the fold-out in her office.

The RIATA CEO, still perspiring from his daily seven-mile run, scanned the list of the Davis Regional Hospital board of trustees.

'Which two did he meet with?' he asked.

'The top two on that sheet: Bourque and Crook. He told me just now that the session went well and that both men were as good as in the bag.'

'Those were his words?'

'Precisely. The only problem is that Stan Ogilvie, our man on the board, told me last night that Judge Iverson had contacted all of them, and that Bourque and Crook had both given their word to go along with anything he recommended.'

'So maybe Frank talked them into changing their position?'

'Possible, but doubtful. Ed, he's scrambling. I just know it. He refuses to admit that he's in over his head. No matter how big the writing on the wall becomes, he keeps thinking he's going to pull this off.'

She filled two crystal goblets with fresh orange juice and passed one over.

'This is your baby, Leigh,' Blair said.

Leigh nodded grimly. Three more New England hospitals were close to coming over, but all of them were holding out until the Davis Regional sale was final. Blair was watching her performance as closely as she was watching Frank's. And the genius behind RIATA International was hardly one to tolerate a failure of this magnitude from anyone.

'Well,' she said, 'I guess it's time I took a little trip up north.'

'I think, my friend, that is a wise decision. You've done an excellent job with Frank Iverson – an amazing job, all things considered. But it's becoming increasingly clear that the man is limited. It would seem he has gone about as far as he can go.'

'And then some,' she observed. She sighed.

'What is it?' Blair asked. 'Surely you can't be upset about pulling the plug on a man who's so blatantly put his own concerns ahead of yours or our company's?'

'No,' she said. 'But I can't help thinking that I'll miss him at all the regional meetings.'

'Miss him?'

'Yes.' She smiled wistfully. 'Frank Iverson may be a little short on principles and a little long on ego, but he's been great visuals.'

*

The pain, a gnawing, empty ache centered beneath the very tip of Frank's breastbone, had begun soon after his fight with Lisette and had instensified throughout the night. He had thrown up several times, and he suspected – although he had not turned on the bathroom light to check – that the last time had been blood.

A bottle and a half of Maalox had helped calm the burning some and enabled him to shave and dress and make it to his office in reasonable shape, but he sensed that it was only a matter of time before the searing pain resurfaced.

It was Lisette's own damn fault that he had hit her. If she had only been more patient, more understanding of the stress he was under, she could have been a wife, and not just another strain on his life.

Zack, the Judge, Mainwaring, Leigh Baron – as if he didn't have enough balls in the air without Lisette taking potshots at him; what goddamn nerve, telling him he needed to get some help when she should have been giving it to him. It was a miracle his stomach hadn't gotten fucked up long before this.

He snatched up the phone and dialed the hospital pharmacy.

'Sammy, it's Frank Iverson. What's the name of the stuff that's good for stomach troubles? . . . No, no, not that stuff, the pills . . . Cimetidine. Yeah, that's it. Listen, could you bring me up a week's supply? . . . I know it's a prescription drug, dammit. I don't need any lectures. What I need are those pills. . . . Good. And not a word about this to anyone, right?' All he needed was a rumor going around that Frank Iverson had a bleeding ulcer.

He slammed down the receiver and took another long swig of Maalox. It might have been a mistake not to have leveled with Leigh Baron about Bourque and Crook, but this battle was between him and the Judge, and the encounter with those two spineless yes-men was no more than a skirmish. By the meeting, he would have more than enough votes to block the buyback.

He thought about calling Mainwaring for a progress report. If anything could help calm down his stomach, it was a few reassuring words from him. Two hundred fifty thousand back in the Ultramed-Davis account and $750,000 left over to build on. Just the notion of that kind of money was enough to ease the queasy sensation.

He simply had to calm down, ignore Lisette's behaviour, and concentrate on the Judge and the board. The ultimate success, both within the company and without, was so close he could taste it.

He culled Mainwaring's Atlanta number from his Rolodex and was in the process of dialing when his secretary cut in on the intercom.

'Mr. Iverson, it's Annette.'

Her voice instantly stirred up images of their sensual, uncomplicated, unselfish evenings together – evenings in sharp contrast to those he had been enduring with Lisette. Annette was the perfect low-stress woman for high-stress times, and Frank made a mental note to have her work late again as soon as possible.

'Yes, Annette,' he said, 'go ahead.'

'Mr. Iverson, Dr. Jack Pearl is here to see you. He knows he doesn't have an appointment, but he says it's quite important.'

Pearl. Frank could think of nothing the distasteful little fairy could have to say that he would ever possibly want to hear.

'Annette, ask Dr. Pearl if whatever it is can wait until later on this – oh, never mind. Have him just come on in.'

Pearl, looking, as usual, as if he hadn't shaved in two days, entered Frank's office with a sheaf of papers in one hand and a cup of coffee in the other, and immediately caught his foot on the doorjamb and stumbled, sloshing most of his coffee onto the Persian rug.

'Oh shit . . . oh fuck,' he mumbled, dropping to his knees and dabbing at the spill with a handkerchief that was far from virginal.

Frank was about to insist that he simply get up and leave the mess to housekeeping. Instead, he threw Pearl a towel from the bathroom and watched with some amusement as the physician crawled about the floor, alternately swearing to himself and clucking like some obscene, gigantic chicken.

'Enough, Jack, enough,' Frank said finally. 'Take a seat. I'll have Annette get you a replacement for your coffee – unless you want to wring that towel out into your cup.' He laughed heartily. 'Sorry, Jack, I was just kidding, just kidding. Seriously, do you want some more?'

'N-No, Frank. No, thank you.'

'Okay, then. So, what is the matter of such earthshaking importance?'

Pearl shifted uncomfortably.

'Go ahead,' Frank said. 'I'm not going to bite you.'

'There's . . . um . . .'

Pearl coughed and cleared his throat.

'There've been a couple of things that have come up . . . problems . . . with Serenyl.'

Frank's eyes grew narrow and hard.

'What the fuck are you talking about, Jack?'

The anesthesiologist began to tremble.

'Well,' he managed, 'what I meant was, not problems, exactly . . . um, a . . . more like *potential* problems. I really needed to talk to you, Frank. You haven't been around.'

'Business, Jack, I had business. For Chrissake, get to the point.'

'I had a visitor in my office Monday morning, Frank' – his words began to come a bit more easily – 'a doctor who is on the verge of figuring out that Mainwaring and I aren't using the anesthetics my operative notes say we are.'

'That's impossible,' Frank said, his mind already churning through the implications of discovery at this final stage of the game.

Awkward, certainly, he concluded; perhaps even expensive if some sort of payoff was needed. But not catastrophic. The testing was complete. The whole project had been designed to make Jason Mainwaring comfortable enough with Serenyl to buy it, and in that sense, the project was already a total success.

'I warned you this might happen,' Pearl was saying. 'I warned both of you.'

'What are you talking about, Jack?'

'The recovery time. I told you and Mainwaring someone might pick up on it, but you wouldn't listen to me. And now, someone has.' His words, initially stuttered and uncertain, began spilling out like a slot machine payoff. 'And that's not all, either. There's this kid we operated on last January for a hernia, and . . . and he's been having these nightmares, and –'

'Okay, okay,' Frank said, holding his hands up, 'enough of this bullshit. I want you to slow down, calm down, go back, and start at the beginning. Got that? . . . Good. Now, first of all, Jack, exactly who are we talking about?'

'Well, Frank, it . . . it's your brother. Your brother Zachary.'

Zack again! For Frank, the minutes that followed were the purest torture. He listened impassively, struggling to maintain his concentration and composure in the face of the grotesque little man and the fireball of hatred that was tearing at his gut.

He studied the notes Pearl had brought – Zack's review of the gallbladder cases and the hospital record of Toby Nelms. Then he insisted Pearl go through the entire story again, step by step.

Midway through that recounting, he excused himself for a few minutes, citing the need to get some papers signed and in the mail to Boston. Then he strolled placidly through his outer office and down the hall to an empty men's room, where he threw up.

Twenty minutes later, he had picked up the Cimetidine and some more Maalox at the pharmacy and stood confronting himself in another men's room mirror.

As a quarterback, he had learned that plays seldom went exactly as the coaches had diagrammed them in the playbook. A lineman stumbles, and everybody's timing is thrown off; a halfback is thinking about a fight he has had with his girlfriend, and misses a crucial block.

The quarterback worth his salt always kept his head; always expected the unexpected. And it was in this area, Frank reminded himself – the instinctive, reflex ability to react and to adjust – that Frankie Iverson had been the very best.

This time, as in so many sticky situations on so many playing fields, his edge would lie in keeping a cool head. He had picked through Pearl's story a piece at a time, and realized that things weren't yet nearly as bleak as he had initially perceived.

When he returned to his office he was scrubbed, combed, and outwardly calm.

Annette Dolan, dressed in a short-sleeved pink sweater with a band of fine beadwork flowing over her breasts, looked even more alluring than usual.

Much work to do. Keep tonight open if you can.

Frank scribbled the words on a scrap of paper, signed the note with a smiley face, and set it by her elbow as he passed.

She glanced at it and, almost imperceptibly, smiled and nodded.

Now there, Frank thought, as he opened the door to his office, *was an understanding woman*.

The office was empty.

'Annette, did Dr. Pearl leave?' he asked over his shoulder.

'No. Just you,' she said.

At that moment, the toilet in his private bathroom flushed. The notion of Jack Pearl sitting on his john was enough to start the acid percolating again in Frank's gut. He would have to get housekeeping to scrub the whole place down before he so much as stepped foot in there again.

Pearl emerged from the room wiping his nose with one hand and tugging at his still-open fly with the other.

'Hope you didn't mind my using your head,

Frank,' he said. 'This whole business has really messed up my insides, and I've got the shits something awful.'

Frank smiled plastically and vowed that after the sale of Serenyl was completed, sending Jack Pearl as far from Sterling as possible would rank in priority only slightly below dealing with Zachary.

'Okay, Jack,' he said, 'tell me what it is, exactly, that you want.'

Pearl cleared his throat.

'Well, the more I've thought about the properties of the drug I built Serenyl from – the more I realize that it's possible your brother might be right about that kid.'

'That's ridiculous.'

'Why?'

'Jack, you and Mainwaring have done five hundred cases. *Five hundred!* Have you encountered even one problem?'

'No, but –'

'But what, Jack?'

'If the kid's problem is due to the drug, then it's some sort of delayed reaction. A flashback – that's what your brother called it. If he's right, maybe some others *are* having them, but they just haven't connected the episodes with the anesthetic. If I knew for sure that was going on, I could fix it, Frank. I know every molecule in that drug. I could do it.'

'Jack, please,' Frank said. 'The whole thing is absolute nonsense. The kid is having nightmares from something he saw on TV – probably on that goddamn *Nova* show. They're always showing babies being delivered and people being operated on and shit like that, for Chrissake. It's a wonder more kids haven't gotten screwed up.'

'Frank, we can check. A hundred or so calls, and we can see if anyone's having –'

'No!'

'But –'

'Jack, I've tried to be patient with you, but now I've just about had it. . . .'

Frank snapped a pencil in two for emphasis.

'Mainwaring's going to finish presenting Serenyl to his partners, and he's going to come back here, and he's going to give us each . . . half a million dollars, and we're going to give him the drug. That's how we planned it, and that's what we're going to do.'

'But –'

'No fucking buts, Jack. If you don't want to believe me when I tell you that kid is just a coincidence, that's your problem. But I'll be damned if you're going to make it mine. Now listen, and listen good: if you say one word about all this to Mainwaring or anyone else, *one fucking word*, the Akron authorities will be here to scoop up what's left of you quicker than you can blink. I got them off your back, and I can get them back on. Clear?'

Pearl wiped his nose with the handkerchief he had used on the coffee spill and lit a cigarette. Frank Iverson had him between a rock and a hard place. It was a spot he knew well.

'C-Clear,' he said.

'It had better be.' Frank shook a finger at him as he spoke. 'Because I'm telling you, Jack, I want that drug sold, and I want that money in the bank. Don't fuck with me on this one.'

'I won't,' Pearl said. 'But . . .'

'But what?'

'Frank, what harm would it do to make a few

calls? If there's a problem with Serenyl, I can fix it.
I know I ca –'

Frank sprung around the desk, grabbed the
anesthesiologist tightly by the shirt, and pulled him
up onto his tiptoes.

'Dammit, Jack, I said no!'

He shook the little man like a terrier breaking a
rat, and then slammed him back into his seat.

Pearl cowered before the onslaught.

'Okay, okay,' he whined, shielding his face.

*Why did his life always come down to scenes like
this? Why?*

'That's better,' Frank said. He patted Pearl on the
shoulder. 'That's much better. . . .' He returned to
his desk chair. 'Hey, buddy, don't look so glum.
Like I said, the kid is just a coincidence. That
Serenyl of yours is just as perfect as you told me it
was.'

'What about your brother?'

'You let me worry about my brother. Just stay
away from him. If he tries to confront you again, tell
him to speak to me or . . . or to call your lawyer.
Here . . . here's a name to give him. But unless you
want a long-term vacation in Akron *after* your
long-term stay in an ICU, that's all you give home,
right? . . . Well, right? . . . That's perfect, Jack. Just
like that little anesthetic of yours – absolutely
perfect.'

'Okay, Frank,' Pearl said, stubbing out his
cigarette and shuffling to the door, 'you win.'

The door opened and closed, and Pearl was gone.

You win. . . . That's right, Frank thought
excitedly. *I do.*

He had handled the distasteful little pervert
brilliantly. After tough go-rounds with Leigh, the

Judge, and the two board members, it felt splendid to be back in control again.

All he had to do now was keep Zack at bay and off balance for another week. And whatever it took to accomplish that, he would do.

Meanwhile, some well-placed pressure on a couple of weak trustees, and the future of Ultramed – and of Frank Iverson – at the hospital would be secure. After that, he would be in a position to deal in a more definitive way with both his goddamn vindictive brother *and* Pearl.

. . . Frank, Frank, he's our man. If he can't do it –
The intercom crackled on.

'Mr. Iverson, it's Annette again. There's a Mr. Curt Largent on three. He says he's a neighbor of yours.'

Major Curtis Largent, USArmy, Ret. was the way the aging war hero had painted his mailbox. Confined to a wheelchair by an errant piece of shrapnel during a battle for some village or church in Italy, Largent was the unofficial security guard of Frank's neighborhood, surveying the area for hours at a time from his upstairs porch and noting down in a book all suspicious comings and goings, as well as virtually every license number of every car he did not know.

Twice over the years his vigilance actually *had* thwarted crime – in one case, the theft of a bicycle, and in the other, the illegal dumping of some landfill off the end of the turnaround.

'Hello, Major, it's Frank Iverson.' The last words of the cheer were still reverberating in his thoughts. 'What can I do for you?'

Largent, despite a college education – engineering of some sort, Frank thought – still spoke with a pronounced down-east accent.

'Well, Frank,' he said, 'I called mostly 'cause I hadn't hud anythin' about yoah movin'.'

'That's because we're not.'

'Well, that's strange; that's very strange.'

'What, Major? What are you talking about?'

'Well, I'm up he-ah on m' po-arch. You know, where I like to sit? . . . Well, down the street, right in front of yo-ah house, is a truck. And a couple of young bucks been loadin' stuff into it for more'n an ow-ah now.'

'Are you sure it's *our* place, Major?'

'Do bay-ahs shit in the woods? Course I'm shu-ah.'

'Do you see any sign of Lisette around?'

'Nope . . . Wait now, maybe I do. . . . Let me get my bi-nocs just to be certain. . . . Oh, it's her all right. She's with them cute little ones of yo-ahs, right by the truck, watchin' 'em load.'

'Major, thank you,' Frank said. 'Thank you for calling me.'

He hung up and dialed home. Twenty or more rings brought no answer.

Fifteen minutes later he brought the Porsche screeching around the corner and up the hill to his house.

'. . . Fucking Lisette,' he had kept muttering throughout the trip home. 'Goddamn, fucking Lisette . . .'

Lisette, the children, and the truck were gone. Most of the house was still intact, but she had taken her jewelry, the microwave, the largest television, hers and the twin's bureaus, their toys, bicycles, and beds, and had left all the liquor bottles she could find smashed to bits in the kitchen sink, including

343

the two-hundred-dollar bottle of Chateau Lafite Rothschild he had given her on her birthday and was saving to celebrate the Serenyl sale.

The note, carefully printed on Lisette's lavender stationery, was pinned to a pillow on their bed.

You will never hit me again. Please do not try to find us. I'll contact you when I'm good and ready. . . . Was it worth it?

Frank slapped the bedside lamp to the floor and then balled the note in his fist and threw it across the room.

'You'll see,' he muttered angrily. 'A million fucking dollars from now, you'll see what was worth it and what wasn't, you disloyal bitch.'

He started for the liquor cabinet, but then remembered the mess in the kitchen sink and, instead, stormed from the house and drove off.

As he spun out of the driveway, from the corner of his eye Frank caught a glimpse of Major Curtis Largent, U.S. Army, Ret., sitting on his upstairs porch, rocking and watching.

The afternoon felt as close to normal – as close to the way afternoons once were – as any Barbara Nelms could remember. Sunlight was streaming through the bay windows in the living room and kitchen, bathing a house that was spotlessly clean. Stacked on the dining room table were the dishes she would use to serve dinner to the first company she and Bob had invited over in more than half a year.

Toby lay on his belly on the living room carpet, leafing through the pages of a glossy, coffee-table book on the history of aviation. On an impulse, Barbara had stopped and bought the book on the way home from the boy's outdoor session with Dr. Iverson. That impulse had proven to be inspired.

Over the days that had followed, Toby had spent hours quietly examining the photographs and paintings. And more importantly, he had not had a single seizure since then. Predictably, Bob had wanted to rush right out and buy a model kit to begin building with their son, but she had cautioned him to go slow, and for the moment, to leave well enough alone.

Even the psychiatrist, Phil Brookings, had been a help. Although he had declined to see Toby until after Dr. Iverson had finished his evaluation, he had seen Barbara herself for two sessions and was encouraging her to bring Bob in for some family counseling as well.

As she straightened out the bookshelves and polished the already glistening clock on the mantel, Barbara mentally ticked through the meal she had planned and the music she would choose. Perhaps after dessert and coffee, if she could nudge someone into a request, she might even play for them herself. It had been so long since she had allowed herself the luxury of such mundane thoughts.

'Toby,' she ventured, 'how would you like to help me put together the dinner we're going to make for Billy's mom and dad tonight?'

Toby continued to flip through his book, occasionally reaching out to run his fingertips over one of the planes.

'Okay,' she said cheerfully. 'Suit yourself. Just let me know if you get bored with your book. I'll be right in the kitchen.'

It had been worth a try.

Minutes later, as Barbara stood by the sink washing vegetables, she heard a soft noise behind her. Suddenly tense, she whirled. Toby was standing by the kitchen door, the corners of his mouth crinkled upward in something of a smile. Barbara felt a surge of excitement.

'Hi,' she said, swallowing against the forceful beating of her heart. 'Want a job?'

The boy hesitated. And then, ever so slightly, he nodded.

'Great! . . . I mean, that's fine, honey. I could really use the help. Here, let me get your little stool.'

She put the wooden stool by the sink and handed Toby the peeler.

'Okay,' she said. 'Now all you have to do is scrape this over the carrots until they all look like this one, see? . . . That's it. Perfect. Listen, I'm going to the laundry room to fold some clothes. When you finish with the carrots, I'll get you started on the potatoes.'

Normal. Barbara had never dreamed she would cherish the feeling so much. As she headed toward the laundry room she glanced at the wall clock.

'Hey, Tobe,' she said, returning to the kitchen, 'guess what it's time for.'

She snapped on the twelve-inch black-and-white set that she kept on the counter to watch soap operas.

The cartoon intro for *Robin the Good* was just ending.

Toby stood on his stool, scraping the carrots, washing them in the cool, running water, thinking about airplanes, and looking over from time to time at Robin and his men.

'Now, maids and men,' Friar Tuck was saying, 'it's time to learn about our Letter of the Day. Today, it's a very special letter, because it's the only one that always has the same letter come after it. It's the letter that starts the words *quick* and *quail* and *quart*. Can you guess what it is?'

'Q,' Toby said absently.

'How many said Q?' the friar asked. 'Well, if you did say Q, you're right! So now, without further ado, here's Robin and Alan to sing about what letter? Right, our good friend, Q.'

Alan-a-Dale strummed his huge guitar several times. Then Robin the Good leapt onto a giant rock and, hands on hips, began to sing.

'Alas, my lo-ove, you do me wro-ong, I do not thi-ink that thou art true. For thou has ye-et to sing a so-ong, abou-out the le-e-ter Q-oo. . . .'

With the first few notes of music, Toby stopped his scraping and began staring at the tiled wall. The peeler slipped from his fingers and clanked into the steel sink. He rubbed at his eyes as the blue and gray tiles grew brighter.

It was beginning to happen. Just like all the other times, it was beginning to happen.

'Mommy . . .'

He called out the word, but heard no sound.

They were coming for him. The nurse and the man with the mask. They were coming for him again.

'Mommy, please . . .'

His eyes drifted downward toward the sink, toward the splashing water.

Stop them! his mind urged. *Don't let them touch you again.*

His hand closed about the black handle of a knife that lay beside the peeler.

Stop them!

As he lifted the knife, sunlight flashed off its broad, wet blade.

Over the half year since her son's attacks first began, Barbara Nelms had developed a sixth sense about them. It was as if something in the air changed – the electricity or the ions. There had been false alarms – times when she had raced through the house, terrified, only to find Toby sitting in the bay window and staring out at the lawn, or lying in the den, mechanically watching a show that held absolutely no interest for him.

But there were other times, especially of late, when she had found him thrashing wildly on the floor, or pressed into a corner, his frail body cringing from the recurring horror that was engulfing him from within.

Barbara was folding the last of the linen when she began to sense trouble. It started as no more than a tic in her mind – a notion. The house was too quiet, the air too still. Like a deer suddenly alert to the hum of an engine still too distant for any man to hear, she cocked her head to one side and listened. All she could hear was the soft splash of water in the sink and the sound of the television.

Robin the Good was singing his alphabet song – a series of absurd, ill-rhymed tributes to each letter, sung to the tune of 'Greensleeves.' It was a melody Barbara had actually loved before encountering the portly actor's version. Now, it grated like new chalk.

'Toby? . . .' she called out. 'Toby, can you hear me?'

There was no answer.

'Toby, honey? . . .'

She set aside the sheet she had been about to fold and took a tentative step toward the door. Then she began to run.

She bolted through the deserted kitchen and was halfway to the living room when she heard the crash of a lamp and her son's terrified scream.

'Noooo! Don't touch me! Don't touch me!' he howled. 'If you touch me there, I'll cut you. I will. . . . Stop it! Stop it!'

Toby was backing toward the far end of the living room, thrashing his arms furiously at assailants only he could see. It took several seconds for Barbara Nelms to realize that he was wielding a knife – a carving knife with an eight-inch blade.

Then she saw the blood.

Inadvertently, Toby had cut himself – a wide slash on the front of his thigh, just below his shorts. Crimson was flowing down his leg from the wound, but he was totally heedless of it.

'Toby!'

Barbara raced toward him, then slowed a step as his wild-eyed fury intensified.

'Stay away from me! Don't touch me!'

'Toby, please. It's Mommy. Please give me that knife.'

He backed into the hallway, still slashing at the air. His lips were stretched apart, his teeth bared in a frightening, snarling rictus. There was no sign that he recognized her.

His flailing sent a pair of framed photographs spinning from the wall. The glass exploded at her feet.

'Toby, please.'

All Barbara Nelms could see now was the blood,

cascading down her son's leg and over his foot, leaving grotesque crimson smears on the carpet. He was nearing the bathroom. If he reached it and locked himself inside . . .

There was simply no way she could let him do that.

The hallway was too narrow for any kind of attack from the side. Focusing as best she could on the knife, which Toby was slashing in wild, choppy arcs, Barbara ducked against the wall and dove at him. The point of the blade flashed down, catching her just at the tip of her shoulder and tearing through her flesh and the muscle of her arm.

Shocked by the viciousness of the pain, she dropped to her knees, clutching the wound with one hand and trying to hold onto Toby's T-shirt with the other. Blood gushed from between her fingers.

Again, the eight-inch blade slashed down. Reflexively, she pulled away her arm. The glancing blow sliced another gash in the skin by her elbow. Before she could recover, Toby had spun away from her and lurched into the bathroom.

'Toby, no!' she screamed as the door slammed shut and the lock clicked.

Woozily, she got to her knees and pounded on the door.

'Toby, open up! Open up, please! It's Mommy.'

The only response was the shattering of glass against tile.

Through a sticky trail of her own blood, Barbara Nelms crawled to her bedroom and dialed 911.

'This is Barbara Nelms, 310 Ridgeview,' she panted. 'My eight-year-old son has locked himself in the bathroom. He has a knife and he's already cut himself. Please, please send help.'

The walls had begun to spin.

She hung up and glanced at her arm. The larger wound, three inches or four, gaped obscenely. Beefy, bleeding muscle protruded from the cut.

The room began to dim, and Barbara knew that she was close to passing out.

She lay on her back and dialed the hospital.

'This is an emergency,' she gasped, forcing hysteria from her voice as best she could. 'Please help me. I must speak to Dr. Iverson. Dr. Zachary Iverson. It is a matter of life and death. . . .'

Chapter 25

The afternoon was oppresively warm and humid. Much to Judge Clayton Iverson's relief, several continuances and a no-show had led to the completion of the docket of the Clarion County Court far earlier than usual.

Returning to his chambers, he slipped off his black robe and tossed it onto the brass coat rack near his desk. With two unanticipated free hours before Leigh Baron was due at the farm, he was rapidly becoming obsessed with thoughts of a shower and a cold drink or two.

His white shirt was soaked through with perspiration, and his underwear felt as though it were glued to his body.

Over the summer, BTU by BTU, the courthouse air-conditioning system had been dying. Even worse, the chances of getting it replaced before several more summers had come and gone were, the Judge knew, remote. There was a time when he would have laughed at such inconveniences. But now, he could barely keep his mind off his own discomfiture and concentrate on the cases at hand.

Perhaps, he reasoned, in what had become a recurring internal dialogue, it was time to consider retiring.

Despite frequent promises to his wife and to himself to cut back – to travel more and work less –

the pace of his life had, if anything, speeded up. Since buying the house in West Palm six years before, he and Cinnie had spent exactly two weeks there, and had finally leased it out. They had no real need for the rental income, but it had made no sense to leave the place vacant.

The Judge knew that with her arthritis worsening, and her childhood roots in North Carolina, Cinnie would jump at the chance to sunbathe away at least some of the grueling New Hampshire winter. They had friends who had already made the move south and sounded ecstatic about their choice. And goodness knew, his golf game could always use some attention.

Retirement . . . Such a soothing notion, he thought *. . . such a frightening reality.*

It was one thing to consider leaving the bench. He had done about as much as he could do, seen about as much as he could see in that position. But it was quite another to pack up and move to the land of oversized tricycles and afternoon tea dances.

The Judge sank into his chair and mopped at his brow with a towel.

For the time being, at least, Cinnie and her arthritis would just have to make do. Bum air-conditioning or not, he had yet to reach the point where the liabilities of giving everything up and retiring to Florida were outweighed by a few less aches and pains for her and a few more rounds of golf for him.

Besides, he reflected excitedly, for the foreseeable future he had business to attend to in Sterling – important business. In what could well become a landmark move in slowing the advancing juggernaut of corporate medicine, he had elected to spearhead the repurchase of Davis Regional Hospital from the Ultramed Hospitals Corporation, and then to supervise its reorganization and transition back to community control.

Meetings . . . politicking . . . bargaining . . . rearranging . . . bending . . . standing firm . . . winning . . . losing . . . Clayton Iverson felt an almost sexual rush at the thoughts of what the months ahead held in store.

It was an ironic harbinger of things to come that, even without knowing he had already made up his mind, Leigh Baron was making the four-hour drive from Boston 'just to talk.' It was also, he knew, probably not the last time Ultramed and RIATA corporate leaders would be dashing up to Sterling for a session with him.

It would be interesting to see the ploys they chose to try – interesting *and* amusing, for whatever they were, he had absolutely no intention of changing his mind.

Not that his decision to convince the board of trustees to annul the Davis sale had come easily. In fact, it had been one of the most difficult he had ever had to make. And the stickiest part of all was Frank.

Engrossed in thoughts of his son, the Judge packed Guy Beaulieu's folder and some related documents into his briefcase and left the courthouse for the drive home.

Zack was right, he acknowledged, as he rolled down Main Street and then out of town along the Androscoggin road, toward the turnoff to the farm; Frank *had* done an excellent job as administrator of the hospital. It wasn't his fault he was working for a company whose policies were so self-serving that that could ultimately cause catastrophes such as

Annie's. Nor was it his fault, at least according to Zack, that the corporation had set out deliberately to destroy Guy Beaulieu.

Handling Frank just right through all of this would be a test . . . perhaps the hardest test of all. Still, the man was worth the effort. He had fallen on some hard times, true, made some bad decisions, but nevertheless . . .

The initial warning blast of the approaching tractor trailer entered Clayton Iverson's thoughts as nothing more intrusive than the familiar drone of a distant foghorn. He was driving by rote, looking without seeing. The second blast, far more desperate and insistent, startled him from his reverie with an ugly and terrifying suddenness.

The left side of the Chrysler had drifted far across the two-lane road – so fat, in fact, that the solid dividing line was streaking along underneath the very center of the car.

The semi, a monstrous, red GMC was hurtling toward him, its air brakes screeching, its grillwork gaping down at him like the balleen of a whale.

In the clamorous, surreal, frozen moments that followed, the Judge processed countless minute details of the scene before him: the high, Slavic cheekbones of the burly trucker, who was staring down at him in wide-eyed terror and fury . . . his green baseball cap – its gold brim . . . the sun, glinting off the truck's windshield . . . the white script *Tenby's* on the crimson wind deflector above the cab. . . .

The horn . . . the air brakes . . . the face . . . the grill . . . the sun . . . the screeching tires . . .

With no conscious realization of what he was doing, Clayton Iverson whipped the wheel of the

Chrysler to the right, spinning into one ninety-degree turn and then another before skidding to a stop on the gravelly soft shoulder.

Lurching and heaving from its efforts, the behemoth rig barreled past, shaking the Chrysler viciously in the vacuum of its wake.

The Judge glanced in the rearview mirror in time to see the trailer stop its pitching and level out as the trucker gradually regained control. Gasping for breath, he continued staring at the mirror until the crimson reflection disappeared around a bend.

Then he sat by the roadside, trembling mercilessly and waiting either for his heart and lungs to burst or for the adrenaline surging through his body to subside.

He had had more than his share of close calls on the road before, although none much closer than this one. And after each one, as now, he silently thanked his Higher Power for giving him reflexes quick enough to compensate for being one of the most easily distracted drivers ever set behind the wheel of a car.

He also paid brief tribute to his own foresightedness in purchasing one of the heavier models on the road.

After several minutes, his pulse had slowed and his shaking had let up enough for him to swing back onto the roadway. The rest of the drive, he promised, would be made at fifteen, twenty at the most.

The trucker, whoever he was, had earned a pass to heaven with his masterful driving.

. . . and masterful it was, too, he thought . . .

He fished a handkerchief from the dashboard pocket and wiped the drenching sweat from his face and hands.

. . . absolutely masterful. . . .

He savored a deep breath, then another. His pulse returned to normal.

Now, he thought, *where was he? . . . Ah, yes, Frank . . .*

It had been a joy to hear from both Whitey Bourque and Bill Crook of their dinner session with him.

One hell of a guy. Those had been Bourque's exact words. *Smart, well prepared, and persuasive as the Dickens . . .*

It was almost like the old days – the reporters, the TV people, the calls from friends every week. . . .

Judge, that's one hell of a kid you've got there. . . . One hell of a kid . . . Judge, can we get a shot of the two of you together? . . . What were you thinking when your boy took off and headed for the end zone like that? . . .

As far as the Judge was concerned, the moment Annie Doucette had tumbled off the end of her bed, the fate of the Ultramed Hospitals Corporation in Sterling had been sealed. But speaking to Bourque had helped him see that although the company had to go, there was no reason Frank had to go with it.

A few calls to select trustees had convinced him that the board would go along with him in keeping Frank on as administrator.

Now, he had only to convince Frank. . . .

The Judge had sped a hundred or so yards beyond the oversized silver mailbox marking the dirt drive to his farm before he realized that he had missed it.

'Damn you, Iverson,' he cursed out loud.

He slowed, giving momentary thought to a U-turn or to backing up. Then, before he could talk himself into chancing either maneuver, he

357

accelerated over the five hundred additional yards to the next driveway. Twice, trying turnarounds on that stretch of narrow road, he had backed into the drainage ditch. The last thing he needed at that moment was to spend a sweltering hour perched on the split-rail fence, waiting for Pierre Rousseau and his damn tow truck.

He had a date with a shower and a gin-and-tonic, and then with a lovely businesswoman who would try, unsuccessfully, to get him to reconsider his decision.

Leigh Baron wasn't all that tough, but she was bright and certainly diverting. And she would surely provide a decent warm-up for the encounters to come with the real heavy hitters.

Once again, he felt the scintillation – the rush – at the prospect of what lay ahead. It was hardly difficult for him to understand why generals gave up their commands so reluctantly.

Retirement? . . . Nonsense, he thought.

The game was on, and Clayton Iverson was right in the middle of it.

As he eased the Chrysler to a stop by his barn, stepped out, and surveyed his land and the mountains beyond, the Judge made a mental note to send a renewal off to their Florida tenant before Cinnie realized that the man's lease had run out.

The atmosphere in the intensive care unit was somber and extremely tense. A child was in trouble – serious trouble.

The nurses moved from one patient cubicle to another efficiently, but more quietly than usual, stopping from time to time at the doorway to number 7 to see if the nurse working on Toby Nelms needed any assistance.

Behind the nurses station, next to the bank of monitors, Zack checked over the latest set of laboratory figures with the boy's pediatrician, Owen Walsh, a soft-spoken man in his late fifties with close-cropped, graying hair, and deep crow's feet at the corners of his eyes which gave him a perpetually cheerful expression.

Across from them, in cubicle 7, Toby lay thrashing on a cooling blanket, totally unresponsive to his environment. His core temperature, despite aggressive measures, remained well above 104.

The fire/rescue squad had broken into the Nelms's bathroom and found the boy draped over the side of the tub, barely conscious, with multiple, self-inflicted slices and stab wounds on his arms, abdomen, and legs.

Barbara Nelms, conscious but in shock, lay in the bedroom, blood still oozing from the gashes in her arm.

Zack had arrived at the house in time to help with the first aid and the insertion of intravenous lines in both mother and child. Then he had accompanied the ambulance to the hospital and had turned Barbara Nelms, whose blood pressure had responded nicely to a fluid push, over to the general surgeon, Greg Ormesby.

Finally, after getting Toby up to the ICU and onto the cooling blanket, Zack had begun to repair his wounds, none of which involved tendons or vital structures. And, frightening as the lacerations appeared, Zack knew that they were of little importance compared to the fever and the deterioration of the boy's central nervous and

359

cardiovascular systems – a constellation of signs that were almost certainly a reflection of brain swelling.

'Do you think Boston?' Owen Walsh asked.

Like many community pediatricians, especially older ones, Walsh was far more comfortable dealing with patients in his office than in the hospital, and was not comfortable at all with a critically ill child in the intensive care unit.

'At this point, I'm not even sure he could make it,' Zack said. 'Although I guess that's what we should be shooting for.'

He's been a patient there in the past, you know.'

'I know, Owen, I know. And I know you're nervous about having him here. The truth is, I'm not so comfortable with it myself. But believe me, as someone who a month ago might have been called in to see this kid *after* his transfer to Boston, our fluids are just as good as theirs. So're our cooling blanket and our Tylenol and our steroids. And we've got a hell of a cardiologist in Suzanne Cole. So it's not like we're doing nothing. I think we should alert the people down there about what's happening and put one of the chopper teams on standby. But there's something we ought to attend to first.'

'The anesthetic?'

'Exactly.'

Zack had shared Toby's history with the pediatrician, withholding only his suspicion that some sort of secret anesthetic might have been used during his hernia operation.

'Can you explain it to me again?' Walsh asked.

'Sure. In a second.'

Zack stood and peered across at Toby. Swathed in bandages, surrounded by the monitor, the clipboards, the intravenous, gastric, and oxygen tubings, and the large cooling blanket console, the child looked terribly frail and vulnerable.

'Any change?' Zack called out to the nurse attending him.

'Temp's down to 104, Doctor,' she said. 'No other change.'

'Pupils?'

'Still equal and reactive, but sluggish.'

'Thank you . . .'

He glanced at the monitor in time to catch several ominous, premature heartbeats.

'See if you can locate Dr. Cole, please,' he said to the unit secretary. 'Ask her if she can come down here.'

He turned back to the pediatrician.

'Okay, Owen. Now, if what we're seeing is some sort of central, toxic reaction to an anesthetic, then as far as I'm concerned, the actual molecules of the drug, or at least their chemical imprints, are still there in Toby's brain, clogging up neuro pathways and periodically firing off messages without any warning or control from him.'

'The seizures.'

'Or flashbacks, or whatever you want to call them. Somehow, the messages these molecules are transmitting are violent ones – ones related to the surgery.'

But why? Zack found himself asking for perhaps the millionth time. *Why do they happen when they do? Why not to every patient, or at least to more of them?* The answer, he felt certain, had to be some sort of neuroactivator – a trigger, or more likely, given the rarity of the condition, a specific sequence of triggers. No other explanation made sense. . . .

'Zack, you were saying?' Owen Walsh was looking at him curiously.

'Oh, sorry.' Zack made a mental note to go over with Barbara Nelms the minute details of the events preceding Toby's attacks. He would also write down his best recollection of the minutes preceding and following Suzanne's bizarre episode. 'Do you follow all this?'

'So far,' Walsh said.

'Okay . . .'

Zack drew a sketch of several nerve endings on a piece of scratch paper, and used the diagram to illustrate his theory.

'So, what we might consider doing, is putting Toby back under again in a perfectly controlled, sensory-deprived situation. One of those isolation tanks would be ideal, but I understand that's just not possible with him being so sick. Anyhow, we just make things as dark and as quiet as we can, and we administer the same anesthetic he received originally.'

'And what we'd be trying to do,' Walsh said, 'would be literally to wash out the molecules that are sending violent sensory messages, and replace them with molecules transmitting – what, blanks?'

'Precisely.'

'You just thought of this?'

'Actually,' Zack said, 'there was some work done in the late sixties and early seventies using the isolation tank technique on patients who had become psychotic from recurring LSD flashbacks.'

'You mean they treated LSD psychoses with LSD?'

Zack nodded. 'A neurologist in Europe. Scotland, I think.'

'Successfully?'

'Successfully enough to be encouraging.'

This time, it was Walsh who stood and gazed in at their patient. The crow's feet by his eyes deepened with what he saw.

'Dangers?' he asked.

'Given the disaster you're observing in there,' Zack said, 'I don't see how giving the child some anesthesia can do much harm, as long as the anesthesiologist is standing by to intubate him if necessary.'

'Will Jack Pearl go along with it?'

'That, my friend, may well turn out to be the sixty-four-dollar question. He and I haven't exactly seen eye to eye on this anesthesia business.'

Owen Walsh nibbled at the edge of one fingernail.

'Perhaps we should present this to the boy's parents, and get their consent,' he said.

'I can do that, provided his mother is still stable.'

'And maybe your brother ought to know what's going on, too. He's a good man, and an excellent administrator, but he doesn't like surprises.'

Zack felt the prickle of irritation and impatience. He reminded himself that one of the reasons he had opted to become a surgeon, while others, like Walsh, had chosen pediatrics or internal medicine, was the speed with which they went about making decisions. More often than not, the primary care people and the surgeons ended up at the same spot. They simply arrived there by different routes. He motioned toward Toby's cubicle.

'Owen,' he said, 'we don't exactly have a lot of time to play around with this thing. I can understand your reluctance, but we either do this or we don't.'

363

Again, the man hesitated.

'Okay, Zack,' he said finally. 'You deal with Pearl and Barbara Nelms, and I'll take care of alerting Boston, getting the helicopter people on standby, and notifying your brother. We'll meet back here at, say, six-thirty.'

'Six-thirty it is. And, Owen?'

'Yes?'

'It's the right decision.'

Chapter 26

Although Clayton Iverson deeply appreciated his wife of nearly forty years, and had actually endured a recent series of nightmares revolving around her premature death, the truth was that he had never had great use for any woman.

The oldest of five children, and the only boy, he had attended an all-male prep school and college, and had known no woman intimately before his wedding night, nor any other than Cinnie Iverson since.

Long before his wife had become pregnant, he had selected the names of his sons, and once suggested to her that, should the unimaginable come to pass, that they consider naming their daughter Ruth after Rutherford B. Hayes.

Despite his pride in describing himself as 'an emerging liberal' on the subject of women's rights, the Judge still had difficulty taking women seriously in any business dealings of substance. And with no woman was that difficulty more intensely manifested than with Leigh Baron.

Evening had settled in around the farm, bringing with it a persistent, windswept drizzle. The Judge sat with Leigh in his study, sharing coffee and some of Cinnie's apple pie and talking in only the vaguest terms about Ultramed and its plans for the future.

It was nearing eight o'clock. The conversation

with the woman was, in his opinion, becoming somewhat tedious. In addition to Ultramed, they had touched on the stock market (her ideas were innovative, but charmingly naive, he thought); children (she and her husband, who spent most of his work week in New York, had decided not to have any!); criminal justice (her notions about the issues surrounding capital punishment were rather simplistic and poorly substantiated); and sports (she had the temerity to compare golf to croquet, and to state that she would consider taking up the game only after she was physically no longer able to play tennis!).

'So, my dear,' the Judge said, completely ignoring a question from her about the differences between putting greens in various parts of the country, 'I assume that the powers that be in Ultramed didn't send someone as bright and charming as you are just to pass the time with this old north woods war-horse.'

'No,' she said, smiling at him curiously. 'No, they didn't.'

The Judge waited for her to continue.

'Well, then,' he said finally, clearing his throat. 'I suppose they wish you to lay some of the ground-work for tomorrow's board meeting.'

'In a manner of speaking.'

'Are you always this evasive and . . . and mysterious, Mrs. Baron?'

'Judge Iverson,' she said, 'exactly who do you think I am?'

'That's a rather strange question, don't you think? I certainly know who you are.'

'Do you?'

There was a firmness in Leigh Baron's voice – a

steely brightness in her eyes that Clayton Iverson had not noticed before. Still, the ploy of asking questions rather than answering them was an amateurish tactic, and one she would have to improve upon if her aim was to control their conversation.

'Okay,' he said after some thought, 'I'll play. You're Leigh Baron, vice president of the Ultramed Hospitals Corporation. Your division is, correct me if I'm wrong, operations.'

'Judge, I hope this doesn't come as too much of a shock, but I haven't been a vice president at Ultramed since, oh, just a few months after I nego-tiated our arrangement with Davis Regional. We were restructured by our parent company. My formal title now is Managing Director. That translates into CEO.'

Startled, the Judge pulled from his briefcase the Ultramed organizational chart Guy Beaulieu had compiled.

'Well, then, who's, um . . . Blanton Richards?'

Leigh smiled enigmatically.

'Judge Iverson,' she said, 'Blanton Richards hasn't been part of Ultramed for several years. I don't know who put that list together – Dr. Beaulieu, I presume; he was always putting lists together – but whoever it was didn't do his home-work. I know how much you expect to be dealing with the good old boys on matters such as this, but I'm afraid that as far as Ultramed is concerned, *I'm* the good old boy.'

'Now just a minute, young lady –'

'Young lady . . .' Leigh Baron's expression was not a little patronizing. 'Judge Iverson, I appreciate the compliment – really I do. But I think it will make things easier for both of us if you understand that my young lady days are well behind me. I'm thirty-seven years old. I was second in my MBA class at Stanford more than a decade ago, I spent two years studying economics at Oxford, and I managed several smaller operations for RIATA International before I was brought into Ultramed. My income last year – not counting bonuses and stock options – was slightly over half a million dollars. Now, if that little misunderstanding is taken care of to your satisfaction, I would suggest we get down to work. You and I have some important business to attend to.'

'Yes,' he said, clearing his throat again. 'Yes, I suppose we do. How about some more coffee first?'

The Judge suddenly felt edgy, and anxious to do something – anything – that would disrupt the woman's rhythm. What he had anticipated would be a preliminary sparring match with Ultramed had turned out to be the main event.

'No, thank you,' she answered. 'But go ahead if you want.'

'I think I will.'

He walked to the kitchen, poured himself a cup, laced it with a stiff slug of brandy, and took a long sip. The warm, velvet rasp had a calming, reassuring effect, reminding him that, although Leigh Baron had him back on his heels, this was the sort of game he loved to play – the one in which he held all the trump cards. He was still the chairman of the board of the hospital. And in the end, regardless of who Leigh Baron was, how much she earned, or what she had to say, *he* was the one who controlled the votes.

His next swallow drained the cup. He poured himself another before returning to the den.

'Okay, *Ms*. Baron,' he said, with ever-so-slight emphasis, 'what's your pitch?'

'No pitch, Judge. Simply put, I would like to know what your plans are for the meeting tomorrow.'

He tried for a bemused expression, but sensed that he missed. He held all the cards. She knew that as well as he did. And yet she continued looking at him as if whatever he had to say really made no difference. He sought another taste of his brandied coffee, but realized that he had once again drained his cup.

'You have my letter,' he said. 'In it, I stated that it was quite possible the board and Ultramed would be able to work things out.'

'Judge, we have reason to believe that the situation up here, at least in your eyes, has changed since you wrote that. I'd like to know what's going on.'

'Nothing's going on. I've done what I was supposed to do as chairman of the board here, and sent you a letter. The meeting's tomorrow. We expect you'll be there to represent Ultramed's interests. At the end of the meeting there'll be a vote. *C'est tout.*'

He held his hands out, palms up.

Leigh Baron rubbed at her eyes wearily.

'Judge, that list you just consulted, was that compiled by Dr. Beaulieu?'

'As a matter of fact, it was.'

'Then I can assume that you have all the other material he had been scraping together against our company.'

'You did try to drive him out of practice.'

'That, Judge, is ridiculous. Ultramed has grown

faster than any company of its size in the field. We know exactly what we are doing. So does our parent company. If we wanted somebody out, believe me, they'd be out. Where did you get the idea that we would do such a thing?'

'Well, actually, it was from my – Actually, it's none of your business. You can find out everything you want to know at tomorrow's meeting.'

'Your son Zachary was a pall bearer at Dr. Beaulieu's funeral. Is he the one who's taken up Beaulieu's cause?'

'If he has, then like I said, you'll find out tomorrow.'

'If he has, then he's wrong. If Guy Beaulieu was being driven from practice, it was not by us.'

'Perhaps,' the Judge said, sensing a shift in control back toward himself. 'If that's true, that should come out at the meeting also.'

'Tell me something, Judge. You've already made up your mind, haven't you?'

'I wouldn't say that at all.'

She flashed that same disquieting smile.

'You don't have to,' she said. 'Judge, if your board does vote to repurchase Ultramed-Davis from us, what were you planning to do about Frank?'

'Do? Why, keep him on, of course. If – and mind you, I said, if – we do vote to return the hospital to the community, we'll need him. He's done a terrific job. You told me that yourself.'

'And I meant it, too,' Leigh said, 'with one slightly enormous exception. . . . Here, Judge, I think you'd better look this over carefully.'

She removed a thin folder from her briefcase and handed it to him.

'While you're doing that,' she went on, 'if you could just point me toward your bathroom . . .'

'Huh?' He had already started scanning the material. 'Oh, it's over there. Down that hallway and on the left . . .'

'Thanks.'

Clayton Iverson finished reading the first page. Written by a well-established, highly respected Boston accounting firm, it was basically an explanation and summation of the material to follow.

Before going on, he went again to the kitchen. This time, he poured brandy into his cup but did not bother adding coffee.

By the time Leigh Baron returned to the study, he had reread the cover letter and begun to skim the lists of figures and transactions, all of which seemed to bear up the accountants' contention that almost three years before, Frank had embezzled nearly a quarter of a million dollars from the Ultramed accounts.

Whether it was the hour or the brandy or the acid anger welling in his throat, the Judge was having increasing difficulty concentrating on the specific financial transfer maneuvers, which were characterized by the bookkeepers as 'rather superficial efforts to obscure the missing funds; efforts which any reasonable audit would uncover, and therefore ones which suggest Mr. Iverson's intention of making good the shortfall at some near date.'

'So,' Leigh Baron said. 'Suddenly this all becomes very serious business, wouldn't you agree?'

'Why haven't you done anything about this before now?'

'Oh, come now, Judge. It's unbecoming for you to ask a question with so obvious an answer.

Besides, as we've both been saying, Frank's done a terrific job for us. It's apparent that he just got a little greedy back there three years ago. He does have a way of being headstrong sometimes. But I guess you know that. . . . Well, I had actually decided that once the sale of Davis to our company was a fait accompli, I would write off the $250.000 as sort of a bonus for his good work. After all, anyone can make a mistake. . . .'

'Sure, sure. And now you're saying that I would be making a mistake to vote against turning our hospital over to you.'

'You won't have left us much choice, Judge, other than to press charges. And believe me, the evidence against Frank is solid – absolutely rock solid.'

In keeping with his overall outlook, Clayton Iverson had always reserved his strongest emotions – positive *and* negative – for men. But at that moment he hated the woman sitting across from him with more passion than he had ever hated anyone.

Who in the hell did she think she was?

The question echoed impotently, over and over again in his mind. She looked like some sort of high fashion model, and discussed issues with the naiveté of a schoolgirl; and yet, there she sat, smiling quietly as she viciously blackmailed him.

The life of his son and, by inference, the lives of his daughter-in-law and granddaughters, in exchange for a vote. He should have retired, he thought. He had clearly lost his edge. He should have stepped down from such dealings long ago.

His head was spinning.

'I . . . I need time to think,' he said.

'I understand. . . . Unfortunately, you have only until tomorrow.'

'I was right in wanting your company out of our town, Mrs. Baron. You're a very callous and self-serving woman.'

'Let's not lower ourselves to name-calling, Judge. It's so unprofessional.' She stood. 'So, then. Tomorrow at one minute after noon everything will be' – she shrugged – 'exactly as it is right now. Only more permanent. Yes?'

Clayton Iverson, his weathered face flushed, his eyes smoldering, could not respond.

'Oh, and Judge,' she said, 'there is one other thing. I would like to review that material Guy Beaulieu accumulated. I promise its return in . . . a few days.'

'You can't have it,' the Judge snapped.

'Judge Iverson, I know I don't have to spell it all out for you, but let me do it anyway. If you go along with our request, your son will be exonerated from all he has done, and we will complete our purchase of the hospital. If you do not, your son will probably end up in prison, and his family will be disgraced. Your influence in Sterling will be greatly diminished, if not destroyed, and we shall almost certainly end up with Ultramed-Davis just the same.'

'This is insane!'

'Perhaps,' Leigh Baron said. 'Perhaps it is. . . . That material, please?'

'Dammit . . .'

'Judge Iverson, face it. It's going to happen. Our business arrangement is going to be consummated as it was laid out. Either easily and cleanly, or very, very messily. But it's going to happen. Now . . .'

Reluctantly, the Judge passed Beaulieu's folder across. Leigh Baron slipped it into her briefcase.

'As I promised,' she said, 'I'll return this in a few days. Don't bother to show me out. I know the way.'

His face buried in his arm, Clayton Iverson sat alone in his study, listening to the soft spattering of night rain against the shutters. In all his business dealings, in all his years on the bench, never had he been manhandled so brutally or efficiently as he had by Leigh Baron this night.

Desperately, he struggled to keep his anger in check – anger directed as much at his son as at the Ultramed CEO. At this point, he reminded himself, he had only Leigh Baron's side of the story.

Before he made another move, before he spoke to one more member of the board, he and Frank had to talk. If Frank could adequately explain why he took the money, how he lost it, how he was planning on replacing it, perhaps they could work something out. If not . . .

Went to Frank's. Please don't worry.

Clayton Iverson set the note for Cinnie on his desk and walked, somewhat shakily, to the Chrysler, wondering if perhaps he had had a bit too much to drink.

His thoughts tumbled about as he tried to focus on what his options might be. He needed the fresh air of a drive as much as anything . . . needed to clear his head . . . needed to confront Frank. . . .

He put the car in gear, turned around with more difficulty than usual, and sped down the winding drive.

Frank would have an explanation, he thought. He would have an acceptable explanation for everything, and together they would find a reasonable way out.

But if there was no explanation . . . if Frank had nothing to offer except greed . . .

The Judge sped through the turn onto the Androscoggin access road. A station wagon speeding south swerved sharply, narrowly avoiding a collision.

Clayton Iverson did not notice.

. . . Of all the ungrateful, inconsiderate things Frank had ever done, he was thinking, this was absolutely the worst. . . . Perhaps it was time he put his foot down. . . . Prison or no prison, disgrace or no disgrace, perhaps it was time. . . .

His eyes open, but unseeing, Toby Nelms lay twitching on the cooling blanket, jerking one restrained hand from time to time in what might have been an attempt to get at the breathing tube Jack Pearl had inserted into his trachea. His core temperature, despite the blanket, intravenous cortisone, and several doses of rectally-administered Tylenol, was still 103.

'. . . Absolutely not,' Pearl was saying. 'There's absolutely no way I am going to put a critically ill child under anesthesia for some off-the-wall theory.'

'Jack, let me go over this again,' Zack pleaded, making no attempt to mask his exasperation. 'What I'm proposing is not off the wall. Just because it isn't a widely used technique doesn't mean that it's wrong. Hell, the problem hasn't been studied enough to be certain one way or the other. But there *is* the LSD article. Why do you think I drove all the way home to get it from my files for you?'

'No way,' Pearl said.

Suzanne joined the two other physicians at the bedside. For more than an hour she had been battling one flurry of irregular cardiac rhythms after another in the boy. Now, for the moment at least, the situation seemed to have stabilized, but the dusky shadows enveloping her eyes were mute testimony to the tension of the struggle.

'So, where do we stand?' she asked, sipping tepid coffee.

Throughout the crisis she had made no overt reference to Zack's theories regarding Mainwaring and Pearl, although several times her expression had warned – or begged – him against any confrontation with the anesthesiologist.

'Well,' Zack said, 'we're right where we were before the arrhythmias started. Cerebral edema. Nothing more. Could be caused *by* the fever; could be the cause of it; could be both.'

'Well, for what it's worth, his arrhythmias seem to be under control.'

'It's worth plenty. Nice going.'

'Thanks. So, have you two decided? Are you going to put the boy back to sleep?'

The two men exchanged glances. Then Pearl looked away.

'Well, Jack,' Zack said, 'go ahead and tell her. Tell her what we – tell her what *you* have decided. Look down at that child there, think about what I've told you, what I've shown you, and tell her.'

'Zack, please,' Suzanne said. She turned to the anesthesiologist.

'Sorry,' he mumbled.

'Jack?' she asked.

'I refuse to do it,' Pearl said simply. 'The evidence that this child's anesthesia had anything to do with his present condition is flimsy enough by itself. Used as justification for a highly questionable maneuver, such as Iverson here is proposing, is absurd. I positively refuse to do it.'

'Do what?'

Frank Iverson appeared near the foot of the bed. He glanced from one physician to the next and then, with some discomfort, at the thrashing boy.

'Do what, Jack?' he asked again.

'Frank,' Pearl said, 'earlier in the week I filed an official report and complaint about a visit I had from your brother, here. At that time, he accused me of any number of things, including improperly anesthetizing this child.'

'Why, that's ridiculous,' Zack said. 'I never –'

'Zack, will you please let him finish. . . . Thank you. Go ahead, Jack.'

'Well, now the boy's got cerebral edema – that's brain swelling – from God knows what. Maybe some form of encephalitis or something. Your brother has this theory that if this *is* some nervous system reaction to the anesthesia he received, my putting him under again with the same drugs might reverse the effect.'

'And?' Frank said.

'And I won't do it.'

'Why?'

'Why?! Well, because it . . . it won't work, Frank. That's why.'

'Zack, has this been done before?'

'In analogous circumstances, yes. I brought in an article describing the theory behind it.'

'Then, Jack,' Frank said calmly, 'what harm would it do to put this boy to sleep again as Zack is suggesting? You put critically injured and ill patients under all the time, don't you?'

'Well yes, but –'

'Suzanne, do you think this child would be able to handle being put to sleep?'

'I . . . well, his cardiac problems seem to have quieted down, and he *is* already on a ventilator, so actually, I don't see why not.'

'But –'

'No buts, Jack. I'm sorry I didn't get over here sooner to discuss all this, but I was tied up trying to reach some people in Akron. Now listen. We're in the business of helping people. That's why we're here. If there's a chance that what Zack is suggesting will help this kid, I think you should try it. My brother's a pain in the neck sometimes, but he's hardly foolhardy. If he says he has evidence, then by God, he's got evidence.'

Witnessing the bizarre exchange from his spot by the head of Toby's bed, Zack sensed an intense nonverbal interplay occurring between his brother and the anesthesiologist. He could also tell from Pearl's expression that the strange little man was no longer going to object to administering the drugs.

'What *were* the anesthetics again?' Suzanne asked.

'Pentothal and isoflurane,' Pearl said.

'Ah, yes.'

'Are you going to do it?' Zack asked.

'How long do you think we'll have to keep him under?'

'Eight minutes. That's how long they did it in the article.'

Pearl glanced once again at Frank.

'Okay,' he said unenthusiastically. 'Give me a couple of minutes to get my equipment together.'

'Good. I'll try and get this place set up.' Zack leveled his gaze at the man. 'Jack, whatever the kid got for that hernia of his, that's what he should get now. Understand?'

'He got Pentothal and isoflurane,' Pearl responded with exaggerated firmness. 'Now, are we going to do this or not?'

'Suzanne?'

'No objections,' she said.

'Okay, then. Let's go for it,' Zack said.

The eerie scene was one that nobody in the ICU that night would ever forget. Throughout the unit, all unnecessary lights were extinguished and every noncritical piece of equipment that produced a noise or vibration was shut off. Nurses sat silently and grimly beside their patients or by the nurses' station.

In cubicle 7, the only lights were flashes of Zack's and Jack Pearl's small penlights and the shimmering monitor readouts of Toby Nelms's cardiac pattern and blood pressure.

Toby himself, anesthetized first with Pentothal, and now with the gas, isoflurane, lay motionless and peaceful, his eyes patched and taped shut, his ears plugged with oil-soaked cotton and covered with bandages. His feet were encased in lamb's wool. Two thin cotton blankets covered him on top, and the water-filled cooling blanket lay underneath him.

Zack had checked both the new, unopened vial of Pentothal and the label on the isoflurane tank before okaying their administration. Now, watch in hand, he sat to one side of the darkened cubicle, waiting. Jack Pearl's willingness to administer the two anesthetics had dispelled some of his suspicions regarding an experimental drug, but doubt remained.

And even if this treatment was the right one, even

if the anesthetics were correct, even if Jack Pearl was as pure and honorable a physician as Galen, Zack knew they might have waited too long. Cerebral edema was, all too often, a one-way street.

Five minutes, six . . . the time seemed endless. . . . Blood pressure, ninety and holding; pulse 120 . . . Seven minutes.

Zack watched the last thirty seconds tick off, glancing over briefly at Suzanne, whose attention was riveted on the monitor screen.

'Okay, Jack,' he said. 'That's it. Eight minutes.'

He threw back the draperies to the room and motioned the nurse back in.

Her first move was to reinsert the rectal probe attached to the cooling blanket console.

'It's 103,' she said.

Slowly, Toby began to stir, as concentrated oxygen washed the isoflurane from his lungs and bloodstream. Zack bent over him and checked his pupils. They were, if anything, more sluggishly reactive than before. Otherwise, a top-to-bottom neurologic exam showed no change.

'Anything?' Suzanne asked.

'Nothing.'

Zack left the cubicle and circled the counter to where she was stationed.

'Satisfied?' she whispered.

'Not really, but I guess there's nothing more I can do.'

Across from them, Jack Pearl had removed Toby's eye patches and was conducting his own exam.

'I really appreciated your restraint in dealing with Jack.'

'It wasn't easy.'

'I could tell.'

'You still don't believe me about all this, do you?'

She shook her head.

'As I said in your office,' she whispered, glancing first at the monitor and then at Pearl, 'one other case, and I'll at least listen.'

'I'm going to find it.'

'You know, you are without a doubt the most headstrong man I've ever met.'

'I'm the most headstrong man *I've* ever met,' he said. 'It's my finest attribute.'

She looked at him coolly.

'Well, Zachary, that may be. But unfortunately, it's also your most frightening one.'

She brushed past him and joined Pearl at the bedside.

Zack stood alone at the nurses' station, fighting the hollowness in his chest, trying to cling to the notion that for the moment, at least, he had done all he could for Toby Nelms – he had done his best.

'Dr. Iverson,' the ward clerk called to him from her desk. 'The call on line two is for you. It's Mr. Iverson.'

'Zack,' Frank said breathlessly, 'I'm down in the E.R. We've got trouble. Maybe big trouble.'

'What?'

'Auto accident. Two cars. Both drivers injured.'

'Bad?'

'Dunno about one of them – apparently they're still trying to cut him out of his pickup. Marshfield's in with the other one right now.'

'Let me just wash my face and I'll be right down.'

'Make it quick, Zack. The guy Marshfield's working on is the Judge.'

Chapter 27

The emergency ward was bedlam. Nearly every bed was full, as was the waiting room. Nurses, some of whom Zack recognized as having been called down from the floors, were hurrying between patients, the med locker, and the supply room. EKG and portable X-ray technicians were standing by their equipment in the hallway. Several blue-clad rescue team members were assisting the nurses while several more sat perched on countertops filling out forms.

Two of the rooms seemed to be the foci of most of the activity.

'The Judge is over there, in eight,' Frank said as he and Zack crossed the lobby.

'What in the hell was he doing driving around at this hour without Mom, anyhow?'

'I don't know, Zack. You can ask him. He's all bandaged and splinted up, but he's perfectly with it. He must be. He's already told me that if we couldn't get a hold of his-son-the-neurosurgeon, he wanted to be transferred to another hospital.'

'Frank, it's okay not to be snide right now, all right? Who's with him?'

'Not sure. Marshfield was, but I see him over there in trauma. The other guy from the accident has just been brought in.'

'Well, do you want to call Mom now, or wait until we know what's going on?'

'The later the better as far as I'm concerned.'

'Okay. Well, maybe you can call Lisette and have her go over and get her.'

'Lisette's . . . gone.'

Zack checked his watch.

'Well, when will she be back?'

'No,' Frank said. 'She's gone, as in: gone. It's a temporary thing. Listen, you go ahead in with the Judge. I'll take care of Mom. . . . And Zack?'

'Yes?'

'Too bad things aren't working out for that kid.'

Without waiting for a response, Frank turned and crossed the emergency ward to where two uniformed troopers were speaking with a reporter from the *White Mountains Gazette*.

'Yeah, Frank,' Zack muttered, flashing briefly on the bizarre, sub rosa interplay between his brother and Jack Pearl. 'Too bad.'

He was heading toward room 8 when the curtain drew back and the nurse, Doreen Lavalley, emerged.

'Oh, Dr. Iverson, I'm glad you were able to get down here so quickly,' she said. 'They called me down because I used to do E.R. work, but it's been a few years and –'

'I'm sure you're doing great. What's the story?'

'Well, I've been in there since just after they brought your father in. The rescue people found him sitting propped against a tree about fifty feet from the crash. They suspect he was thrown out of the car and then walked or crawled over there. He almost certainly has a fractured wrist. The rescue people also report there's a huge gash in his lower back, but nobody's had the chance yet to move him off the board to check it. Dr. Marshfield had to go in with the fellow from the other car. From a distance, at least, that guy doesn't look good at all.'

Zack moved to a spot just outside the doorway to room 8. Through it, he could see his father, strapped to a transfer board, with his head and neck secured in excellent first aid fashion. One arm was wrapped and splinted, the other fitted just above the wrist with an IV line. A monitor was in place and chronicling a perfectly normal rate and rhythm.

'Did Dr. Marshfield have the chance to get any films?'

Doreen Lavalley consulted a scrap of paper.

'He got a portable shoot-through of his neck and a view approximately over where that gash is. I had the lab draw a blood count and chemistries.'

'Blood bank, too?'

'Yes. I asked them to type him and crossmatch him for four units.'

'Nice going, Doreen. I'm glad to see you're still working here.'

'Just one more week,' she said, somewhat sadly. 'I've taken a job with the Visiting Nurse Association.'

'Well, that's going to be Davis's loss.'

'Thank you. I'll miss this place. At least the way it used to be, I will. I'll see if I can get those films.'

If Clayton Iverson was relieved to see his son, he showed little evidence of it. Zack was not surprised. It had always been that way, and regardless of the circumstances, it would be that way this night.

'H'lo, Judge.'

Zack leaned against the bed rail, assessing his father – the slight pallor about his lips, the deepened creases at the corner of his eyes. The man was in some pain, and probably still bordering on shock. Reflexively, Zack reached across and increased the intravenous flow.

'Zachary . . .' The Judge spoke through teeth nearly clenched by the bandages pulled tightly across his forehead and beneath his chin to stabilize his neck. 'Do you think you could get rid of this damn stuff?'

'As soon as I've seen the film of your neck, Judge. Apparently you weren't all that coherent when the police arrived. You could have hurt your neck and not know it. You in much discomfort?'

'Mostly my back – right through here. . . .' He motioned with his unsplinted hand at a spot just above his navel. 'Does your mother know I'm here?'

'Frank went to take care of that.'

'Have him tell her to wait at home, and that I'll call her later.'

'Judge, just relax and let us take care of things. Okay? Now, what happened?'

'I don't know. I was on my way over to . . . ah . . . to talk with Frank and Lisette about some investments they're thinking of making. And just as I was passing by Cedar Street, boom. The next thing I really remember was the inside of the ambulance.'

. . . to talk with Frank and Lisette? . . . Lisette's gone Judge. Who's lying? Frank to you, or you to me?

'Did you hit your head?'

'Not that I know.'

'Zack?' Suzanne stood by the doorway, the X rays in her hand. 'I came down to see if I could be of any help. The nurse said she'd be next door if you need her.'

'How's the boy?'

'Not awake at all, but still reasonably stable. Owen Walsh is trying to arrange a transfer, but I don't think he's been able to find a bed yet.'

'Well, I'm glad you could get down. Have you seen the films?'

It was only then that he noticed the tension in her face. Something was wrong in the X rays.

'Flip 'em right up there,' he said, motioning her to the two view boxes on the wall beside the Judge's litter.

She illuminated the lateral shoot-through of the Judge's neck. Zack counted to be certain that all seven cervical vertebrae were displayed, and then checked the alignment and spacing of each.

'Normal,' he said. 'Perfect. Looks like we're in luck, Judge. We'll get a complete set of films, just to be certain, but I suspect they'll be fine. I don't see any reason not to remove this harness they've rigged up.'

He reached for the restraint.

'Zack, you may want to wait on that,' Suzanne said, snapping the second film into place. 'There was a load of scrap metal in the pickup. The police wonder if maybe he fell on something.'

'What is that thing?' the Judge asked.

Still constrained by the harness, he was forcing his eyes far to the left in order to see the X ray.

'It's a chunk of metal, Dad,' Zack said, studying the piece, which was stubby, wedge-shaped, and pointed on all three corners. The longest, sharpest point of the three was directly between two vertebrae, the twelfth dorsal and first lumbar. 'A pretty big chunk, too. I'll need a lateral view to know how deep it is. Are you having any numbness or tingling in your legs at all?'

'I . . . I don't think so.'

'Well, just the same, I think I'll leave you strapped in for now.'

'If you have to. Am I going to be all right?'

'Of course you are. But I'll feel happier when we know exactly where that metal is and we've gotten someone to take it out.'

'*You're* not going to do it?'

'Judge, first things first, okay? Suzanne, can you send in the portable unit for a lateral view? Meanwhile, I'll go over the rest of him.'

'. . . Suction, I need suction!' . . . 'Doctor, do you want another line?' . . . 'His pupil's dilating' . . . 'Christ, I asked for suction. . . .'

The snatches of exchange between Wilton Marshfield and a nurse came from the trauma room.

'. . . He's vomiting again. Doctor, I think he's seizing' . . . 'Get me ten of Valium for an IV push' . . . 'Did you know that Dr. Iverson is in with his father?'

'Sounds like trouble,' the Judge said. 'Are you going in there?'

'If they need me, they'll come and get me,' Zack said. 'I'm not leaving you alone. Suze, while you're out there can you please check on what's going on? If that's the other driver from the accident, find out who he is.'

Zack was completing a rapid exam when the curtain flew back and Frank entered.

'Oo-ee, what a zoo out there,' he said. 'Police, reporters, the works. What gives here?'

'He's got a chunk of metal in his back – see? It looks like it shot in there during the crash, but maybe he fell on it or rolled over it. I won't know exactly where it is until I see some more views, but it obviously has to come out.'

'Well, Judge,' Frank said, 'even if it does, you got

387

the better end of the deal in this one. Ol'Beau in there is a mess.'

'Beau Robillard?' Zack and the Judge said the name in unison.

'Yeah, didn't you know? Public nuisance number one is right in the next room. That was his rust-bucket pickup you hit. If he's operating true to form, that scrap metal in the back of it was probably hot. Hey, Zack, remember how Robillard and his buddies used to follow you home after school and kick the daylights out of you?'

'Frank, that was junior high, for goodness sakes.'

'He hasn't changed,' the Judge said. 'I see him in my court every other week, it seems. He's as nasty as ever. Nastier. I should have put him away the last time I had the chance. Was there anyone in the truck with him?'

'Nope,' Frank answered. 'The police say that while they were cutting him out of the cab he kept screaming that you ran the light at the bottom of the Mill Street hill.'

'That's ridiculous.'

At that moment, Suzanne reappeared at the doorway with the X-ray technician.

'Zack,' she said, 'Wilton asked if you could help him next door. The guy from the truck has a bad head injury. He's started seizing. His name's Robillard.'

'Beau Robillard. We know. He used to beat me up in junior high.'

'He's trash,' the Judge said. 'Petty theft, assault, disturbing the peace. Zachary, I don't want you going in there.'

'What?'

'You heard me. Tell Marshfield you're tied up in here and you can't help him.'

388

'Judge, I can't do that. . . .'

Zack paused, waiting for support for his position from Frank and Suzanne. There was none.

'Listen,' he said finally, 'I've got to go in and at least honor his request for help. Besides, you need more X rays and maybe a CT scan, and . . . and the O.R. team's got to be mobilized. By the time all those studies are completed, I should be done in there, okay?'

'I already told you how I felt,' the Judge said. 'Why are you asking if it's okay?'

'Zack,' Frank said, 'let me talk to you outside for a minute.'

'Okay, in just a second. . . .' Zack felt shaken. 'Please go ahead with a lateral of his thoraco-lumbar region and a shot of his wrist,' he said to the X-ray technician. 'On second thought, why don't you forget the portable. Take him over and get a really good set of films. Suze, can you go with him?'

'Sure. Owen Walsh'll call me if anything develops in the unit.'

'You might want to go over him for pre-op clearance. I don't think they've had time yet to get a full EKG.'

'I'll take care of that.'

'Also, find out who's on for orthopedics, if you can.'

'Zachary, I meant what I said about Robillard,' the Judge said as Suzanne and the technician wheeled him from the room. 'I never meant anything more.'

Zack could only shake his head.

'Hey, listen,' Frank said when the two of them were alone. 'Just go in there and see Robillard, and do whatever you have to do. Leave the Judge to me.'

'I know he's hurt and angry, Frank, but all the same, I can't believe he would talk like that. I just can't believe it.'

'You've been away from here – away from the man – for a long time. Remember, buddy, we're not the only ones he keeps passing judgment on. Years and years of sentencing the same stiffs over and over again has done something to him. Listen, don't worry about him. I can handle things. Just go on in there and play doctor.'

'Did you call Mom?'

'I have one of the state troopers going to get her.'

'Okay. I'll be next door. Frank, thanks for your help. I hope things with Lisette get straightened out.'

'Not to worry. Just get on in there and do whatever you have to.'

The two of them left room 8. Zack entered the trauma room and Frank crossed the E.R. to the X-ray department.

The Judge had been moved, on the transfer board, to the X-ray table.

'I need a minute alone with him,' Frank said, motioning Suzanne and the technician away.

'Judge, listen,' he whispered, when the others were out of earshot. 'I tried to reason with Zack about not seeing Robillard, but he just won't listen. I'm on your side on this one. One hundred percent. Just relax and let them take your pictures. I'll keep trying to make Zack see what's right.'

The rescue team, nurses, and emergency physician cleared a path as Zack entered the trauma room. His programming in the evaluation of nervous system damage was in reflex operation before he reached the bedside.

Beau Robillard, lying nude on the trauma room litter, was disheveled, covered with cuts and abrasions, and even worse off than Zack had anticipated.

Comatose . . . respirations shallow, minimally effective . . . barely responsive to deep pain . . . right pupil, two millimeters; left pupil, five millimeters, sluggishly reactive . . .

'Was he ever awake, Wilton?'

'Absolutely,' Marshfield said. 'He was awake when the police found him, and moaning and incoherent when he arrived here. Then he seized.'

. . . Some purposeless movement on the left side, no movement on the right. . . . Babinski reflex absent both sides . . . deep scalp laceration left parietal region . . .

'Could I have a pair of gloves, please. Size eight. Also, get set to intubate him. Number seven point five tube. Wilton, can I see his films?'

'We haven't had a chance to get them, what with your father coming in first and this creep looking a helluva lot better than he does right now. Do you know who he is?'

'Yeah, yeah,' Zack said. 'I know.'

'When this . . . this thing here was a boy,' Marshfield said, 'he and his cronies beat up on my nephew so many times that my brother finally ended up having to send the kid to St. Michael's Academy. I'm telling you, he was really a creep. So were those two older Robillard boys.'

Zack explored the deep scalp gash with his gloved fingers, and felt the distinctive click of bone fragments.

'Well, I don't care if he's the reincarnation of Jack the Ripper and Attila the Hun rolled into one,' he said. 'He's got a subdural or epidural hematoma expanding on the left. He needs Burr hole drainage, and quickly. Also, see if you can get Greg Ormesby in here just in case something's going on in his abdomen.'

The nurse set a tray of equipment by Zack's right hand. He hunched over the head of the litter, positioned the steel blade of the laryngoscope against Robillard's tongue, and in seconds slid the polystyrene breathing tube through the man's vocal cords into his trachea.

'Hyperventilate him, please,' Zack said, connecting a breathing bag to the tube and turning it over to the respiratory technician.

Burr holes! An hour in the operating room. More if there was trouble.

Zack backed away from the bed, a stranglehold of indecision tightening about his chest. Both Beau Robillard and the Judge needed surgery that, of those at Ultramed-Davis, he was by far the most qualified to perform. From a purely medical perspective, there was no dilemma, no doubt about the priorities of the moment. Without immediate intervention, Robillard would die. It was that simple.

But thanks to Judge Clayton Iverson, it wasn't that simple at all.

'Keep bagging him,' Zack mumbled, rubbing at the ache that had suddenly materialized between his temples. 'Be sure there are two teams available for the O.R. I'll be right back.'

He glanced into room 8. It was still empty.

Please, he was thinking as he headed toward the

X-ray department. *Let that chunk of metal be just below the skin. Let it be someplace where anyone with a scalpel and a little training can get it out.*

Suzanne was standing by one of the department's banks of view boxes, studying the films.

Even from a distance, Zack could see that the position of the metal fragment was trouble.

'How's he doing?' he asked.

'Okay. He's complaining of some heaviness in his legs, but I think you might have put that symptom in his head. Your mother's here. Frank's got her in the quiet room, I think. That metal's not in such a good spot, huh?'

'It's in near the cord, if that's what you mean. See right here how it's chipped the edge of the vertebral transverse process? Removing it should be reasonably straightforward, but it certainly won't be any smash and grab. The area's got to be explored to be sure there's no bleeding around the cord. Damn, but I wish this wasn't happening. That Robillard is going out. A Burr hole procedure now is his only chance, and not such a huge one at that.'

'Are you going to do it?'

'Suzanne, I don't have any choice. Of course I'm going to do it. Did you find out who's on for orthopedics?'

'Sam Christian's the only one around, but he's in the O.R. over at Clarion County. Apparently he just started an open reduction.'

'Damn. Well, listen, keep your eye on the Judge, okay? I'm going to call John Burris in Concord. He's an excellent neurosurgeon, and with that Beechcraft of his, he can be up here in an hour or less. Meanwhile, go ahead, call in the radiologist and get a CT scan of the area. See if we can assess the extent of bleeding. This day is really the pits, do you know that?'

'Zack?'

'What?'

'The Judge and Frank told me what kind of a person this Robillard is. If he's really as bad off as you say, maybe you should accept the inevitable and devote your energy to making sure your father's all right.'

'Suzanne, I can't believe you're saying that.'

'Really? Well, what if it were *me* lying in there with a piece of metal up against my spinal cord? Zack, this is your father we're talking about.'

'Suzanne, that man in there's dying.'

'You know, there are such things in this world as love and loyalty. They're allowed. According to some people, they're even worthwhile virtues to have. Even physicians are allowed to be human. That man you want to operate on steals and beats up on people, Zachary. That's what he does. The police say that the cab of his pickup was littered with empty beer cans. . . .'

Zack glared at her.

'I can't believe you're saying that. I just can't believe it.'

He turned and stalked into the room where his father lay beneath the X-ray camera.

'Dad, how're you doing?'

'My back aches, and my legs feel a little heavy.'

Zack tapped his reflex hammer against the Judge's Achilles' tendons, documenting once again through the reassuring flick of each foot that the ankle to spinal cord and spinal cord-to-ankle circuits were intact.

'Wiggle your toes, please. . . . Good. Other foot . . . good.'

'What's the story?' the Judge asked.

'Well, your wrist is broken, but it will keep until Sam Christian gets done at Clarion County. However, that piece of metal in your back ought to come out soon.'

'I thought so. You going to do it?'

Zack hesitated, and then shook his head, triggering a jackhammer pain between his eyes.

'No, Dad,' he said. 'I've got to do that man first or he's dead. Besides, we're not encouraged to operate on our own family if we can avoid it. I'm going to call John Burris up from Concord.'

'I want you.'

'Judge, please, don't make this any harder. You're quite stable right now. Robillard's dying.'

'Let him die.'

'I can't do that. . . .'

Clayton Iverson stared stonily at the ceiling.

In the silence, Zack became aware of others in the room. He turned. Frank and Suzanne stood just inside the doorway, watching and listening.

'Suzanne, please arrange the CT scan,' Zack said, trying to ignore the disapproval in her eyes. 'I've got to call Burris and then get into the O.R. I can see by your face what you want to say to me. Don't bother. I'm doing the one thing we are taught always to do – I'm doing what I think is right. . . . Judge, I love you, and I'll be keeping track of things. With luck, by the time Burris gets here I'll be done with what I have to do, and I can assist him. Meanwhile, just hang in there.'

He turned and left, brushing past Suzanne. She followed him for several steps, but then, shaking her head in resignation and frustration, headed for the radiology office.

'Ma's here,' Frank said, approaching the bed. 'Judge, I'm sorry. I tried to help him see reason.'

'Forget it, Frank,' Clayton Iverson said. 'Just leave me alone.'

'But Judge –'

'Dammit, Frank, I said leave me alone.'

Nothing felt normal or comfortable. The room, O.R. 4, seemed far too warm, the surgical team far too quiet. The blades and scissors and drill bits were too dull, the hemostats and needle holders unacceptably stiff or loose.

Zachary struggled to ignore his throbbing headache and his sodded scrub suit and to focus on the situation at hand. The circulating nurse, no longer waiting for his request, was mopping perspiration from his forehead and cheeks every two or three minutes.

They were nearly an hour into the Burr hole drainage procedure on Beau Robillard, and still there was no word that John Burris had arrived from Concord. Down the hall, in O.R. 2, a second surgical team stood ready.

'Valerie,' Zack said to the circulator, 'could you go on down to the E.R., please, and see what you can find out about Dr. Burris. He should have been here by now.'

Beneath his green paper mask, Zack's jaw was clenched. He was right in what he was doing, dammit. He was a physician, a surgeon, not judge and jury. Why, then, was everyone acting as if his decision were some sort of mortal sin? Surely they understood that he wasn't choosing this man's life over his father's. The Judge was stable, perfectly stable. Beau Robillard was dying.

'Pressure's down a bit,' Jack Pearl cautioned.

The words brought Zack's thoughts back in tune with his hands.

'Feel free to transfuse him a unit if you need to,' he responded. 'I've aspirated a fair amount through these Burr holes, but his brain's not showing any signs of reexpanding. If there's no action in a few more minutes, we're going to have to push ahead with a full craniotomy.'

The circulating nurse, Valerie, reentered the O.R. through the scrub room.

'Dr. Iverson,' she said, 'there's a problem downstairs.'

Zack shuddered.

'Yes, go ahead. . . .'

'I was told to tell you that Judge Iverson's feet have gone numb. He's unable to move his toes.'

'Who's with him?'

The urgency in his voice bordered on panic. He glanced down at the persisting space between Beau Robillard's skull and brain surface, and begged himself to calm down.

'Dr. Cole and Dr. Marshfield,' the woman answered.

'*And where in the hell is –*'

Zack breathed deeply and exhaled.

'Where is Dr. Burris?' he asked more evenly.

The eyes of everyone on the surgical team were fixed on him. There was, they all knew, little chance he could break scrub and leave the operating room without killing Robillard.

'The weather's gotten worse. Apparently there was a problem with Dr. Burris's plane,' the nurse explained. 'He's gotten someone to fly him up, but they lost some time.'

'How much till he's here?'

'Twenty minutes.'

'Damn,' Zack murmured.

It would take another hour to complete the craniotomy – the open procedure he now felt certain was necessary. And even with the procedure, Beau Robillard's chances of survival as anything more than a vegetable were growing dimmer each second.

'Have them give Judge Iverson five amps of Narcan IV, and get him up to the operating room now.'

'Five? But the usual dose is –'

'Dammit, I know what the usual dose is.' He took a deep breath. 'Sorry. I didn't mean to snap at you. The high dose is to help keep down the swelling in his cord. Also, please ask Dr. Cole if she can come up here and tell me exactly what's going on.'

In truth, Zack had little doubt as to what was going on. An epidural bleed, not predictable at all from his initial exam, was compressing the Judge's spinal cord.

Had he missed something? Had there been a clue?

Uncertainty and self-doubt hardened around Zack's hands like cement.

With Burris less than twenty minutes away, could any significant change be effected now by scrubbing out on Robillard and going after the Judge's bleed?

Zack gazed down at the man for whose life he had chosen to be responsible. Having made that choice, did he even have the right now to renege on it?

The doors to the O.R. burst open, and Suzanne, dressed in scrubs, stepped inside.

'The Judge can't move his legs,' she said. 'Burris is about to land. A cruiser's waiting for him at the airport.'

'Reflexes?'

'A flicker,' she said. 'It would seem, Doctor, that unless John Burris works a minor miracle, your father might well end up paralyzed from the waist down.'

At that moment, Jack Pearl called out, 'Dr. Iverson, his rate's dropping. I can't get a pressure.'

'Give him an amp of epinephrine.'

'Already done.'

'Get ready for CPR.'

'Pulse is dropping. Dropping more.'

'Damn . . . Begin CPR.'

'Doctor, he's straight line. . . .'

'Another amp of epi. Give him another amp of epi. . . .'

Chapter 28

It was after two in the morning. The fine, misty rain drifting over the valley for hours had sapped most of the warmth remaining from the day.

Zack lay sprawled on his living room floor, staring at nothing in particular. The only illumination in the room was from half a dozen candles and the red and green lights on his stereo receiver.

For the two hours since his return from the hospital, he had been listening to Mendelssohn and Mahler, talking almost nonstop to Cheapdog, and drinking – at first several beers, then beer plus shots of Wild Turkey, and finally, the 110-proof Wild Turkey alone.

'I didn't ask mush, y'know, Cheap? . . . Peace and quiet, some rocks to climb, a place to do my work without any hassles, the chance to make a difference. . . . Don't look at me that way. I know I said that before. So what? . . . You're the dog, so you just have to sit there and listen. . . . That's the way it is. . . .'

Zack could count on the fingers of one hand the number of major-league drinking bouts he had ever had, but he felt determined to add this night to the list.

Beau Robillard had survived his cardiac arrests on the operating table, only to experience several more arrests in the recovery room. Zack had called off the resuscitation after intensive efforts failed to bring back any functional cardiac activity.

In retrospect, given the extent of the cerebral contusion and hemorrhage Zack had discovered during surgery, it seemed that the die was cast for Robillard the moment the side of his head had connected with whatever it had.

Unfortunately, in the heat of battle, with no time to spare and a life on the line, there was simply no way for him to know that ahead of time.

'. . . You know what medicine's like, boy? 'S like you come to rely on this wonderful woman who has promised you that if you treat her right, she'll always be there when you need her. . . . So you do. . . . You study, and no matter how exhausted you are, you don't take any shortcuts. . . . And then, when you need her the most, when your own goddamn father's involved, you follow the system and use your clinical judgement, and do just what you're supposed to do, and *poof!* She's gone. . . . Gone! Damn women . . . Damn medicine . . .'

Zack had pronounced Beau Robillard dead just as John Burris was completing the removal of a jagged chunk of rusty metal from deep within the muscles of Clayton Iverson's back. Although there was no evidence that the fragment had pierced the dural lining of the spinal canal, apparently there had been some impairment of blood flow to the cord, because the Judge's paralysis had progressed and was now being regarded by Burris as total paraplegia.

Whether the condition was permanent or not, Burris would not speculate, although both he and Zack knew all too well that the prognosis following such a development was not good.

Word of Zack's decision, the Judge's paralysis,

and Beau Robillard's death had spread through the hospital like wildfire. That Robillard's blood alcohol level had come back well below that of legal intoxication, while the Judge's was above the 0.1 cutoff, was a fact lost in the rumors and the stories of the accident, and the virtually universal condemnation of Zack's disloyalty to his father.

Suddenly, it seemed, there was not a soul in all of Ultramed-Davis who did not have a bone or two to pick with Beaudelaire Robillard, Jr., nor one who had not been helped at one time or another by Judge Clayton Iverson.

Throughout the hideous evening, which ended with a tense, one-way conversation at his father's bedside, Zack did not hear so much as one word of support from anyone for the difficulty of his position or the rightness of his decision.

With Suzanne and Owen Walsh watching Toby, and John Burris staying the night in the guest room at the hospital, there was no reason for him to stay around. And there was every reason to come home and get drunk. In the morning, he would in all likelihood pack up and leave. If only there were some way he could take off for parts unknown without bringing himself along.

With the heat turned off, and no fire in the hearth, the house had begun to absorb the chill of the night. Zack pushed himself up and shuffled to the bedroom for a sweater. He was surprised that although he had had more to drink over a shorter period of time than he could ever remember, he felt quite steady on his feet.

There was a certain irony that on this particular night he was unable even to do a decent job of getting drunk.

Returning to the living room, he laid a small fire, put on a slightly less morose album, and sipped another ounce of Wild Turkey. He could understand the Judge's stony castigation of him, and even his mother's. They had every right to be upset. But Suzanne's reaction was a bitter pill.

She was a physician, to say nothing of being his lover. Even if no one else did, she should have had some compassion and understanding for his predicament.

He poured another ounce.

Years before, in the very beginning of his training, he had wrestled with the issues of making decisions in medicine, and had chosen to adopt the careful, objective, by-the-book approach over any of the more flamboyant, headline-grabbing tactics embraced by many of his surgical colleagues.

The decision had not been that difficult.

He was a second child, a plodder. He had done his best with what tools he had. Why couldn't Suzanne understand that? Frank was the buccaneer in the family. He was a scholar. Frank danced on the wind. He needed a system.

The room was growing stuffy and uncomfortably warm. If he closed his eyes for any length of time, it began to spin. His stomach felt queasy, his head like modeling clay.

Perhaps he had had enough to drink. Perhaps it was time to . . .

Zack fought the unpleasant feelings, crossed to the window and opened it a slit. The cool air felt wonderful.

Toby Nelms about to be shipped off to Boston . . . The Judge, paralyzed . . . The man he had chosen to treat instead, dead . . . He himself anathema at the hospital. Could things have possibly turned out any worse?

There are such things in this world as love and loyalty. They're allowed. . . .

Suzanne's words. He should have listened to her.

He was simply too stiff, too inflexible. Connie had told him that more than once, before she had checked out of his life. Now, Suzanne was trying to tell him the same thing.

Too many rules. Not enough person.

He gazed out across the glistening yard, past the low thicket, to the wall of jagged rock that he had named There, hoping someone, someday, would ask him why he climbed it. The granite face, perhaps three hundred feet up and five hundred across, was the single aspect of the house that had most appealed to him when the Pine Bough realtor was first showing him around.

Sloping upward at seventy-five to eighty degrees, the face crested at a broad plateau with a better than decent view of the valley. The climb, though somewhat tricky, was one he had already made several times.

But always, he suddenly realized, he had climbed in the sunlight and with equipment. Always, he had done it by the rules. . . .

He negotiated a few heel-to-toe steps without any difficulty, and stood on one foot for several seconds. The alcohol would be no problem, he decided. Probably he hadn't even drunk as much as he thought.

Rules . . . systems . . .

Zack strode to the hall closet, pulled on his rubber-soled climbing shoes and his windbreaker, and stuffed a small but potent flashlight into his pocket.

It was time to stop being a second child. . . . Time to loosen up and shatter the mold . . . Time to break some rules . . .

'Because it's There,' Zack cackled as he slipped out the back door and into the chilly night. 'Just because it's There.'

What in the hell other reason did he need?

The air held little more than a hint of the fine, black rain, but it was still cool and heavy. Several times as Zack crossed the yard and thrashed his way through the dense thicket, he swore he could see his breath. By the time he reached the base of the rock face, his climbing shoes were soaked through.

Climbing alone, at night, after a few drinks, in the rain . . . how many more rules could he think of to break? Perhaps, he mused, he should go up blindfolded as well. No reason to do things halfway. After a brief debate, he rejected that notion. What he was doing was quite enough for the moment – the first in a series of steps that would ultimately lead to his tranformation as a person and a physician.

He moved laterally through the tall grass until he located a decent starting point, and then peered upward along the ebony granite. Above the rim, the heavily overcast sky was only slightly less black than the stone itself. It was going to be a hell of a climb.

And when it was over, when he had proven what he needed to prove, he would lie beneath the trees on the plateau overhead and watch as dawn floated in over the valley.

The exhilaration of the adventure coursing through him, Zack reached out and pressed his palms against the damp, cool stone. Then, with a final glance above, he was off.

Five feet . . . ten . . . twenty . . . forty . . .

The climb, even with the alcohol and the darkness and the rain, was a piece of cake.

Fifty . . . sixty . . . seventy . . .

Every time he needed a sound hold, his fingers found one. He was 'zoned' – climbing with a beautiful smoothness and synchrony. If he had wanted to, he *could* have done it blindfolded. Below – now far below – he could see the candlelight flickering in the windows of his house. His street, the winding road toward the river, the occasional car, the night lights of town; with each new hold, each upward step, his vista broadened.

It was a magnificent climb, he told himself. . . . Absolutely magnificent . . . Connie was right. . . . So was Suzanne. . . . He should have been breaking rules like this long ago. . . . While it had been reasonable to operate on beau Robillard – reasonable and medically sound – in the final, metaphysical analysis, perhaps it might not have been right.

Ninety feet . . . one hundred . . . maybe more . . .

Below, the steeply sloping rock had no features. Above, there was only blackness. His progress was slower now, but steady still. The wind had picked up a bit, and a fine spray was, once again, spattering him through the night.

Minute by minute, Zack began feeling his breath becoming shorter, his grips not quite as firm. Foul-tasting acid started percolating into his throat and up the back of his nose. How much, exactly, *had* he had to drink?

Concentrate, he begged himself. *Use your adrenaline, your experience, and focus in. . . .*

The handholds became more slippery, smaller, and more difficult to find. He was traversing more as he searched for safe leverage, ascending less. His fingers were beginning to stiffen up. Behind him, nestled in the gloom, was his house – so tantalizingly close, so incredibly far. Without lines, descent in the dark and the rain was simply out of the question.

Then, without warning, he slipped.

His foot went first, skidding off the edge of a niche he thought was safe. Instantly, his grips gave way as well. He slid ten or fifteen feet, slamming his elbow against a small outcropping and skinning his knee and his chin. He reacted instinctively, using technique and years of practice to stem the fall.

Clawing and kicking at a shallow crevice, he was able to bring himself to a stop.

Then, gasping, he clung to the rock until, inch by inch, he was able to work himself to a more secure spot. His elbow and his knee were throbbing, but not broken. His lungs were on fire. Waves of cramping pain had begun to shoot from his stomach through to his back.

He looked below him. The rock face, what little of it he could discern, seemed almost smooth. It was ascend or find some way to strap himself in where he was, and remain there until morning.

Then he remembered the flashlight. How could he have forgotten it? He loosened his grip and gingerly reached down and patted his windbreaker pocket. The light was gone – probably lost during the fall.

At that moment, searing pain knifed through his gut and he vomited, retching again and again. Foul, whiskey acid poured through his mouth and out his nose, spattering onto his clothes and shoes and cascading down the rock.

For five minutes, ten, he could only hang on and struggle for breath. He was in trouble. He had broken the rules, and he was in more trouble, more danger, than he had ever been in his life.

Gradually, his head began to clear, and his gasping respiration slowed. He was at least a hundred fifty feet up, he guessed; maybe more. Certainly, he was more than halfway. He could use his jacket or his belt to secure himself against the rock, but in the dark, there was no real spot he could count on. His only option was to climb, and to pray.

Once again, hold by hold, inch by inch, he started upward. The rain and the wind were real factors now, making every grip more treacherous, every ledge less dependable. The taste in his mouth and throat was abominable, the stiffness in his fingers, elbow, and knees worsening every second.

Still, he climbed.

It was all so stupid. He had taken on the cliff to . . . to what? He couldn't even remember. All that was clear was that he had taken a bad situation and made it much, much worse.

He glanced behind himself. His house was a toy, a shadow, vaguely discernible against the glow of a nearby streetlight. Peering up the rock face, through the rain overhead, he could almost swear he saw the edge of the plateau.

The pitch seemed steeper, the handholds even smaller. Zack scanned the rock face to his right, looking for a traverse that would set up the last segment of his climb. Damn, but he needed that light. It had been stupid, arrogant, and careless not to have tied it on.

Stupid, arrogant, careless . . . That thought brought the wisp of a smile. Before his great decision to break free of his personal constraints, he had been none of the three.

One limb at a time, he worked his way across the rock, searching with his fingertips for the changes that would, once again, guide him upward.

Almost there, he urged himself on. . . . *Almost there . . . Almost . . .*

Before he could adjust or even react, his right foot missed its plant and skimmed off the rock. His arms snapped taut. His hands, both with reasonable grips, held; but they were already stiffened and weak.

Straining his head back and to one side, he looked down. His feet were dangling a foot or so below the nearest purchase.

Oh God, was all he could think of at that moment. *Oh God . . . Oh God . . .*

Reluctant to put any additional pressure on his fingers by struggling, he lifted one foot, gingerly scraping it along the rock, searching for a ledge or a crevice. Below him, at a pitch that was almost sheer, the granite face disappeared into blackness.

Oh God, please . . . Oh God . . .

His foot caught the edge of a minuscule ledge. On a dry day, the tiny space would have been a virtual platform for him – more than enough. But now, there was no way to tell.

Desperate to take some of the pressure off his fingers, Zack planted the toe of his shoe on the ledge and carefully shifted his weight to the foot.

Hold, damn you . . . Please ho –

For a moment, the foot felt solid. Then, as he added more of his weight, it slipped off the edge, tearing his right hand free of the rock. For five seconds, ten, his left hand held.

Then, with a painful snap, his fingers gave way and he was falling, tumbling like a rag doll, over and over again down the sheer rock, screaming as he hurtled against granite outcroppings, shattering one bone after another. . . .

'Nooooo!'

His final scream, the howl of an animal, echoed in his mind, and then blended with another sound . . . a voice . . . Suzanne's voice.

'Zack? For God's sake, Zack, can you hear me?'

He felt a cool, wet towel sweep across his face.

Slowly, he opened his eyes. A cannon was exploding in his head. He was on the living room floor, soaked in fetid vomit. The lights were on. Suzanne was kneeling over him, concern darkening her eyes.

Nearby, resting on its side, was an empty bottle of Wild Turkey.

Across the room, watching intently, sat Cheapdog.

Chapter 29

'Never again. I swear it. Not a drop. Not ever.'

Over the span of two and a half hours, with Suzanne as guide, Zack had wandered from the terror of his alcohol-induced hallucination, through a valley of tearful self-deprecation, across a brief stretch of cheery self-deprecation, and finally into an abysmal hangover.

'Never again?' she asked. 'Do you want me to put that in writing? You can sign it and hang it on the wall.'

Zack pressed against his temples.

'Write whatever you want,' he said, 'as long as the pen doesn't scratch too loudly on the paper. I just hope you can tell that I'm a total amateur at abusing my body like this.'

'Oh, I can tell.'

He did not clearly remember the shower, or the shampoo, or the first sips of tea, but he knew that Suzanne had taken him through each. Now, although his head still transposed each heartbeat into mortar fire, his thoughts had cleared enough at least to carry on a workable conversation.

He risked a deeper swallow of tea, and nearly wept with the realization that it was going to stay down.

'You've done an amazing job of putting me back together again,' he said. 'Thanks.'

She smiled sadly.

'No big deal. Unfortunately, my ex-husband gave me a lot of practice.'

'Great. I'm sorry.'

'Don't be. It was bad, but like everything else, it came to pass. . . .'

'Have you been up all night?'

'Uh-huh. Helene's with Jen.' She handed him a cool washcloth. 'Here, wipe your face off with this. You want some aspirin?'

'Soon. How are things at the hospital?'

'No real change – at least as of half an hour ago. Toby's still in coma. His temp's around 102. Walsh thinks he'll have a bed for him at either Hitchcock or Children's by noon.

'And my father?'

'No change either, as far as I know. I think that neurosurgeon from Concord – what's his name?'

'Burris. John Burris.'

'Yes, well, I think John Burris is planning to have him transferred later today as well.'

'What a mess.'

Suzanne pulled back the curtain. Across the backyard, the first hint of dawn was washing over the face of There.

'So,' she said, motioning toward the granite escarpment, 'the dreaded scene of your midnight climb.'

'That's not so funny, Suzanne. I died on that rock. I really did.'

'Well, I certainly hope so. Because from what I've been able to extract from your babble these past two hours, I don't think I would have much liked the guy who crawled up there in the first place. Confused, self-loathing, arrogant, the perennial victim – too close to Paul Cole for my taste.'

'Hey, come on. I was just seeing things the way they are. There wasn't a single person in that hospital who had one encouraging word for me. Fifty thousand Frenchmen and all that . . . Well, those particular fifty thousand Frenchmen were saying that I screwed up. And don't forget, you were one of them.'

'I know. I'm sorry for that. . . .'

'Don't apologize. You were right – all of you were right. I did screw up. By the time I got home, I couldn't stand who I was. And hallucination or not, when I went up on that cliff back there, I was honestly trying to break free of myself, to . . . to become more, I don't know, more flexible, more human in my approach to medicine. And to everything else, for that matter.'

'I understand that.'

'And?'

'And I was wrong for saying the things I did. Zachary, you have no reason to change. You're an excellent surgeon, a decent, caring son, and a wonderful friend to me. And I had no right to unsinuate that you were otherwise. It was selfish and cruel of me. And it was wrong – very wrong. That's why I called in the first place – to tell you that. I felt so guilty for what I said to you at the hospital – for leaving the way I did – that I couldn't sit still. Then, when you didn't answer, I got frightened. That's why I drove out here.'

'I'm glad you did,' he said. 'But there was no need to feel guilty. You were right.'

'I was wrong, dammit! Stop saying that. . . .'

She took a deep breath to calm herself and rubbed at the shadowy strain that enveloped her eyes.

'Zachary, as I told you, Paul was . . . a very sad, very sick man, totally lacking in any center to his life, any perspective. He never, ever put me or Jen ahead of himself, of his booze, or his drugs, or his other women. Never. I still have trouble believing that I could have misjudged anyone so badly. That's why I've been so reluctant to get involved with you. But those things I said in the hospital last night – about loyalty, about what if it was me lying there – what I didn't appreciate until after you left was that I was really saying them to a man I was trying not to fall in love with, not to another doc with a terrible decision on his hands. I was punishing you for being the first man since Paul that I wanted to trust. I was wrong, and I'm sorry.'

Zack stared down at his hands.

'Thanks,' he said. 'But you weren't wrong. The truth of the matter is that my father is crippled, and I probably could have prevented it.'

'Zack, the truth of the matter is that you did what you thought was right. You didn't cripple your father; an automobile accident and a piece of metal did. Can't you see that? You did all you ever will be able to do. You did your best.'

Zack could only shake his head. Hadn't he once said precisely the same thing to Wil Marshfield? Why couldn't he believe it now, hearing it from her?

'. . . Doing what we do for a living isn't easy,' Suzanne was saying. 'Nobody ever promised us it would be. Nobody ever told us that everyone we took care of would get better, or that every decision we made was going to turn out to be the right one. Medicine isn't a board game with a set number of cards and answers. Every situation is different.'

Zack looked over at her glumly.

'How in the hell am I ever supposed to trust my own medical judgment again?' he asked. 'Can you answer that for me?'

'God,' she groaned. 'Listen, Zachary. Have another cup of tea. Then try a cold shower. Then, if you want to continue to castigate yourself, maybe you can try *really* climbing that wall out there. Do it with your hands tied behind your back, though. Put razor blades in your shoes. No sense in making it easy for yourself.'

'Hey, there's no reason to snap at me like that.'

'Yes, there is,' she said, sounding close to tears. 'There are plenty of them.' She snatched up her jacket and purse. 'I came over to make sure you were all right, to tell you I was sorry, and to let you know that I was falling in love with you. I've done all that. It hurts too much to stick around and watch you sink out of sight in your own little bog of self-pity. So if you'll excuse me . . .'

'Wait.'

She turned back to him. Her eyes were dark and filmy, and as drawn and sad as he had ever seen them.

'What is it?' she asked wearily.

'I . . . I'm sorry.'

'Don't apologize to me, Zack,' she said. 'What you're doing, you're doing to yourself. You've got nothing to apologize to anyone else for.'

'I'm sorry for not listening to what you're trying to say. How's that?'

'Whatever.'

'Suzanne, you don't understand.'

'Don't I? You forget that I was married to the master of melancholy. Unfortunately for you – for us – I understand *too well*. I feel terrible about what

415

happened to your father. I would no matter *who* he was. And I don't blame you for being upset – but it should be at the situation, Zack, not at yourself . . . at the vagaries of life and of medicine, not at the fact that you're not perfect. I'm sorry, but after all those years of Paul, I have no patience for this kind of talk. Life's too short. I simply have no patience for this at all.'

She headed for the door.

'Suzanne, please. Don't go.' He crossed to confront her. 'I don't like the way I've been sounding, either. Really I don't. But I've never had anything backfire on me like this before, and . . .'

'And what?' She was keeping her distance.

'And . . . nothing. I understand what you're saying. Let's leave it at that. It's all beginning to sink in. And . . . and I'm going to be okay. Really, I am. . . . Could you stay? Just for a bit?'

She eyed him warily. And then, for the first time all morning, she smiled. It was a tired, five A.M. smile, but it was vintage Suzanne Cole.

'Sure, Doc,' she said. 'I can stay for a bit if you want me to. You know, what goes around comes around. That definition of friend you once wrote for me cuts both ways: the one who helps you find the tools when you can't seem to find them for yourself.'

She led him to the couch and laid his head on her lap.

'You've got to face it, Zack,' she whispered, stroking his forehead. 'No matter how much you want to take off, no matter how much you're hurting, you've got to go back into that hospital, pick up the pieces, and get on with business. There's too much at stake not to. Way too much.'

'Way too much,' he murmured.

Slowly, his eyes closed. His breathing grew deeper and more regular. In seconds, he was out.

'Please, Zachary,' she urged softly. 'Please don't run.'

She lowered his head onto a pillow, brought his clock radio in from the bedroom, and set it for nine. A call to the O.R. would delay or postpone anything he had scheduled, and one to his office nurse would buy him time there as well. The next move would be up to him.

She was gathering her things when she spied a copy of one of her favorite pieces of medical writing: Davenport's classic treatise on the principles and art of clinical medicine. The slim monograph was wedged on the bookshelf between several huge surgical tomes. She opened it to a passage that she had read enough over the years to know nearly by heart, marked the page for Zack, and then slipped out the front door into the cool, hazy July morning.

Provided Toby Nelms was reasonably stable, there was still time to have a cup of coffee with Helene, to get Jennifer dressed and off to day camp, and to shower, before making rounds. She was nearing twenty-four hours without sleep, but as she so often told her anxious patients, nobody ever died from lack of sleep.

'Hello, Whitey? . . . Frank Iverson here. I'm glad I found you in. I know you're due to open in a bit, so I won't keep you. . . . Yes, well, I guess everyone in Sterling knows about it by now. Goddamn Beau Robillard. Never did a single decent thing his whole life, and now, he can't even die without hurting

someone.... The Judge is doing okay, Whitey. John
Burris, the neurosurgeon who operated on him, is
sending him down to Concord early this afternoon
by ambulance.... Well, I'm afraid you heard right.
As things stand, he's paralyzed from the waist
down. But Burris isn't making any predictions, and
we're all hopeful as hell this is just a temporary
condition. The Judge is tough, as we both well
know. If anyone can beat this thing, he can.... Say,
Whitey, actually there're two reasons I'm calling.
First was to touch base with you about the Judge,
and second was to tell you that I spoke to Sis Ryder
in dietary about next month's meat order. She's
agreed to try allowing your place to handle the
whole thing rather than going through the
Ultramed purchasing office. Just to see how it all
works out.... Oh, you're welcome. You deserve the
chance. Oh, listen, there is one other thing.
Needless to say, the Judge is in no shape to make
that meeting this morning.... No, I'm afraid there's
no way to delay the meeting. The contract calls for
the sale to be finalized at noon unless there's a
buyback vote by the board. I did speak briefly with
him a few minutes ago, and he seemed content just
to let each board member vote his conscience on this
thing, and let the chips fall where they may. But
Whitey, since you'll be running the meeting, there's
one big favor you can do for me. I'd really appreciate it if that vote later this morning could be by
closed ballot.... I know that's not how you usually
do it, but don't you think that would be the fairest
way? Do this for me, Whitey, and I promise you
that dietary contract will be just the beginning....
Excellent, excellent. Hey, then, I'll see you at the
meeting. And Whitey, thanks.'

Frank replaced the receiver in its cradle, sipped his morning coffee, and then drew a careful line through Whitey Bourque's name on the block-printed list of business he had to attend to that morning.

Before becoming administrator of Ultramed-Davis, Frank had never in his life made a list of things to do. Lists were for morning people, for grinds and drudges; for catchers and linebackers, not for quarterbacks. They were for draught horses, needing to know in advance precisely where they would be clopping to and when, not for thoroughbreds.

However, four years of exposure to the efficiency and effectiveness of UltraMA's data banks, plus the pressures of juggling a dozen or more difficult situations at once, had changed him. Now, he began each day with a carefully drawn-up menu.

Frank liked to look on his emergence as a list-maker as one of the more visible manifestations of his adaptability and maturity.

And of all the lists he had ever made, the one for this morning was easily the most exciting.

He scanned the roster of members of the board to assure himself that everything was in order for the meeting. It had taken a hell of an effort, but with the Judge's influence virtually neutralized, he had used the promise of a closed-ballot vote, plus certain other inducements, to capture the additional members he had needed to block the buyback. The votes – six in all – had not come cheaply, but he had done what he had to do.

The sudden turn of events had him giddy. The whole thing was unbelievable – absolutely incredible: Zack teetering on the edge of oblivion at Davis, waiting only for the smallest nudge; the Judge eliminated from attending the decisive board meeting.

He couldn't have scripted it better if he had tried. With Mainwaring due back from Georgia any time, everything had fallen into place – everything, that is, but one minor exception.

After brief thought, Frank took a black magic marker from his drawer and eliminated *Call Lisette* from his list.

'Fuck her,' he muttered.

The woman deserved neither the call nor the apology he had considered making. In fact, if there were to be any apologies, they would come from her. She would see the truth on her own – come to understand what she had pushed him to do – or she would lose out. The house, the car, the children. She would lose out big. He had more than enough friends in high places to ensure that she paid for her desertion. This was simply not the day for dealing with a whiny, passive bitch like Lisette. This was a day of triumph. If she didn't choose to be available to share it with him, that was her problem.

He took his list and carefully added: *Check with A.D. re: tonight.*

Perfect, he thought. Annette Dolan was the ideal choice to help celebrate the remarkable turn of events.

He keyed the intercom. Moments later, Annette knocked softly and slipped into his office. She was wearing a tight plaid skirt and a beige, short-sleeved angora sweater that seemed to be straining to cover her breasts.

'G'morning,' he said.

'Morning, yourself.'

She stood primly beside his desk, her hands folded in front of her skirt, her arms pulled tightly downward, lifting her breasts together in a way that made them look even more spectacular.

'I . . . um . . . I have some Xeroxing I need done,' Frank managed.

He passed some papers across to her.

'Twenty copies. No, make that thirty. You . . . ah . . . that's a great sweater.'

'Thanks.'

'Do you think you might be able to wear it to work tonight? Say at eight?'

'Oh, Frank, I don't know. My mom's not feeling too well.'

'I'm sorry to hear that . . .'

He hesitated, and then reached into his desk and brought out the diamond necklace he had planned to give Lisette for her birthday.

'. . . because I was kind of hoping you'd wear this at the same time.'

Annette's eyes widened.

'Oh, Frankie, it's beautiful,' she said. 'It's the most beautiful necklace I've ever seen. You're so good to me.'

'That's because you're so good to me. About tonight? . . .'

She ran her fingers over the piece.

'How could I say no?'

'I don't know. . . . How could you?'

He pulled her to him and kissed her, sliding his hand over her skirt and then up to her breast.

'Annette, honey, I don't want to wait until tonight. Just a little. Right here. Right now.'

'Fra-ank, please,' she said. 'You've *got* to wait. I have work to do, and all the Xeroxing, and that door isn't locked. And besides, he might hear us.'

'Who might hear us?'

'Why, your brother, of course. Didn't I. . . ?' She held her hand to her mouth and looked at him sheepishly. 'Oh my. I was about to tell you.'

Frank's expression darkened.

'How long has he been out there?'

'Just a few minutes. I'm sorry, Frank.'

'Hey, no need to apologize,' he said, giving her breast a squeeze. 'Just wear that sweater tonight . . . and your necklace. Okay?'

'S-Sure.'

'Perfect. Tell my brother I know he's here, and I'll be with him shortly.'

'Okay. I'm sorry.'

'Actually, now that I think about it, he couldn't have come at a better time.'

The receptionist brightened noticeably. 'Really?'

'Really,' Frank said. 'This will be the icing on the cake.'

He patted her behind as she turned to leave, and followed it with his eyes as she sashayed from his office. Then he added another item to his list in the same, perfect block print as all the others: *Fire Z.I.*

He paused, studying the notation thoughtfully, and then drew a small happy face next to it.

Chapter 30

'Dr. Iverson, Mr. Iverson said to tell you that he knows you're here and will be with you as soon as he can. Are you sure I can't get you something?'

'No, no, thank you.'

Zack managed to prevent himself, at the last possible instant, from augmenting his response with a shake of his head. Actually, the tympani that had been rehearsing in his brain had given way to the French horn section, and the tempest in his stomach had been downgraded to mere queasiness. Physically, it appeared, he was on the mend.

With a little assistance from Cheapdog, he had awakened well before the time set on his clock radio by Suzanne. On the coffee table beside him was a glass of water, a packet of Bromo Seltzer, and his old copy of Davenport, held open by his stethoscope and marked with a note from Suzanne which said, simply, *Be strong.*

Now, as he waited for his brother to decide that he had been kept waiting long enough, Zack withdrew the monograph from his briefcase and reread the passage.

Be diligent. Be meticulous. Be honest. Account for every variable. Acknowledge that which you do not know, and then, at the first opportunity, learn it. Believe in yourself.

423

That is our system.

Honor it, and it will support you like a rock.
Honor it, and even the death of a patient will be
no failure.

Zack had been especially grateful for those words
when he'd arrived at the hospital that morning and
been informed by his father's private duty nurse
that except for his wife, the Judge was seeing no
visitors, and that he had specifically included his
sons in that group.

Even Annie Doucette, facing surgery on her hip in
twenty-four hours, was less than cordial to him.
After being barred by the Judge's nurse, Zack had
gone directly to her room, hoping – naively, it turned
out – to be the first to tell her of what had happened.

'I am not pleased with you, young man,' she had
said. 'You save an old lady like me, who wants to
die, and then let something like this happen to a man
like your father. What kind of doctor is that?'

Zack had started to respond, but then had simply
shrugged and left. Another time, perhaps.

Nor was the hospital staff any more amiable.
Wherever he went, eyes were averted; greetings of
any kind were mumbled or withheld altogether.
Nurses and other physicians hurried in the opposite
direction as he approached.

He had decided to stick things out at Davis, but
reestablishing himself was clearly going to be an
uphill struggle.

Be strong . . . Be strong . . . Be—

'Annette,' Frank's voice crackled over the intercom, 'would you please ask Dr. Iverson to come on
in? And hold all calls – unless they're regarding our
father's condition. Thank you.'

Zack walked into his brother's office, wishing he were anyplace else.

'Have a seat, Bro,' Frank said. 'I was wondering when you were going to show up here again. Where've you been?'

'Oh, here and there. Mostly on the floor or on the toilet.'

'I know.'

Zack looked at him curiously.

'John Burris told me,' Frank explained. 'Apparently he called to give you a progress report on the Judge. He says you were obviously intoxicated and totally incoherent.'

'Aw, he was just being kind.'

'Zack, this isn't funny. Burris said something about it to one nurse, and already the whole hospital knows. Once they're lost, reputations around the hospitals don't get found again very often. Ask Guy Beaulieu.'

'Now who's being funny, Frank?'

'You know what I meant.'

'Well, one of the reasons I stopped by was to tell you that I was sorry for causing so much disruption around this place. I see now that I've got to back off a little if I'm going to get by here, even though I've only been doing what I thought was right.'

'Have you?'

'Dammit, Frank, you're an excellent administrator, but that doesn't mean you're on top of everything that's going on around here.'

'For instance?'

'For instance, that sleazy anesthesiologist, Pearl, and his sidekick, Mainwaring. They're up to something, Frank. They're using something other than what they say they are in the operating room. I swear it.'

'That's ridiculous.'

'I have proof.'

'Do you?'

'Well, not exactly. But I have some data about recovery times that are pretty damn suggestive. And I've learned some things about Mainwaring's past that even you might not be aware of. I'm telling you, there's a connection between that poor Nelms kid's seizures and whatever the two of them have been giving patients in the O.R. Frank, this hospital could be headed for terrible trouble. We've got to find out what's going on.'

'No, we don't, Zack-o,' Frank said simply.

'What are you talking about?'

'Well, first of all, we're not going to find out because there's nothing to find out. Those two men worked here for two years before you arrived, and there was not so much as a whisper of anything but praise for either of them. How do you explain that?'

'I . . . I can't really. At least not yet. But I'm right, Frank. I just know I am. Mainwaring's got a past that involves testing drugs illegally, and Pearl's hiding something. Couldn't you tell that from the way he behaved last night? He's so frightened of being found out that he was willing to put that kid to sleep with anesthetics he had never used on him in the first place. Something's going on, and dammit, I'm going to find out what.'

'No, you're not,' Frank said again. 'You're not going to find out because you're not going to be stirring up any more trouble around here. And you're not going to be stirring up trouble because you're through . . . finished . . . fired. You're done at this hospital as of right now.'

Zack stared at him in disbelief. Frank looked back at him, smiling placidly.

'Frank, that's crazy. I'm a physician on the staff. You can't fire me. Only the medical staff can do that, and then only after due process.'

'Oh, really? Here, Doctor. Here are the corporate bylaws. You don't work for the medical staff. It's on page seven. Check it out. You work for Ultramed. And Ultramed can fire anyone they goddamn well please. And I'm Ultramed, and you're fired.'

He held his hands out palms up. '*C'est tout, mon frère.*'

Be strong. . . . Suzanne's encouragement was growing hollower by the moment.

'Frank, you can't do this.'

'I can, and I did. You see, Bro, that's been your big mistake all along – not understanding that this is my hospital and that I can do whatever the hell I want to. I wanted Beaulieu out, and he was out. And now I want you out.'

'Frank, you forget that even though you might not have wanted Beaulieu here, you didn't fire him. He was being systematically and deliberately driven out by—'

'By who?'

Zack hesitated, remembering his promise to Maureen Banas. Then he decided that she would simply have to understand. His situation was too desperate.

'It was Ultramed, Frank. He was being driven out by Ultramed. Just look at that letter from Maureen Banas. That's proof you don't know everything that's going on around here. Do you think she wrote that of her own free will? She was coerced, Frank, by that company we work for. By Ultramed.'

'Was she?'

'Yes, she received a copy of that letter along with a note that—'

'That said if she told me about receiving it, both she *and* I would be fired?' Frank's gloating leer was at once disgusting and terrifying.

'Jesus,' Zack muttered.

'Nice touch, don't you think?'

'Oh, Frank. You are really sad. Why didn't you just fire him like you're trying to do to me?'

'He was an obstreperous sonofabitch, that's why. I didn't want him making a big stink. I was just learning the ropes then, Zack-o, learning how far I could go. I know them now, and they tell me that it's okay to fire you, so . . . you're fired. God, I really love hearing that.'

'You're crazy, Frank. Do you know that? You are absolutely nuts.'

'Maybe,' Frank said. 'But I am also employed. Which is more than can be said for you.'

'I'm going to fight you.'

Frank shrugged.

'Do whatever you want. As far as the company or the medical staff is concerned, you're a drunken, disloyal troublemaker. I doubt that even your little cardiology fluff will stick up for you.'

'Frank, Guy Beaulieu died because of what you did to him. *Died!* Doesn't that mean anything to you?'

'You have a good day, now, Zack.'

'And don't you even care that it's possible some madmen are poisoning patients in the operating room of this hospital? What are you?'

'I'll be speaking with the folks at Pine Bough

Realty. I'm sure they'll be more than happy to give you, oh, two or three days at least to get out of their house.'

'Jesus. I'm coming to that board meeting, Frank. I'm coming, and I'm going to tell the board and Ultramed what's going on here. The Judge may be paralyzed, but he saw what Ultramed and its policies did to Annie. He's had time to review Beaulieu's evidence and to convince people how to vote. I'm going to be there to reinforce his position.'

'Well, I spoke with him earlier this morning, and he's promised to keep hands off the whole affair.'

'Frank, that's a fucking lie. I was just up there. The nurse told me the Judge won't see either of us.'

Frank winked.

'Then let's just say that if he *had* spoken with me, that's what he would have promised.'

'You crazy bastard, Frank. . . . You crazy, crazy bastard.'

'I'll be happy to write you a letter of recommendation, provided the place you apply to is far enough away. Now, if you'll excuse me, I have a hospital to run.'

'I'll be seeing you later at the meeting.'

'Try it if you want to, Zack-o. The security guards will know exactly how to handle things if you show up there. And now, little brother, how about either you leave or I remind you of how much hurt you ended up with every time we fought behind the barn. I probably would enjoy that almost as much as I've enjoyed firing you. . . . You take care, now. Y'hear?'

Numbly, Zack wandered from his brother's office and through the busy corridors of the hospital.

The polished linoleum, the tile, the nurses bustling from one patient to the next in their starched whites, the framed prints in every room – how clean it all appeared on the surface, how perfect. The set of a movie.

Zack smiled grimly at the thought. Davis Regional had become a gleaming, movie-set hospital – Hollywood veneer with no soul. It was a nightmare. And now, a nightmare he could do no more than walk away from. He drifted into the intensive care unit.

Suzanne, wearing surgical scrubs beneath her lab coat, was in Toby's cubicle, moving about the heavily bandaged child in a way that could only mean trouble. At the foot of the bed, Owen Walsh, the pediatrician, watched, his perpetually cheerful expression darkened by concern.

'Hi,' she said, glancing over only momentarily. 'Glad you could make it.'

She studied the monitor, and then emptied the contents of a syringe into Toby's IV line.

'Problems?' Zack asked.

Having just been fired from the staff, he found himself strangely reluctant to approach the bedside.

'These last sixteen hours have been like a crash refresher course for me in pediatric pharmacology,' she said without looking up. 'Every time his temp goes up, his rhythm goes crazy. What we're doing here amounts to nothing more than a holding action. I sure wish we knew what was going on.'

I do know, he wanted to say. Instead, he forced himself to the head of the bed, where he made a quick check of Toby's pupils, eye grounds, and reflexes. While there was still no definite evidence of irreversible damage, there was certainly no sign of improvement.

'We've got the promise of a bed for him in Boston,' Owen Walsh said. 'But they can't transfer him until late this afternoon or this evening.'

Take him away from this place, away from Jack Pearl, and you take him away from his only chance.

Again, Zack's thought went unspoken.

'Anything I can do in the meantime?' he asked.

'You can review the steroids he's getting.' Suzanne checked the temperature reading from the rectal probe. 'Back down to one-oh-two. And look, Zack – his rhythm's stable again. Damn, what's going on?'

'If you're able to leave,' he said, 'I'd like to talk to you for a minute.'

Suzanne checked the monitor and Toby's chest, and then glanced over at Walsh.

'Just don't go too far,' the pediatrician said.

'We'll be right outside in the waiting room, Owen,' she replied. 'Besides, you're doing fine here.'

Walsh smiled. 'She saves this child's life at least five times in one night, and she says *I'm* doing fine.'

'Nonsense. I'll be back in a little bit. Hang in there.'

As soon as the door to the ICU waiting room clicked shut, Suzanne threw her arms about Zack's chest and buried her head against his shoulder.

'I knew you'd come back,' she said. 'I'm so damn proud of you – of both of us. Listen, as soon as we get Toby off to Boston, let's go to my place for dinner. Helene's going to take Jen for the night, and I have a batch of shrimp in the fridge and—'

'Suzanne—'

'No, listen, it's my guilt for acting the way I did in the E.R. last night, and only shrimp sauteed in garlic butter will—'

He held her by the shoulders and moved her away.

'Suzanne, Frank just fired me.'

'He what?'

'Effective immediately.'

'He can't do that.'

'Can and did. He even was kind enough to present me with a set of the corporate laws to prove he can.'

He held up the book for her to see. Only then did he realize how totally drained she looked. Her face was pale and drawn, her eyes reddened with strain and fatigue.

'This is crazy,' she said. 'What reason did he give?'

'Actually, according to page seven here, he doesn't need a reason. But just to be fair, he provided a couple: being drunk while on call – technically, I was, you see – being a disruptive influence. Hell, I can't even remember everything he said. Listen, you look really wasted. Why don't you find an empty bed and crash for an hour or two? I'll watch Toby. Frank won't even know I'm in the hospital. And even if he finds out, he won't do anything about it. Owen's too panicked about being left alone to allow that. We'll talk later, after we get the child to Boston.'

'No, Zack. I'm fine. Really,' she said. 'But Zack, we can't let him do this.'

'You don't understand. This isn't a hospital the way we were trained to know one. It's a merchandise mart that hires doctors and nurses and technicians.

And Frank is the president of that company – at least here in Sterling he is. He hires, and he can fire. Except with someone like Guy Beaulieu. In Guy's case, Frank didn't want the hassle Beaulieu was threatening him with, so he just took the route of destroying the man by rumor and innuendo. He admitted being responsible for all of that.'

'To you?'

'He had already fired me. What did he have to be afraid of? He was actually boasting when he told me.'

Suzanne sank onto the sofa.

'Oh, Zack,' was all she could manage.

'Listen, Suze, this is my problem, and I'll work it out.'

'No,' she said suddenly.

'What?'

'No, it's not your problem – at least not yours alone. It's all of ours. The medical staff, I mean. We're going to fight this.'

'Suzanne, I don't want anyone else getting hurt because—'

'No, listen to me. For years now, at least as long as I've been here, the doctors in this hospital have been acting like . . . like ostriches. This isn't the first time there's been a problem between Frank or Don Norman and staff doctors, Zack. It isn't the first time one of us has clashed with the system here and then suddenly found himself out. Don't you remember what Wil Marshfield said that first night? And I've been as much of an ostrich as anyone – so grateful for getting out of the trouble I was in that I've turned my back on any number of company decisions that might not have been in the best interests of our patients. I didn't feel committed enough to any one issue to make waves. But dammit, I feel committed now.'

'Suzanne, I don't want you—'

'Please. You had the guts to come back and face the music. And now, dammit, I'm going to see to it that the medical staff gets behind you. It's time we stood up for this community – time that we stood up for our own. . . .'

She rose and took his hands.

'Zack, hang in here. Please. Do it for all of us. If I can just get us to present a unified front, I'm sure the medical staff can stand up to the corporation. And if we can't get Ultramed to listen, then . . . then we'll just take our case to the community.'

'You think you could pull that off?' he asked.

'I'm tougher than I look.'

He touched her cheek.

'That's not saying much, you know.'

'Well, you just watch. Can you stand the heat?'

'Suzanne, I don't want to leave here. I don't want to leave you.'

'Okay, then. It's decided. As soon as I finish with my office appointments, I'm going to start twisting some arms.'

'It's not going to be easy.'

She kissed him lightly.

'It's not going to be as hard as you think. Listen, I ought to get back in there. What are you going to do right now?'

'I think I'm going to try and get in to see my father. He refused to see me earlier, but I think it's worth one more try. I was planning on putting in an appearance at that board meeting later today, but Frank has promised to have the hospital security people ready for me if I do.'

'Damn him. Zack, I think your brother and I are about due for a little meeting of the minds.'

'You would do that?'

'Would and will. I have too many friends around here, and make too much money for this place for him not to listen to me. You must be strong. . . . God, Zachary, it feels so good to realize that all of a sudden I'm not afraid anymore.'

'You were afraid of the corporation?'

'No,' she said, kissing him once again. 'Of you.'

Chapter 31

Brief operative note (full note dictated): . . .
Four-inch gash over T-10, 11, and 12 debrided
. . . hemostasis attained . . . wound explored. . . .
Jagged five centimeter by three centimeter
piece of rusty metal removed without difficulty
. . . dura appears intact . . . No collection of
blood noted. . . . Wound irrigated copiously,
and then closed with drain in place. . . . Patient
sent to recovery room in stable condition, still
unable to move either lower extremity. . . .
Tetanus and antibiotic prophylaxis initiated.
. . . Preoperative impression: foreign body, low
midback; postoperative impression: same,
plus paraplegia – etiology uncertain, possibly
secondary to spinal cord disruption or cir-
culatory embarrassment. . . .

Seated to one side of the nurses' station, Zack read
and reread the account of his father's surgery, and
confirmed through John Burris's terse progress
note and two much more detailed nurse's notes, that
there had been little change in the Judge's condition
since his surgery.

Dura intact . . . No collection of blood . . .

Zack chewed on the nub of his pen as he stared
out the window at the Presidential Range. Something was off. The Judge's symptoms seemed out of

proportion to the extent of his injury – way out of proportion. The pieces of this clinical puzzle simply weren't locking together.

Sheering forces snapping fibers in the cord, arterial spasm with enough interruption of blood supply to cause nerve damage – there were a number of logical explanations for the Judge's paraplegia, but none of them sat just right.

At one end of the Formica counter, a small plastic tray was piled high with pens and pencils, as well as a stethoscope and several other pieces of medical equipment. Zack slipped an ophthalmoscope, reflex hammer, and straight pin into his pocket and headed for his father's room.

It wasn't that he was questioning Burris's findings and opinion, he rationalized, it was just that . . . that a physician was taught never to completely trust anyone's findings or conclusions other than his own.

Now, if he could only get the Judge to allow him close enough to do an exam . . .

Cinnie Iverson was seated on a low, hard-backed chair in the hallway outside of her husband's room. She was, as always, dressed immaculately – this day in a plain blue dress, with a white cardigan draped over her shoulders. Lipstick and an ample amount of rouge failed to completely obscure her pallor. Her ever-present lace handkerchief was balled in one fist.

'Hello, Mom,' Zack said as he approached.

She stood, and allowed him to kiss her on the cheek. Her expression was cool, but not angry, which was to say, as disapproving as Zack had ever known it to be.

'How's he doing?' he asked.

'The nurse is giving him a bed bath.'

'Any change?'

Cinnie Iverson bit at her lower lip and shook her head.

'Mom, I . . . I'm sorry this has happened. You can't know how terrible I feel.'

'I'm sure you do,' she said quietly. 'We all do. . . .' She hesitated, then went on.

'Zachary, I'm quite sure that in time I'll see things more charitably, but right now, with the Judge lying in there like that, you'll have to forgive me if—'

'I understand,' he said. 'All I want you to know is the same thing I came up here to tell him, and that is that I was only trying to do what I thought was right.'

'I believe that. I don't think he'll speak with you, though,' she added. 'He's very upset – at everybody. And he's very depressed.'

'He doesn't have to speak, Mom. He just has to listen. Who sent the flowers?'

He motioned toward an enormous vase of lilies, orchids, and birds of paradise that he estimated must have cost one hundred fifty dollars – probably even more.

'It just arrived from Frank,' she said. 'Whether you know it or not, you owe your brother quite a thank-you. He was very helpful in keeping us all under control last night. Very helpful.'

'I'll . . . I'll thank him just as soon as I can, Mom.'

'I just don't know what we would have done without him.' She dabbed her handkerchief at the corner of one eye.

'I understand,' Zack said, fighting off a wave of rage.

'I only wish Lisette were around. At least then I'd know he was getting a decent meal once in a while.'

'He told you about Lisette?'

'He told me she and the girls are in Virginia visiting an old friend of hers, if that's what you mean.'

'Sure, Mom,' Zack said through nearly clenched teeth. 'That's what I meant.'

At that moment, the private duty nurse, an expansive woman with pendulous upper arms and thick ankles, wheeled her cart from the room.

'He's all set, dear,' she said. 'Sorry to take so long, but that husband of yours is a big man. . . .' She eyed Zack warily. 'Still no visitors, Doctor,' she said. 'I'm sorry.'

'Mom, I need to go in to talk to the Judge.'

Cinnie took a moment to size up the exchange.

'It's okay, Mrs. Caulkins,' she said. 'I'll take care of things here. You go do whatever it is you have to.' She waited until the woman had gone. 'Zachary, I'll ask your father if your visit would be okay, but I don't expect him to say yes.'

'Mom, it's important – very important that I speak with him.'

She hesitated.

'Mom, please . . .'

'You won't say anything to upset him?'

'Promise.'

'Well, then, I suppose you should be allowed to go in there and say your piece.'

'Mom, thank you.'

'And Zachary?' She continued to work her handkerchief over and over in her hands. 'I know you didn't mean things to turn out this way.'

'That's right, Mom,' he said, knowing that she

would miss the understatement – the sad irony in his voice. 'I certainly didn't.'

Muted sunlight, filtering through the nearly closed blinds, provided the only illumination in the room. The Judge, wearing a blue hospital johnny, lay on his back, staring at the ceiling. An intravenous line was draining into one arm.

'Hello, Judge,' Zack said.

Clayton Iverson glanced over at him, and then looked away.

'Are you in much pain?'

There was no response.

'Judge, it won't hurt to talk to me. Believe me, it won't. . . . Okay, okay, suit yourself.'

It might have been a mistake to have come. Zack could see that now. Merely going against the man's wishes was enough to warrant the silent treatment, let alone going against his wishes and achieving such disastrous results. He reminded himself that the Judge could be as petulant and inflexible as Frank.

Zack turned to go, but then he stopped. There were things he had to get out – if not for his father, then for himself.

'Okay, Judge, you don't have to say a word. I won't stay long. I just wanted to tell you that I feel very badly for the way things have turned out. I was only doing what I spent so many years training to do – using my judgment, and trying to do my best.'

He pulled a chair over as he spoke, and sat down by his father's hand. The Judge continued to stare at the ceiling.

'Judgment, Dad . . . that's what you have to rely on, too, now that I think about it. Maybe in time, that will help you understand the dilemma I was in. . . .

'Judge, you're my father. I love you for that – for the things you've done for me, for the kind of person you've helped me become. I would never want to see you hurt. Never. I honestly believe that I would give up my life, if necessary, to protect you. But that's *my* life. . . .

'Anyhow, I guess what I really want you to know is that although I'm sorry as hell for the way everything turned out, given the information I had to work with last night, if the same situation arose again, I would make the same choices. That's the sort of person my parents raised me to be, and the sort of surgeon I was trained to be. I came up here to ask for understanding, not absolution.'

He paused, hoping for some sort of reply. There was none. In that moment, he decided to say nothing of what had transpired with Frank. Soon, the Judge would learn it all anyhow, but this was not the time to attack the man's myth of his quarterback son.

'Well, then,' he said. 'I guess that's that.' He rose. 'Oh, except for one other thing. I'm going to that meeting today to present Guy's case to the board. I don't expect to sway many votes, but I think Guy was right. I think we need to take a hard look at what we're willing to give up in exchange for a few shiny pieces of equipment and some black ink on the bottom line. So if you could just talk to me enough to tell me where that folder of his is, I'll—'

'It's gone,' Clayton Iverson said flatly, still not looking at this son.

'What!'

'I said the folder is gone. I . . . I gave it to the Ultramed people to examine. They have it. Now please, go.'

Zack sighed.

'You certainly underwent one heck of a change of heart there, Dad,' he said.

'I asked you to leave.'

'I'm going. I'm going.'

As he turned, Zack's hand brushed against the instruments in his pocket. He hesitated, took several steps toward the door, and then turned back.

'Judge, I know you want me out of here,' he said, 'but . . . but I'd like to examine a couple of things on you if I could before I go.'

Tentatively, he returned to the bedside, waiting for the man's outburst. There was none. He lifted the sheet off his father's legs.

'Thank you, Dad,' he whispered, gauging the muscle tone of one calf with his fingertips. 'Thank you for trusting me this much. This will only take a minute.'

In fact, Zack's examination, carried out mostly with his touch and reflex hammer, took just over five minutes. Clayton Iverson watched him work in stony silence, although there was a spark of curiosity in his eyes.

By the time Zack had finished, by the time he had dropped down on a corner of the bed, shaken and mentally drained, the loose-fitting pieces of the clinical puzzle had been pulled apart and rearranged in the strangest of patterns.

'Mom, can you come in here, please?' he called out, after he had regained some composure. 'There's something I want both of you to hear together.'

Cinnie Iverson entered, took the chair next to the Judge, and held his hand.

Zack paced from one side of the room to the

other, choosing each word carefully, suddenly frightened that the tendon and muscle activity he had detected were not true neurologic indicators at all, but rather the phantoms of his own hopes.

'Judge, Mom,' he began, 'have either of you ever heard of a conversion reaction?'

Cinnie Iverson shook her head. Clayton did not move.

'An older term for it was conversion hysteria, but I never liked that phrase, because hysteria implies craziness, and a conversion reaction is much more an intense, involuntary focusing of emotional energy than it is a sign of anything crazy.'

'Zachary, what are you saying?' Cinnie asked.

'I'm saying that there are certain reflexes that disappear when the spinal cord is damaged, and others that show up. The pattern I'm finding now isn't consistent with that.'

'I'm not sure I understand,' Cinnie said.

'Judge, I know this may not make total sense to you at the moment, but I'm picking up signs – fairly strong signs – that your paralysis may be due to factors other than spinal cord damage – emotional factors.'

'Emotional factors?'

Cinnie sounded incredulous. The Judge showed no reaction at all.

'I know it sounds far out,' Zack said, 'but believe me, it isn't. It happens all the time. One of my first cases on my neurology service was a man with psychologically induced blindness. There was absolutely nothing wrong with his eyes, yet he positively couldn't see. In fact, after hynotherapy, much of his vision returned.

'Heart attacks in Type A personalities, gastric

ulcers in situations of high stress – our emotions have power over every organ in our bodies. There's even a well-documented condition called pseudo-cyesis in which a woman who desperately wants to become pregnant has her periods stop, her breasts grow large, and her abdomen swell. Only a blood test or an ultrasound or X ray can prove she's not pregnant.'

'And you think your father may be having one of these – what are they called?'

'Conversion reactions. Yes, Mom, I do. Judge, your neurologic findings simply don't jibe well with any other explanation.'

The Judge looked away.

'But why?' Cinnie asked.

Zack shrugged.

'I'm not certain,' he said. 'Anger at me is the most likely possibility. There are other factors that could be at work, too, I guess: fear, grief, guilt. Only you can fill in the blanks, Judge. But whatever it is, is very powerful stuff. At the moment, even you might not know. Many times, though, as soon as the source of the conversion is identified, the symptoms begin to resolve.'

'Are you sure about this?' Cinnie asked.

'No, Mom, I'm not. It's just that the other diagnoses don't fit with the operative findings and Dad's clinical picture, and conversion reaction does. I might be wrong. All I can do is hope that I'm not, and tell you what I think.'

'Clayton?' she asked.

The Judge, tight-lipped, would not answer.

'Zachary,' she said, 'perhaps you'd better go now. We can talk about this again soon.' She rose and kissed him on the cheek, her expression begging him to leave them be – to allow them the chance to digest what he had said.

'Sure enough,' he said. 'When is the ambulance due?'

'Any time now, I think.'

'Fine . . . Dad, I—' He looked down at his father's pallid, emotionless face. 'I'll be thinking of you.'

As he reached the doorway, Zack checked the corridor for his brother or a security guard, and then headed for a room at the far end of the hall. If, as it seemed, he was running out of time within the walls of Ultramed-Davis, he would use what little he had left to make one last run at a clinical puzzle that was no less perplexing than his father's, and far more lethal.

'I knew it,' Barbara Nelms said as Zack finished recounting his interview with her son and the theories he had developed as a result. 'You are not a very good liar, Dr. Iverson. I could see it in your eyes that night in your office. I should have called you on it then, dammit. You know, holding out on me like that was a very cruel thing to do.'

'I know, and I'm sorry. But I had no proof.'

'Dr. Iverson, Toby is my son.'

'I understand.'

Barbara was propped up in her hospital bed by several pillows. Her right arm was in a sling and her left was fixed to an intravenous line that was infusing a potent antibiotic. Despite her pallor and the heavy shadows engulfing her eyes, her glare was piercing.

'I'm not sure that you do, Dr. Iverson,' she said after some thought. 'But I'm willing to give you the benefit of the doubt – at least for now.'

'Thank you.'

'You said that you held back information from me and my husband because you had no proof of your theories. Am I to assume that situation has changed?'

Zack hesitated.

'Dr. Iverson, please,' she said. 'Don't try to lie to me again. My son nearly stabbed me to death yesterday without even knowing I was there.'

'Okay,' he said. 'Okay. The truth is, as things stand, I have no direct proof of anything. But the circumstantial evidence supporting my belief is quite strong – at least to me it is.'

'Tell me.'

Zack reviewed his impressions of Pearl and Mainwaring's gallbladder cases, and summarized his conversation with Tarberry at Johns Hopkins. He could see the anger smoldering in Barbara Nelms's eyes. In time, whether Toby survived or not, she would be out for blood. And where once that notion had been the impetus to have him lie to her, now it goaded him to share every detail. Frank had been given his chance to clean house, but he had ignored it.

'I wouldn't blame you a bit for being skeptical,' Zack said as he concluded his account, 'but that's the way I see it.'

'Dr. Iverson,' Barbara Nelms responded, her fury barely contained, 'this is the first time since this nightmare began that an explanation has fit with the facts as I know them. I believe every word you've told me. Every word.'

She turned and stared out the window. Resting on the rim of her sling, her fist was clenched. Slowly, her fingers relaxed. The tension in her neck and back lessened. When she turned back to Zack, the anger had given way to determination.

'Now then, Dr. Iverson,' she said, 'what can we do to save my son?'

Zack took a moment to sort his thoughts.

'Well, first of all,' he said finally, 'it would help tremendously if we could find the trigger.'

'You mean the thing that sets Toby off?'

'Exactly.'

'But how?'

'I want you to close your eyes, lean back, listen to my voice, and begin to tell me everything you can think of surrounding Toby's attacks. Everything, no matter how trivial it may sound.'

'Are you going to hypnotize me?'

'I can. And I will, if it seems appropriate. But I believe all you'll need is a little help. Now, relax as much as you can, open your mind, and let it drift back to Toby's very first episode.'

'He . . . he was in his pajamas. . . .'

'Good. Go on.'

'It was before bed . . . He was playing. . . .'

'Playing what?'

'I . . . I can't remember.'

'Was he in his room?'

'Yes . . . No, no, wait. He ended up in his room, but I don't think he started there. He . . . he was in the den. He was watching television. Yes, that's right. That's exactly right.'

'Good. Very good. Now, what was he watching?'

'The show?'

'Yes.'

'I . . . I can't remember.'

'Just relax, Barbara. You're doing fine. . . . Now, just open your mind to that evening and think about what he might have been watching. . . . See it. . . . Just relax, open your mind, and see it. . . .'

The muscles in Barbara Nelms's face went slack. Her breathing became deeper and more regular.

'That's good,' Zack whispered. 'That's very good.'

Zack's words brought a strange, enigmatic smile to Barbara's mouth.

'I know what he was watching,' she said. 'Each time, I know what he was watching. . . .'

Chapter 32

Zack raced down the corridor at nearly a full run, hesitating only to glance into his father's room. The bed was stripped, and an aide was washing down the plastic mattress cover. He bolted through the stairway door and vaulted down to the first floor.

A major piece in the puzzle had fallen into place – a piece that irrefutably connected Toby Nelms, Suzanne, and Jason Mainwaring. Now, Frank would have to listen.

'My brother in?' he panted to the buxom, blond receptionist.

Annette Dolan looked at him strangely.

'He is, but—'

'Thank you,' Zack said, already on his way through Frank's office door.

Frank, behind his desk, working at his computer, looked up coolly.

'You don't work here anymore,' he said.

'Frank, I've got to talk to you. I've learned something – something important.'

'Mr. Iverson, I'm sorry. I tried to stop him,' Annette Dolan said from the doorway.

Frank smiled at her emotionlessly.

'That's okay, Annette,' he said. 'I know how persistent my little brother can be. I'm sure you did your best to stop him. Before you get back to work, though, why don't you go on home and change that sweater. It's not appropriate for the office.'

The receptionist hesitated a beat, her lower lip quivering. Then she turned and hurried away.

'Now, then,' Frank said, glancing at his watch, 'what on earth could be important enough to take you away from your packing?'

Zack moved to sit down, but Frank stopped him with a raised hand.

'Don't get comfortable, sport,' he said. 'Just say what you want to say and leave.' He motioned to the computer. 'Number six now, Zack-o. Six out of nearly two hundred administrators nationwide. Not bad, if I do say so myself. No, siree, not bad at all.'

'Well, then you'd better listen to me, Frank. Because I've learned something that could bring this place crashing down about your ears if you don't do something about it.'

There was no more than a flicker of interest. 'Oh?'

'It's that anesthetic, Frank. The one I tried to tell you about before.'

'Go on.'

'I just came from speaking with Mrs. Nelms, the mother of the boy in ICU.'

'I know who she is,' Frank said.

'Well, I was going over some of my concerns with her, and—'

'You what?'

'Frank, just calm down and listen.'

'No, *you* listen. Do you have any idea how much of a nuisance that woman will be if you fill her with all that human experimentation bullshit of yours?'

'Frank, it's not bullshit. It's really happening, and you'd better help me do something about it or this place will be crawling with lawyers, hospital-certification people, and police. I promise you.'

'Don't you dare threaten me.'

'Well, then, will you please listen, for Chrissake? Suzanne's life may be on the line here, to say nothing of that poor kid in the ICU. We don't have much time.'

Frank toyed with a paper clip for a few moments, straightened it, and then snapped it in two.

'Okay, Bro,' he said finally. 'You've got five minutes.'

'They're experimenting with something, Frank – Mainwaring and Pearl. They're fooling around with some sort of new general anesthetic, and they think it's working fine, only it isn't. The patients look asleep during their surgery and even think they *were* asleep afterward. But at some level, just below their conscious surface, they were wide awake, experiencing the whole thing – the cutting the blood, the pain, everything.'

'Sport, I didn't believe you this morning, and I don't believe you now.'

'Well, you'd better. I have proof.'

'Oh?'

'It's the music, Frank. "Greensleeves" – the music Mainwaring operates to.'

'What in the hell are you—'

'Mainwaring nearly always works to one piece of music. It's a classical version of "Greensleeves" – you know, the folk song from—'

'I know the tune,' Frank said testily.

'Well, according to Mrs. Nelms, every time her kid had one of his seizures, he was watching a children's show where they play that melody.'

'That's your proof?'

'There's more. Last week Suzanne and I were together, when suddenly she went blank, totally blank.'

'So?'

'Frank, that tune was playing on the radio. As soon as I shut if off, she snapped out of whatever place she was in, and kept on talking as if nothing had ever happened. I didn't put together what was going on until just now. She was on her way, Frank. I'm sure now that if I had left the radio on a little longer, she would have had a seizure just like the kid's. She was on her way to reliving her breast operation – probably in some bizarre, distorted way – just the way Toby kept reexperiencing his hernia repair.'

'This is ridiculous.'

'It's fact, Frank. Listen, you've got to help me find Mainwaring, or at least help me try and reason with Pearl.'

'No way.'

'That child is dying. We need to know what they gave him.'

Frank picked up the phone and dialed.

'Chief Clifford, Frank Iverson here,' he said. 'That restraining order I asked you for ready yet?'

'Jesus, Frank, you *are* crazy,' Zack said.

'That's fine, Chief, fine. So it's effective immediately?'

'I'm going to tell the board what's going on here, Frank – the board *and* Ultramed. And as soon as I find Mainwaring, I'm going to—'

'Chief, could you do me a big favor and send a couple of men around now? He's here, and he's refusing to leave. . . .'

'Dammit, Frank.'

452

'Thanks, Cliff. . . . Oh, he's doing as well as could be expected. It's nice of you to ask. John Burris, the neurosurgeon from Concord, has transferred him down there. . . .'

'Frank, for Chrissake—'

'Hopefully, we'll be getting a new neurosurgeon in town soon, so that we won't have to send folks out who need our help. . . . Exactly. Well, thanks again, Cliff. When can I expect those men of yours? . . . Excellent. You run a crack operation, Cliff. The best . . . You bet. Take care now.'

Frank laid down the receiver with exaggerated deliberateness.

'You've got about three minutes to get your ass out of my hospital,' he said, 'and less than a day to get it out of our house. I'd suggest you get home and start packing. And I promise you, if you so much as set foot in this place, or say one word to any of our patients, you will be in deep, deep shit. Is that clear?'

'Frank, you're making a big mis—'

'I said, is that clear?'

Without responding, Zack headed toward the door. When he opened it, a hospital security guard – if anything, even larger than the guard, Henry – was standing there.

'It's a little button right down here,' Frank explained, gesturing to the base of his desk. 'I never had to use it until now, but it just paid for itself. Tommy, would you please see to it that Dr. Iverson here is out of the hospital and off hospital property right away.'

'Yessir.'

'No stops.'

'Yessir.'

'It's not going to work, Frank,' Zack said.

'I'll take my chances.'

'What about that kid?'

'That kid will be better off having a doctor who doesn't get drunk when he's on call, sport. Now, I see by the ol' clock on the mantel that your five minutes are about up.' He looked out the window. 'Oh, and there are our friends from the constabulary, right on time.'

'You are something, Frank. You really are.'

Frank smiled broadly.

'Yes,' he said, 'I know.'

'Greensleeves.'

Curious, Frank fished through his desk drawer for the cassette Mainwaring had given him and popped it into his tapedeck. It was syrupy, spineless music – certainly far from being any sort of lethal weapon. Clearly, Zack had flipped over the edge, grasping at any straw in an effort to disrupt his brother's finest hour.

'No way, Zack-o,' Frank murmured. 'No fucking way.'

He snapped off the tape and then watched through his office window as his brother was led across the hospital parking lot to his car by two policemen and the hospital guard. It was a scene he would carry with him forever. The days of sports trophies and star-struck coeds might be part of the past, but this triumph would do quite nicely.

As he followed Zack's battered orange camper down the hill toward town, Frank knew that the last obstacle toward his achieving every one of his goals was all but disappearing. With the Judge out of the way, and Bourque having agreed to a closed vote, the final purchase of the hospital by Ultramed was a virtual lock. And with Zack out of the way, there was nothing to interfere with the satisfactory conclusion of his dealings with Mainwaring.

He felt at once exhilarated and exhausted. It had been a brutal game, but with time running out, he had just run in for the go-ahead touchdown and then recovered the fumble on the ensuing kickoff. Now, he had only to hang on to the ball and run out the clock. He glanced at his watch. The board meeting was less than an hour away. He reminded himself that no matter how exhausted he felt, this was not the time to let down.

'Loose ends . . .' he murmured. 'Loose ends . . . loose ends . . .'

He called the guard room and ordered an extra man brought into patrol the outside of the hospital, on the off chance his brother tried anything foolish. Then he phoned two fence-sitting board members to tell them about the closed-ballot vote and to call in favors he was owed. Finally, he called Atlanta and learned that Jason Mainwaring had left for New England the previous evening and was expected back in Atlanta the next day. Perfect, he thought. If the secretary's information was correct, Mainwaring had to be planning to conclude their transaction that afternoon.

Again, Frank checked the time. For the moment, there was nothing he could think of to do but wait. He returned his attention to the still-open hookup with UltraMA. Soon, perhaps within a day, his access code would be upgraded to that of a regional director and he would be made a party to some of Ultramed's most sensitive information.

Regional director, with a cool three quarters of a million dollars in the bank. Frank Iverson was within a cat's whisker of making it all the way back and then some. When she walked out on him, Lisette had made the biggest fucking mistake of her life. By the time the dust settled, he would have it all – the position, the money, the house and, goddamn it, the children, too. She'd see. He had handled the board, he had handled his brother, and he would handle her just as well.

Only when the knock on his office door grew persistent did Frank notice it.

'Who is it, Annette?' he asked through his intercom. 'Annette?'

There was no answer. Then he remembered having sent the woman home, and cursed himself for forgetting that his other secretary was on vacation.

'Come in,' he called out. 'For crying out loud, stop that pounding and come in.'

Jason Mainwaring, wearing his customary beige plantation owner's suit, entered, carrying his briefcase.

'Little shy on office help, aren't we?' he said, heading directly for Frank's liquor supply.

'You know me, Jason. Slice off the excess fat. Everything goes down to the bare bone.'

Mainwaring ran his fingertips over the glistening mahogany surface of Frank's desk.

'Yes,' he drawled. 'I can see that philosophy at work all around me'

'I called Atlanta a while ago. Your secretary said she expected you back there tomorrow. You're welcome to use your house for a few more days if you want.'

'Thanks all the same, but I've been here about two years too long already. My replacement lined up?'

'Ready to cut. He's due here next Wednesday.'

Frank felt determined to keep his eagerness in check. He knew that Mainwaring wanted Serenyl at least as much as he wanted Mainwaring's million. If this was their last skirmish, he was damned if he was going to let the man leave with the upper hand. He crossed to his bookcase and poured himself a glass of tonic. Then he deliberately set aside Mainwaring's 'Greensleeves' tape, which he'd been listening to, and snapped on a Mantovani in its place.

The surgeon flinched.

'Iverson,' he said, 'are you tryin' to bait me?'

'Hardly, Jason. I just thought that since this might be our last meeting together, I might see if I could change your opinion about Mantovani. This album's called *Roman Holiday*. What do you think?'

'I think we should get his business of ours over with. That's what I think.' Irritably, the surgeon rose and shut off the tape.

Frank unlocked a drawer of his desk and withdrew a thick envelope.

'Here it is, Jason,' he said. 'Signed, sealed, and ready to be delivered.'

'Just as we had it drawn up?'

'You were there.'

'Well, then . . .' Mainwaring set his briefcase on his lap and opened it. 'Our chemists have approved Dr. Pearl's work, and my company has authorized payment to you of the sum we agreed upon.'

'That being?'

'That being the sum we agreed upon. Iverson, don't play games with me, or I swear, I'll be out that door.'

'In that case, Jason, you'll be out two years of your life as well.'

Frank was feeling glorious. It was the sort of scene he had watched his father play any number of times over the years. Now, there was a new Iverson pulling the strings – a new Iverson at the top of the heap.

Mainwaring hesitated, then flipped an envelope onto the desk.

'Barclay's Bank, Georgetown, Grand Cayman Islands,' he said, somewhat wearily. 'They won't release the money to you until they hear from me. But if you have doubts about the account numbers, feel free to call them.'

'That won't be necessary, Jason. I trust you. Besides, I've arranged for my man at the Cayman National Bank to transfer the funds to accounts there as soon as he hears from me. So, if you'll just check over those papers, we can each make a call.'

'You are quite the most distasteful man I have ever had dealings with, Iverson.'

'Thank you,' Frank said. 'From you, I'll take that as a compliment. Now, if you'll be so kind.'

He slid the phone across to the surgeon, then sat back as calmly as he could manage and waited. When the calls were completed, he dropped Mainwaring's envelope in his drawer and watched as the surgeon tucked the bill of sale and the patent rights to Serenyl into his briefcase. A million dollars, Frank was thinking. Just like that – a million dollars.

'I hope this means we're about to see the last of one another,' Mainwaring said.

'We'll miss you, Jason,' Frank replied with a straight face. 'We surely will.'

458

The surgeon stood and gave Frank's proffered hand an ichthyic shake. Then he whirled and was gone.

Frank walked to his bathroom, washed his face, and studied himself in the mirror.

'Funny,' he said, straightening his tie and then winking at his reflection, 'you don't look like a millionaire.'

Judge, you're my father. I love you for that – for the things you've done for me. . . . I would give up my life, if necessary, to protect you. . . .

Lying on his stretcher, Judge Clayton Iverson watched the foliage flash past through the rear windows of the ambulance as he reflected on his son's words. They had passed through Conway five or ten minutes before, he guessed, so almost certainly they had split off from Route 16 and were heading southwest on 25, toward Moultonborough and the northern rim of Lake Winnipesaukee. Beside him, the paramedic, a woman with Orphan Annie hair and an eager, child's face, was carrying on a running conversation with the driver, pausing occasionally to check his pulse and blood pressure.

It was all so painful, the Judge acknowledged; so confusing. One moment, he was on top of the world, the next he was speeding through town to confront his older son with the facts of his dishonesty and embezzlement, and with the reality that, once again, the man had been given every opportunity and had failed. And even more distressing, Frank's perfidy had, in effect, ripped control of the Ultramed-Davis situation from the community board and handed it to Leigh Baron on a plate.

. . . Paralysis may be due to factors other than spinal cord damage. . . . Guilt, fear, grief. Only you can fill in the blanks, Judge. . . .

There was no cause for guilt, the Judge reasoned desperately. Beau Robillard hadn't done one thing of value his entire life. Clayton Iverson had been elected Sterling Man of the Year six times. Six! Besides, if blame were to be placed, it should go to Frank, not to him. If it weren't for Frank, there would have been no accident. If it weren't for Frank, there would have been no drinking, no lapse in concentration, no missed red light.

. . . Given the information I had to work with last night, if the same situation arose again, I would make the same choices. . . .

If it weren't for Frank, Zachary would never have been put in the position of having to make such a terrible decision. At least Zachary had had the guts to face him – to face him and to hold his ground. *Why hadn't he appreciated his younger son more before?* Explanations, but no excuses. That was the way of a real man. Frank always had excuses.

Now, because of Frank, Ultramed would have control of Davis forever, and with that control, a stranglehold on Sterling that even Clayton Iverson would be unable to break.

There was no sense lingering over the spilled milk that was Beau Robillard. That milk was soured to begin with. But the hospital was a different story. John Burris had told him that trying to attend the board meeting was out of the question, and in truth, he had wanted to get as far away from both of his sons as possible. But now . . .

If only he weren't so damned helpless. If only he could move. . . .

'Judge Iverson,' the paramedic said.

'Yes, what is it?'

'Sir, you just crossed you legs.'

'What?'

Clayton Iverson looked down at his feet. They were, in fact, crossed – his left ankle resting on his right. Gingerly, he lifted the upper leg and set it down on the stretcher. Then he lifted the other. His pulse began to pound.

'What time is it?' he demanded.

'Eleven, sir.'

'Where are we?'

'Just outside of Moultonborough.'

'Tell the driver to turn around.'

'Excuse me?'

'Turn around, dammit. Turn around. I've got to get back to the hospital.'

'Sir, we can't—'

'Do you know who I am? . . . Well then, I said turn around. I don't have time to argue. I'm paying for this ambulance, and I swear, if you don't do as I say, there will be hell to pay for both of you!'

'But—'

'Now!'

'Y-Yessir.'

The woman knelt beside the driver, and after a brief exchange, the ambulance swung into a drive-way and turned around.

'Use your lights and siren, and step on it,' the Judge said.

'But sir, we're not allowed to—'

'The siren, dammit! I assure you nothing bad will happen if you do, but everything bad will happen if you don't. Quickly now, let's move.'

The driver hesitated, and then switched on the lights and siren and accelerated.

Behind him, Judge Clayton Iverson crossed and uncrossed his legs again.

'Well, I'll be damned,' he muttered. 'I'll be goddamned.'

Chapter 33

Shortly after she had seen the first several office patients of the morning, Suzanne sent word to her nurse to try and reschedule as many of the rest as possible. It was, perhaps, the most killing aspect of private practice that a day's patients had no way to adjust to their physician having been awake most or all of the previous night. And, indeed, it was doubtful most of them would even want to try. They had waited days or even weeks for their appointments, and they expected – and deserved, as far as Suzanne was concerned – to have their physician be one hundred percent theirs for the short time they had together.

Normally, even after a grueling night she could rev herself up for her office work. This morning, though, try as she might, she simply could not hold her concentration together. A seventy-five-year-old lady who was taking double the amount of digitalis prescribed, had nearly slipped past her. A housewife had gotten cross with her for not seeming to take her complaints of fatigue more seriously. A pharmacy called because she had neglected to write the strength of a cardiac medicine on one of her prescriptions.

And, she knew, her difficulty was not simply one of fatigue. A child she felt responsible for and a man she was growing to love were both in serious trouble. Her thoughts kept ricocheting from one to the other. Twice, already, she had called the unit to check on Toby's status, despite knowing that she would be contacted by Owen Walsh or the nurses at the first sign of trouble. Twice, already, she had interrupted the workday of medical staff members to gauge their response to some sort of job action should Frank refuse to back down on his dismissal of Zack.

And overriding even her concern for Zack and Toby Nelms was her growing indignation at the treatment Guy Beaulieu had apparently received from Frank, and the mounting likelihood that unauthorized chemical experimentation was being conducted at the hospital. For more than two years, gratitude for her salvation from Paul and her legal entanglements had kept her from voicing any criticism of Frank's decisions or Ultramed policies. Now it was time to take a stand.

She buzzed her nurse.

'Janice, how are we doing with those reschedulings?'

'You're clear for the next hour, Dr. Cole,' the woman said. 'I haven't been able to reach Mr. Braddock or that new referral from Hanover, but I'll keep trying.'

'Excellent. Listen, I'll be in the unit or on page if you need me. There are a few things I've got to get done.'

She left her office and took the glass-enclosed walkway from the Physicians and Surgeons Building to the main hospital. On her way to the ICU, she passed the Carter Conference Room. Two dietary aides were busily arranging the tables for a luncheon meeting – almost certainly, she realized, the meeting of the community board and the people from Ultramed. There could be no better time to confront Frank with her concerns than right now. He would listen, and make some major concessions, or face the embarrassment and conflict of having her present those misgivings to the meeting.

Frank's outer office door was closed. Suzanne opened it and stepped into the deserted reception area.

'Hello? Frank?' she called as she tapped on the inner door. 'It's Suzanne Cole. . . . Frank?'

'It's open, Suzanne.' She was startled to hear his voice through the intercom on one of the desks behind her. 'Come in.' She opened the door and he rose from behind his desk.

'Well, now,' he said, shaking her hand. 'This is a pleasant surprise.'

'Thanks, Frank. I'm sorry to barge in on you like this, but I need to talk with you.'

He glanced at the Lucite clock.

'That would be fine, Suzanne, but this just isn't the time. You see, I have a b—'

'I know what you have, Frank,' she said, taking a seat in one of the pair of oak-armed chairs facing his desk. 'You have a meeting with the community board and the people from Ultramed. Before you go into that meeting, I think you should hear what I have to say.'

'Oh, you do.'

His buoyant expression chilled, perhaps, a degree.

'Yes. But first, I wanted to find out why you fired Zachary.'

'Because I always do what is in the best interests of my hospital, and getting rid of a disruptive, drunken troublemaker was clearly in the best interests of my hospital. Speaking of which, would you like a drink?'

'Frank, listen to me, please. Two years ago you helped me out of a huge jam. I'm grateful for what you did, and ever since I've been here, I've done my best to support you.'

'And I appreciate it, Suze. You've been great. Tell you what: as soon as this board business is taken care of, let's you and I do dinner on Ultramed and talk about some sort of increase in your pay.'

Suzanne felt her irritability quicken.

'Don't patronize me, Frank. I came here to get some issues straight – to voice some concerns Zack has shared with me. And Frank, if you can't respond to those concerns, I intend to go in and raise them at that meeting.'

I'm afraid I can't let you do that, Frank was thinking, rapidly sorting through his options. The votes to finalize the sale were almost certainly there now, but they were shaky. And of even greater concern were the clauses Mainwaring's corporate lawyers had forced into their contract, requiring legal reprisals or an immediate return of their investment should there be any deception – or even suggestion of deception – regarding the properties of Serenyl. *No, siree, baby*, he concluded, *I'm afraid I can't let you do that at all.*

He propped his elbows on the desk and his chin on his hands.

'Okay, shoot,' he said.

'That's better. Well, I have two requests I would like your word on, Frank.'

'Go on.'

'First of all, I want your promise to allow the

medical staff to determine whether or not Zack has been disruptive enough to be fired from the hospital.'

'Done,' he said.

'What?'

'You have my word. As soon as possible, next Wednesday's meeting if you want, we'll present our cases to the medical staff and let them decide. Satisfied?'

'I . . . I guess so.'

'Good. Now, what's number two?'

'Well, number two has to do with some concerns Zack has raised regarding Jason and Jack Pearl.'

'Ah, yes, the infamous anesthetic.'

'You don't believe him?'

'Of course I don't believe him, Suzanne. But I am investigating his allegations.'

'You are?'

Frank was hardly acting like the man Zack had described meeting with earlier that morning. And despite herself, Suzanne once again felt a spur of doubt regarding what she had been told.

'Absolutely,' Frank was saying. 'I have already contacted the members of the medical ethics committee, as well as Jason and Jack, and have scheduled a meeting for the first thing next week. Call them and check on that if you want. I'll be happy to have both you and my brother present if you wish.'

'I wish. But what about Toby Nelms?'

'What about him?'

'Frank, if what Zack believes is true, that child might not have until the first thing next week. Is there any way you could try and reason with Jason and Jack, just in case?'

'Jason's away, but if it will make you feel better

about things, you and I can meet with Jack at, say, five o'clock today, right here.'

'Thank you. Would you mind if Zack comes, too?'

'If you insist. Suzanne, you're one of the best things that has ever happened to this place. I would do anything I could to keep you here and happy. But now, if you'll pardon me, there is a meeting room filling up with people. We can plan on getting together again at five o'clock.'

By then, his thoughts continued, *I'm sure I will have come up with some more permanent way of dealing with both you and my brother.*

'Frank, I appreciate all of this very much,' she said, rising.

In that moment, inexplicably, she began to sense that something was wrong – very wrong. The whole session had gone much too smoothly. There was too great a difference between the man Zack had described firing him and the one she was confronting now.

'Hey, no problem,' Frank was saying, his hand extended. 'I'm as committed as you are to making sure this place is the best.'

Suzanne took his hand and, for just a few seconds, continued to hold it. There was an unnatural feel to it – a coolness, a tension.

'Frank, tell me on last thing,' she said, releasing his hand but keeping her eyes firmly fixed on his. 'Were you responsible for all those rumors and stories that circulated about Guy?'

Frank held her gaze unwaveringly. 'Absolutely not,' he said.

In that instant, Suzanne knew. The unflinching darkness in his eyes, the earnest set of his face – it was a look that had confronted her before. Many times before. *It was Paul!*

'Frank, you're lying to me, aren't you?' she said.

'Nonsense.'

He forced calm into his voice, but beneath his lightweight suit, he had begun to sweat. There was no way, he reaffirmed even more strongly, that Suzanne Cole was going to that board meeting.

In the back of his desk drawer was a small revolver. Carefully, Frank eased the drawer open. Then he stopped. If Zack was right, there was an easier, far easier, means of regaining control of the situation. It was certainly worth a try.

'Suzanne, sit down, please,' he said calmly, rising from his own chair.

Puzzled, she did as he asked.

'There's something I want you to listen to.'

'Okay, but I don't see what—'

'Please.'

'A-All right.'

She followed him with her eyes as he crossed to his stereo, switched on the tape deck, and replaced the cassette that he had listened to earlier. After just a few notes, she recognized the music.

'Have you heard this before?' Frank asked, returning to his desk and opening the drawer another inch.

Suzanne did not answer. Instead, she began to stare at the large aerial photo of the hospital complex. The colors were growing more and more intense.

Get up! her mind screamed. *Get up and run!*

Her legs would not respond.

'Well, have you?' he asked again.

His voice was rumbling and muted, his face twisted in a strange, bemused smile.

'Well, I'll be damned,' she heard him say.

Suzanne rubbed at her eyes. The sounds in the room – Frank's breathing, her own, gave way to the music, which itself drifted farther and farther away.

Then she heard the voice – slow and patient and reassuring.

'All right, Suzanne, now I want you to count back from one hundred. . . .'

'One hundred,' she heard herself say.

'Go on . . . go on.'

'Ninety-nine . . . ninety-eight . . .'

The blue johnny covering her was pulled away, exposing her breasts. She shivered at her nakedness and the sudden chill.

'Ninety-seven . . . ninety-six . . .'

'She's under, Jason.'

'Excellent. Let's get started, then.'

'No, Jason,' she begged, as russet anesthetic was swabbed over her breast. 'Please wait. It hasn't worked yet. The anesthetic hasn't worked.'

'Turn the music up a bit. Fine, that's fine. Okay, then, knife.'

'No, wait! Ninety-five! . . . Ninety-four! Please hurry, please work.'

Overhead, the bright, saucer light flashed on. Gloved hands appeared just below Jason Mainwaring's sterile, blue eyes. Nestled in the right hand was a scalpel. In agonizing slow motion it drifted down toward her.

'Jason, no!' she screamed as the blade cut into the skin by her shoulder, releasing a spurt of crimson.

The pain intensified as the scalpel began slicing a slow arc around the base of her breast. But before she could scream, a gag was pulled tightly between her teeth and tied behind her head, and her arms were bound just as vigorously to her sides.

Soundlessly, praying for the relief of unconsciousness, Suzanne endured the agony of the surgical removal of her breast. And when the dissection was complete, she looked down at herself in wide-eyed terror. Where once there had been skin and breast tissue and a nipple, now there was only a gaping, bloody crater.

In that moment, amidst a final, silent scream, blackness mercifully intervened.

Fascinated by what he was observing, Frank set the stereo playing *Fantasia on Greensleeves* for automatic repeat and turned up the volume. For once, at least, his goddman brother had been something of a help.

Suzanne lay semiconscious on her back on the rug, twitching and shuddering from time to time, and crying out as much as the handkerchief tied tightly through her mouth would allow. Frank loosened the sleeves of his suitcoat, which he had used to bind her arms, and then cut a bath towel into strips. It was probably overkill, he realized, even to bother tying her up. Mainwaring's syrupy music was doing as fine a job of immobilizing her as any truss. Still, at least until she could be removed from the hospital to some safe – and permanent – resting place, it was worth the extra precaution.

He rolled her onto her side and bound her hands tightly behind her. Then he laid her back and secured her ankles. Her eyes remained closed, but her restless movements had increased – almost in reflection to the intensity of the music.

Frank knelt beside her. Even under such difficult

circumstances, she was a real beauty. Brains and looks – Leigh Baron without the hard edge. When Suzanne had first come to Sterling, he had made several carefully gauged attempts to start something up between them. Each time, she had politely but firmly refused him. It angered him that, after just a few weeks in town, his brother was already getting inside her pants.

Well, so be it, he thought. *The two of them deserved one another.*

And as soon as the board meeting was over, he would set about seeing to it that they got to spend an eternity together. He had tried to play it easy with both of them, but that approach had nearly blown up in his face. They had forced him to take off the gloves, and now they would see what kind of competitor Frank Iverson really was. He had always played to win, and now there was far, far too much at stake even to think of backing off.

He reached down and ran his fingertips over Suzanne's face and then down over her breasts. She really did have a phenomenal body. *Phenomenal!* Lisette, Suzanne – Zack was spiteful enough to be planning on screwing them both, if he hadn't done so already.

No way, Zack-o, Frank thought as he dragged Suzanne into his bathroom and set her on the damp floor of his shower stall. *No way you're ever going to humiliate me like that.*

He smoothed out his suitcoat and combed his hair. The music reverberated through the tiled room. Behind him, reflected in the mirror, Suzanne continued to jerk spasmodically.

Perhaps, Frank thought, after the meeting, before he set about arranging an accident of some sort for her and his brother, he would take a few minutes to enjoy the favors she had denied him. To miss such an opportunity would be a shame.

Besides, he mused as he checked himself in the mirror, a moment before setting off for the board meeting, it would be a crime to waste such romantic music.

Chapter 34

'I'm sorry, Dr. Iverson, but as I told you before, I'm under strict instructions from Mr. Iverson that no calls from you are to be put through to anyone at the hospital except him.'

'But all I want you to do is to page Dr. Cole for me. Ask her to call me.'

An hour had passed since Zack had been fired and ushered out of the hospital he had expected to work in for the rest of his professional life. He had driven home with the patrol car following him right into his driveway, and then had tried to reach Suzanne at her office. After a number of busy signals, he had gotten a tape saying that the office would be closed until one. He had tried his own office, but the line had already been disconnected. Now, after a fruitless call to the hospital switchboard and a no-answer try at Suzanne's home, he was giving the page operator one last shot.

'I understand what you are asking, Doctor,' the operator said.

'And even when I tell you it's a medical emergency you won't do it?'

'Mr. Iverson was quite specific.'

'What's your name?'

'Janine.'

'Well, Janine, I appreciate that you have your orders, but how is Mr. Iverson to know if you just put this one call through for me?'

'You'd be amazed at the things Mr. Iverson finds out, Doctor. And if he does, it's my job. Now please, I've got to get back to my board.'

'Janine, wait – Damn.'

Zack slammed the receiver down and then snatched it up for another attempt. This time, he stopped before the switchboard operator could even answer. Frank had put an airtight seal on the hospital that no simple phone call was going to breach. Nor did it help matters that his decision to forsake his father's care in favor of the town derelict had reduced his influence around Ultramed-Davis to near zero.

Still, he had to get back into the hospital – to tell Suzanne of the trigger, and, he hoped, to enlist her help in confronting Jack Pearl. He had given up on even trying to speak at the board meeting. Frank would have him in a cell before he could get close to the door. But Toby Nelms was a different matter. Without cooperation from Pearl, without the man's willingness to admit what he and Mainwaring were doing, he felt quite certain the boy was as good as dead.

Perhaps, he began to think, the board meeting might be the key. With Frank inside the conference room, and his security people stationed nearby, there might be some other, unguarded way inside the hospital. He scratched out a crude drawing of the building as best he could remember it. There was, he was nearly sure, a delivery entrance outside the cafeteria – one that had to be open. Assuming Suzanne was in the ICU, he could enter the hospital through the kitchen and reach the ICU by a back staircase.

He checked the time. The board meeting, if not

already under way, would be starting any minute. He could park on the highway and circle through the woods to the delivery entrance. Police or no police, it was worth a try.

He tied Cheapdog on his run and then lurched the camper out of the drive and down the hill toward the hospital, hoping that the time for Toby's transfer to Boston had not been moved up. As he drove he pictured the boy sitting cross-legged on the rug in his house, watching his favorite hero cavorting across the screen, urging him to join in a song extolling the virtues of the letter P.

'Alas my love, you do me wrong . . .'

How many others, Jack? he said to himself, practicing the words he would use. *How many other time bombs have you and Mainwaring planted in your patients?*

The hospital was located on the opposite side of town from Zack's house. Ordinarily, he took the highway bypass around Main Street. This day, lost in thought, he missed the turnoff and was well into town before he realized it. Traffic was heavier than usual, and it seemed, from the long line of cars at the corner of Birch, that the light was malfunctioning. After a moment's debate, he backed up a foot and made a U-turn, narrowly missing a two-tone Oldsmobile that was speeding past.

It took several seconds before he realized that the driver of the Oldsmobile was Jason Mainwaring.

Zack began honking and waving, but it was several blocks before Mainwaring became aware of him and pulled over. They confronted one another in a small streetside park, circumscribed by an arc of slatted benches arranged about a marble pedestal and bust of one of Sterling's founding fathers.

Several grizzled men sat on two of the benches, smoking cigarettes, watching the passing scene, and occasionally sharing surreptitious sips from a brown bag. They watched curiously as the two well-dressed men approached one another.

'Jason,' Zack began, somewhat breathlessly, 'God, am I glad to see you.'

The surgeon looked at him strangely.

'I'm sorry, Iverson,' he said after a beat, 'but I've signed out to Greg Ormesby. If y'all need any surgical help, I'm afraid you'll have to call—'

'This has nothing to do with surgical help. Jason, we need to talk. I've been trying to locate you for several days.'

'I've been at home in—'

'Georgia. I know.' He glanced over at the old men, and then motioned to the bench farthest from them. 'Please, Jason, what I need to speak with you about is pretty urgent and very private. Could we talk over there?'

'Well, Iverson, I'm afraid I'm in a bit of a rush. Why don't we get together say—'

'It's about the anesthetic.'

Mainwaring's color drained.

'I beg your pardon?' he said.

'Over there?' Zack again motioned toward the bench.

By the time they sat down, the surgeon appeared as composed as ever.

'Now, then,' he drawled, 'just what anesthetic are you talkin' about?'

'It's the one you and Jack Pearl have been using on your cases, Jason. The one that allows them to get out of the recovery room three times faster than anyone else's cases.'

'I'm afraid I don't understand,' Mainwaring said. But Zack could see from his eyes that he did.

'I don't have time to play games,' he said. 'A child is dying, and I have reason, good reason, to believe that your anesthetic is at fault.'

A minute tic developed at the corner of Mainwaring's eye. The hint of understanding disappeared from his face. This time, Zack felt certain, the man was genuinely surprised.

'Look, Iverson,' he said, 'I just don't have time for this nonsense. If you have something to accuse me or Jack Pearl of, then I'd suggest you do it through channels. I would also suggest you have a shitload of proof.'

'Jason, please,' Zack said, trying desperately to keep civility in his tone. 'This isn't ethics or charges we're talking about. It's a child's life. Please listen.'

Item by item, in a near whisper, he reviewed his investigation into the case of Toby Nelms. Mainwaring listened impassively. Only at the mention of Darryl Tarberry did Zack detect any reaction.

'So that's where things stand,' he concluded. 'The boy's mother is certain that at least several times he was watching this children's show when he had his seizures. It's a show that features a version of "Greensleeves" – the same music you use in the operating room. If I could just get my hands on whatever it is you were using for anesthesia, I think I might be able to help that kid.'

'Oh, you do?'

'It's a long shot, but right now, it's his only chance.'

'Well, then,' Mainwaring said, 'it would appear

that the boy has no chance at all. Because, y'see, Iverson, there is no mystery anesthetic.'

Zack stared at the man in disbelief.

'Iverson, just who have you shared these charges with?' the surgeon asked.

'Jason, these aren't charges. A child is dy—'

'Who?'

'The child's mother.'

'That all?'

'Suzanne.'

'She believe you?'

'She was willing to listen. But I spoke to her before I learned about the trigger – the music. Now Jason, please—'

'I asked if she believed you.'

'Not completely, but after I tell her what I've learned, I'm certain she'll—'

'Not completely,' Mainwaring cut in snidely. 'Iverson, I sure hope you have one hell of a lawyer. Have you mentioned this nonsense to your brother?'

Zack glanced at his watch. The board meeting was already under way.

'Mainwaring, this isn't nonsense. If that child dies, if anyone who received that drug dies, then it's murder.'

'Don't threaten me,' the surgeon said, shaking a finger at Zack. 'Don't you ever threaten me. Now, I asked if you had shared this hokum with your brother.'

'I did. Dammit, Mainwaring, doesn't any of this have an impact on—'

'When did you tell him?'

'Just a while ago.'

'And his response?'

'Mainwaring, there's no time for this—'

'*What was his response?*'

'He ignored me.'

'Just as I intend to do,' Mainwaring said. 'Now, if you'll excuse me.' He rose.

'Mainwaring, you can't do this,' Zack said loudly.

The grizzled observers' interest heightened, and one of them sputtered on the contents of the brown bag.

'Can, and am,' Mainwaring said just as loudly. 'Now you just quiet down, Iverson, or you'll have even more charges to deal with than you already do.'

'Mainwaring, are you some kind of fucking monster?'

The surgeon turned and headed for his car.

'Well, are you?' Zack screamed after him.

Mainwaring, now at his car, turned back and shook a finger at him.

'Watch it,' he said venomously. 'Just fuckin' watch it.'

The sun, which had been gliding in and out of hiding all morning, slid behind a dense billow of gray cloud, instantly cooling the air. Zack pulled the camper onto a dirt track off the Androscoggin road and worked his way upward through a forest still sodden by the midnight rain. He felt ill over his unsuccessful encounter with Mainwaring, and could not dispel his anger – not only at the surgeon, but at his own handling of the man.

Had he been too aggressive? Too abrasive? Would his arguments have been more effective if he had simply brought Mainwaring to the hospital and let him see Toby Nelms for himself? The questions burned in his thoughts as he picked his way uphill toward the north side of the hospital.

Only one thing was certain now. With Frank an enemy, and Mainwaring unwilling to expose himself to charges, Jack Pearl was all the hope the child had left. And without either of the other two men to back him up in a confrontation with the anesthesiologist, that hope was slim, indeed.

Through the trees ahead, Zack could see the top two floors of the hospital. The broad glass windows were, he noticed for the first time, tinted just enough to give them an ebony cast. The effect was cold and uninviting.

He moved up to the edge of the forest and flattened himself against a thick beech tree. To his left, just beyond an expanse of grass and past the corner of the building, was the patio of the cafeteria. A group of nurses sat laughing and talking at the only table in his line of sight. The entire north side of the hospital was deserted.

Cautiously, he picked his way along the treeline toward the corner farthest from the patio. He would have to dash across, perhaps, twenty yards of lawn to reach the delivery door. From there, he would walk nonchalantly through the kitchen, searching for a route to the corridor that did not take him through the crowded cafeteria itself.

Ahead of him the tinted windows of the hospital glinted ominously in the muted midday light. If there were faces behind those windows watching him, he would have no way of knowing. His heart was pounding in his ears, more so than even on the most treacherous climbs.

A crouch, a final check of the building line, and Zack bolted ahead. He saw the blur of movement and color to his right at virtually the same moment he heard the barked command.

'Stop! Right there, right now!'

Startled, Zack stumbled forward, slamming heavily against the brick facing and nearly falling as he spun toward the voice. Standing not ten feet away, brandishing a heavy nightstick, was the security guard, Henry, the pockmarked behemoth who had been present at Guy's death and again at his funeral.

'I been following you, Doc,' he said, rubbing a hand over the side of his nearly nonexistent neck. 'From that window right there, I been following you all the way across.'

'Jesus, Henry, you just scared the hell out of me,' Zack said, still gasping for breath.

His shoulder was throbbing viciously at the point where it had collided with the building. Gingerly, he raised his arm. Pain stopped it just below a horizontal position. He'd almost dislocated it. A first-degree separation at least, he guessed.

'Didn't mean to scare ya, Doc,' the huge guard said, lowering his stick nearly, but not completely, to his side. 'Just to stop ya.'

'Henry, I've got to get in there,' Zack said.

'Mr. Iverson left strict orders not to let you. That's why I was called in.'

'There's a kid dying in there, Henry. A kid that only I can help. You've got to let me pass.'

'Can't,' the man said simply. 'If I do, it's my job. No discussion, no excuses. That's what my boss said. I got three kids, and nothin' to support 'em with exceptin' what God gave me from the neck down. Jobs like this one don't come along that often to a man like me.'

Zack started to argue, but then, just as quickly, stopped himself. He pictured the guard at Guy's funeral – his ill-fitting blue suit, his quiet, anxious little wife. The man was right. The job probably *was* a godsend to them and their children. And too many people had been hurt already. He would find another way to contact Suzanne, or perhaps a way to lure Jack Pearl outside the protection of the building.

'All right, Henry,' he said. 'I won't try to argue with you.'

He turned and started back toward the woods.

'Doc, wait. . . .'

Zack looked back over his injured shoulder.

'How old's the kid?'

'He's eight, Henry.'

'I see. . . . My Kenny's almost nine. . . . Doc, what in the heck happened between you and your brother, anyhow?'

Zack laughed ruefully.

'It's a long story, Henry.'

'You know, he's not a very nice man, your brother.'

'No, Henry,' Zack said. 'I guess he isn't.'

'He doesn't think much of people like me.'

'Perhaps he doesn't.'

For a few moments, there was only the sound of the wind through the leaves overhead.

'Doc,' the guard said suddenly, 'why don't you just go ahead on in there and do whatever it is you have to do.'

Zack eyed the man.

'You mean that?'

'Talking to me and my wife the way you did at Doc Beaulieu's funeral – that was a really nice thing to do.'

'Henry, your job may be on the line.'

'I'll find another one if I have to. You know, I really did think I was responsible for Doc Beaulieu's death. I'm big, and I'm tough when I have to be, but I'm not mean. I couldn't eat or sleep after he died – that is, until you talked to me.'

'If anyone was responsible, Henry,' Zack said, 'it was my brother. He's the one who started all those rumors about Dr. Beaulieu.'

'I believe it. You go on in there.'

Zack started toward the door.

'You sure?' he asked.

'Do it for Doc Beaulieu,' Henry said.

Chapter 35

Forty-nine years.

Had Guy lived, Clothilde Beaulieu suddenly realized, they would have celebrated their forty-ninth anniversary in just one week. How strange that now, standing behind her chair, surveying the room of blank, bored, and patronizing faces, she should feel as close to her husband as she had at any time during those five decades.

He had stood in rooms like this one many times over the past two years, confronting these faces, or faces like them. And although she had never been there with him, Clothilde knew that she was feeling exactly as he had. She knew, too, that even though there was little or no chance she would prevail, he was, at that moment, by her side, and he was proud.

'. . . For many years after my husband opened his practice in Sterling,' she was saying, 'he was one of only three doctors in town, and the only surgeon for almost a hundred miles. He was a kind and skilled and caring man, who did nothing – nothing – to deserve the kind of treatment he was to receive from the administration of this institution and the corporation whose philosophy it has adopted. . . .'

Seated across from the woman, Frank Iverson shaded in portions of the geometric design he was developing on a napkin, and checked the time. It would be a laughable irony if Guy Beaulieu's widow were allowed to drone on past the twelve o'clock deadline, rendering the vote of the board legally meaningless, regardless of its outcome. No, not laughable, he decided – perfect. It was all he could do to keep from smiling at the notion.

The Carter Room was set up in its conference mode – thirty chairs arranged around an open rectangle of sandlewood tables. At the back of the room, near the gallery of past medical staff presidents, a serving table was set with coffee, Danish, and bowls of fruit.

Hidden beneath the draping linen cloth of that table, awaiting the inevitable, several bottles of premium French champagne were chilling in sterling silver ice buckets.

The magic number was ten. Of the twenty-two members of the Davis Hospital board of trustees, nineteen were present. Absent from the group were a real estate agent who was vacationing in Europe; the CEO of the Carter Paper Company, who had never attended a board meeting since his first one years before; and Board Chairman Clayton Iverson. In the Judge's absence, Whitey Bourque had been presiding over the meeting.

Frank sat beside Leigh Baron at the corner of the arrangement farthest from Bourque. They were flanked by a trio of lawyers, two representing Ultramed and the third, the hospital.

Across from them stood Clothilde Beaulieu.

'. . . Someone must realize that in a civilized society such as ours,' she was saying, 'the best available medical care must not be doled out as a privilege. The right to live one's life as free from disease as possible must be extended to all, regardless of their ability to pay. It was my husband's

486

belief, and it is mine, that the Ultramed Hospitals Corporation has failed in that sacred obligation. By selecting only those who can pay for treatment, by influencing the therapeutic decisions of physicians who have studied many years to develop their craft, the corporation has reduced the delivery of medical care to the level of ... of automobile mechanics. ...'

Frank glanced over at Gary Garrison, proprietor of Garrison's Chevrolet Sales and Service, just in time to see the man smile and whisper a remark to the board member seated next to him. More irony. Garrison's vote was one of those that Frank had not absolutely locked up. Given enough time, it was possible that Clothilde Beaulieu could insult enough members on the board to make the vote unanimous.

Frank made his fifth head count of the session. When he had left his father's office, less than a week before, he was certain of only five votes, six at the most. Now, thanks in large measure to the Judge's absence and his refusal to use his influence on the board, he had eleven – one over the magic number. Gary Garrison would make twelve. And with the closed ballot Whitey Bourque had promised him, there might even be one or two more.

'You look concerned,' Leigh whispered.

Frank smiled.

'No sweat,' he whispered back.

'I hope so, Frank. We're counting on you.'

'That's the way I like it.'

'... Over the past two years, Guy Beaulieu fought back against the attempts of Ultramed to drive him from practice. Unfortunately, as I said earlier, much of the evidence he accumulated is not available today. I have done my best without it to present our position to you. I leave you now with this petition, signed by sixty-seven residents of this area, requesting the return of our hospital to community control.

'I greatly appreciate the opportunity you have given me to represent my husband's interests this day. I know, just as he did, that the age of the country doctor making house calls and sharing the most intimate details of his patients' lives is all but over in this country. But I issue to you, in his name, and in the name of those on this petition, one final plea that you do what you can to stop the juggernaut of technology and profit from robbing medicine of so much of its dignity, compassion, and sacred trust. Thank you, and God bless you for listening so patiently to this old woman.'

Several members of the board applauded lightly, and Bill Crook, seated on Clothilde's right, patted her on the arm.

Whitey Bourque, who had unabashedly checked his watch half a dozen times during the final few minutes of her speech, sighed audibly and tapped his gavel on the table as he stood by his chair.

'So,' he said. 'There you have it. Frank has had his say, and now Mrs. Beaulieu has had hers. Any other comments in the few minutes we have left? . . . Good enough. Well, in view of the seriousness of this repurchase matter, it has been suggested, and I agree, that we vote on the issue by closed ballot. Any objections? . . . Okay, then. You'll each find a ballot in your folder. Just mark whatever you think is right, and pass your vote over to me.'

Across the room, Frank subconsciously nodded his approval. Beneath the table, his leg was jouncing in nervous anticipation. After immobilizing

Suzanne Cole, he had called Annette Dolan and insisted that she stay home for the remainder of the day. Next, he had worked out an exquisite scenario for Zack and Suzanne, which would take both of them out of his hair for good and place the blame for their accident squarely on the shoulders of his brother.

He couldn't have scripted things better. First Mainwaring's million, now the vote, and later, a call to Zack and one final test of Serenyl – this time at the edge of the four-hundred-foot drop-off at Christmas Point. It would be the perfect ending to a perfect day. The game hadn't been easy, but he had met and overcome every obstacle. And now, at long last, Frankie Iverson was about to be on top again.

In the back of his mind, the cheerleaders' chant had begun to build.

Frank, Frank, he's our man. . . .

With Henry checking the corridors and stairways ahead of him, Zack moved easily through the kitchen and up the north stairway to the ICU. The pain from his shoulder, while tolerable, was continuing to make its existence known, especially when he tried to raise his arm.

'Good luck in there, Doc,' the guard said, barely able to contain his enthusiasm at the decision he had made. 'I'll be around the hospital if you need me. Just have me paged.'

Zack shook his hand gratefully.

'You've done a good thing, Henry,' he said. 'A really good thing. I'll page you if I need you. . . .'

Readying himself for the struggle ahead, he turned and entered the ICU.

The unit was virtually as he had left it two hours

before, except that neither Suzanne nor Owen Walsh was there. Half of the glass-enclosed cubicles were empty, and what activity there was continued to center about Toby Nelms.

The nurses eyed him uncomfortably as he approached. Off to this right, he saw the unit secretary snatch up the receiver of her phone and then slowly set it back down again, as if unwilling to take sole responsibility for reporting his appearance in the hospital.

Bernice Rimmer, the nurse assigned to Toby's care, had actually been a classmate of Zack's from early childhood through high school. She was the mother of three children now, but still looked nearly as slim and buoyant as she had during her teens. She was also a nurse's nurse, tough on the outside, but with a core of honey – and smart. Her presence this day was, Zack realized, no less fortunate for him than his encounter with Henry. If any nurse would give him a break, it was she.

As he approached, Bernice, almost as if reading his thoughts, sent the aide who was working with her out of Toby's cubicle.

'Hi, Bernie,' Zack said.

'Funny,' she responded, 'you don't look like public enemy number one.'

'I'm not.'

'Tell that to your brother. I never thought the two of you got along all that well, but this is something else.'

She took a folded sheet of paper from her uniform pocket, smoothed it out on Toby's bed, and passed it over.

Zack was not surprised at the content of the memo, only at its viciousness. In essence, Frank had outlined a set of charges against him that would have made Attila the Hun proud, and had threatened summary dismissal for anyone not immediately reporting his presence in the hospital.

'Frank and I are having a few problems,' he said.

'I guess.'

'How's Toby doing?'

'About the same. His temp's staying around 101. Pupils are still equal. No change in his consciousness.' She gestured at the memo. 'You do all those things?'

Zack shook his head.

'Frank doesn't want to believe that the anesthesia this child received for his hernia operation is responsible for his problem.'

'Is it?'

'Yes.'

Bernice Rimmer studied him for a time, and then she gazed down at her charge, reached over, and stroked the boy's forehead. Finally, she looked past Zack to the unit secretary and shook her head.

'So, what do you propose to do about it?' she asked.

Zack started to thank her, but the look in her eyes stopped him. She wanted action, not platitudes.

He conducted a brief neurologic check of Toby.

'I need to have a few words with Jack Pearl,' he said.

'He's in the O.R.'

'That's okay. But before I see him, I need to go over some things with Suzanne. Do you know where she is?'

'No idea. She called a while ago to say she'd be down here shortly, but she hasn't showed. I think Dr. Walsh paged her once, but as far as I know, she never answered. He's gone to his office.'

'Could you have her paged again, please? Also, try the E.R., just in case she's tied up there.'

They waited several minutes for Suzanne to answer. Then, once again, Zack tried calling her at home.

'This is very weird,' he said. 'Does she fail to answer pages often?'

'Never.'

'Hmm. Bernice, could you do me one more favour and page Henry Flowers, the security guard. Ask him to come here.'

'You *want* security?'

'Not security – Henry. It's okay. And please thank the rest of the staff for holding off on reporting me.'

Henry Flowers arrived at the unit in less than two minutes.

'How'm I doing?' Zack asked.

The massive guard shrugged.

'As far as I can tell, no one knows you're here.'

'I'm trying to find Dr. Cole. You know her?'

'Of course. I just heard her paged.'

'That was me. She didn't answer.'

'So?'

'So I'd like you to start looking around for her, if you could. I don't think I'd last very long out there.'

'Okay.'

'Check her office in the P and S building first. Then maybe the cardiac lab.'

Henry stroked his pocked cheeks.

'I saw her,' he said thoughtfully.

'When? Where?'

'Not too long ago. I . . . I can't remember where, though, Doc.'

'Try.'

'Let's see. . . . I started my rounds on the front lawn, and then crossed through the lobby, and then . . .' Suddenly, he brightened. 'I remember, now. I remember where I saw her.' Then, just as suddenly, his expression darkened.

'Henry, where?' Zack asked.

'It wasn't in the west wing,' he said distantly. 'She . . . she was going into Mr. Iverson's office.'

Zack felt an instant chill.

'Henry, get me there,' he said. He turned to the nurse. 'Bernie, could you please find out who's on for anesthesia beside Dr. Pearl? Call whoever it is and ask them to stand by. Don't tell them it's for me.'

With Henry resuming his role as scout, they left the unit and made their way down to the sub-basement, then across the hospital to the west-wing staircase and up. Zack flattened himself against the stairwell wall.

'Henry,' he whispered, 'I think my brother is in a meeting, but he was two receptionists.'

'Yeah, I know. The knockout twins.'

'Exactly. Talk to them. See if they remember when Suzanne left, or better still, where she might have gone. Also, find out if Frank was with her when she went.'

Subconsciously, the huge guard straightened his tie, adjusted the lapels on his uniform, and pushed his massive shoulders back a notch. Then he slipped out the stairway door to confront the knockout twins.

Half a minute later, he was back.

'No one there,' he said.

'No one?'

'Nope.' He appeared disappointed. 'Not the blonde. Not the dark-haired one. No one. I even took a chance because there was music playing inside, and unlocked the outer office door and listened at Mr. Iverson's door for voices.'

'Music?'

'Violins. Pretty music, but it must be on awful loud to be able to hear it through two closed doors.'

'Henry, I want to go back there.'

'Okay, but—'

Zack was already through the stairway door. The guard shrugged and followed closely.

Just outside Frank's outer office, Zack stopped and listened. As Henry had said, the music coming from the inner office was quite audible.

It took just a few seconds for Zack to recognize the piece.

'Jesus, Henry, open this up, please!'

The guard did as asked.

The music, much louder now, brought a sickening tightness to Zack's gut. He knocked on the door and called out once, but knew there would be no answer.

'This door, Henry. Open it, please!'

'Can't.'

'Henry, it's important. I think Dr. Cole's in there, and I think she's in trouble.'

'No key. Only Mr. Iverson has a key to that door.'

'Henry, we've got to get in there. . . .'

The guard hesitated.

'Please . . .'

'Well,' he said finally, 'I guess I can't get fired more than once, can I?'

He took a single step forward and then hit the

heavy door with such force that the entire frame shattered. The door itself, crushed where his shoulder had made contact, fell to the floor like a playing card.

Fantasia on Greensleeves was playing at a near-deafening level.

Zack snapped off the tape, glanced about the office for a moment, then raced into the bathroom.

'Henry,' he yelled. 'Get in here!'

No longer mindful of being seen, Zack raced ahead as Henry carried Suzanne through the corridors of the hospital and up the stairs to the ICU. She was motionless, unresponsive, and soaked with perspiration. Her level of coma was deep, and her elevated temperature quite apparent.

Bernice Rimmer's surprise at their arrival lasted only seconds before she was in action, stripping Suzanne's clothes off, getting a blood pressure cuff around her arm, and ordering a Ringer's Lactate IV from one of the other nurses.

'She remind you of anyone, Bernie?' Zack asked. 'She got the same anesthesia as Toby. You believe me now?'

'I believed you before,' the nurse said, listening to Suzanne's chest. 'You probably don't remember this, but I once asked you to cheat on a Latin translation for me, and you refused. I figured that if you were such an honest nerd then, you couldn't have changed all that much.'

'Who's Pearl's backup?'

'The nurse anesthetist. She's in obstetrics.'

'Call her, please. Tell her to meet me by the operating room doors in two minutes. Tell her it's a life-and-death emergency. Also, order some labs and blood gases on Suzanne – everything stat. And give her Decadron. Ten milligrams IV.'

'Done.'

'I'll be back shortly. . . . Get ready, Pearl, you bastard,' he murmured as he slammed through the unit doors. 'This crap has gone on long enough. I'm coming for you!'

Chapter 36

Frank knew, as he watched Whitey Bourque separate the ballots into two piles, that the vote was going to be closer than he had wanted. He counted exactly ten ballots in one pile and nine in the other. By insisting on a closed vote, it had been his hope to minimize any influence the Judge might still have had on certain members. Now, it appeared, he had succeeded more in minimizing his own.

Fuck you, Garrison, he thought, watching the last of the ballots smoothed open. *Starting next year, it will be Fords for this hospital. Bank on it.*

'Well,' Bourque said as he and the member seated next to him finished a cooperative tabulation of the votes. 'I make it ten to nine. You get that, too, Charlie? . . . Good.' He banged his gavel. 'In that case, I am pleased to announce that the Davis – er, excuse me, the Ultramed-Davis board of trustees has, by a vote to ten to nine, approved the finalization of the sale of this hospital to the Ultramed Division of RIATA International.'

Several members applauded; many others simply shrugged. Leigh Baron accepted the congratulations of the attorneys and then turned to Frank.

'That was close,' she said.

Frank smiled.

'Hand grenades and horseshoes,' he said giddily.

'Pardon?'

'Oh, just a little phrase my father drummed into my head.'

'Well, Frank, it would appear that you are to be—'

'Excuse me, but I wondered if the acting chairman could delay the celebration long enough to listen to one more point of view.'

Like the gallery at a tennis match, every head in the room swung, in unison, toward the door.

The Judge, a blanket over his lap, sat in a wheelchair just inside the room, pale but smiling grimly.

Whitey Bourque raced around and shook his hand.

'God, Judge, it's good to see you up like this. You all right? I mean, can you—'

'I can move 'em, Whitey. Not very much yet, but more every minute.'

Somewhat painfully, he demonstrated by lifting his right foot several inches off its support.

Frank, too stunned by the sudden intrusion even to react, glanced down at his watch. It was eight minutes till noon. At that moment, he realized his father was watching him.

'Good to see you, Judge,' he managed hoarsely.

The Judge nodded at him and then exchanged a prolonged look with Leigh Baron.

'I'd like to address the board, if I might,' he said.

'Of course, Judge,' Whitey Bourque replied. 'Why don't you just let me wheel you up front.'

'Judge,' Frank said, 'the voting's over.'

'Is it?'

'I'm afraid so, Judge,' Bourque said. 'Ten to nine it was, in favor of Ultramed.'

'Well, perhaps I can change a mind or two.'

'That's not legal, sir,' one of the Ultramed lawyers said. 'The vote's done.'

Clayton Iverson fixed him with a glare that would have melted block ice.

'Don't you dare tell me what's legal and what's not, young man,' he rasped. 'I was a lawyer and a judge while your mommy was still wiping your behind. Our contract with you people says that we have until noon today to repurchase this hospital by a majority vote of the board. That's what it says. No more, no less. And unless something's wrong with my timepiece, here, I make it seven of.'

Ashen, Frank watched as his father was wheeled up to the chairman's table. He was desperately sorting through disruptions he could instigate that might carry the meeting past the deadline. But before he could light on a specific action, the Judge was speaking.

'I'll make this short,' he began. 'I had promised many of you that I would do the legwork necessary to ensure that it was to the benefit of our community to finalize our temporary arrangement with the Ultramed people. Because of my accident, and for other reasons which I have neither the time nor inclination to go into now, I decided to withhold my conclusions about this business and let the chips fall where they may. Well, I have come back at this time to tell you that my reaction was unfair – to you, my friends and colleagues, and to the city of Sterling as well.

'I have learned enough to appear before you now and tell you categorically that while we may have benefited in the short run from Ultramed's involvement with our hospital, it would be a grave mistake to turn Davis Regional over to them permanently. My housekeeper, Annie Doucette, almost died because of a policy – an Ultramed corporate policy

– that rewards physicians for transferring patients out of the hospital as early as possible, and rewards them even more if that transfer is to an Ultramed-owned nursing home. Patients who helped build this hospital are being shunted off to Clarion County because they haven't got enough insurance. There's more – much more' – he glanced at Leigh Baron— 'but because of the time, I'm going to ask you to trust me on that. Now, we have three minutes until noon. If it is agreeable with Whitey, here, I would like to call for another vote on this question.'

'Any objections?' Bourque asked.

'Yes,' Frank said, standing. 'I object.'

'Well, I'm sorry, Frank,' Bourque countered, 'but you're not a board member, 'n' we don't have time for any outside objections.'

Frank hesitated, and then sank numbly to his seat.

'Okay, then,' Bourque said. 'You all have a second ballot in your folders. I put one there knowin' that at least some of you were bound to screw up the first one.'

A brief volley of laughter gave way to dense silence as the twenty board members marked their ballots, folded them, and passed them toward the front of the room.

Leigh Baron, her back to Frank, sat staring stonily at the gallery of presidents.

As the last of the ballots reached Whitey Bourque and was counted, the steeple bells of St. Anne's began tolling the noon hour.

Sara Newton, the nurse anesthetist, was a mousy young woman with braces that had yet to correct a striking overbite. She had been asleep in maternity, awaiting a delivery, and arrived at the doors to the operating suite only moments after Zack, breathless, bleary-eyed, and disheveled.

'Where's the emergency?' she panted, tugging at a kink in her bra.

'In the unit,' Zack said.

His shoulder was throbbing from the dash through the hospital, and he had resorted to partially splinting it by jamming his thumb through a belt loop.

'The unit? Well, then, let's get going. Say, are you okay? You look a little pale.'

'I'm fine. A little stressed out is all.'

'That's right. There was a notice sent around that you've been fired.'

'I've been rehired. Sara, I need Jack Pearl. It's a case he's familiar with. I'd like you to take over his case in O.R. 1 so he can leave.'

The woman was astonished.

'Dr. Iverson, I can't do that.'

'Listen, Sara,' Zack said sharply, 'I don't have time to argue. I know you're very good at your job, and if I thought you could do what I need, I wouldn't hesitate. But this is Pearl's affair. His and mine. And at least two lives are on the line. Now please.'

'Wh-What can I do?' she asked, shaken.

'Get a fresh set of scrubs on and be outside O.R. 1 as quickly as you can. I'll signal you when it's okay to come in.'

'Jack will never agree to something like this.'

'You leave Jack to me. Now, please, hurry.'

Zack raced into the surgeon's locker room and painfully undressed. He threw his clothes into his locker and pulled on a scrub suit, a paper hair cover, mask, and shoe covers, and he hurried past the sinks

501

in the prep room and into O.R. 1. Greg Ormesby, the surgeon on the case, looked up and took several seconds to recognize who he was.

'Iverson?' he asked somewhat coolly. 'That is you under there, isn't it?'

At the mention of Zack's name, all activity in the room came to an instant halt. Jack Pearl, who was hunched over his instruments, looked up and paled.

'Sorry to bust in like this, Greg,' Zack said with forced calm, 'but I need to talk to Jack, here.'

'I'm busy,' Pearl muttered.

'Well, whatever it is will just have to wait,' Ormesby said. 'We'll be done in half an hour. Now, if you please, Iverson.'

Zack bent over Pearl and laid his right hand at the base of the man's neck.

'Jack,' he whispered, 'it's Suzanne. She's in the ICU right now, and she's having a seizure just like Toby's. She's reliving her operation and she's screaming out your name. Yours and Jason's.'

Even wearing a mask and hair cover, the frail anesthesiologist looked ill. 'That can't be,' Pearl whispered back.

'I want you up there with me right now.'

'You're crazy.'

Zack slipped his fingers around the sides of Pearl's neck and applied just a bit of pressure.

'She's the second case, Jack. The one you were holding out for.'

'I'm not going anyplace. Now let go of me! You're hurting me!'

Zack looked up just as Sara Newton appeared outside the door. He motioned her in with a snap of his head, and tightened his grip, digging his sinewy fingers into the nerves alongside Pearl's neck.

502

'Iverson, what in the hell is going on here?' Ormesby demanded. 'Are you crazy? Somebody call security. Iverson, for crying out loud, there's a goddman woman opened up on the table here. Can't you see that?'

'I'm sorry to do things this way, Greg,' Zack said, raising the little anesthesiologist to his feet, 'but there's trouble in the ICU that only Jack can help with.'

'That's crazy!' Pearl cried out. '*He's* crazy! Ow! You're hurting me, Iverson! Let go!'

Greg Ormesby and the surgical team watched in stunned silence as Zack pulled the little man away from his console and gestured Sara Newton into his place.

'Iverson, stop this right now!' Ormesby shouted. 'You're endangering my patient.'

'Nonsense. Sara, here, is an excellent anesthetist, and you know it. She'll take good care of your patient. I'm sorry to have to do things this way, but I just don't have time to explain right now. I will, though, Greg. I promise.'

'Oh, for God's sake. Will somebody call security? Iverson, this is madness.'

Zack did not respond.

The pain in his shoulder partially numbed by his own adrenaline, he dragged Pearl through the scrub room and slammed him against the bank of lockers, pinning him by the throat so that he was up on the tips of his toes.

'Iverson,' Greg Ormesby hollered, 'I see now that what everyone is saying about you is true. I'll get you for this! I'll see you up on charges!'

'Okay, Jack,' Zack said, ignoring the surgeon's bellowing. 'This is it. Now tell me: There *is* an experimental drug, isn't there? . . .'

He augmented his grip with his injured arm, and hoisted the anesthesiologist up another fraction of an inch. Pearl's toes came off the carpet.

'Well, isn't there?'

Pearl, either too frightened or too obstinate to answer, did not respond. His face was violet. His eyes, now nearly level with Zack's, were bulging.

At that moment, a security guard burst into the locker room, and without a word, struck Zack with his nightstick – a blow that glanced off the side of his head and landed squarely on his injured shoulder. Crying out from the pain, Zack dropped heavily to the carpet, clutching his arm, as Jack Pearl slithered down the locker and, moaning, collapsed in a heap nearby.

The guard knelt on the small of Zack's back and raised his stick, preparing for another blow.

'Stop that! Right now!'

Startled, the guard came off Zack and whirled toward the voice. Zack reacted more slowly. He turned, and through tears of pain saw Jason Mainwaring, hands on hips, standing by the door.

'Mainwaring,' he gasped, 'it's Suzanne. She's in the unit, and—'

'I know. I just came from there.' Mainwaring turned to the guard. 'Everything's under control here now. You can go.'

'But—'

'I *said*, things are under control.'

'Y-Yessir.'

The guard backed from the room, with Mainwaring's ice-blue eyes helping him along.

'Okay, Jack,' the surgeon said as the door swung shut, 'give Iverson whatever he wants.'

'Jason, I can't—'

'Dammit, Jack, do it! There are two people in deep trouble in the unit up there. I may have made some mistakes in this business, but I'm no murderer. If Serenyl's responsible for their condition, then I want Iverson here to get whatever he needs to help them . . . Now!'

Pearl stumbled to his feet.

Zack tried to rise, fell heavily, and then tried again – this time with shaky success.

'Thanks, Mainwaring,' he said. 'I didn't think I'd gotten through to you.'

'Just remember, Iverson, that just because I'm here doesn't mean I'm admitting to anything.' He glanced over at the anesthesiologist, and then added in a voice too soft for the man to hear, 'I'm no monster, Iverson. If Pearl's drug has hurt some people, I want to do whatever I can to help out. You remember that, now. You remember I did that.'

'Yeah, sure, Mainwaring,' Zack said. 'I'll remember.'

Frank sat alone to one side of the Carter Conference Room and watched as Whitey Bourque, the last remaining board member, wheeled his father away for readmission to the hospital. The re-vote had been an impressive fourteen to six in favor of repurchase.

As he neared the door, the Judge looked back at him and mouthed the words, 'I'm sorry, Frank.'

Across from Frank, Leigh Baron shared a final exchange with her lawyers and sent them off. Then she turned and surveyed the near-empty room and the vestiges of the meeting just past.

'Well, he beat you,' she said finally.

'He beat you, too,' Frank retorted.

'He's one of the hardest men I've ever dealt with.'

'Tell me about it.'

Leigh paced to one side of the room and then back.

'Unfortunately,' she said, 'that is, unfortunately for you, your father's actions have placed me in a rather ticklish position.'

'Oh?'

'You see, Frank, three years ago you did a very stupid, very amateurish thing. You took money from us. A good deal of money.'

Shocked, Frank stared up at her.

'I . . . I don't know what you're talking about,' he managed.

'Oh, Frank,' she said sardonically, 'you disappoint me so.' She crossed the room and laid the accountant's report in front of him. 'We were a little worried about this vote today,' she explained, 'so last night I visited with your father.'

'You what?'

'I shared the contents of that folder with him, and promised that it would be incinerated as soon as the sale of the hospital was complete.'

'That's insane.'

'No, Frank,' she said calmly, 'that's business.'

'What kind of person are you? Do you know that you probably were the cause of his accident?'

'I know nothing of the kind. But what I do know is that your father made his choice, and now we must make ours. You can expect charges of embezzlement to be brought against you first thing next week.'

'You can't do that.'

'Can, and will,' she said.

'I . . . I was about to put that money back. I have the cash. Right now. Right in the bank.'

'Too late.'

'You're an insensitive bitch.'

'Oh, that's wonderful, Frank. So witty, so articulate.'

'I'll . . . I'll double what I took,' he said. 'Five hundred thousand. I can have it in your hands this afternoon.'

'Frank, you don't understand. If it was the money, you would have been buried three years ago, when we first became aware of what you had done.'

'In that case,' he said, suddenly seeing a crack of daylight and racing toward it, 'if I go down, your company goes down with me, big time.'

'What are you talking about?'

'I'm talking about some work that has been going on at this hospital – at *your* hospital. The testing of a new and unapproved anesthetic. It's work involving *your* administrator, and one of *your* surgeons, and one of *your* anesthesiologists, and it hasn't come out too well. If you need proof, stop by the ICU and check out a kid named Nelms. And I promise you that if I get charged with anything, I'll smear Ultramed's name until your stock isn't worth using as toilet paper.'

'I don't believe you,' she said.

But Frank could tell that she did.

'Like I said, just stop by the unit. I'm sure the child's parents and their lawyers would love to know that a multi-billion-dollar company was responsible for their son's condition.'

'You've been allowing this to go on without our knowledge?'

Frank felt the shift in momentum.

'Allowing it? Hell, I've been in charge of it. How do you think I was planning on coming up with that much money? In fact, the work is already done. I've been paid off. And fortunately – for all of us – only I know that it hasn't come out all that well. . . . Now, do we have a Mexican standoff or not?'

Leigh Baron spent several seconds sizing him up, but he knew that he had won.

'How many patients?' she asked.

'Oh, five hundred,' he said, 'give or take.'

'I intend to check up on what you've told me.'

'Feel free. Just be careful when you do. If this blows, it blows in your face.'

'Frank, you're pathetic.'

'Ah, ah. Now who's being articulate?'

'One word, Frank, if so much as one word about this . . . this stupidity touches Ultramed, I swear I'll bury you. What you've done is horrible.'

Frank grinned broadly.

'No, it's not,' he said with a wink. 'It's business.'

Chapter 37

The article, 'Studies in the Reversal of the Delayed Toxicity of Lysergic Acid Diethylamine (LSD),' had been written by a Scottish neurologist named Clarkin, and published almost fifteen years before in the little-read British *Journal of Neuropsychology*. It was an anecdotal report, not a scientific study in the true sense of the word. Zack had stumbled onto the work during his first year of residency and had saved it because the notion of treating LSD flashbacks with LSD both amused and fascinated him.

In most of his cases, Clarkin had used a high-density, saline-flotation isolation tank. With no such device at hand, they would simply have to make do. And while the Scotsman's concepts were intriguing, the data presented were too scant to justify many of his conclusions. It was frightening to realize that with no other promising options, Clarkin's theories were all that Suzanne and Toby Nelms had going for them.

As he supervised the nurses' transfer of Suzanne to a water mattress – the first step in reducing her sensory input to the absolute minimum – Zack wondered about the neurologist and his work. *Was it a mistake not to try and locate him? Was he even still alive? Still practicing? Was he a scholar, or a fraud? Had he received acclaim for his theories, or scorn?*

But most of all, Zack wondered if he might be endangering his two patients by what he was attempting to do. Over the years of his training he had developed total, implicit faith in his clinical judgment. Now, having difficulty focusing past the pain in his shoulder, and with the nightmare of the past twenty-four hours so fresh in his mind, he was having doubts.

Be diligent. Be meticulous. Be honest. Account for every variable. . . .

Zack stared down at Suzanne, bound for the moment by four-point, leather restraints. Shortly after arriving in the ICU her coma had lightened and she had become combative and disoriented. Her symptoms were identical in many ways to Toby's, but were clearly evolving more rapidly and virulently – the result, Zack was certain, of Frank's vicious treatment of her.

Although she was groggy from Valium she had received, it was apparent that she was still locked in her psychosis, totally out of touch with reality. Her temperature had risen to almost 101.

Was there another way? He had been so sure of himself before the Judge's accident; sure enough to charge in and insist on applying Clarkin's anecdotal work to Toby Nelms. Now, even with Mainwaring's and Pearl's validation of his theories about an experimental drug, he felt himself on the knife's edge of panic.

Be meticulous. . . . Account for every variable. . . .

Zack rubbed at his shoulder. The swelling was increasing. Even the slightest movement of his arm was now sending numbing, metallic pain up into his neck and down to his fingertips. Fatigue and tension were battling for control of his mind.

510

Across from him, in quiet resignation, Jack Pearl was readying his instruments and syringes. Off to one side, Jason Mainwaring stood alone, watching.

As Zack finished placing patches over Suzanne's eyes and oil-soaked cotton in her ears, Mainwaring motioned him over. He looked uncharacteristically rumpled, gray, and drawn, and the concern in his eyes was, it seemed, genuine.

'Iverson, you know, I'm sorry this is happening,' he whispered.

'You should be.'

'I've never been one to make excuses for myself, but before you 'n' Pearl get started, there are two things I'd like you to know.'

'Oh?'

'First of all, that woman you learned about from Tarberry – the one who died in my office . . .'

'Yes . . .'

'She died of a coronary, not any allergic reaction. She never got anything but plain ol' Xylocaine. And that's the truth. I had some . . . some enemies at the hospital who had learned about my involvement with a pharmaceutical company. They were determined to get me, and Mrs. Grimes's unfortunate death gave them the chance. I won't deny doin' some work in my office with an experimental local anesthetic, but Mrs. Grimes got Xylocaine.'

Zack glanced over at Suzanne.

'Mainwaring,' he said coolly, 'I appreciate your coming back here the way you did. But don't look for any exoneration from me. What you two – *you three* – have done here was beyond stupid, and beyond wrong.'

'I've never been one to cut corners, but our company was failing. We . . . we were desperate.

511

Serenyl would have saved us.'

Zack gestured toward the two comatose patients.

'Do you think they care?' he asked.

Mainwaring had no response.

'Zack, we're all set,' Bernice Rimmer called over.

'Coming.'

Throughout the ordeal the nurse had been a rock, quietly stemming the concerns of the rest of the unit staff, and promising to take full responsibility should anything go wrong. She was so quick, so efficient and compassionate. Zack found himself trying to remember what she had been like during their years together at school. The only image he could conjure was of a plain, soft-spoken girl, pleasant enough, but well outside of the in crowd. How meaningless all of that seemed now.

'All right,' he said to the staff. 'Before we start, I want you all to know how much I – how much all three of us – appreciate what you're doing here. I know you have questions about what's going on, and I promise that when things settle down we'll answer as many of them as we can. The plan is to put Suzanne to sleep with a new anesthetic in hopes of ending her seizure. After we're done, we'll do the same thing to Toby.'

'Exactly what do you expect to have happen?' one of the other nurses asked.

'Ideally? Well, I guess we hope that whatever chemical molecules are poisoning their central nervous systems will be washed away, and they'll both just wake up. But it may take some time.'

'Are there dangers?'

Zack looked over at Jack Pearl, who was drawing up the contents of one of his vials into a syringe.

'Well, Jack?'

Pearl shook his head.

'No,' he muttered. 'No dangers.'

The nurse seemed satisfied.

'Okay, then,' Zack said, feeling his pulse beginning to quicken, 'let's go. Remember, no light, no sound, no movement.'

The nurses began cutting the lights and equipment noise to a minimum.

Zack motioned Jack Pearl off to one side.

'Remember, Jack,' he said. 'Play this straight.'

'Serenyl's not responsible for this,' Pearl growled.

'Jack, don't start with me. Just do this right, dammit.'

'It won't work, Iverson. You're crazy.'

'You're absolutely right, Jack.' His back to the others, Zack glared down at the man. 'I am crazy. And don't you for one goddamn second forget that.'

Together, they returned to Suzanne's bedside. The nurses settled down in the darkness as Pearl inserted a needle into the rubber bulb of Suzanne's IV line. Then he hesitated.

'Do it, Jack,' Zack rasped. 'This may be your only ticket out of hell. For God's sake, do it now!'

The anesthesiologist's hands were trembling so badly he needed both of them to hold the syringe.

'Dammit, Jack . . .'

Slowly, Pearl depressed the plunger.

Frank perched on one of the tables of the Carter Conference Room and watched as Leigh Baron gathered her things. She would, no doubt, stop by the unit to verify his claims about Toby Nelms. But then, with any luck, she would be out of his life for good.

513

His heartbeat continued to race, and there remained a persistent, sandpaper tightness in his throat, but that was understandable. He had narrowly dodged a bullet. Still, as he had learned countless times over his years as the quarterback, although his last-second victory wasn't a pretty one, a win was a win. And a win this most certainly was. His expectations of a regional directorship were gone, but the additional money in his bank account more than compensated for the termination of his association with Ultramed and Leigh Baron.

It was interesting, he mused, how suddenly unattractive the woman looked in defeat. The bridge of her nose; the shape of her hips; the stiff, unfeminine way she moved. It was absurd that at one time he had found her so desirable. He could do better – much better.

'Remember, Frank,' Leigh said, snapping her briefcase closed, 'assuming what you've told me is true, I don't want one word of it to get anywhere near Ultramed.'

'Sure, baby. Sure.'

Even her orders sounded different – groveling, hollow.

'Damn you, Frank,' she muttered.

Before he could respond, she turned and was gone.

Gradually, the unpleasant tightness in Frank's throat began to subside. He was pleased to find he could breathe deeply again. He even managed a thin smile. He was on a roll. Another challenge had arisen and been dealt with. Still, he cautioned himself, this was no time to celebrate. Not yet.

Soon, though, he thought. As soon as Suzanne Cole and one Zachary Iverson had been dispatched, there would be all the time in the world.

He pushed himself off the table and headed toward his office, reviewing the plan he had devised. Removing Suzanne from the hospital was the only tricky part, and that could easily be accomplished with one of the hospital's laundry hampers. He had always been a 'hands-on' administrator. It was hardly unusual for him to be seen carrying tools to a job, or moving a piece of furniture. So even if he *were* seen with the hamper, it was doubtful any questions would be raised.

The rest was elegantly simple: a call to Zack, a meeting at Christmas Point, and an accident. He had even thought to stop by central supply and appropriate some intravenous alcohol. Starting an IV line – especially one that needed to last only minutes – was no big deal. Once Zack was immobilized, either with an injection of Serenyl or the butt of his revolver, he would infuse enough of the alcohol to leave no doubt in anyone's mind what had happened – especially since he had already seen to it that Zack's drinking the night before was common knowledge around the hospital.

Inspired. Elegant. Simple.

Lost in thought, Frank hurried along the first-floor corridor toward the new wing, nearly colliding with the Judge's wheelchair as it was pushed out of the admissions office. Clayton Iverson eyed him grimly and then turned to the young candy striper who was transporting him.

'Kathy, dear, this is my son. If you don't mind, I need to talk to him. I'll send for you if I need you again. Thank you.'

He waited until the girl had left, and then used his cast and his good hand to wheel himself past the doorway.

'I want you to know that it hurt me to do what I had to do in there, Frank,' he said.

'Nonsense, Judge,' Frank said. 'I wouldn't have expected anything less of my father.'

Clayton Iverson looked up at him in surprise.

'I'm pleased to hear you say that, Frank. Unfortunately, I wish that was all there was to it.'

Once again, Frank saw daylight.

'Dad, listen,' he said. 'I just finished speaking with Leigh Baron. I know the spot she put you in.'

'You do?'

'Three years ago, some people from Boston came to me with a once-in-a-lifetime chance to get in on a land deal. They were so goddamn smooth, so well organized, that I fell for their crap hook, line, and sinker. I borrowed the money from the hospital expecting to pay it back in a matter of a week or two. It . . . it was the stupidest thing I've ever done. . . .'

Frank knelt on one knee and forced a tremble into his voice.

'. . . I was so frightened, so ashamed, I—'

'Frank, you should have come to me.'

'I know that, Dad. I know that now. . . .' *Easy. Not too much. Not too thick.* 'But . . . but you'd already helped me out of that mess in Concord, and—' His voice broke as he stared down at his hands.

'What did Leigh Baron say?' the Judge asked.

'Say?'

'About the money.'

'Oh. Well, she was pretty reasonable, all things considered. You see, I've been working on some deals – a second mortgage on the house, the sale of that lot on Winnipesaukee – and I can get together at least part of what I owe. She understands that I

516

meant to repay the money and that I'm probably out of a job, so she's promised to put the matter to rest providing I can come up with the full amount in the next few weeks.'

'And can you?'

'I . . . I can try.'

'How short are you?'

Frank struggled to mask his excitement.

'I . . . Judge, I want to handle this myself.'

'And just how do you expect to do that with a wife and two children and no job?'

'I'll manage. *We'll* manage. I'll catch on somewhere. I may have made a stupid mistake, but I'm still a damn good administrator.'

'The best.'

'Thanks for saying that.'

'And Leigh Baron has promised that if you replace the money, she'll be off your back?'

'That's what she said.'

'How much?'

'Judge, please.'

'How much more do you need?'

'A-About a hundred thousand.'

'I see . . .'

'Dad, it's my problem.'

'Nonsense. Frank, I'm very pleased with the way you're dealing with all this. I was angry as hell at you, but now I understand. You made a mistake, you admitted it, and you're trying to make good. That's all I could ever ask of you. I'll see to it that you get the money as soon as I get out of here.'

'But . . .' Again, Frank stared down at his hands. First Mainwaring, then Leigh Baron, and now the Judge himself!

'No buts,' the Judge went on. 'You can pay me

back when things get better. Believe me, it will be worth it not to have to explain all of this to your mother.'

'Judge, I . . . I don't know what to say.'

'Well, for starters, you can stand up and promise me that as the administrator of Davis Regional Hospital, you'll never let anything like this happen again.'

Slowly, Frank straightened up, carefully monitoring every muscle of his face.

Who says you can't have it all? he was thinking. *Who says you can't have it all, and more?*

'You mean that?' he asked, with just the right mix of incredulity and gratitude.

'Frank, I don't think there's a single member of the board who wouldn't vote to retain you – that is, provided you'd agree to stay on.'

Finally, Frank allowed himself a smile.

'I think I'll be able to manage that,' he said. 'Now I think it's time you got out of that chair and into a bed. You look a little pale. What room did they give you?'

'I asked for the third floor. They gave me 301.'

'Perfect. The best in the house. Come on. I'll wheel you up.'

Frank pushed his father toward the elevator. As they reached the corridor to the new wing, he stopped.

'Listen, Judge,' he said. 'If you don't mind waiting here for just a moment, there's something I need to check on in my office.'

'No problem,' the Judge said. 'Take your time.'

The door to Frank's outer office was less than twenty feet away. Frank left the wheelchair against a wall, crossed to the door, and inserted the key.

518

At the same moment he realized there was no music coming from within, Henry Flowers entered the corridor from the stairway.

'She's not there, Mr. Iverson,' he said.

'What?'

Frank felt a sudden, vicious chill.

'Dr. Cole. She's not there.'

Frank threw open the door, revealing the gaping hole to his inner office.

'She's in the intensive care unit with Dr. Mainwaring and your brother,' the giant guard explained. 'And you ought to be ashamed of the way—'

'No!'

'—you tied her up and—'

Frank shoved the man aside and bolted past him.

'Nooo!' he bellowed again as he slammed through the stairway door.

Chapter 38

'Two minutes.'

Seated beside Toby Nelms's bed, Zack mouthed the words and held two fingers in the beam of his penlight for Jack Pearl to see. Pearl nodded, and let up on the Serenyl infusion.

They had kept Suzanne anesthetized with the drug for nine minutes. Besides the cessation of all voluntary movement, the only sign of any change had been an almost immediate drop in her pulse rate from 120 to sixty. And although it was now more than twelve minutes since the anesthetic had been stopped, she had not awakened.

Rather than wait, Zack had decided to leave Bernice Rimmer in with her and to move on to Toby. The child, too, had responded to his anesthesia with a dramatic drop in pulse. Now, he lay in the eerie darkness, motionless except for the minute respiratory rise and fall of his chest beneath two thin blankets.

As Zack monitored the surreal scene, he struggled against the mounting foreboding that it was already too late for the boy, and possibly for Suzanne as well. Desperately, he tried reminding himself that he was too tired and in far too much pain to maintain any semblance of a positive, objective outlook. Perhaps it would take several hours to see any real change. Perhaps several days. And perhaps, he acknowledged, it was better, anyhow, to expect the worst.

'One minute.'

He signaled with his flash, and glanced about the unit. Mainwaring . . . Pearl . . . Suzanne . . . Toby . . . It was all so bizarre, so sad. He had come back to Sterling with such high hopes, so many expectations.

'Thirty seconds . . .'

Never, he vowed. *No more expectations.*

He heard the doors to the darkened ICU glide open. Then there were footsteps.

'Fifteen seconds.'

He turned and peered through the darkness, past Mainwaring, toward the doors. Just inside the glass, he could see the silhouette of a woman in a business suit. Barreling past her was Frank.

'Wake him up, Jack!' Zack whispered urgently. 'Quick! Wake him up.'

'What in the hell is going on here?' Frank bellowed. 'Turn these lights on! Turn them on right now!'

Jack Pearl stepped back from Toby's bed. The plastic syringe slipped from his fingers and clattered to the floor just as the lights in the unit came on.

Frank, his fists balled at his side, stood beside the nurses' station.

'You've been fired,' he snapped at Zack. 'Get the fuck out of this hospital before I call the police.'

'No way, Frank.'

Frank turned to the unit secretary.

'Call security, and then call the police. Tell them that a physician who has been fired from this hospital is refusing to leave.'

The woman did not move.

'Do it!'

Beneath his tan, Frank was livid.

One nurse rushed to close the glass partitions to other patients' rooms.

Zack stepped from Toby's cubicle to confront his brother.

'Frank, listen,' he said.

'Shut up!' Frank shouted, looking wildly about.

Leigh Baron moved a few steps closer. Behind her, a wheelchair appeared.

'I tried to tell you, Frank,' Jack Pearl whined. 'I tried to tell you we should have waited. . . .'

'Jack, shut up . . .'

'. . . We should have been doing a retrospective study. . . .'

'Goddamn you, Jack!'

'. . . But you wouldn't listen. You wouldn't give me a chance to fix my Serenyl.'

Frank stepped forward and punched the anesthesiologist squarely in the face. Pearl's head shot back. Blood sprayed across his face as he dropped to the floor.

Frank's fine features were twisted and distorted with rage.

'Get out!' he screamed. 'All of you. You're fired! This is my hospital, dammit! You're all fired!'

'Frank, stop,' Zack said quietly. 'It's over. Stop and listen. You've done terrible things here – sad and very terrible things. . . . Frank, don't you see? Look around. Look at all these people. Don't you see that it's over for you know? It's over.'

'Damn you!' Frank shrieked as he hurtled over a chair and leapt at his brother. 'I'll kill you! I swear, I'll fucking kill you!'

The force of his attack sent both men smashing through the plate-glass partition of any empty cubicle. A nurse screamed. Zack's injured shoulder struck the floor, exploding with nauseating pain. Dazed, he rolled to one side, over a mass of broken glass that cut into his arms and back. He stumbled to his feet, staggering drunkenly. Before his vision could clear, Frank was on him again, snarling like an animal, his hands viselike around Zack's throat, driving him backward.

Powerless, Zack's arms went limp. The pressure of Frank's thumbs against his windpipe was inexorable, and he knew, as he listened for the snap of his own larynx, that he was going to die.

At the moment that his legs gave out, he soiled himself. The pain gave way, and he sensed himself falling, drifting. Then the back of his head slammed against the corner of the metal bedframe. There was a blinding, searing flash. And then, instantly, there was nothing.

The light, a soft, warm glow, washed over the darkness in waves. One by one, faces began floating through the void. Zack followed the images with a detached curiosity, pleased when he was able to spot an old teacher or relative or classmate among them. Gradually, the faces grew more defined – and more current. An anatomy professor at Yale . . . a Wellesley coed from – from where? . . . a climbing partner in Wyoming. . . Then Annie Doucette . . . Toby . . . Suzanne . . . and finally, Frank, his face, pinched and crimson with hatred, spinning through the glow like a dervish.

I'll kill you . . . I'll kill you. . . .

'I'll kill you. I'll kill you.'

At first the voice was Frank's. Then, it was Zack's own, moaning the words over and over again.

'Iverson. Iverson, open your eyes. It's all right. You've had a concussion.'

'Concussion?'

'That's right, Iverson. Look up here.'

Zack's eyes fluttered and then opened.

For several seconds, the face above him remained blurred. Then its features grew more distinct.

'Ormesby?'

The surgeon nodded.

'You hit your head. You've been out for over an hour.'

'An hour? Suzanne . . .' He struggled to rise, but quickly fell back.

'Easy, Iverson. Easy.'

Ormesby put a calming hand on his arm.

Zack's thoughts began to clear. He was in bed, on a monitor, in the intensive care unit. An IV was draining into his arm.

'Did I have a seizure?'

'From what I hear, you did. Probably from the concussion. The CT scanner's warmed up and waiting for us right now.'

'Don't need one.'

'Iverson, you're the patient here, not the doctor. Got that? I've changed my mind about your being a nut case. Don't make me change it back.'

Zack nodded meekly. His head was throbbing, and jabs of pain were beginning to spark from half a dozen other places on his body. The discomfort helped clear his mind.

'Suzanne . . .' he said. 'Did she—'

'Right there, Iverson. Just turn your head to the right.'

Through a brief, machine-gun burst, Zack did as the surgeon asked. Suzanne, wrapped in a blanket, her IV on a transport pole, waved at him from a chair not four feet away. She looked pale, but otherwise seemed none the worse for her ordeal.

'Hi, Doc,' she said. 'You come here often?'

'God bless you, Clarkin,' Zack murmured.

'What?'

'Oh, nothing. How's Toby?'

'Still out, Zack. But he's lighter. I think he may be coming around, but it's hard to tell. The people from Boston are due here any minute to get him.'

Behind Suzanne, near the nurses' station, Zack could see the Judge watching intently.

'Listen,' Ormesby said. 'I'm going to get them ready for your scan. Afterward, I have a few dozen stitches to put in you.'

'My shoulder, I think it's—'

'We know. Sam Christian's already seen you. Now just relax, will you?'

'Where's Frank?'

'In jail by now, I would guess. You owe that big guard over there a hell of a thank-you, Iverson. Apparently everyone was sort of paralyzed. If he hadn't pulled Frank off you when he did, I think your ticket might have been canceled.'

'Bless you, Henry,' Zack rasped, rubbing at the soreness in his neck.

'Now, just stay put. I'll be back.'

'Stay put,' Zack echoed.

He waited until the surgeon had left and then reached over for Suzanne's hand.

She inched her chair closer to him.

'Sorry I can't get up,' she said. 'I get dizzy when I try.'

'Why don't you go back to bed. We'll talk later.'

'You okay?'

'I feel like shit, if you want to know the truth. But I'm okay. Fucking Frank nearly killed us both.'

'Almost. But it's over now, Zack.'

'What time is it, anyway?'

'Two. Almost two.'

'Damn.'

'What is it?'

'The board meeting . . . Do you know what happened there?'

She squeezed his hand.

'I think your father wants to talk to you about that. I'll see you after your test.'

'Sure. Meanwhile, stay away from the radio.'

Suzanne smiled.

'Not to worry,' she said. 'Sooner or later, though, I'm going to have to, um, face the music.'

She motioned to Bernice Rimmer, who brought a wheelchair over, took her IV pole and wheeled her from the room.

Moments later, the Judge appeared at Zack's bedside.

'You were right about my legs,' he said.

'I'm glad.'

'Zachary, don't feel bad about Frank.'

'I do. Judge, he hurt a lot of people. He's very sick.'

'I know. He stole a great deal of money from the hospital. Apparently this business with Jack Pearl and that Mainwaring was an attempt to replace it.'

'Lord.'

'I found out about it for sure yesterday, but I've suspected he was in trouble for some time. Frank never could put anything over on me. I . . . I just don't know where he could have gone so wrong.'

Try at birth, Zack wanted to say. He looked at the

bewilderment in his father's face, and knew that there was no percentage in responding.

'Judge, the board meeting,' he said. 'Did you go?'

'I went. They had already voted to sell out, but I had just enough time to turn things around. After the vote Frank had the temerity to ask me if we might keep him on as administrator. Much as it hurt me, I told him absolutely not.'

'Great,' Zack said with no enthusiasm.

'He should have known better than to try and hide the truth from me. He was always trying. He never could. I have no tolerance for his kind of deceit. No tolerance at all.' He sighed. 'I had such hopes for him. I gave your brother every chance, Zachary. Every chance. You know that, don't you?'

Zack closed his eyes, and instantly he was on the slalom run, tumbling over and over again down the snowy mountainside, his knee screaming with pain. The accident had eliminated him from competitive sports and, it seemed, from much of his father's interest as well. At the time it was the worst thing that had ever happened to him. Now, he could see, it well might have been his salvation.

'Of course you did, Judge,' he said, looking away. 'Of course you did.'

Epilogue

As if they could quantitate a miracle leaf by leaf, the meteorologists had proclaimed October 10 *the* peak day of the foliage season in northcental New Hampshire. And in fact, as the day – a Wednesday – evolved, with acre upon acre of crimson, orange, burgundy, and gold sparkling beneath a cloudless, azure sky, not even those old-timers who always had a different opinion of such things could argue.

In the small, atriumlike auditorium of the Holiday Inn of Sterling, sunlight streamed through glass panels, bathing the hundred or so hospital officials, board members, and physicians in a warmth that made the northern New England winter seem still remote. Throughout the hall, there was an air of excitement and history. They had come together from communities across the northern part of the state, and had met for three days around conference tables and in back rooms, hammering out the framework of a new consortium of hospitals.

Now, in minutes, the fruits of those efforts would be presented to the gathering, and a new era in community medicine would begin. The hospitals involved – seven in all – would be banded together in a way that would give them enormous purchasing power without the sacrifice of one bit of autonomy.

Judge Clayton Iverson, his wife at his side,

wandered about the milling crowd, exchanging greetings and handshakes with the other attendees, most of whom knew that he was about to be announced as the first chairman of the board of the consortium. His selection for the post had been virtually unanimous. The search committee had established experience and absolute integrity as the prime qualifications for the post, and through his handling of the Davis Regional-Ultramed disaster, the Judge had proven himself amply endowed with both.

Most impressive to the group had been the Judge's refusal to intervene in the trial and sentencing of his son Frank on myriad charges ranging from co-conspiracy in testing the unauthorized drug, Serenyl, to assault with intent to murder.

Then there was his handling of the surgeon, Jason Mainwaring. After demanding and obtaining the surrender of Mainwaring's medical license, the Judge had gotten the charges against the man diminished in exchange for the liquidation of his pharmaceutical company; from the proceeds a fund would be set up to aid those patients found to have been harmfully affected by the anesthetic.

And finally, there was the leadership role he had played in the reclamation of Davis Regional Hospital from Ultramed. Not only had the Judge supervised the transition back to community control, but, dissatisfied with the amount raised from the sale of Mainwaring's beleaguered drug firm, he had convinced the Ultramed directors of the sagacity of augmenting the Serenyl settlement fund with a multimillion-dollar contribution of their own.

Though he was constantly smiling, and seemed

relaxed, in between handshakes the Judge continued to glance toward the doors at the rear of the hall.

'Do you see him?' Cinnie asked.

'No. You did speak to his girlfriend, didn't you?'

'Yes, dear, I did. I told her you had been selected, and asked her to try and convince Zachary to be here for the announcement.'

'And?'

'And she said she'd try, but that she doubted he would come.'

She drew him off to one side, away from the crowd.

'Clayton, please,' she said. 'There's still time. Please reconsider this, and let's go to Florida. Just for the winter.'

'No.'

'But why? Lisette has moved away with the girls, and Zachary almost never comes by anymore. We haven't had a Sunday dinner in I don't know how long. We have friends down there. I . . . Clayton, I don't want to spend another winter here. Please.'

'Absolutely not. Zachary will come around. You'll see.'

'I don't know. He's been so distant since that terrible business with Frank. I ask him why almost every time we speak, and all he ever says is that there are things he has to work out. He says he's not even sure yet that he's going to stay in Sterling.'

'Oh, he'll stay. He's moved in with that Suzanne. Does that sound like he's planning to leave?'

'No,' she said. 'No, I suppose it doesn't.'

'Take your seats, everybody. Please take your seats,' the conference chairperson announced, tapping on her microphone. 'This is what you've all been waiting for.'

'He'll be here, Cynthia,' the Judge said. 'You'll see. His brother never appreciated the things I did for him, but in the end, Zachary will. He'll be here to share this.'

'Clayton, please . . .'

'No. And not another word about it.'

'Ladies and gentlemen, it gives me great pleasure to officially announce the birth of the Northern New Hampshire Community Hospital Consortium.'

There was a burst of applause. Again, the Judge turned toward the rear doors.

'Face it, Clayton,' Cinnie said. 'He's not coming.'

'Damn him,' Clayton muttered. 'The ungrateful . . . Damn them both.'

'. . . And as our first order of business, I would like to introduce to you the man chosen by our search committee to head our new consortium. He is a man of accomplishment and integrity, a man known to many in this room for his tireless work on behalf of his community and his hospital. He is a devoted man, dedicated uncompromisingly to the principles of fairness. . . .'

Six miles south of the Holiday Inn, resting on the deserted field known as the Meadows, the engine of a crimson model plane screeched to life. A young boy raced across the golden autumn grass, hand in hand with a young girl.

'Jennifer wants to learn, Zack,' he said, clutching the radio control box. 'Can I show her? All by myself. Can I show her how to fly it?'

'How about another quick coin trick first?'

'Oh, no – I mean, how about later on? Zack, she really wants to learn.'

Zack leaned back on his elbows and breathed in

the fragrant mountain air. Then he turned to Suzanne and brushed his lips against her ear

'I think the kid's got a crush on your daughter,' he whispered.

'So it would seem,' she replied. 'Toby, do you have a license to fly that thing?'

'A what?'

'Nothing, nothing.'

'Can I, Zack?' the boy asked again.

'Sure, kiddo,' Zack said. 'Of course you can.'

With Jennifer Cole watching intently, Toby Nelms eased back on the tiny control stick. Instantly, the Fleet shot forward, across the field and up into the perfect noonday sky.